P. D. JA

The Lighthouse

FABER & FABER

First published in 2005
by Faber & Faber Ltd
Bloomsbury House
74–77 Great Russell Street
London WC1B 3DA

Published by Penguin Books in association
with Faber & Faber in 2006
This Faber & Faber paperback edition first published in 2015

Pinted and bound by CPI Group (UK) Ltd, Croydon CR0 4YY

A CIP record for this book
is available from the British Library

ISBN 978–0–571–32510–8

FSC
www.fsc.org
MIX
Paper from
responsible sources
FSC® C013604

2 4 6 8 10 9 7 5 3

In memory of my husband
Connor Bantry White
1920–1964

Contents

Author's Note

Great Britain is fortunate in the variety and beauty of her offshore islands, but the setting for this novel, Combe Island off the coast of Cornwall, will not be found among them. The island, the deplorable events which took place there and all the characters in the story, living or dead, are entirely fictitious, existing only in that interesting psychological phenomenon, the imagination of the crime novelist.

P. D. James

Prologue

I

Commander Adam Dalgliesh was not unused to being urgently summoned to non-scheduled meetings with unspecified people at inconvenient times, but usually with one purpose in common: he could be confident that somewhere there lay a dead body awaiting his attention. There were other urgent calls, other meetings, sometimes at the highest level. Dalgliesh, as a permanent ADC to the Commissioner, had a number of functions which, as they grew in number and importance, had become so ill-defined that most of his colleagues had given up trying to define them. But this meeting, called in Assistant Commissioner Harkness's office on the seventh floor of New Scotland Yard at ten fifty-five on the morning of Saturday, 23 October, had, from his first entry into the room, the unmistakable presaging of murder. This had nothing to do with a certain serious tension on the faces turned towards him; a departmental debacle would have caused greater concern. It was rather that unnatural death always provoked a peculiar unease, an uncomfortable realisation that there were still some things that might not be susceptible to bureaucratic control.

There were only three men awaiting him and Dalgliesh was surprised to see Alexander Conistone of the Foreign and Commonwealth Office. He liked Conistone, who was one of the few eccentrics remaining

3

in an increasingly conformist and politicised service. Conistone had acquired a reputation for crisis management. This was partly founded on his belief that there was no emergency that was not amenable to precedent or departmental regulations but, when these orthodoxies failed, he could reveal a dangerous capacity for imaginative initiatives which, by any bureaucratic logic, deserved to end in disaster but never did. Dalgliesh, for whom few of the labyrinths of Westminster bureaucracy were wholly unfamiliar, had earlier decided that this dichotomy of character was inherited. Generations of Conistones had been soldiers. The foreign fields of Britain's imperialistic past were enriched by the bodies of unmemorialised victims of previous Conistones' crises management. Even his eccentric appearance reflected a personal ambiguity. Alone among his colleagues he dressed with the careful pinstriped conformity of a civil servant of the Thirties while, with his strong bony face, mottled cheeks and hair with the resilient waywardness of straw, he looked like a farmer.

He was seated next to Dalgliesh opposite one of the wide windows. Having sat through the first ten minutes of the present meeting with an unusual economy of words, he sat, his chair a little tilted, complacently surveying the panorama of towers and spires, lit by a transitory unseasonable morning sun. Of the four men in the room – Conistone, Adam Dalgliesh, Assistant Commissioner Harkness and a fresh-faced boy from MI5 who had been introduced as Colin Reeves – Conistone, the one most concerned with the matter in hand, had so far said the least while Reeves, preoccupied with the effort of remembering what was being said without the humiliating expedient of being seen to take notes, hadn't yet spoken. Now Conistone stirred himself for a summing up.

'Murder would be the most embarrassing for us, suicide hardly less so in the circumstances. Accidental death we could probably live with. Given the victim, there's bound to be publicity whichever it is, but it should be manageable unless this is murder. The problem is that we haven't much time. No date has been fixed yet, but the PM would like to arrange this top-secret international get-together in early January. A good time. Parliament not sitting, nothing much happens just after Christmas, nothing is expected to happen. The PM seems to have set his mind on Combe. So you'll take on the case, Adam? Good.'

Before Dalgliesh could reply, Harkness broke in, 'The security rating, if it comes off, couldn't be higher.'

Dalgliesh thought, *And even if you're in the know, which I doubt, you have no intention of telling me who will be meeting at this top-secret conference, or why.* Security was always on a need-to-know basis. He could make his guesses, but had no particular curiosity. On the other hand, he was being asked to investigate a violent death and there were things he needed to be told.

Before Colin Reeves had time to realise that this was his cue to intervene, Conistone said, 'All that will be taken care of, of course. We're not expecting problems. There was a similar situation some years ago – before your time, Harkness – when a VIP politician thought he'd like a respite from his protection officer and booked two weeks on Combe. The visitor stood the silence and solitude for two days before realising that his life was meaningless without his red boxes. I should have thought that that was the message Combe was established to convey but he didn't get it. No, I don't think we'll be worrying our friends south of the Thames.'

Well that, at least, was a relief. To have the security services involved was always a complication. Dalgliesh reflected that the secret service, like the monarchy, in yielding up its mystique in response to public enthusiasm for greater openness, seemed to have lost some of that half-ecclesiastical patina of authority bestowed on those who dealt in esoteric mysteries. Today its head was known by name and pictured in the press, the previous head had actually written her autobiography and its headquarters, an eccentric oriental-looking monument to modernity which dominated its stretch of the south bank of the Thames, seemed designed to attract rather than repel curiosity. To surrender mystique had its disadvantages; an organisation came to be regarded like any other bureaucracy, staffed by the same fallible human beings and liable to the same cock-ups. But he expected no problems with the secret service. The fact that MI5 was represented at middle-grade level suggested that this single death on an offshore island was among the least of their present concerns.

He said, 'I can't go inadequately briefed. You've given me nothing except who's dead, where he died and apparently how. Tell me about the island. Where exactly is it?'

Harkness was in one of his more difficult moods, his ill humour imperfectly concealed by self-importance and a tendency to verbosity. The large map on the table was a little crooked. Frowning, he aligned it more accurately with the edge of the table, pushed it towards Dalgliesh and stabbed it with his forefinger.

'It's here. Combe Island. Off the coast of Cornwall, about twenty miles south-west of Lundy Island and roughly twelve miles from the mainland, Pentworthy in this case. Newquay is the nearest large town.' He looked over at Conistone. 'You'd better carry on. It's more your baby than ours.'

Conistone spoke directly to Dalgliesh. 'I'll waste a little time on the history. It explains Combe and if you don't know it you may start under a disadvantage. The island was owned for over four hundred years by the Holcombe family who acquired it in the sixteenth century, although no one seems clear exactly how. Probably a Holcombe rowed out with a few armed retainers, hoisted his personal standard and took it over. There can't have been much competition. The title was later ratified by Henry the Eighth once he'd got rid of the Mediterranean pirates who'd established it as a basis for their slave-trading raids along the Devon and Cornish coasts. After that Combe lay more or less neglected until the eighteenth century when the family began to take an interest in it, and visited occasionally to look at the bird-life or spend the day picnicking. Then a Gerald Holcombe, born in the late eighteen-hundreds, decided to use the island for family holidays. He restored the cottages and, in 1912, built a house and additional accommodation for the staff. The family went there every summer in those heady days before the First World War. The war changed everything. The two elder sons were killed, one in France, the other at Gallipoli. The Holcombes are the kind of family who die in wars, not make money from them. That left only the youngest, Henry, who was consumptive and unfit for military service. Apparently, after the death of his brothers he was oppressed by a sense of general unworthiness and had no particular wish to inherit. The money hadn't come from land but from fortunate investments and by the late Twenties they had more or less dried up. So in 1930 he set up a charitable trust with what was left, found some wealthy supporters and handed over the island and the property. His idea was that it should be used as a place of rest and seclusion for men in positions of responsibility who needed to get away from the rigours of their professional lives.'

Now, for the first time, he bent down to open his briefcase and took out a file with a security marking. Rummaging among the documents, he brought out a single sheet of paper. 'I've got the exact wording here. It makes Henry Holcombe's intentions clear. *For men who undertake the dangerous and arduous business of exercising high responsibility in the service of the Crown and of their country, whether in the armed forces, politics, science, industry or the arts, and who require a restorative period of solitude, silence and peace.* Engagingly typical of its age, isn't it? No mention of women, of course. This was 1930, remember. However the accepted convention is held to apply, that the word "men" embraces women. They take a maximum of five visitors whom they accommodate at their choice either in the main house or in one of the stone cottages. Basically what Combe Island offers is peace and security. In the last few decades the latter has become probably the more important. People who want time to think can go there without their protection officers in the knowledge that they will be safe and completely undisturbed. There's a helicopter pad for bringing them in, and the small harbour is the only possible landing place by sea. No casual visitors are ever allowed and even mobile phones are forbidden – they wouldn't get a signal there anyway. They keep a very low profile. People who go there are generally on personal recommendation, either from a Trustee or from a previous or regular visitor. You can see its advantage for the PM's purpose.'

Reeves blurted out, 'What's wrong with Chequers?'

The others turned on him the brightly interested gaze of an adult prepared to humour a precocious child.

Conistone said, 'Nothing. An agreeable house with, I understand, every comfort. But guests who are invited to Chequers tend to get noticed. Isn't that the purpose of their going there?'

Dalgliesh asked, 'How did Downing Street get to know about the island?'

Conistone slid the paper back into his file. 'Through one of the PM's newly ennobled chums. He went to Combe to recover from the dangerous and arduous responsibility of adding one more grocery chain to his empire and another billion to his personal fortune.'

'There are some permanent staff, presumably. Or do the VIPs do their own washing up?'

'There's the secretary, Rupert Maycroft, previously a solicitor in Warnborough. We've had to confide in him and, of course, inform the Trustees that Number Ten would be grateful if some important visitors could be accommodated in early January. At present it's all very tentative but we've asked him to make no bookings after this month. There are the usual staff – boatman, housekeeper, cook. We know something about all of them. One or two of the previous visitors have been important enough to warrant security checks. It's all been done very discreetly. There's a resident physician, Dr Guy Staveley, and his wife, although I gather she's more off than on the island. Can't stand the boredom apparently. Staveley's a refugee from a London general practice. Apparently he made a wrong diagnosis and a child died, so he's got himself a job where the worst that can happen is someone falling off a cliff and he can't be blamed for that.'

Harkness said, 'Only one resident has a criminal conviction, the boatman Jago Tamlyn in 1998 for GBH. I gather there were mitigating circumstances but it must have been a serious attack. He got twelve months. He's been in no trouble since.'

Dalgliesh asked, 'When did the current visitors arrive?'

'All five in the last week. The writer Nathan Oliver, together with his daughter Miranda and copy-editor Dennis Tremlett, came on Monday. A retired German diplomat, Dr Raimund Speidel, ex-Ambassador to Beijing, came by private yacht from France on Wednesday, and Dr Mark Yelland, director of the Hayes-Skolling research laboratory in the Midlands which has been targeted by the animal liberation activists, arrived on Thursday. Maycroft will be able to put you in the picture.'

Harkness broke in, 'Better take the minimum of people, at least until you know what you're dealing with. The smaller the invasion the better.'

Dalgliesh said, 'It will hardly be an invasion. I'm

still awaiting a replacement for Tarrant but I'll take Inspector Miskin and Sergeant Benton-Smith. We can probably manage without a SOCO or official photographer at this stage, but if it proves to be murder, I'll have to have reinforcements or let the local force take over. I'll need a pathologist. I'll speak to Kynaston if I can reach him. He may be away from his lab on a case.'

Harkness said, 'That won't be necessary. We're using Edith Glenister. You know her, of course.'

'Hasn't she retired?'

Conistone said, 'Officially two years ago, but she does work occasionally, mostly on sensitive overseas cases. At sixty-five she's probably had enough of trudging gum-booted through muddy fields with the local CID, examining decomposing bodies in ditches.'

Dalgliesh doubted whether this was why Professor Glenister had officially retired. He had never worked with her but he knew her reputation. She was among the most highly regarded of women forensic pathologists, notable for an almost uncanny accuracy in assessing the time of death, for the speed and comprehensiveness of her reports and for the clarity and authority with which she gave evidence in court. She was notable, too, for her insistence on maintaining the distinction between the functions of the pathologist and the investigating officer. Professor Glenister, he knew, would never hear details of the circumstances of the murder before examining the body, ensuring, presumably, that she came to the corpse with no preconceived ideas. He was intrigued by the prospect of working with her and had no doubt that it was the FCO who had originally suggested using her.

All the same, he would have preferred his usual forensic pathologist.

He said, 'You're not implying that Miles Kynaston can't be trusted to keep his mouth shut?'

Harkness broke in. 'Of course not, but Cornwall is hardly his patch. Professor Glenister is stationed at present in the South West. Anyway Kynaston isn't available, we've checked.' Dalgliesh was tempted to say, *How convenient for the FCO.* They certainly hadn't lost any time. Harkness went on, 'You can pick her up at RAF St Mawgan, near Newquay, and they'll arrange a special helicopter to take the body to the mortuary she uses. She'll treat the case as urgent. You should get her report sometime tomorrow.'

Dalgliesh said, 'So Maycroft rang you as soon as possible after finding the body? I suppose he was following instructions.'

Harkness said, 'He was given a phone number, told that it was top secret and instructed to phone the Trustees if anything untoward happened on the island. He's been warned that you'll be arriving by helicopter and to expect you by early afternoon.'

Dalgliesh said, 'He'll have some difficulty explaining to his colleagues why this particular death should attract a Metropolitan Police commander and a detective inspector instead of being dealt with by the local CID, but I suppose you've covered that.'

Harkness said, 'As well as we can. The Chief Constable has been put in the picture, of course. There's no point in arguing over which force should take responsibility until we know whether we've got a murder to investigate. In the meantime they'll cooperate. If it is murder and the island is as secure as they claim, there'll be a limited number of suspects. That should speed up the inquiry.'

Only someone ignorant of a murder investigation, or who had conveniently forgotten the less successful incidents of his past, could have been so misjudging. A small group of suspects, if each was intelligent and prudent enough to keep his or her counsel and resist the fateful impulse to volunteer more than was asked, could complicate any investigation and bedevil the prosecution.

At the door Conistone turned. 'The food's all right on Combe Island I suppose? The beds comfortable?'

Harkness said coolly, 'We've had no time to enquire. Frankly it didn't occur to me. I should have thought that whether the cook knows her job and the state of the mattresses is more your concern than ours. Our interest is in a dead body.'

Conistone took the barb with good humour. 'True. We'll check on the amenities if this conference comes off. The first thing the rich and powerful learn is the value of comfort. I should have mentioned that the last surviving Holcombe is a permanent resident on the island, Miss Emily Holcombe, aged eighty plus, a former Oxford academic. History, I believe. Your subject, wasn't it, Adam – but weren't you at the other place? She'll either be an ally or a perfect nuisance. If I know anything about academic women it will be the latter. Thank you for taking this on. We'll be in touch.'

Harkness rose to escort Conistone and Reeves out of the building. Leaving them at the lifts, Dalgliesh went back to his office. First he must phone Kate and

Benton-Smith. After that there was a more difficult call. He and Emma Lavenham were to have spent tonight and tomorrow together. If she planned to spend the afternoon in London, she might already be on her way. He'd have to reach her on her mobile phone. It wouldn't be the first call of its kind and, as always, she would be half-expecting it. She wouldn't complain – Emma never did. Both of them had occasional urgent commitments and their time together was the more precious because it could never be relied upon. And there were three words he wanted to say to her which he found he could never speak over the phone. They too would have to wait.

He put his head round the door of his PA's room. 'Get DI Miskin and Sergeant Benton-Smith for me, will you, Susie. Then I'll need a car to go to Battersea Heliport, picking up Sergeant Benton-Smith first, then Inspector Miskin. Her murder case is in her office. See that it's put in the car, will you.'

The call could hardly have come at a less convenient time. After a month of working a sixteen-hour day tiredness had caught up with him and, although he could manage tiredness, what he longed for was rest, peace and, for two blessed days, the company of Emma. He told himself that he had only himself to blame for the spoilt weekend. He wasn't compelled to undertake a possible murder investigation, however politically or socially important the victim or challenging the crime. There were senior officers who would have preferred him to concentrate on initiatives with which he was already closely involved, the complications of policing a multiracial society in which drugs, terrorism and international crime conglomerates were the major challenges, the proposal for a new detective force to deal with serious crimes best investigated nationally. The plans would be bedevilled with politics; top-level policing always had been. The Met needed senior officers who were at ease in that duplicitous world. He saw himself as in danger of becoming one more bureaucrat, a committee member, adviser, co-ordinator – not a detective. If this happened, would he any longer be a poet? Wasn't it in the rich soil of a murder investigation, in the fascination of the gradual unveiling of truth, in shared exertion and the prospect of danger, and in the pitiableness of desperate and broken lives that his poetry put out its shoots?

But now, with Kate and Benton-Smith on their way, there were things to be done and quickly, meetings to be tactfully cancelled, papers to be locked away, the public-relations branch to be put in the picture. He kept a bag always packed for these sudden emergencies, but it was in his Queenhithe flat and he was glad that he needed to call in there. He had never yet phoned Emma from New Scotland Yard. She would know as soon as she heard his voice what he was about to say. She would make her own arrangements for the weekend, perhaps excluding him from her thoughts as he was from her company.

Ten minutes later he closed the door of his office and for the first time with a backward glance, as if taking leave of a long familiar place he might not see again.

2

In her flat above the Thames, Detective Inspector Kate Miskin was still in bed. Normally, long before this hour, she would have been at her office and, even on a rest day, showered, clothed and breakfasted. Early rising was habitual for Kate. It was partly by choice, partly a legacy of her childhood when, burdened with the daily dread of imagined catastrophe, she would drag on her clothes at the moment of waking, desperate to be ready to cope with the expected disaster: a fire in one of the flats below preventing rescue, a plane crashing through the window, an earthquake shattering the high-rise, the balcony rail trembling then breaking in her hands. It was always with relief that she would hear her grandmother's frail and querulous voice calling for her early-morning tea. Her grandmother had a right to be querulous: the death of the daughter she hadn't wanted to bear, cooped up in a high-rise flat where she hadn't chosen to live, burdened by an illegitimate granddaughter she didn't want to care for and could hardly bear the pain of loving. But her grandmother was dead, and if the past was not dead and never could be, she had learned painfully over the years to recognise and accept the best and the worst of what it had done to her.

Now she looked out on a very different London. Her riverside flat was at the end of the building with a double outlook and two balconies. From the sitting room she looked south-west over the river with its incessant traffic – barges, pleasure boats, the launches of the river police and the Port of London Authority, the cruise liners making their way upstream to berth at Tower Bridge. From her bedroom she saw the panorama of Canary Wharf, its top like a gigantic pencil; the still water of West India Dock; the Docklands Light Railway with its trains like childhood clockwork toys. She had always loved the stimulus of contrast and here she could move from the old to the new, surveying the life of the river in all its contrasts from first light until dusk. At nightfall she would stand at the balcony rail watching the city transform itself into a shining tableau of light, eclipsing the stars, staining the sky with its reflected crimson glare.

The flat, long-planned, prudently mortgaged, was her home, her refuge, her security, the dream of years solidified in bricks and mortar. No colleague had ever been invited to the flat and her first and only lover, Alan Scully, had long departed for America. He had wanted her to go with him but she had refused, partly out of fear of commitment, but mainly because her job came first. But now, for the first time since their last night together, she had not been alone.

She stretched in the double bed. Beyond the transparent curtains the morning sky was a clear pale blue above a narrow smudge of grey cloud. Yesterday's forecast had predicted another late autumnal day of alternate sun and showers. She could hear small agreeable sounds from the kitchen, water hissing into the kettle, the closing of a cupboard door, the clink of china.

Detective Inspector Piers Tarrant was making coffee. Alone for the first time since they had arrived together at the flat, she relived the last twenty-four hours, not with regret, but with amazement that it should have happened.

The phone call from Piers had come to her at her office early on Monday. It was an invitation to have dinner on Friday night. The call had been unexpected; since Piers had left the Squad to join the anti-terrorist branch they hadn't spoken. They had worked together on Dalgliesh's Special Investigation Squad for years, respected each other, been stimulated by a half-acknowledged rivalry which she knew Commander Dalgliesh had made use of, had occasionally argued, passionately but without acrimony. She had found him – and still did – one of the most sexually attractive men she had ever worked with. But even had he sent out tentative well-recognised signals of sexual interest, she wouldn't have responded. To have an affair with a close colleague was to risk more than one's competence; one of them would have had to leave the Squad. It was her job that had freed her from Ellison Fairweather Buildings. She wasn't going to jeopardise all she had achieved by going down that seductive but ultimately messy path.

She had pocketed her mobile, a little surprised by her ready acceptance of the invitation and puzzled by what lay behind it. Was there something, she had wondered, that Piers needed to ask or to discuss? It seemed unlikely. The Met rumour mill, usually efficient, had disseminated hints of his dissatisfaction with the new job, but men confided their successes to women, not their misjudgements. And he had suggested that they meet at seven-thirty at Sheekey's after asking her whether she liked fish. The choice of a highly regarded restaurant, which couldn't be expected to be cheap, had sent out a subtle if confusing message. Was this to be in some way a celebratory evening, or was this extravagance usual for Piers when he entertained a woman? After all, he had never given the impression that he was short of money and he was rumoured never to be short of women.

He had been waiting for her when she arrived and as he rose to greet her she caught his quick appraising glance and was glad that she had taken trouble, intricately piling up her strong fair hair which, when working, she always brushed firmly back and wore either in a pigtail or tied on the nape of her neck. She was wearing a shirt in dull cream silk and her only expensive jewellery, antique gold earrings each set with a single pearl. She was intrigued and a little amused to see that Piers had taken trouble too. She didn't remember ever having seen him in a suit and tie and was tempted to say, 'Scrub up nicely, don't we?'

They were seated at a corner table, safe for confidences, but there had been few. Dinner had been successful, a protracted enjoyment without constraints. He had spoken little of his new job but that she had expected. They had talked briefly of the books they had recently read, films they had found time to see, conventional exchanges which Kate sensed were no more than the careful social chat of two strangers on a first date. They had moved to more familiar ground, the cases they had worked on together, the latest Met gossip, and from time to time confided small details of their private lives.

At the end of the main course of Dover sole, he had asked, 'How is the handsome sergeant making out?'

Kate was secretly amused. Piers had never successfully concealed his dislike of Francis Benton-Smith. Kate suspected that it had less to do with Benton's extraordinary good looks than with a shared attitude to the job: controlled ambition, intelligence, a carefully calculated route to the top based on the confidence that they brought advantages to policing which, with luck, would be recognised with fast-streaming to promotion.

'He's all right. A bit over-anxious to please perhaps, but weren't we all when AD took us on? He'll do.'

'It's rumoured that AD might have him in mind for my job.'

'Your old job? It's possible, I suppose. After all, he hasn't filled it yet. The top brass may be waiting to decide what to do about the Squad. They could shut it down, who knows? They're always after AD for other and bigger jobs – this national CID they're planning, you must have heard the rumours. He's always tied up with one top-level meeting or another.'

By the time they were eating their puddings the talk had become desultory. Suddenly Piers said, 'I don't like drinking coffee too soon after fish.'

'Or after this wine, but I need sobering up.' But that, she thought, had been disingenuous. She never drank enough to risk losing control.

'We could go to my flat. It's near enough.'

She had said, 'Or mine. I've got a river view.'

The invitation, his acceptance, had been totally

without strain. He said, 'Then yours. I just need to call at my place en route.'

He had been absent for only two minutes and at her suggestion she had stayed in the car. Twenty minutes later, unlocking her flat, coming with him into the wide sitting room with its wall of windows overlooking the Thames, she had seen it with fresh eyes: conventional, all the furniture modern, no mementoes, no evidence that the owner had a private life, parents, a family, objects passed down through generations, as tidy and impersonal as a show flat cunningly arranged for a quick sale. Without a glance around, he had moved to the windows, then through the door on to the balcony.

'I can see why you chose it, Kate.'

She didn't go out with him, but had stood watching his back, seeing beyond him to the black heaving water, scarred and slashed with silver, the spires and towers, the great blocks on the opposite bank patterned with oblongs of light. He had come into the kitchen with her while she ground the coffee beans, set out the two mugs, heated milk from the fridge. By the time, sitting together on the sofa, they had finished drinking and he had leaned forward and kissed her gently but firmly on the lips, she knew what would happen. But then, hadn't she known from that first moment in the restaurant?

He said, 'I'd like to shower.'

She laughed. 'How matter-of-fact you are, Piers! The bathroom's through that door.'

'Why not join me, Kate?'

'Not enough room. You go first.'

It had all been so easy, so natural, so devoid of doubt or anxiety, even of conscious thought. And now, lying in bed in the gentle morning light, hearing the rush of the shower, she thought back over the night in a sweet confusion of memory and half-spoken sentences.

'I thought you only liked mindless blondes.'

'They weren't all mindless. And you're blonde.'

She had said, 'Light brown, not yellow blonde.'

He had turned again towards her and had run his hands through her hair, a gesture unexpected, not least in its slow gentleness.

She had expected that Piers would be an experienced and skilful lover, what she had not expected was how uncomplicated and unstressed had been their joyous carnality. They had lain down with laughter as well as with desire. And afterwards, a little distanced in her double bed, hearing his breathing and feeling the warmth of him flowing towards her, it had seemed natural that he should be there. She knew that their love-making had begun to soften a hard core compounded of self-mistrust and defensiveness which she carried on her heart like a weight and which, after the Macpherson Report, had acquired an accretion of resentment and a sense of betrayal. Piers, cynical and more politically sophisticated than she, had shown little patience.

'All official committees of inquiry know what they're expected to find. Some of the less intelligent do it a little overenthusiastically. It's ridiculous to lose your job over it or to let it destroy your confidence or your peace.'

Dalgliesh, with tact and sometimes wordlessly, had persuaded her not to resign. But she knew that over the past years there had been a slow draining away of the dedication, commitment and naïve enthusiasm with which she had entered the police service. She was still a valued and competent officer. She liked her job and could contemplate no other for which she was either qualified or suitable. But she had become afraid of emotional involvement, too self-protecting, too wary of what life could do. Now, lying alone and hearing the faint sounds of Piers moving about the flat, she felt an almost forgotten joy.

She had been the first to wake, and for the first time without that childhood vestigial anxiety. She had lain relishing her body's contentment for thirty minutes, watching the strengthening light, aware of the first river sounds of the day, before slipping out to the bathroom. The movement had woken him. Stirring, he had reached out for her, then sat up suddenly like a tousled jack-in-the-box. They had both laughed. In the kitchen together he had squeezed the oranges while she made tea, and later they had taken hot buttered toast out to the balcony and thrown the crusts to the shrieking seagulls in a whirl of wildly beating wings and snapping beaks. Then they had gone back to bed.

The rush and gurgle of the shower had ceased. Now it was time finally to get up and face the complications of the day. She had swung her legs out of bed when her mobile phone rang. It jolted her into action as if she had never heard it before. Piers came out of the kitchen, a towel wrapped round his waist, cafetiere in hand. She said, 'Oh God! Right on cue.'

'It might be personal.'

'Not on this phone.'

She put out her hand to the bedside table, picked up the phone, listened intently, said 'Yes sir', and switched off. She said, knowing that she couldn't hide the excitement in her voice, 'It's a case. Suspected murder. An island off the Cornish coast. It means a helicopter. I'm to leave my car here. AD is sending one to pick up Benton and then me. We're to meet at Battersea Heliport.'

'Your murder kit?'

Already she was moving, swiftly, knowing what had to be done and in what order. She called from the bathroom door, 'It's in the office. AD'll see it's put in the car.'

He said, 'If he's sending a car I'd better move quickly. If Nobby Clark's driving and sees me, the drivers' mafia will have the news within minutes. I don't see why we should provide entertainment for the canteen gossips.'

Minutes later, Kate dumped her canvas bag on the bed and began her quick methodical packing. She would wear, as usual, her woollen trousers and tweed jacket with a roll-top cashmere jumper. Even if the mild weather continued, there was no point in packing linen or cotton – an island was seldom uncomfortably warm. Stout walking shoes went into the bottom with one change of pants and bra. These could be washed daily. She folded a second warmer jumper into the bag and added a silk shirt, carefully rolled. On top came pyjamas and her woollen dressing-gown. She tucked in the spare toilet bag which she always kept ready with the things she needed. Last of all she threw in two new notebooks, half-a-dozen ball-point pens and a half-read paperback.

Five minutes later both of them were dressed and ready to leave. She walked with Piers to the underground garage. At the door of his Alfa Romeo he kissed her on the cheek and said, 'Thank you for your company at dinner, thank you for breakfast, thank you for everything in between. Send me a postcard from your mysterious island. Six words will be enough – more than enough if they happen to be true. *Wish you were here, love Kate.*'

She laughed but didn't reply. The Vauxhall leaving the garage before him had a notice in the rear window, *Baby on board.* It always aroused Piers to fury. He grabbed a handwritten card from the glove-box and stuck it against the glass. *Herod on board.* Then he raised his hand in farewell and was gone.

Kate stood looking after him until, hooting a final goodbye, he turned into the main road. And now a different, less complicated but familiar emotion took over. Whatever problems this extraordinary night might produce, thinking about them would have to wait. Somewhere, as yet only imagined, a body was lying in the cold abstraction of death. A group of people was waiting for the police to arrive, some distressed, most apprehensive, one surely sharing her intoxicated mixture of excitement and resolve. It had always worried her that someone had to die before she could experience this half-guilty exhilaration. And there would be the part she most enjoyed, the team get-together at the end of the day when AD, herself and Benton-Smith would ponder over the evidence, picking up, discarding or clicking the clues into place as they might the pieces of a jigsaw. But she knew the root of the small sprig of shame. Although they had never spoken of it she suspected that AD felt the same. With this jigsaw the pieces were the broken lives of men and women.

Three minutes later, waiting bag in hand outside the flat, she saw the car turn into the driveway. The working day had begun.

3

Sergeant Francis Benton-Smith lived alone on the sixteenth floor of a post-war block to the north-west of Shepherd's Bush. Beneath him were fifteen floors of identical flats and identical balconies. The balconies, which stretched the whole length of each floor, afforded no privacy but he was only rarely disturbed by his neighbours. One used his flat as a *pied-à-terre* and was seldom there, and the other, engaged in some mysterious work in the City, left even earlier than did Benton and returned with conspiratorial quietness in the small hours. The block, previously local-authority housing, had been sold off by the council, renovated by private developers and the flats then put on the market. Despite a reconstructed entrance hall, the modern unvandalised lifts and the new paint, the block was still an unhappy compromise between prudent economy, civic pride and institutional conformity, but at least architecturally it was inoffensive. It aroused no emotion other than surprise that anyone should have bothered to put it up.

Even the wide view from the balcony was unremarkable. Benton looked out on a drab industrial landscape patterned in black and greys and dominated by rectangular slabs of high-rise flats, featureless industrial buildings and narrow streets of obstinately surviving nineteenth-century terraces, now the carefully preserved habitat of aspiring young professionals. The Westway rose in a curve above a closely packed caravan-park of transients who lived under the concrete pillars, rarely venturing out. Beyond them was a yard piled high with the crumpled metal of derelict cars, the spiked tangle a rusting symbol of the vulnerability of human life and hope. But when night fell the view was metamorphosed, made insubstantial and mystical by light. Traffic signals changed, cars moved like automata on liquid roads, the high cranes with their single top lights were angled like praying mantises, grotesque Cyclops of the night. Aircraft descended silently towards Heathrow from a blue-black sky bruised with garish clouds and, as dusk deepened, floor-by-floor as if by a signal, the lights came on in the high-rise flats.

But neither by night or day was this uniquely a London landscape. Benton felt that he could be looking out over any large city. None of the familiar landmarks lay beneath him – no glimpse of the river, no painted floodlit bridges, no familiar towers or domes. But this carefully chosen anonymity, even the landscape, was what he had wanted. He had put down no roots, having no native soil.

He had moved into the flat six months after joining the police and it could not be more different than his parents' home in the leafy street in South Kensington: the white steps up to the pillared front door, the gleaming paint and immaculate stucco. He had decided to leave the small self-contained flat at the top of the house, partly because he felt it demeaning to be still living at home after the age of eighteen, but chiefly because he couldn't imagine inviting a colleague to his flat. Even to walk through the main door of the house was to know what it represented: money, privilege, the cultural assurance of the prosperous liberal upper-middle-class. But he knew that his present apparent independence was spurious; the flat and its contents had been paid for by his parents – on his salary he couldn't otherwise have afforded to move. And he had made himself comfortable. He told himself wryly that only a visitor knowledgeable about modern furniture would have guessed how much the deceptively simple pieces had cost.

But there had been no visitors among his colleagues. As a new recruit he had trodden carefully at first, knowing that he was on a probation more rigorous and protracted than any provisional assessment from senior officers. He had hoped, if not for friendship, for tolerance, respect and acceptance, and to an extent he had earned them. But he was aware that he was still regarded with wary circumspection. He felt himself to be surrounded by a variety of organisations, including the criminal law, dedicated to protecting his racial sensitivities, as if he could be as easily offended as a Victorian virgin confronted by a flasher. He wished that these racial warriors would leave him alone. Did they want to stigmatise minorities as over-sensitive, insecure and paranoid? But he accepted that the problem was partly of his making, a reserve that was deeper and less forgivable than shyness and which inhibited intimacy. They didn't know who he was; he didn't know who he was. It wasn't, he thought, only the result of being mixed-race. The London world he knew and worked in was peopled with men and women of mixed racial, religious and national backgrounds. They seemed to manage.

His mother was Indian, his father English, she a paediatrician, he the headmaster of a London comprehensive school. They had fallen in love and married when she was seventeen, his father twelve years older. They had been passionately in love and they still were. He knew from the wedding photographs that she had been exquisitely beautiful; she still was. She had brought money as well as beauty to the marriage. From childhood he had felt an intruder into that private self-sufficient world. They were both over-busy and he had learned early that their time together was precious. He knew that he was loved, that his welfare was their concern, but coming quietly and unexpectedly into a room where they were alone, he would see the cloud of disappointment on their faces quickly change into smiles of welcome – but not quickly enough. Their difference in religious belief seemed never to worry them. His father was an atheist, his mother a Roman Catholic and Francis had been brought up and schooled in that faith. But when in adolescence he gradually let it go as he might relinquish a part of childhood, neither parent appeared to notice, or if they did, felt that they were justified in questioning him.

They had taken him with them on their annual visits to Delhi, and there too he had felt an alien. It was as if his legs, painfully stretched across a spinning globe, could find no secure footing in either continent. His father loved to revisit India, was at home there, was greeted with loud exclamations of delight, laughed, teased and was teased, wore Indian clothes, performed the salaam with more ease than he shook hands at home, left after tearful goodbyes. As a child and adolescent, Benton was made a great fuss of, exclaimed over, praised for his beauty, his intelligence, but he would stand there ill at ease, politely exchanging compliments, knowing that he didn't belong.

He had hoped that selection to Adam Dalgliesh's Special Investigation Squad would help to make him more at home in his job, perhaps even in his disjointed world. Perhaps to some extent it had. He knew himself to be lucky; time spent in the Squad was a recognised asset when it came to promotion. His last case – which was also his first – a death by fire in a Hampstead museum, had been a test that he felt he had successfully passed. With the next call there could be problems. Inspector Piers Tarrant was known to be a demanding and occasionally tricky senior officer but Benton had felt that he knew how to cope with Tarrant, recognising in him that touch of ambition, cynicism and ruthlessness that he understood and which mirrored his own. But with Tarrant transferred to the anti-terrorist branch, he would be working under Detective Inspector Kate Miskin. Kate Miskin was a less straightforward challenge and not just because she was a woman. She was always correct and less openly critical than Tarrant, but he sensed that she was ill at ease with him as a colleague. It had nothing to do with his colour, his sex or his social status, although he sensed that she had some hang-ups over class. She just didn't like him. It was as simple and intractable as that. Somehow, and perhaps soon, he would have to learn how to deal with it.

But now his thoughts turned to his plans for this free day. He had already cycled to the farmers' market at Notting Hill Gate and bought organic fruit, vegetables and meat for the weekend, some of which he had arranged to take to his mother during the afternoon. He hadn't been home for six weeks and it was time he showed his face, if only to assuage a nagging guilt that he was a less than punctilious son.

And in the evening he would cook dinner for Beverley. She was a twenty-one-year-old actress who, straight from drama school, had landed a small part in a long-running television serial set in a Suffolk village. They had met in a local supermarket, a well-known pick-up resource for the solitary or temporarily deprived. After studying him covertly for a minute she had made the first move by asking him to lift down a tin of tomatoes conveniently beyond her reach. He was enchanted by her looks, the delicate oval face, the straight black hair cut in a fringe above the slightly slanting eyes, which gave her an engaging look of oriental delicacy. She was in fact robustly English and from much the same professional background as himself. She would have been perfectly at home in his mother's drawing room. But Beverley had cast off her middle-class social nuances and accent and changed her unfashionable first name in the service of her career. Her part in the serial, the wayward daughter of the village publican, had caught the public imagination. There were rumours that the character would be developed with exciting possibilities – a rape, an illegitimate child, an affair with the church organist, perhaps even a murder, though not, of course, of her or the baby. Audiences, she told Benton, didn't like to see murdered babies. In the glitzy ephemeral firmament of popular culture, Beverley was becoming a star.

After sex, which Beverley liked to be inventive, prolonged but inconveniently hygienic, she would practise her yoga. Propped up on his arm in the bed, Benton would watch her extraordinary contortions with fascinated and indulgent affection. At these moments he knew himself to be dangerously close to love, but he had no expectation that the affair would last. Beverley, who was as vocal as a hellfire preacher about the dangers of promiscuity, preferred serial monogamy but with a carefully defined time limit for each partner. Boredom usually set in after six months, she explained helpfully. They had now been together for five and although Beverley hadn't yet spoken, Benton had no expectation that either his lovemaking or his cooking had qualified him for extra time.

He was still unpacking his purchases and finding room for them in the fridge when the designated mobile he kept on his bedside table began to ring. He would put out his hand each night to reassure himself that it was still in place. In the morning, setting out for his interim job at the Met, he would slip it in his pocket willing it to ring. Now, slamming the refrigerator door, he dashed to answer it as if fearful that the ringing might stop. He listened to the brief message, said 'Yes, sir', and switched off. The day was transformed.

His bag, as always, was already packed. He had been told to bring his camera and binoculars, both of which were superior to those owned by other members of the team. So they were to be on their own, calling in no back-up, no photographer or SOCO unless it proved necessary. Mystery deepened his excitement. And now he had nothing to do but make two quick phone calls, one to his mother, the second to Beverley. Both, he suspected, would cause minor inconvenience, but no pain. In happy but half-fearful expectation, he turned his mind to the challenge that awaited him on that as yet unknown offshore island.

BOOK ONE

Death on an Offshore Island

I

At seven o'clock on the previous day in Atlantic Cottage on Combe Island, Emily Holcombe stepped out of her shower, tied a towel round her waist and began smoothing moisturising cream into her arms and neck. It had become a daily routine for the last five years since her seventy-fifth birthday, but she had no sanguine expectation that it could do more than temporarily alleviate the ravages of age, nor did she greatly care. In youth and middle-age she had taken little trouble with her looks and she occasionally wondered whether it might not be both pointless and a little demeaning to begin these time-consuming rituals when the results could gratify no one but herself. But then, whom else had she ever wished to gratify? She had always been handsome, some thought beautiful, certainly not pretty, strong-featured with high cheekbones, large hazel eyes under straight brows, a narrow slightly aquiline nose and a wide, well-shaped mouth which could look deceptively generous. Some men had found her intimidating; others – among them the more intelligent – were challenged by her barbed wit and responded to her latent sexuality. All her lovers had given her pleasure, none had caused her pain, and the pain she had caused them had long since been forgotten, and even at the time had left her unburdened by remorse.

Now, with all passion spent, she had come back to the

beloved island of her childhood, to the stone cottage on the cliff edge which she intended should be her permanent home for the rest of her life. She had no intention that anyone – certainly not Nathan Oliver – should take it from her. She respected him as a writer – he was, after all, acknowledged to be one of the world's greatest novelists – but she had never considered that major talent, even genius, entitled a man to be more selfish and self-indulgent than was common in the majority of his sex.

She strapped on her watch. By the time she went back to her bedroom Roughtwood would have removed the early-morning tea tray, which arrived promptly at six-thirty each morning, and breakfast would have been laid out in the dining room: the home-made muesli and marmalade, the unsalted butter, the coffee and the warm milk. Toast wouldn't be made until he heard her passing the kitchen door. She thought of Roughtwood with satisfaction and some affection. She had made a good decision for both of them. He had been her father's driver and when, the last of her family, she had been at the family house on the edge of Exmoor, arranging the final details with the auctioneer and selecting the few items she wished to retain, he had asked to speak to her.

'As you are taking up residence on the island, madam, I would like to apply for the post of butler.'

Combe Island was always referred to as 'the island' by the family and servants, as Combe House on the island was spoken of only as 'the house'.

Getting to her feet, she had said, 'What on earth would I want with a butler, Roughtwood? We haven't had a butler here since my grandfather's day, and I shan't need a driver. No cars are allowed on the island except the buggy for delivering food to the cottages, as you well know.'

'I used the word butler, madam, as a generic term. What I had in mind were the duties of a personal servant but, conscious that the words could be taken to imply that I was serving a gentleman, butler seemed a more convenient if not entirely appropriate description.'

'You've been reading too much P. G. Wodehouse, Roughtwood. Can you cook?'

'My range is limited, madam, but I think you'll find the results satisfactory.'

'Oh well, there probably wouldn't be much cooking. An evening meal will be provided at the house and I'll probably book in for that. But how healthy are you? Frankly, I don't see myself as a nurse; I have no patience with illness either in myself or others.'

'I haven't found it necessary to consult a doctor for twenty years, madam. And I'm twenty-five years younger than yourself, if you'll excuse my mentioning it.'

'Naturally in the course of things I can expect to predecease you. When that happens, there probably won't be a house for you on the island. I wouldn't want you to find yourself homeless at sixty.'

'That would present no problem, madam. I've a house in Exeter which at present is let furnished on short-term leases, usually to academics from the university. I propose to retire there eventually. I have an affection for the city.'

Why Exeter? she had wondered. What part had

39

Exeter played in Roughtwood's mysterious past? It was not, she thought, a city to provoke strong affection except in its residents.

'Then we might try the experiment. I'll have to consult the other Trustees. It will mean that the Trust must provide me with two cottages, preferably adjacent to each other. I imagine neither of us wish to share a bathroom.'

'I'd certainly prefer a separate cottage, madam.'

'Then I'll see what can be arranged and we could try it for a month. If we don't suit each other, we can part without acrimony.'

That had been fifteen years ago and they were still together. He had proved to be an excellent servant and a surprisingly good cook. Increasingly she ate her evening meal in Atlantic Cottage, not at the house. He took two holidays a year, each of ten days exactly. She had no idea where he went or what he did, nor did he ever confide in her. She had always assumed that long-term residents on the island were escaping from something even if, as in her case, the items on her list were too commonly accepted by the malcontents of her generation to be worth dwelling on: noise, mobile phones, vandalism, drunken louts, political correctness, inefficiency and the assault on excellence by renaming it elitism. She knew no more about him now than she did when he had driven her father and then she had seen him rarely, a square immobile face, his eyes half-hidden by the brim of his chauffeur's cap, his hair unusually blond for a man, precisely cut in a half moon on the thick neck. They had established a routine agreeable to both. Every evening at five o'clock they would sit down together in her cottage for their daily game of Scrabble, following which they would have a glass or two of red wine – the only time they ate or drank with each other – and he would return to his own cottage to prepare her dinner.

He was accepted as part of the island's life but she sensed that his privileged, hardly overworked existence caused some unspoken resentment among the other staff. He had his own unwritten job specification but even in the rare emergencies never offered to help. They thought he was devoted to her as the last of the Holcombes; she thought that unlikely and wouldn't have welcomed it. But she did admit to herself that he was in danger of becoming indispensable.

Moving into her bedroom with its two windows giving a view both over the sea and across the island, she walked to the northerly window and opened the casement. It had been a blustery night but the wind had now moderated to a lively breeze. Beyond the land leading to the front porch the ground rose gently and on the ridge stood a silent figure, as firmly rooted as a statue. Nathan Oliver was gazing fixedly at the cottage. He was only some sixty feet distant and she knew that he must have seen her. She drew back from the window but still watched him as intently as she knew he was watching her. He didn't move, his motionless body contrasting with his swirling white hair tossed into wildness by the wind. He would have looked like an anathematising Old Testament prophet except for the disconcerting stillness. His eyes were fixed on the cottage with a concentrated desire that she felt went beyond the rational reason he put forward for wanting the place – that he came to Combe Island accompanied always by

his daughter Miranda and his copy-editor Dennis Tremlett and required adjacent cottages. Atlantic Cottage,
the only one which was semi-detached, was the most
desirable on the island. Did he also need, as did she, to
live on this dangerous edge, to hear night and day the
crash of the tide hurling itself against the cliff face thirty
feet below? This, after all, was the cottage in which he
had been born and where he had lived until, at sixteen,
he left Combe without explanation and began his
solitary quest to become a writer. Was that at the heart
of it? Had he come to believe that his talent would
wither without this place? He was twelve years younger
than she, but did he have a premonition that his work,
and perhaps his life, were nearing the end and that he
couldn't find rest for his spirit except in the place where
he had been born?

For the first time she felt threatened by the power
of his will. And she was never free of him. For the past
seven years he had established a habit of coming to the
island every three months, staying for two precisely
timed weeks. Even if he didn't succeed in dislodging
her – and how could he? – his recurring presence on
Combe disturbed her peace. Little frightened her
except irrationality. Was Oliver's obsession an ominous
symptom of something even more disturbing? Was he
going mad? And still she stood, unwilling to go down to
breakfast while he was standing there, and it was five
minutes before, finally, he turned and walked away over
the ridge.

2

Nathan Oliver lived by routine when in London and this varied little when he made his quarterly visits to Combe Island. While on Combe he and his daughter followed the general practice of visitors. A light lunch, usually of soup, cold meats and salad, was delivered each morning by Dan Padgett in accordance with Miranda's telephoned instructions to the housekeeper, Mrs Burbridge, who conveyed them to the cook. Dinner could be taken either in the cottage or in the main house, but Oliver preferred to eat in Peregrine Cottage and Miranda did the cooking.

For four hours on Friday morning he had worked with Dennis Tremlett, editing his latest novel. He preferred to edit on preliminary proofs typeset from the manuscript, an eccentricity that, at some inconvenience, his publishers accepted. He edited extensively, even making alterations to the plot, writing on the backs of the typeset pages in his minuscule upright hand, then passing the pages to Tremlett to be copied more legibly on to a second set. At one o'clock they stopped for lunch and by two the simple meal had been eaten and Miranda had finished the washing up and placed the containers on the shelf in the outside porch for later collection. Tremlett had earlier left to eat with the staff in their dining room. Oliver usually slept in the afternoon until half-past three when Miranda would wake him for afternoon tea. Today he decided to forgo the rest and walk down to the harbour to be there when the boatman, Jago, brought in the launch. He was anxious to reassure himself that a blood sample taken by Joanna Staveley the previous day had reached the hospital pathology department safely.

By two-thirty Miranda had disappeared, binoculars slung round her neck, saying that she was going bird-watching on the north-west coast. Shortly afterwards, carefully replacing both sets of proofs in his desk drawer and leaving the cottage door unlocked, he set off along the cliff edge towards the steep stone path which led down to the harbour. Miranda must have walked quickly – scanning the scrubland he could see no sign of her.

He was thirty-four when he married and the decision was less an impulse of sexual or psychological need than a conviction that there was something slightly suspect about a heterosexual who remained openly celibate, a suggestion either of eccentricity or, more shaming, of the inability to attract a suitable mate. Here he expected no great difficulty but he was prepared to take his time. He was after all a catch; he had no intention of suffering the ignominy of a refusal. But the enterprise, undertaken without enthusiasm, had proved unexpectedly quick and straightforward. It had taken only two months of shared dinners and the occasional overnight visit to a discreet country inn to convince him that Sydney Bellinger would be an appropriate choice, a view she had made it plain that she shared. She had already gained a reputation as a distinguished political journalist; the confusion occasionally caused by her ambivalent forename had been, if anything, an advantage. And if her histrionic good looks owed more to money, expert make-up and an impeccable taste in clothes than to nature, he asked for nothing more, certainly not romantic love. Although he kept his sexual appetite too much in control ever to be ruled by it, their nights together gave him as much pleasure as he expected to receive from a woman. It was she who made the running, he who acquiesced. He assumed that she saw an equal advantage in the match and this seemed to him reasonable; the most successful marriages were always based on both partners feeling that they had done rather well for themselves.

It might have lasted until now – although he had never relied on permanence – if it hadn't been for Miranda's birth. Here he accepted the major responsibility. At thirty-six, and for the first time, he had detected in himself an irrational desire: the wish to have a son, or at least a child, the acceptance that, for a convinced atheist, this should at least provide the hope of vicarious immortality. Parenthood was, after all, one of the absolutes of human existence. His birth had been outside his control, death was inevitable and would probably be as uncomfortable as birth, sex he had more or less brought under control. That left parenthood. Not to engage in this universal tribute to human optimism was, for a novelist, to leave a lacuna of experience which could limit the possibilities of his talent. The birth had been a disaster. Despite the expensive nursing home, the labour had been protracted and mismanaged, the final forceps delivery spectacularly painful, the anaesthesia less effective than Sydney had hoped. The visceral tenderness, which had sparked feebly at his first sight of his daughter's slimy and bloody nakedness, quickly died. He doubted whether Sydney had ever felt it. Perhaps the fact that the baby had been taken away immediately into Intensive Care hadn't helped.

Visiting her, he had said, 'Wouldn't you like to hold the baby?'

Sydney was twisting her head restlessly on the pillows. 'For God's sake, let me rest! I don't suppose she wants to be mauled around if she's feeling as bloody as I am.'

'What do you want to call her?' It was not something they had discussed.

'I thought Miranda. It seems a miracle she's survived. It's a bloody miracle that I have – and bloody is the appropriate word. Come back tomorrow, will you, I've got to sleep now. And tell them I don't want any visitors. If you're thinking of the family album, wife sitting up in bed, flushed with maternal triumph and holding a presentable infant, put it out of your mind. And I'm telling you now, I'm finished with this brutal business.'

She had been a largely absent mother; more affectionate than he would have expected when she was with the child in the Chelsea house, but more often abroad. He had money now, so with their joint incomes there was enough for a nurse, a housekeeper and for daily help. His own study at the top of the house was forbidden territory to the child, but when he did emerge she would follow him around like a puppy, distanced and seldom speaking, apparently content. But it couldn't last.

When Miranda was four, Sydney, on one of her visits home, said, 'We can't go on like this. She needs the companionship of other children. There are schools that take kids as young as three. I'll get Judith to find out about them.'

Judith was her PA, a woman of formidable efficiency. In this she proved not only efficient but surprisingly sensitive. Brochures were sent for, visits made, references taken up. At the end she managed to get husband and wife together and, file in hand, made her report. 'High Trees, outside Chichester, sounds the best. It's a pleasant house with a very large garden and not too far from the sea. The children seemed happy while I was there and I visited the kitchen and later had a meal with the younger ones in what they call the nursery wing. Many of the children have parents serving overseas and the headmistress seems more concerned with health and general happiness than with academic achievement. That may not matter, you did say Miranda shows no signs of being academically gifted. I think she'd be happy there. I can arrange a visit, if you'd like to meet the headmistress and see round the school.'

Afterwards Sydney had said, 'I can find an afternoon next Wednesday and you'd better come. It wouldn't look good if people knew we'd shoved her off to school with only one of us caring enough to see where she was going.'

So they went together, as distanced, as much strangers as if they were official school inspectors. Sydney played the concerned mother to perfection. Her analysis of her daughter's needs and their hopes for her was impressive. He could hardly wait to get back to his study and write it down. But the children did indeed appear uninhibitedly happy and Miranda was sent there within a week. The school took pupils during the holidays as well as in term time and Miranda seemed to miss High Trees on the few occasions when it was convenient for her to spend part of a holiday at home. After High Trees came a boarding school which offered a reasonably sound education with the kind of quasi-maternal care which Sydney thought desirable. The education didn't go beyond a few examinations at GCSE level, but Oliver told himself that Miranda hardly qualified for Cheltenham Ladies' College or St Paul's.

She was sixteen when he and Sydney divorced. He was surprised at the passion with which Sydney catalogued his inadequacies.

'You really are an appalling man, selfish, rude, pathetic. Don't you honestly realise how much you suck the life out of other people, use them? Why did you want to be there when Miranda was born? Blood and mess are hardly your thing, are they? And you weren't there for me. If you felt anything for me it was physical disgust. You thought you might like to write about childbirth, and you did write about childbirth. You have to be there, don't you? You have to listen, and watch and observe. It's only when you've got the physical details right that you can produce all that psychological insight, all that humanity. What did that last *Guardian* reviewer write? As close as we're likely to get to a modern Henry James! And of course you've got the words, haven't you? I'll give you that. Well, I've got my own words. I don't need your talent, your reputation, your money or your occasional attention in bed. We may as well have a civilised divorce. I'm not keen on advertising failure. It's helpful that this job in Washington has come up. That'll tie me down for the next three years.'

He had said, 'And what about Miranda? She seems anxious to leave school.'

'So you say. The girl hardly communicates with me. She did when she was a kid, but not now. God knows what you'll do with her. As far as I can tell, she isn't interested in anything.'

'I think she's interested in birds; at least she cuts out pictures of them and sticks them on that board in her room.'

He had felt a great spurt of self-congratulation. He had noticed something about Miranda which Sydney had missed. His words were an affirmation of responsible parentage.

'Well, she won't find many birds in Washington. She'd better stay here. What on earth could I do with her?'

'What can I do? She should be with her mother.'

And then she had laughed. 'Oh come on, you can do better than that! Why not let her housekeep for you? You could have holidays on that island where you were born. There should be enough birds there to make her happy. And you'd save on a housekeeper's wages.'

He had saved on wages and there had been birds on Combe, although the adult Miranda showed less enthusiasm for bird-watching than she had as a child. The school had at least taught her how to cook. She had left at sixteen with no qualifications other than that and an undistinguished academic record and for the last sixteen years had lived and travelled with him as his housekeeper, quietly efficient, uncomplaining, apparently content. He had never thought it necessary to consult her about the quarterly and almost ceremonial migrations from the Chelsea house to Combe any more than he would have thought it appropriate to consult Tremlett. He took it for granted that both were willing appendages to his talent. If challenged – and he never was, even by the inconvenient inner promptings which he knew others might call conscience – he would have had his answer ready: they had chosen their way of life, were adequately paid, well fed and housed. On his overseas tours they travelled with him in luxury. Neither appeared to want or was qualified for anything better.

What had surprised him on his first return to Combe seven years ago had been the sudden amazed exhilaration with which he had stepped ashore from the launch. He had embraced this euphoria with the romantic imaginings of a boy; a conqueror taking triumphant possession of his hard-won territory, an explorer finding at last the fabled shore. And that night, standing outside Peregrine Cottage and looking out towards the distant Cornish coast, he knew that he had been right to return. Here in this sea-girt peace the inexorable progress of physical decay might be slowed, here his words would come back.

But he knew, too, from first seeing it again, that he had to have Atlantic Cottage. Here in this stone cottage, which seemed to have grown out of the dangerous cliff below, he had been born and here he would die. This overwhelming need was buttressed by considerations of space and convenience but there was something more elemental, something in his blood responded to the ever-present rhythmic pulse of the sea. His grandfather had been a seaman and had died at sea. His father had been boatman in the old days on Combe and he had lived with him in Atlantic Cottage until he was sixteen and could at last escape his father's alternate drunken rages and maudlin affection and set out alone to make himself a writer. Throughout those years of hardship, of travel and loneliness, if he thought of Combe, it was as a place of violent emotions, of danger, an island not to be visited since it held in thrall the forgotten traumas of the past. Walking along the cliff towards the harbour, he thought how strange it was that he should return to Combe with such an assurance of coming home.

3

It was just after three o'clock and in his office on the second floor of the tower of Combe House Rupert Maycroft was at work drawing up estimates for the next financial year. At a similar desk set against the far wall Adrian Boyde was silently checking the accounts for the quarter ended thirtieth September. Neither was engaged on his favourite job and each worked in silence, a silence broken only by the rustle of paper. Now Maycroft stretched back in his chair and let his eyes rest on the view from the long curved window. The warm unseasonable weather was continuing. There was only a light wind and the wrinkled sea stretched as deeply blue as in high summer under an almost cloudless sky. To the right on a spur of rock stood the old lighthouse with its gleaming white walls topped by the red lantern enclosing the now defunct light, an elegant phallic symbol of the past, lovingly restored but redundant. Sometimes he found its symbolism uncomfortable. To the left he could glimpse the curved arms of the harbour entrance and the stunted towers of the harbour lights. It was this view and this room which had informed his decision to come to Combe.

Even now, after eighteen months, he could find himself surprised to be on the island. He was only fifty-eight, in good health, his mind, as far as he could judge, functioning unimpaired. And yet he had taken early retirement from his practice as a country town solicitor and been glad to go. The decision had been precipitated by the death two years ago of his wife. The car accident had been shockingly unexpected, as fatal accidents always are, however predicted and warned against. She had been on her way from Warnborough to attend a book-club meeting in a neighbouring village, driving too fast along a narrow country road which had become dangerously familiar. Taking a corner at speed, she had crashed her Mercedes head-on with a tractor. During the weeks following the accident, the edge of grief had been blunted by the necessary formalities of bereavement: the inquest, the funeral, the seemingly endless consolatory letters to be answered, the protracted visit of his son and daughter-in-law while his future domestic comfort was discussed, sometimes, he felt, as if he was not present. When, some two months after her death, grief unexpectedly overwhelmed him, he was as astonished by its power as he was by its unexpectedness, compounded as it was by remorse, guilt and a vague unfocused longing. The Combe Island Trust was among his firm's clients. The original Trustees had viewed London as the dark heart of duplicitous and crafty machinations designed to entrap innocent provincials and had been happier choosing a local and long-established practice. The firm had continued to act for the Trust and when it was suggested that he might fill the interregnum between the retirement of the resident secretary and the appointment of his successor, he had seized the opportunity to get away from his practice. Official retirement made the break permanent. Within two months of his appointment at Combe Island he was told that the job was his if he cared to take it.

He had been glad to get away. The Warnborough hostesses, most of whom had been Helen's friends, alleviated the mild boredom of provincial domesticity by the euphoria of benevolent intention. Mentally he paraphrased Jane Austen: *A widower in possession of a house and a comfortable income must be in want of a wife.* It was kindly meant, but since Helen's death he had been smothered with kindness. He had come to dread the regular weekly invitations to lunch or dine. Had he really given up his job and come to this isolation merely to escape the unwelcome advances of local widows? At times of introspection, like the present, he accepted that it could have been so. The prospective successors to Helen had seemed so much of a type that it was difficult to tell them apart: his own age or a little younger, pleasant-faced and some of them pretty, kindly, well dressed and well groomed. They were lonely and assumed that he was too. At every dinner party he worried that he would forget a name, ask the same innocuous questions about children, holidays or hobbies that he had asked before, and with the same feigned interest. He could imagine his hostess's anxious telephone calls after a carefully calculated wait: *How did you get on with Rupert Maycroft? He seemed to enjoy talking to you. Has he phoned?* He hadn't phoned, but had known that one day, in a mood of quiet desperation, loneliness or weakness, he would.

His decision to give up his partnership in the practice, to move – at first temporarily – to Combe Island, had been received with the expected expressions of public regret. They had said how much he would be missed, how greatly he had been valued, but it now struck him forcibly that no one had attempted to dissuade him. He comforted himself with the thought that he had been respected – even, perhaps, a little loved by his long-standing clients, most of them inherited from his father. They had seen him as the epitome of the old-fashioned family solicitor, the confidential friend, keeper of secrets, protector and adviser. He had drawn up their wills, dealt efficiently with their property transactions, represented them before the local magistrates, all of whom he knew, when they were summoned for their petty delinquencies, mostly contested parking or speeding offences. Shoplifting by the wife of a local clergyman was the most serious case he could remember, a scandal that had provided enjoyable gossip in the parish for weeks. With his plea in mitigation the case had been compassionately dealt with by the ordering of medical reports and a moderate fine. His clients would miss him, would remember him with sentimental nostalgia, but not for long. The firm of Maycroft, Forbes and Macintosh would expand, new partners would be recruited, new premises equipped. Young Macintosh, who was due to qualify next year, had already put forward his plans. His own son, Helen's and his only child, would thoroughly have sympathised. He now worked in London in a City firm with over forty solicitors, a high degree of specialisation, distinguished clients and a fair share of national publicity.

He had now been on Combe for eighteen months. Cut off from the reassuring routines which had buttressed the inner self, he found himself ironically more at peace and yet more prone to inner questioning.

At first the island had confused him. Like all beauty, it both solaced and disturbed. It held an extraordinary power to compel introspection, not all of it gloomy, but most of it searching enough to induce discomfort. How predictable, how comfortable his fifty-eight years had been, the over-guarded childhood, the carefully chosen prep school, the years until eighteen at a minor but respected public school, the expected upper second at Oxford. He had chosen to follow his father's profession, not from enthusiasm or even, it now seemed, from conscious choice, but out of a vague filial respect and the knowledge that an assured job was waiting for him. His marriage had been less an affair of passion than a choice from the small coterie of suitable girls among the members of the Warnborough Tennis and Dramatic Clubs. He had never taken a really difficult decision, been tortured by a difficult choice, engaged in a dangerous sport, accomplished anything beyond the achievements of his job. Was it, he wondered, one result of being an only child, treasured and overprotected? The words from childhood most often recalled were his mother's: 'Don't touch that, darling, it's dangerous.' 'Don't go there, darling, you might fall.' 'I shouldn't see too much of her, darling, she's not exactly our type.'

He thought that his first eighteen months on Combe had been reasonably successful; no one had said otherwise. But he recognised two mistakes, both new appointments, both he now knew were ill advised. Daniel Padgett and his mother had come to the island at the end of June 2003. Padgett had written to him, although not by name, enquiring if there was a vacancy for a cook and a handyman. The then handyman was about to retire and the letter, well written, persuasive and accompanied by a reference, had seemed opportune. No cook was required, but Mrs Plunkett had hinted that extra help would be welcome. It had been a mistake. Mrs Padgett was already a very sick woman with only months to live, months which she had apparently been determined to spend on Combe Island, seen from the shore as a child during visits to Pentworthy and which had become a fantasy Shangri-la. Most of Padgett's time, helped by Joanna Staveley and occasionally by Mrs Burbridge, the housekeeper, had been spent looking after her. Neither had complained but Maycroft knew that they were paying for his folly. Dan Padgett was an excellent handyman but he managed, although wordlessly, to make it plain that he disliked being on the island. Maycroft had overheard Mrs Burbridge speaking to Mrs Plunkett. 'Of course he's not really an islander and, now that his mother's gone, I don't think he'll be here much longer.' *He's not an islander* was on Combe a damning indictment.

And then there was eighteen-year-old Millie Tranter. He had taken her in because Jago, the boatman, had found her homeless and begging in Pentworthy and had phoned him to ask if she could come back on the launch until arrangements could be made for her. Apparently it was either that, leaving her to be picked up by the first predatory male or handing her over to the police. Millie had arrived and been given a room in the stable block and a job helping Mrs Burbridge with the linen and Mrs Plunkett in the kitchen. That at least was working well, but Millie and her future remained a nagging anxiety. Children were no longer allowed on the island and

Millie, although in law an adult, had the unpredictability and waywardness of a child. She couldn't remain on Combe indefinitely.

Maycroft looked across at his colleague, at the long-boned sensitive face, the pale skin which seemed impervious to sun and wind, the lock of dark hair falling across the forehead. It was a scholar's face. Boyde had been some months on the island when Maycroft arrived, he too a fugitive from life. Boyde had been brought to Combe Island through the auspices of Mrs Evelyn Burbridge; as the widow of a vicar, she still had connections in the clerical world. He had never questioned either of them directly but knew, as he supposed most people on the island knew, that Boyde, an Anglican priest, had resigned from his living either because of a loss of faith or his alcoholism, or perhaps a mixture of both. Maycroft felt himself incapable of understanding either predicament. For him wine had always been a pleasure, not a necessity, and his former Sunday attendance at church with Helen had been a weekly affirmation of his Englishness and of acceptable behaviour, a mildly agreeable obligation devoid of religious fervour. His parents had distrusted religious enthusiasm, and any wild clerical innovations which threatened their comfortable orthodoxy had been summed up by his mother. 'We're C of E, darling, we don't do that sort of thing.' He found it odd that Boyde should resign because of recently acquired doubts about dogma; a loss of faith in dogma was an occupational hazard for priests of the Church of England, judging from the public utterances of some of the bishops. But the church's loss had been his gain. He couldn't now envisage the job at Combe without Adrian Boyde at the other desk.

Guiltily he realised that he must have been staring out of the window for over five minutes. Resolutely he turned eyes and mind to the work in hand. But his good intentions were frustrated. There was a bang on the door and Millie Tranter bounced in. She came to the office seldom but always arrived in the same way, seeming to materialise on his side of the door before his ears caught her knock.

She said, with no attempt to hide her excitement, 'There's big trouble down at the harbour, Mr Maycroft. Mr Oliver said you was to come at once. He's really wild! It's something to do with Dan losing his blood sample overboard.'

Millie seemed impervious to cold. Now she was celebrating the warm day by wearing her heavily buckled jeans low on her hips with a short tee-shirt barely covering the childlike breasts. Her midriff was bare and there was a gold stud in the umbilicus. Maycroft thought that perhaps he had better have a word with Mrs Burbridge about Millie's clothes. Admittedly none of the visitors was likely to see much of her, clad or unclad, but he couldn't believe that his predecessor would have tolerated the sight of Millie's naked stomach.

Now he said, 'What were you doing at the harbour, Millie? Aren't you supposed to be helping Mrs Burbridge with the linen?'

'Done that, haven't I? She said I could bunk off. I went to help Jago unload.'

'Jago's perfectly competent to unload himself. I think

you'd better go back to Mrs Burbridge, Millie. There must be something useful you can do.'

Millie made a pantomime of casting her eyes upward, but went without argument. Maycroft said, 'Why do I always talk to that child like a schoolmaster? Do you suppose that I might understand her better if I'd had a daughter? Do you think she can possibly be happy here?'

Boyde looked up and smiled. 'I shouldn't worry, Rupert. Mrs Burbridge finds her useful and they get on well. It's a pleasure to have someone young about. When Millie's had enough of Combe she'll be off.'

'I suppose Jago is the attraction. She's always at Harbour Cottage. I hope she doesn't cause complications there. He really is indispensable.'

'I think Jago can cope with adolescent passion. If you're worried about possible trouble if Jago seduces her – or she him, which is more likely – don't. It won't happen.'

'Won't it?'

Adrian said gently, 'No Rupert, it won't.'

'Oh well, I suppose that's a relief. I don't think I was really worried. I doubted whether Jago would have the time or the energy. Still, sex is something most people find time and energy for.'

Adrian said, 'Shall I go down to the harbour?'

'No, no. I'd better go.'

Boyde was the last one who should be asked to confront Oliver. Maycroft felt a second's irritation that the suggestion should have been made.

The walk to the harbour was one of his favourites. Usually it was with an uplifting of his spirits that he crossed the forecourt of the house and took the narrow pebble-strewn path towards the steps which led down the cliff to the quay. And now the harbour lay beneath him like a coloured picture from a storybook: the two stunted towers topped with lights on each side of the narrow entrance, Jago Tamlyn's neat cottage with the row of large terracotta pots in which he would plant his summer geraniums, the coiled ropes and the spotless bollards, the tranquil inner water and, beyond the harbour mouth, the restless sea and the distant counter-flow of the riptide. Sometimes he would leave his desk and walk to the harbour when the launch was due, silently watching for its appearance with the atavistic pleasure of islanders down the ages awaiting the arrival of a long-expected ship. But now he walked slowly down the final steps, aware that his approach was being studied.

At the quayside Oliver was standing rigid with fury. Jago, disregarding him, was busying himself with the unloading. Padgett, ashen faced, was pressed against the wall of the cabin as if facing a firing squad.

Maycroft said, 'Is anything wrong?'

Silly question. The peremptory silence, Oliver's white face, implied a more than trifling misdemeanour on Padgett's part.

Oliver said, 'Well, tell him, one of you! Don't just stand there, tell him.'

Jago's voice was expressionless. 'Mrs Burbridge's library books, some shoes and handbags that belonged to Mrs Padgett and which Dan was taking to the Oxfam shop, and Mr Oliver's blood sample have been lost overboard.'

Oliver's voice was controlled but staccato with outrage. 'Note the order. Mrs Burbridge's library books – obviously an irreparable loss to the local public library. Some unfortunate pensioner looking for a pair of cheap shoes at the charity shop will be disappointed. The fact that I shall have to give blood again is of no importance compared with those major catastrophes!'

Jago was beginning to speak, but Oliver pointed to Padgett. 'Let him answer. He's not a child. It was his fault.'

Padgett made an attempt at dignity. He said, 'I had the packet with the blood sample and the other things in a canvas bag slung over my shoulder. I was leaning over the rail looking at the water and the bag slipped off.'

Maycroft turned to Jago. 'Didn't you stop the launch? Couldn't you get a billhook to it?'

'It was the shoes, Mr Maycroft. They were heavy and they sunk quickly. I heard Dan shout out, but it was too late.'

Oliver said, 'I want to speak to you, Maycroft. Now, please, and in the office.'

Maycroft turned to Padgett. 'I'll talk to you later.'

That schoolmaster's voice again. He was about to add, *Don't worry about it too much,* but knew that the comfort implied in the words would only antagonise Oliver further. The look of terror on Padgett's face worried him. Surely it was disproportionate to the crime. The library book would be paid for; the loss of the shoes and handbags hardly warranted more than a sentimental regret that could only be felt by Padgett himself. Oliver might be one of those unfortunates with a pathological hatred of needles, but if so, why had he asked to have blood taken on the island? A mainland hospital would probably have had the more modern thumb-pricking method of taking blood. The thought brought back memory of the blood tests on his wife some four years earlier when she had been treated for a deep-vein thrombosis following a long flight. The memory, coming at such an incongruous moment, brought no comfort. Confronting Oliver's white and rigid face on which the jutting bones seemed to have solidified into stone, the memory of their joint visits sitting together in the hospital outpatients department only reinforced his sense of inadequacy. Helen would have said, *Stand up to the man. You're in charge. Don't let him bully you. There's nothing seriously wrong with him. No harm's been done. Giving another sample of blood isn't going to kill him.* So why at this moment did he have an irrational conviction that somehow it could?

They made their way up the pathway to the house in silence, Maycroft accommodating his strides to Oliver's pace. He had last seen the man only two days previously when there had been the expected encounter in his office about Atlantic Cottage. Now, glancing down at him, at the fine head which reached only to Maycroft's shoulder, the strong white hair lifted by the breeze, he saw with reluctant compassion that even in that short time Oliver seemed visibly to have aged. Something – was it confidence, arrogance, hope? – had seeped out of him. He was now toiling painfully, that much photographed head looking incongruously heavy for the short enfeebled body. What was wrong with the man? He was only sixty-eight, hardly more than late middle-aged by modern reckoning, but he looked over eighty.

In the study Boyde got to his feet and, at a nod from Maycroft, silently left. Oliver, refusing a chair, supported himself by clasping its back and confronting Maycroft across the desk. His voice was in control, the words calmly delivered.

'I have only two things to say and I shall be brief. In my will I have divided what the Treasury is graciously pleased to leave me equally between my daughter and the Combe Island Trust. I have no other dependants and no charitable interest, or indeed any desire to relieve the State of its obligations towards the less fortunate. I was born on this island and I believe in what it does – or in what it used to do. Unless I can be given an assurance that I shall be welcome here as often as I choose to come, and that I shall be provided with the accommodation I need for my work, I shall change my will.'

Maycroft said, 'Isn't that rather a drastic response to what was clearly an accident?'

'It was not an accident. He did it on purpose.'

'Surely not. Why should he? He was careless and stupid but it wasn't meant.'

'I assure you it was meant. Padgett should never have been allowed to come here and to bring his mother with him. She was obviously dying at the time and he misled you about her condition and her competence to work. But I'm not here to discuss Padgett or to teach you how to do your job. I've said what I wanted to say. Unless things change here my will shall be altered as soon as I return to the mainland.'

Maycroft said carefully, 'That, of course, is your decision. I can only say I'm sorry if you feel we have failed you. You have the right to come whenever you choose, that is clear under the deed of the Trust. Anyone born on the island has that right and as far as we know you're the only living person to whom that applies. Emily Holcombe has a moral right to Atlantic Cottage. If she consents to move, then the cottage will be yours.'

'Then I suggest you let her know the cost of her obstinacy.'

Maycroft said, 'Is that all?'

'No, it is not all. I said there were two matters. The second is that I propose to take up residence permanently on Combe as soon as the necessary arrangements can be made. I shall, of course, require the appropriate accommodation. While I am waiting for a decision on Atlantic Cottage, I suggest additions are made to Peregrine Cottage to make it at least temporarily acceptable.'

Maycroft desperately hoped that his face didn't convey the dismay he felt. He said, 'I shall, of course, tell the Trustees. We'll have to look at the Trust deed. I'm not sure if permanent residents other than those actually working here can be allowed. Emily Holcombe, of course, is provided for in the deed.'

Oliver said, 'The wording is that no person born on the island can be refused admission. I was born on Combe. There is no prohibition on the length of stay. I think you'll find that what I propose is legally possible without the need to change the terms of the Trust.'

Without another word he turned and was gone. Staring at the door which Oliver had shut with a firmness just short of a slam, Maycroft sank into his chair, a wave of depression as heavy as a physical weight on his shoulders. This was catastrophe. Was the job he had taken as an easy temporary option, a peaceful interval in which he could come to terms with his loss, evaluate his past life and decide on his future, to end in failure and humiliation? The Trustees knew that Oliver had always been difficult, but his predecessor had coped.

He didn't hear Emily Holcombe's knock but suddenly she was crossing the room towards him. She said, 'I've been talking to Mrs Burbridge in the kitchen. Millie's there bleating about some problem down at the quay. Apparently Dan has dropped Oliver's blood sample overboard.'

Maycroft said, 'Oliver's been in here complaining. He took it very badly. I tried to explain that it was an accident.' He knew that his dismay and – yes – his inadequacy were written on his face.

She said, 'An odd kind of accident. I suppose he can give another sample. There must be some blood left even in his grudging veins. Aren't you taking this too seriously, Rupert?'

'That's not all. We've got a problem. Oliver's threatening to cut the Trust out of his will.'

'That will be inconvenient but hardly disastrous. We're not on the breadline.'

'He's made another threat. He wants to live here permanently.'

'Well he can't. The idea's impossible.'

Maycroft said miserably, 'It may not be impossible. I'll have to look at the Trust deed. We may not legally be able to stop him.'

Emily Holcombe made for the door, then turned to face him. She said, 'Legally or illegally, he's got to be stopped. If no one else has the guts to do it, then I shall.'

4

The place that Miranda Oliver and Dennis Tremlett had discovered for themselves had seemed as propitious and unexpected as a small miracle: a grassy depression on the lower cliff, about a hundred yards south of an ancient stone chapel and less than three yards from the sheer forty-foot drop to a small inlet of churning sea. The shallow was bound by high granite rocks on each side and accessible only by clambering and slithering down the steep boulder-strewn incline tangled with bushes. They provided convenient boughs to hang on to and the descent wasn't particularly difficult, even for the partially lame Dennis. But it was unlikely to tempt anyone who wasn't looking for a secret hiding-place and only a watcher peering down from the extreme edge of the friable overhanging cliff would have a chance of seeing them. Miranda had happily discounted that possibility – desire, excitement, the optimism of hope had been too intoxicating to admit what were surely unlikely contingencies and spurious fears. Dennis had tried to share her confidence, had forced into his voice the enthusiasm he knew she expected and needed from him. For her, the closeness to the dangerous cliff edge enhanced the invulnerability of their refuge and gave an erotic edge to their lovemaking.

Now they lay bodily close but distanced in thought, their faces upheld to the blue tranquillity of the sky and a tumble of white clouds. The unusual strength of the autumn sun had warmed the enclosing boulders and they were both naked to their waists. Dennis had pulled up his jeans, still unzipped, and Miranda's corduroy skirt was crumpled over her thighs. Her other clothes lay in a tumbled heap beside her, her binoculars thrown over them. Now, with the most urgent physical need satisfied, all his other senses were preternaturally acute, his ears – as always on the island – throbbed with a cacophony of sound: the pounding of the sea, the crash and swirl of the waves and the occasional wild shriek of a seagull. He could smell the crushed turf and the stronger earth, a faint unrecognised smell, half-sweet, half-sour, from the clump of bulbous-leaved plants brightly green against the silver of the granite, the sea smell and the pungent sweat of warm flesh and sex.

He heard Miranda give a small, satisfied sigh of happiness. It provoked in him an uprush of tenderness and gratitude and he turned his face towards hers and gazed at her tranquil profile. She always looked like this after they had made love, the complacent secret smile, the face smooth and looking years younger, as if a hand had passed over her skin conjuring away the faint etchings of incipient middle-age. She had been a virgin when they first came together but there had been nothing tentative or passive about their desperate coupling. She had opened herself to him as if this moment could compensate for all the dead years. And sexual fulfilment had released in her more than the body's half-acknowledged need for warm responsive flesh, for love. Their stolen hours, apart from the over-riding need for physical love, had been spent in talk, sometimes desultory, more often a spilling out of pent-up, long-repressed resentment and unhappiness.

He knew something of what her life with her father had been; he had watched it for twelve years. But if he had felt pity, it had been only a fleeting emotion untouched by any affection for her. There had been an intimidating unattractiveness about her too obvious efficiency, her reserve, the times she seemed to treat him more like a servant than her father's confidential assistant. She seemed almost at times not to notice he was there. He told himself that she was her father's child. Oliver had always been a demanding taskmaster, particularly when he was undertaking overseas publicity tours. Dennis wondered why he still bothered; they couldn't possibly be commercially necessary. Publicly Oliver said that it was important for a writer to meet his public, to speak to the people who bought and read him, to undertake in return the small service of signing their copies. Dennis suspected that there were other reasons. The tours ministered to a need for public affirmation of the respect, even the adoration, which so many thousands felt for him.

But the tours were a strain compensated for by fussiness and irritation, which only his daughter and Tremlett were allowed to see. Miranda made herself unpopular by criticisms and requests which her father never voiced directly. She inspected every hotel room he was given, ran his baths when the complicated apparatus controlling hot, cold, shower and bath was beyond him, made sure his free time was sacrosanct, ensured that he had the food he liked served promptly even at inconvenient times. He had peculiar foibles.

Miranda and the accompanying publicity girl had to ensure that readers who wanted their books dedicated presented him with the name written plainly in capitals. He made himself endure long signing sessions with good humour but couldn't tolerate being presented, once his pen was put away, with late requests for dedications from the bookstore staff or their friends. Miranda would tactfully collect their copies to take back to the hotel, promising that they would be ready by the next morning. Tremlett knew that she was seen as an irritating addition to the tour, someone whose peremptory efficiency contrasted with her famous father's willingness to put himself out. He himself was always given an inferior room in the hotels. They were more luxurious than anything he had been used to and he made no complaint. He suspected Miranda would have received the same treatment except that she bore the name Oliver and her father needed her next door.

And now, lying beside her quietly, he remembered how the love affair had started. It was in the hotel in Los Angeles. It had been a long and stressful day and at eleven-thirty, when she had at last settled her father for the night, Dennis had seen her at the door of her room, half leaning against it, her shoulders drooping. She seemed unable to get the card into the lock and on impulse he had taken it from her and opened the door. He saw that her face was drained with exhaustion and that she was on the verge of tears. Instinctively he had put his arm round her and had helped her into the room. She had clung to him and after a few minutes – he wasn't sure now quite how – their lips had met and they were kissing passionately between incoherent mutterings of love. He had been lost in a confusion of emotions but the sudden awakening of desire had been the strongest and their move towards the bed had seemed as natural and inevitable as if they had always been lovers. But it was Miranda who had taken control, it was Miranda who had gently broken free and picked up the telephone. She had ordered champagne for two and directed it 'to come immediately, please'. It was Miranda who had instructed him to wait in the bathroom until it was delivered, Miranda who had put a *Do not disturb* notice on the outside of the door.

None of it mattered now. She was in love. He had awoken her to a life which she had seized on with all the obstinate determination of the long-deprived, and she would never let go, which meant never letting him go. But he told himself that he didn't want to go. He loved her. If this wasn't love, what else could he call it? He, too, had been awakened to sensations almost frightening in their intensity: the masculine triumph of possession, gratitude that he could give and receive so much pleasure, tenderness, self-confidence, the shedding of fears that solitary sex was all that he would ever have, or was capable of, or deserved.

But now, lying in mild post-coital exhaustion, there came again the inrush of anxiety. Fears, hopes, plans jostled in his mind like lottery balls. He knew what Miranda wanted: marriage, a home of her own, and children. He told himself that that was what he too wanted. She was radiantly optimistic; for him it seemed a distant, unrealisable dream. When they talked and he listened to her plans, he tried not to destroy them, but he couldn't share them. As she poured out a stream of happy imaginings, he realised with dismay that she had never really known her father. It seemed strange that she, who was Oliver's child, who had lived with him, had travelled with him all over the world, knew less of the essential man than did he after only twelve years. He knew that he was underpaid, exploited, never admitted to Oliver's full confidence except when they were working on a novel. But then, so much had been given: removal from the noise, the violence, the humiliation of his teaching job at an inner-city comprehensive and, later, the uncertainty and poor pay of his job as a freelance copy-editor; the satisfaction of having a part, however small and unacknowledged, in the creative process; seeing a mass of incoherent ideas come together and be formed into a novel. He was meticulous in his copy-editing, every neat symbol, every addition or deletion was a physical pleasure. Oliver refused to be edited by his publishers and Dennis knew that his value went far beyond that of copy-editor. Oliver would never let them go. Never.

Would it be possible, he wondered, to carry on as they were now? The stolen hours which, with cunning, they could increase. The secret life which would make everything else bearable. The thrill of sex heightened because it was forbidden fruit. But that too was impossible. Even to contemplate it was a betrayal of her love and her trust. Suddenly he recalled long-forgotten words, lines from a poem – Donne, wasn't it? *Who is as safe as us where none can do / Treason to us, except one of we two?* Even warmed by her naked flesh, treason slithered like a snake into his mind and lay there heavily coiled, somnolent but unshiftable.

She raised her head. She knew something of what he was thinking. That was the terrifying thing about love; he felt that he had handed over the key to his mind and she could wander in at will.

She said, 'Darling, it's going to be all right. I know you're worrying. Don't. There's no need.' She said again with a firmness close to obstinacy, 'It's going to be all right.'

'But he needs us. He depends on us. He won't let us go. He won't let our happiness upset his whole life, the way he lives, how he works, what he's used to. I know it would be fine for some people, but not for him. He can't change. It would destroy him as a writer.'

She raised herself on her elbow, looking at him. 'But darling, that's ridiculous. And even if he did have to give up writing, would that be so terrible? Some critics are already saying that he's done his best work. Anyway, he won't have to do without us. We can live in your flat, at least to begin with, and go in to him daily. I'll find a reliable housekeeper to sleep in the Chelsea house so he won't be alone at night. It might even suit him better. I know he respects you and I think he's fond of you. He'll want me to be happy. I'm his only child. I love him. He loves me.'

He couldn't bring himself to tell her the truth but at last he said slowly, 'I don't think he loves anyone but himself. He's a conduit. Emotion flows through him. He can describe but he can't feel, not for other people.'

'But darling, that can't be true. Think of all those characters – the variety, the richness. All the reviewers say the same. He couldn't write like that if he didn't understand his characters and feel for them.'

He said, 'He does feel for his characters. He *is* his characters.'

And now she stretched herself over him, looking down into his face, her pendulous breasts almost touching his cheeks. And then she froze. He saw her face, now uplifted, white as granite and stark with fear. With one clumsy movement he broke free from under her and clutched at his jeans. Then he too looked up. For a moment, disorientated, all he could see was a figure, black, motionless and sinister, planted on the extreme edge of the upper cliff and shutting out the light. Then reality asserted itself. The figure became real and recognisable. It was Nathan Oliver.

5

It was Mark Yelland's third visit to Combe Island and, as on the previous occasions, he had asked for Murrelet Cottage, the most northerly on the south-east coast. Although further from the cliff edge than Atlantic Cottage, it was built on a slight ridge and had one of the finest views on Combe. On his first visit two years previously he had known from the moment of entering its stone-walled tranquillity that he had at last found a place where the daily anxieties of his dangerous life could for two weeks be put aside and he could examine his work, his relationships, his life, in the peace which, at work and at home, he never knew. Here he was free from the problems, great and trivial, which every day awaited his decision. Here he needed no protection officer, no vigilant police. Here he could sleep at night with the door unlocked and the windows open to the sky and the sea. Here were no screaming voices, no faces distorted with hate, no post that it could be dangerous to open, no telephone calls threatening his life and the safety of his family.

He had arrived yesterday, bringing the minimum necessities and the carefully selected CDs and books which only on Combe would he have time to listen to and read. He was glad of the cottage's relative isolation and on the two previous visits had spoken to no one for the whole two weeks. His food had been delivered according to written instructions left with the empty canisters and thermos flasks; he had had no wish to join the other visitors for the formal evening meal in the house. The solitude had been a revelation. He had never realised that to be completely alone could be so satisfying and healing. On his first visit he had wondered whether he would be able to endure it, but although the solitude compelled introspection, it was liberating rather than painful. He had returned to the traumas of his professional life changed in ways he couldn't explain.

As on the previous visit, he had left a competent deputy in charge. Home Office regulations required that there should always be a Licence Holder or deputy Licence Holder in the laboratory or on call and his deputy was experienced and reliable. There would be crises – there always were – but he would cope for the two weeks. Only in an extreme emergency would his deputy ring Murrelet Cottage.

As soon as he had begun unpacking the books he had found Monica's letter, placed between the two top volumes. Now he took it from the desktop and read it again, slowly and with careful attention to every word, as if it held a hidden meaning which only a scrupulous re-reading could discern.

Dear Mark, I suppose I should have had the courage to speak to you directly, or at least handed this to you before you left, but I found I couldn't. And perhaps it's just as well. You will be able to read it in peace without needing to pretend you care more than you do, and I shan't feel I have to go on justifying a decision I should have arrived at years ago. When you return from Combe Island I won't be here. To write about 'going home to mother' is humiliatingly bathetic, but that's what I've decided to do and it is sensible. She has plenty of room and the children have always enjoyed the old nursery and the garden. As I've decided to end our marriage, it's better to do so before they start secondary education. There's a good local school prepared to take them at short notice. And I know they'll be safe. I can't begin to explain what that will mean to me. I don't think you've ever really understood the terror that I've lived in every day, not just for myself, but for Sophie and Henry. I know you'll never give up your work and I'm not asking you to. I've always known that the children and I are not in your list of priorities. Well, I have my own priorities. I'm not prepared any longer to sacrifice Sophie, Henry or myself to your obsession. There's no hurry about an official separation or divorce – I don't much care which – but I suppose we'd better get on with it when you return. I'll send you the name of my solicitor when I've got settled. Please don't bother to reply. Have a restful holiday. Monica.

On first reading of the letter he had been surprised how calmly he had taken her decision, surprised too that he'd had no idea that this was what she had been planning. And it had been planned. She and her mother had been allies. A new school found and the children prepared for the move – all that had been going on and he hadn't noticed. He wondered whether his mother-in-law had had a hand in composing the letter. There was something about its matter-of-fact coherence that was more typical of her than of Monica. For a moment he indulged the fantasy of them sitting side by side working on a first draft. He was interested, too, that the regret he felt was more for the loss of Sophie and Henry, than for the end of the marriage. He felt no strong resentment against his wife but he wished she had chosen her moment better. She could at least have let him have his holiday without this added worry. But gradually a cold anger began possessing him, as if some noxious substance were being poured into his mind, curdling and destroying his peace. And he knew against whom with increasing power it was being directed.

It was fortuitous that Nathan Oliver was on the island, fortuitous too that Rupert Maycroft had mentioned the other visitors when he met him on the quay. Now he made a decision. He would change his plans, phone Mrs Burbridge, the housekeeper, and ask who had booked in for dinner at the house tonight. And if Nathan Oliver were among them he would break his solitude and be there too. There were things he needed to say to Nathan Oliver. Only by saying them could he assuage this surging anger and bitterness and return alone to Murrelet Cottage to let the island work its mysterious ministry of healing.

6

He was standing with his back to her, looking out of the southern window. When he turned, Miranda saw a face as rigidly lifeless as a mask. Only the pulse-beat above the right eye betrayed the bitterness he was struggling to control. She willed her eyes to meet his. What had she been hoping for? A flicker of understanding, of pity?

She said, 'We didn't mean you to find out like this.'

His voice was quiet, the words venomous. 'Of course not. No doubt you were planning to explain it all after dinner. I don't need to be told how long the affair has been going on. I knew in San Francisco that you'd at last found someone to fuck. I confess it didn't occur to me that you'd been reduced to making use of Tremlett – a cripple, penniless, my employee. At your age tupping him in the bushes like a randy schoolgirl is obscene. Were you obliged to take the only available man who offered or was it a deliberate choice to inconvenience me? After all, you could have done better. You have certain inducements on offer. You're my daughter, that counts for something. After my death, unless I change my will, you'll be a moderately rich woman. You have useful domestic accomplishments. In these days when I am told it's difficult to find, let alone keep, a good cook, your one skill could be an inducement.'

She had expected this conversation to be difficult, but not like this, not to be faced with this coruscating anger, this bitterness. Any hope that he might be reasonable, that they might be able to talk things over and plan what could be best for them all, died in a welter of despair.

She said: 'Daddy, we love each other. We want to get married.'

She had come inadequately prepared. She knew with a sickening wrench of the heart that she sounded like a querulous child asking for sweets.

'Then marry. You're both of age. You don't need my consent. I take it that Tremlett has no legal impediment.'

And now it all came out in a rush. Their impossible schemes, the happy imaginings which, even as she spoke, seemed small verbal pebbles of hopelessness thrown against his implacable face, his anger and his hatred.

'We don't want to leave you. It needn't change anything. I'd come in to you by the day – Dennis too. We could find a reliable woman to take over my part of the house so that you weren't alone at night. When you're on tour we could be with you as usual.' She said again, 'Nothing need change.'

'So you'd come in by the day? I don't need a daily woman or a night nurse. And if I did, no doubt both can be obtained if the pay is high enough. I take it that you're not complaining of your pay?'

'You've always been generous.'

'Or Tremlett of his?'

'We didn't talk about money.'

'Because you assumed, presumably, that you'd live off me, that life could go on for you as comfortably as it always has.' He paused, then stated, 'I have no intention of employing a married couple.'

'You mean Dennis would have to go?'

'You heard what I said. Since you seem to have talked over your plans and settled my future for me, may I enquire where you intend to live?'

Her voice faltered. 'We thought in Dennis's flat.'

'Except, of course, that it isn't Tremlett's flat, it's mine. I bought it to house him when he came to me full-time. He rents it furnished on derisory terms under a legal agreement which gives me the right to terminate the tenancy at a month's notice. Of course he could buy it from me at its present value. I shall have no use for it.'

'But the flat must be worth double what you paid for it in 1997.'

'That is his and your misfortune.'

She tried to speak but couldn't form the words. Anger, and a grief more terrible because she didn't know whether it was for herself or for him, rose like nauseous phlegm in her throat, choking speech. He had turned again to look out of the window. The silence in the room was absolute but she could detect the rasp of her own breathing, and suddenly, as if the ever-present sound had for a time been silenced, the sonorous murmur of the sea. And then, unexpectedly and disastrously, she swallowed hard and found her voice.

'Are you so sure you can do without us? Don't you really understand how much I do for you when you are on tour – checking the hotel room, running your bath, complaining on your behalf if the details aren't right, helping to organise the signing sessions, protecting your reputation as the genius who's not too famous to bother about his readers, making sure that you get the food and wine you like? And Dennis? All right, he's your secretary and copy-editor, but he's more, isn't he? Why do you boast that your novels don't need editing? That's because he helps edit them – not just copy-editing – editing. Tactfully, so you won't have to admit even to yourself how important he is. Plotting isn't your strength, is it, not in recent years? How many ideas do you owe to Dennis? How often do you use him as a sounding board? Who else would do as much for so little?'

He didn't turn to show her his face, but even with his back to her, the words came to her clearly, but not in a voice that she recognised.

'You'd better discuss with your lover what exactly you propose to do. If you decide to throw in your lot with Tremlett, the sooner the better. I shall not expect you back at the London house and I shall be grateful if Tremlett will hand over the keys to the flat as soon as possible. In the meantime, don't speak about this to anyone. Do I make myself clear? Speak to no one. This island is small but there should be space enough for us to keep out of each other's way for the next twenty-four hours. After that we can go our separate ways. I'm booked in here for another ten days. I can take my meals in Combe House. I propose to book the launch for tomorrow afternoon and I expect you and your lover to be on it.'

7

Maycroft wasn't looking forward to Friday's dinner. He seldom did when any of the visitors had booked in to dine. What caused anxiety was not their eminence, but his responsibility as host to encourage conversation and ensure that the evening was a success. As his wife had frequently pointed out, he was not good at small talk. Inhibited by his lawyer's caution from participating in the most popular chatter – well-informed and slightly salacious gossip – he strove, sometimes desperately, to avoid the banalities of enquiring about the visitors' journeys to Combe or discussing the weather. His guests, all eminent in their different fields, would no doubt have had interesting things to say about their professional lives which he would have been fascinated to hear, but they had come to Combe to escape from their professional lives. Occasionally there had been good evenings when, discretion put aside, guests had spoken freely and with passion. Usually they got on well; the egregiously rich and famous might not always like each other but they were at home in the topography of each other's privileged bailiwicks. But he doubted whether his two guests tonight would gain pleasure from each other's company. After Oliver's eruption into his office and his earlier threats, he was horrified by the prospect of entertaining the man through a three-course meal. And then there was Mark Yelland. This was Yelland's third visit but he had never before booked in for dinner. There might be perfectly understandable reasons for this, such as the wish for a formal meal, but Maycroft saw it as ominous. After a final adjustment to his tie before the mirror in the hall, he took the lift from his apartment in the central tower down to the library for the usual pre-dinner drinks.

Dr Guy Staveley and his wife Joanna had already arrived, he standing, sherry glass in hand, beside the fire while Jo had arranged herself elegantly in one of the high-backed armchairs, her glass as yet untouched on the table beside her. She always took trouble over dressing for dinner, particularly after an absence, as if a carefully enhanced femininity was a public demonstration that she was back in residence. Tonight she was wearing a silk trouser suit with narrow trousers and tunic top. The colour was subtle, a pale greenish-gold. Helen would have known what colour to call it, even where Jo had bought it and how much it had cost. If Helen had been at his side the dinner, even with Oliver present, would have held no fear.

The door opened and Mark Yelland appeared. Although guests could order the buggy, he had obviously walked from Murrelet Cottage. Taking off his topcoat, he laid it over the back of one of the chairs. It was the first time he had seen Jo Staveley and Maycroft made the introductions. There were twenty minutes before the dinner gong would sound but they passed easily enough. Jo, as always in the presence of a good-looking man, exerted herself to be agreeable and Staveley somehow discovered that he and Yelland had both been at Edinburgh University, although not in residence at the same time. Staveley found enough academic chat, shared experience and common acquaintances to keep the conversation going.

It was nearly eight, and Maycroft began to hope that Oliver had changed his mind, but just as the gong sounded, the door opened and he came in. With a nod and a curt 'Good evening' to the company, he took off his coat, placed it beside Yelland's and joined them at the door. Together they went down the one floor to the dining room immediately below. In the lift neither Oliver nor Yelland spoke, merely acknowledging each other with a brief nod like rivals observing the courtesies but saving words and energy for the contest ahead.

As always there was a menu written in Mrs Burbridge's elegant hand. They were to begin with melon balls in an orange sauce with a main course of guinea fowl with roasted vegetables followed by a lemon soufflé. The first course was already in place. Oliver took up his spoon and fork and regarded his plate with a frown as if irritated that anyone should waste time forming melon into balls. The conversation was desultory until Mrs Plunkett and Millie arrived, wheeling a trolley with the guinea fowl and vegetables. The main course was served.

Mark Yelland picked up his knife and fork but made no move to begin eating. Instead, elbows on table and knife raised as if it were a weapon, he looked across at Nathan Oliver and said with dangerous quietness, 'I presume that the character of a laboratory director in the novel you're bringing out next year is intended to be me, a character you've been careful to make as arrogant and unfeeling as you could manage without the man becoming completely incredible.'

Without raising his eyes from his plate, Oliver said, 'Arrogant, unfeeling? If that's your reputation, I suppose some confusion may arise in the public mind. Rest assured there's none in mine. I have never before met you. I don't know you. I have no particular wish to know you. I'm not a plagiarist of life; I only need one living model for my art, myself.'

Yelland put down his knife and fork. His eyes were still on Oliver. 'Are you going to deny that you met a junior member of my staff in order to question him about what goes on in my laboratory? I'd like to know, incidentally, how you got hold of his name. Presumably through the animal liberation people who dangerously disrupt his life and mine. No doubt impressing him with your reputation, you extracted his views on the validity of the work, how he justified what he was doing, how much the primates were suffering.'

Oliver said easily, 'I undertook necessary research. I wanted to know certain facts about the organisation of a laboratory – the staffing levels, the conditions under which the animals are kept, how and what they're fed, how obtained. I asked no questions about personalities. I'm a researcher of facts not of emotions. I need to know how people act, not how they feel. I know how they feel.'

'Have you any idea how arrogant that sounds? Oh, we can feel all right. I feel for patients with Parkinson's disease and cystic fibrosis. That's why I and my colleagues spend our time trying to find a cure, and at some personal sacrifice.'

'I should have thought that the sacrificial victims were the animals. They suffer the pain; you get the glory. Isn't it true that you'd happily see a hundred monkeys die, and in some discomfort, if it meant that you published first? The fight for scientific glory is as ruthless as the commercial marketplace. Why pretend otherwise?'

Yelland said, 'Your concern for animals doesn't much inconvenience your daily life. You seem to be enjoying your guinea fowl, you wear leather, no doubt you'll be taking milk with your coffee. Perhaps you should turn your attention to the ways in which some animals – quite a number, I'm told – are slaughtered for meat. They would die a great deal more comfortably in my lab I assure you, and with more justification.'

Oliver was dissecting his guinea fowl with care. 'I'm a carnivore. All species prey on each other, that seems to be the law of nature. I could wish we killed our food more humanely but I eat it without compunction. That seems to me very different from using a primate for experimental purposes which can't possibly benefit it on the assumption that *homo sapiens* is so intrinsically superior to every other species that we're entitled to exploit them at our will. I understand that the Home Office does monitor the pain levels permissible and usually seeks detailed clarification on the analgesics being used, and I suppose that's a small alleviation. Don't misunderstand me. I'm not a member or even a supporter of the organisations which inconvenience you. I'm not in a position to be since I have benefited from past discoveries using animals and shall certainly take advantage of any future successes. Incidentally,

I shouldn't have expected you to be a religious man.'

Yelland said curtly, 'I'm not. I have no supernatural beliefs.'

'You surprise me. I assumed you took an Old Testament view of these matters. You're familiar, I take it, with the first chapter of the Book of Genesis. *And God blessed them, and God said unto them, Be fruitful and multiply, and replenish the earth, and subdue it: and have dominion over the fish of the sea, and over the fowl of the air, and over every living thing that moveth upon the earth.* That's one divine commandment which we've never had difficulty in obeying. Man the great predator, the supreme exploiter, the arbiter of life and death by divine permission.'

Maycroft's guinea fowl was tasteless, a gunge in the mouth. This was disaster. And there was something odd about the dispute. It was less an argument than an antiphonic contest in which only one participant, Yelland, felt genuine passion. Whatever was worrying Oliver, it had nothing to do with Yelland. He saw that Jo's eyes were bright as they moved from one speaker to the other, as if watching an unusually long rally in a game of tennis. Her right hand was crumbling a bread roll and she fed the pieces unbuttered into her mouth without looking down. He felt that something should be said, but as Staveley sat in increasingly embarrassed silence, he said, 'Perhaps we should feel differently if we suffered from a neurological disease, or if a child of ours suffered. Perhaps these are the only people who have the right to speak on the moral validity of these experiments.'

Oliver said, 'I've no wish to speak on their behalf. I

didn't begin this argument. I've no strong views one way or the other. My characters have, but that's a different matter.'

Yelland said, 'That's a cop-out! You give them a voice, sometimes a dangerous one. And it's disingenuous to pretend you were only interested in routine background information. The boy told you things he had no right to disclose.'

'I can't control what people choose to tell me.'

'Whatever he told you, he's now regretting it. He's resigned his job. He was one of my most able young men. He's lost to important research and perhaps lost to science altogether.'

'Then perhaps you should doubt the level of his commitment. Incidentally, the scientist in my novel is more sympathetic and complex than you seem to have grasped. Perhaps you didn't read the proofs with sufficient understanding. Or, of course, you may have been imposing your character – or what you fear may be perceived as your character – on my creation. And I would be interested to know how you got your hands on the proofs. Their distribution is tightly controlled by my publisher.'

'Not tightly enough. There are subversives in publishing houses as well as in laboratories.'

Jo had decided it was time to intervene. She said, 'I don't think anyone of us likes using primates for research. Monkeys and chimps are too like us to make it comfortable. Perhaps you should use rats in your experiments. It's difficult to feel much affection for rats.'

Yelland fixed his gaze on her as if assessing whether such ignorance deserved a reply. Oliver kept his eyes on his plate. Yelland said, 'Over eighty per cent of experiments are on rats, and some people do feel affection for them. The researchers do.'

Jo persisted. 'All the same, some of the protesters must be motivated by genuine compassion. I don't mean the violent ones who are just getting a kick out of it. But surely some of them genuinely hate cruelty and want to stop it.'

Yelland added dryly, 'I find that difficult to believe, since they must know that what they're doing with their violence and intimidation is to force the work out of the United Kingdom. The research will continue but in countries which haven't our statutory protection for the animals. This country will suffer economically but the animals will suffer a great deal more.'

Oliver had finished his guinea fowl. Now he placed his knife and fork carefully side by side on the plate and got to his feet. 'I think the evening has provided sufficient stimulation. You will excuse me if I leave you now. I have to walk back to Peregrine Cottage.'

Maycroft half rose from his chair. 'Shall I order the buggy for you?' He knew that his voice was propitiatory, almost servile, and hated himself for it.

'No thank you. I am not yet decrepit. You will, of course, remember that I need the launch tomorrow afternoon.'

Without a sign to the company he left the room.

Yelland said, 'I must apologise. I shouldn't have started this. It isn't what I came to Combe for. I didn't know Oliver was on the island until I arrived.'

Mrs Plunkett had entered with a tray of soufflés and was beginning to collect their plates. Staveley said, 'He's in a strange mood. Obviously something's happened to upset him.'

Jo was the only one eating. She said easily, 'He lives in a permanent state of being upset.'

'But not like this. And what did he mean by asking for the launch tomorrow? Is he leaving or isn't he?'

Maycroft said, 'I profoundly hope he is.' He turned to Mark Yelland. 'Will his latest novel create difficulties for you?'

'It will have its influence, coming from him. And it'll be a gift to the animal liberation movement. My research is seriously at risk, and so is my family. I haven't any doubt that his so-called fictional director will be taken as a portrait of me. I can't sue, of course, and he knows it. Publicity is the last thing I want. He was told things which he had no right to know.'

Staveley said quietly, 'But aren't they things we all have a right to know?'

'Not if they're used to jeopardise life-saving research. Not if they get into the hands of ignorant fools. I hope he does intend to leave the island tomorrow. It's certainly not big enough for the two of us. And now if you'll excuse me, I won't wait for coffee.'

He crumpled his table napkin, threw it on his plate and, with a nod to Jo, abruptly left. There was a silence broken by the sound of the lift door.

Maycroft said, 'I'm sorry. That was a disaster. Somehow I should have stopped it.'

Jo was eating her soufflé with evident enjoyment. 'Don't keep apologising, Rupert. You're not responsible for everything that goes wrong on this island. Mark Yelland only booked in for dinner because he wanted to confront Nathan and Nathan played along with it. Get started on the soufflés, they'll go flat.'

Maycroft and Staveley took up their spoons. Suddenly there was a series of booms like distant gunfire and the logs in the fireplace flared into life. Jo Staveley said, 'It's going to be a windy night.'

8

When his wife was in London, Guy Staveley disliked stormy nights, the cacophony of moans, wails and howling was too like an uncannily human lament for his deprivation. But now, with Jo at home, the violence outside the stone walls of Dolphin Cottage was a reassuring emphasis of the comfort and security within. But by midnight the worst was over and the island lay calm under the emerging stars. He looked over to the twin bed where Jo was sitting cross-legged, her pink satin dressing-gown tight under her breasts. Often she dressed provocatively – occasionally shamelessly – without seeming aware of the effect, but after lovemaking she covered her nakedness with the careful modesty of a Victorian bride. It was one of the quirks which, after twenty years of marriage, he found obscurely endearing. He wished that they were in a double bed, that he could reach out to her and somehow convey the gratitude he felt for her unquestioning and generous sexuality. She had been back on Combe for four weeks and, as always, she returned to the island as if she had never been away, as if theirs were a normal marriage. He had fallen in love with her from the first meeting and he was not a man who loved easily or was capable of change. There would never be another woman for him. He knew that for her it was different. She had set out her terms on the morning of their marriage before, defying convention, they had left the flat together for the registry office.

'I love you, Guy, and I think I shall go on loving you, but I'm not in love. I've had that and it was a torment, a humiliation and a warning. So now I'm settling for a quiet life with someone I respect and am very fond of and want to spend my life with.'

At the time it had seemed an acceptable bargain and it did so still.

Now she said, her voice carefully casual, 'I went into the practice when I was in London, and saw Malcolm and June. They want you back. They haven't advertised for a replacement and they don't intend to, not yet anyway. They're terribly overworked, of course.' She paused, then added, 'Your old patients are asking for you.'

He didn't speak. She went on, 'It's all old history now about that boy. Anyway, the family have left the district. To general relief, I imagine.'

He wanted to say, *He wasn't 'that boy', he was Winston Collins. He had a bloody awful life and the happiest grin I've ever seen on a boy.*

'Darling, you can't live with guilt for ever. It happens all the time in medicine, in every hospital for that matter. It always did. We're human. We make mistakes, wrong judgements, miscalculations. They get covered up ninety-nine times out of a hundred. With the present workload what else do you expect? And the mother was an over-anxious demanding nuisance, as we all know. If she hadn't called you out unnecessarily time after time her son would probably be alive. You didn't tell that to the inquiry.'

He said, 'I wasn't going to push the responsibility on to a grieving mother.'

'All right, as long as you admit the truth to yourself. And then all that racial trouble, accusations that it would have been different if he'd been white. It would all have died down if the race warriors hadn't seized on it.'

'And I'm not going to make unfair racial accusations an excuse either. Winston died of peritonitis. Today that's unforgivable. I should have gone when the mother rang. It's one of the first things you learn in medicine – never take chances with a child.'

'So you're thinking of staying here for ever, indulging Nathan Oliver in his hypochondria, waiting for one of Jago's rock-climbing novices to fall off a cliff? The temporary staff have GPs in Pentworthy, Emily is never ill and is obviously set to live to a hundred, and the visitors don't come if they're not fit. What sort of job is that for someone with your ability?'

'The only one at present I feel I can cope with. What about you, Jo?'

He wasn't asking what use she made of her nursing skills when she returned alone to their empty London flat. How empty was it? What about Tim and Maxie and Kurt, names she occasionally mentioned without explanation and apparently without guilt? She would speak briefly of parties, plays, concerts, restaurants, but there were questions which, fearing her answer, he did not dare to ask. Whom did she go with, who paid, who saw her back to the flat, who spent the night in her bed? He found it strange that she didn't intuit the force of his need to know, and his fear of knowing.

Now she said easily, 'Oh I work when I'm not here. Last time it was in A and E at St Jude's. Everyone's overstressed so I do what I can, but only part-time. There are limits to my social conscience. If you want to see life in the raw, try A and E on a Saturday night – drunks, druggies, broken heads and enough foul language to blue the air. We're depending a lot on imported staff. I find that inexcusable – administrators swanning round the world in comfort, recruiting the best doctors and nurses they can find from countries that need them a bloody sight more than we do. It's disgraceful.'

He wanted to say, *They're not all recruited. They'd come anyway for more money and a better life, and who can blame them?* But he was too sleepy for political discussion. Now he said, not greatly caring, 'What's happening about Oliver's blood? You heard, of course, about the furore at the harbour, that idiot Dan dropping the sample overboard.'

'You told me, darling. Oliver's coming tomorrow at nine o'clock to give another sample. He's not looking forward to it and nor am I. He hates the needle. He can thank his lucky stars I'm a professional and like to get a vein first time. I doubt you'd manage it.'

'I know I wouldn't.'

She said, 'I've watched some of the medical staff taking blood in my time. Not a pretty sight. Anyway, Oliver may not turn up.'

'He'll turn up. He thinks he could be anaemic. He'll want the test done. Why wouldn't he turn up?'

Jo swung her legs off the bed and with her back to him let slip her robe and reached for her pyjama top.

She said, 'If he's really planning to leave tomorrow he may prefer to wait and get the tests done in London. It would be sensible. I don't know, it's just a feeling I have. I wouldn't be surprised if I didn't see Oliver at nine o'clock tomorrow.'

9

Oliver took his time returning to Peregrine Cottage. The anger which had possessed him since his encounter with Miranda was exhilarating in its self-justification, but he knew how quickly he could fall from its enlivening heights into a slough of hopelessness and depression. He needed to be alone and to walk off this energising but dangerous tumult of fury and self-pity. For an hour, buffeted by the rising wind, he paced to and fro on the edge of the cliff trying to discipline the confusion of his mind. It was already past his normal hour for bed, but he needed to watch until the light in Miranda's bedroom was finally switched off. He gave little thought to the dispute with Mark Yelland. Compared to the treachery of his daughter and Tremlett, that argument had been a mere exercise in semantics. Yelland was powerless to do him harm.

At last he went quietly through the unlocked door of the cottage and closed it behind him. Miranda, if not asleep, would take care not to appear. Normally, on the rare occasions when he was out alone at night, she would be listening, even if in her bed, for the click of the door latch. A low light would have been left on for him and she would come down to make a hot milky drink. Tonight the sitting room was in darkness. He contemplated a life without her watchful care but convinced himself that it wouldn't happen. Tomorrow she would see sense. Tremlett would be made to go and that would be the end of it. If he had to, he could manage without Tremlett. Miranda would realise that she couldn't give up security, comfort, the luxury of their overseas visits, the privilege of being his only child, the prospect of her inheritance, for Tremlett's salacious and no doubt inexpert fumblings in some dingy one-bedded flat in an insalubrious and dangerous area of London. Tremlett couldn't have saved much from his salary. Miranda had nothing except what he gave her. Neither was qualified for a job which would make enough to enable them to live even simply in central London. No, Miranda would stay.

Undressed and ready for bed, he drew the linen curtains across the window. As always, he left half an inch of space so that the room wasn't completely dark. As the bedclothes settled around him, he lay quietly, exulting in the howling of the wind until he felt himself slipping down the plateaux of consciousness more quickly than he had feared.

He was jerked into wakefulness with a high thin scream which he knew was his own. The blackness of the window was still dissected by the line of light. He stretched out an uncertain hand to the bedside lamp and found the switch. The room blazed with a reassuring normality. Fumbling for his watch, he saw that it was now three o'clock. The storm had spent itself and now he lay in what seemed an unnatural and ominous calm. He had woken from the same nightmare which year after year made his bed a centre of horror, sometimes recurring in clusters, more often visiting so rarely that he began to forget its power. The nightmare never varied. He was mounted barebacked on a great dappled horse high above the sea, its back so broad that his legs had no power to grip, and he was being violently swung from side to side as it reared and plunged among a blaze of stars. There were no reins and his hands scrabbled desperately at the mane, trying to gain a hold. He could see the corner of the beast's great flashing eyes, the spit foaming from its neighing mouth. He knew that his fall was inevitable and that he would drop, his arms helplessly flailing, to an unimagined horror under the black surface of the waveless sea.

Sometimes when he woke it was to find himself on the floor, but tonight the bedclothes were half-tangled round him. Occasionally his awakening cry would alert Miranda and she would come in, matter-of-fact, reassuring, asking if he were all right, whether there was anything he needed, whether she could make them both a cup of tea. He would reply, 'Just a bad dream, just a bad dream. Go back to bed.' But tonight he knew that she wouldn't come. No one would come. Now he lay staring at the strip of light, distancing himself from horror, then gradually edged himself out of bed and, stumbling over to the window, opened the casement to the wide panoply of stars and the luminous sea.

He felt immeasurably small, as if his mind and body had shrunk and he was alone on a spinning globe looking up into immensity. The stars were there, moving according to the laws of the physical world, but their brilliance was only in his mind, a mind that was failing him, and eyes that could no longer clearly see. He was only sixty-eight but slowly, inexorably, his light was fading. He felt intensely lonely, as if no other living thing existed. There was no help anywhere on earth, nor on those dead spinning worlds with their illusionary brightness. No one would be listening if he gave way to this almost irresistible impulse and shouted aloud into the unfeeling night, *Don't take away my words! Give me back my words!*

10

In his bedroom on the top floor of the tower, Maycroft slept fitfully. At each waking he switched on the light and glanced at his bedside clock hoping to find that dawn was near to breaking. Two-ten, three-forty, four-twenty. He was tempted to get up, make himself tea and listen to the World Service on the radio, but resisted. Instead he tried to compose himself for another hour or two of sleep, but it didn't come. By eleven o'clock the wind had risen, not to a prolonged gale but blowing in erratic gusts which howled in the chimney and made the lulls between the onslaughts less a relief than an ominous period of unnatural calm. But he had slept through more violent storms than this in the eighteen months since arriving on the island. Normally the constant throbbing of the sea was soothing to him, but now it swelled into the room, a pounding intrusive bass accompaniment to the howling of the wind. He tried to discipline his thoughts but the same anxieties, the same foreboding, returned with renewed force with each waking.

Was Oliver's threat to live permanently on the island real? If so, how legally could he be stopped? Would the Trustees see him as responsible for this debacle? Could he have handled the man better? His predecessor had apparently coped with Oliver and his moods so why was he finding it so difficult? And why had Oliver ordered the launch for today? Surely he must intend to leave. The thought momentarily cheered him, but for Oliver to leave in anger and bitterness would be an unhappy augury for the future. And it would be seen as his fault. After the first two months his appointment had been confirmed, but he felt himself to be still on probation. He could resign or be asked to leave at three months' notice. To fail at a job, which was generally regarded as a sinecure, which he himself had seen as a peaceful interlude of introspection, would be ignominious both personally and publicly. Despairing of sleep, he reached for his book.

He woke again with a start when the hardback of *The Last Chronicle of Barset* thudded to the ground. Fumbling for his watch, he saw with dismay that it was eight thirty-two, a late start to the day.

It was nearly nine before he rang for his breakfast and half an hour later before he took the lift down to his office. He had by now partly rationalised the nagging anxieties of the night but they had left a legacy of unease amounting to foreboding which, even as he went through the normal comforting rituals of breakfast, couldn't be shaken off. Despite his tardiness, Mrs Plunkett had arrived with his breakfast within five minutes of his ringing her: the small bowl of prunes, the bacon fried crisply but not hardened – just as he liked it – the fried egg on its square of bread fried in bacon fat, the jug of coffee and the hot toast which was brought in at precisely the moment he was ready for it, the home-made marmalade. He ate, but without relish. The meal in its perfection seemed a wilfully contrived reminder of the physical comfort and harmonious routine of his life on Combe. He wasn't ready to make yet another fresh start and dreaded the inconvenience and exertion of finding a property and setting up home on his own. But if Nathan Oliver came to live permanently on Combe, in the end that was what he would have to do.

As he entered the office he found Adrian Boyde at his desk tapping out figures on his calculator. He was surprised to find him at work on a Saturday but then remembered Boyde mentioning that he would come in for a couple of hours to complete work on the VAT return and the quarterly accounts. Even so, it was an unusual start to the day. Both men said good morning and then silence fell. Maycroft looked across at the other desk and suddenly felt that he was seeing a stranger. Was it his imagination that Adrian looked subtly different, the face more tautly pale, the anxious eyes shadowed, the body less relaxed? Glancing again, he saw that his companion's hand wasn't moving over the papers. Had he too suffered a poor night? Was he infected by this ominous foreboding of disaster? He realised again, but with renewed force, how much he relied on Boyde: the quiet efficiency, the unspoken companionship when they worked together, the common sense which seemed the most admirable and useful of virtues, the humility which had nothing to do with self-abasement or obsequiousness. They had never touched on anything personal in either of their lives. Why then did he feel that his uncertainties, his grief for his wife whom he could forget for days at a time and then suddenly yearn for with almost uncontrollable longing, were understood and accepted? He didn't share Adrian's religious belief. Was it simply that he felt himself in the presence of a good man?

All he knew had been learned from Jo Staveley in a moment, never repeated, of impulsive confidence. 'The poor devil fell flat on his face dead drunk while celebrating Holy Communion. Devout old lady, chalice at her lips, knocked off her knees. Wine spilled. Screams, general consternation. The more innocent of the congregation thought he was dead. I gather the parish and the Bish had been tolerant of his little weakness, but this was a drink too far.'

And yet it had been Jo who in the end had saved him. Boyde had been on the island for over a year and had stayed sober until the appalling night of his relapse. Three days later he had left Combe. Jo had been living in her London flat at the time on one of her periodic escapes from the boredom of the island and had taken him in, moved with him to a remote country cottage, dried him out and, just before Maycroft himself arrived, brought him back to Combe. It was never spoken of, but Boyde probably owed his life to Jo Staveley.

The phone on his desk rang, startling him. It was nine twenty-five. He hadn't realised that he had been sitting as if in a fugue. Jo sounded irritable. 'Have you seen Oliver? He isn't with you by any chance? He was supposed to come to the surgery at nine o'clock to have another blood sample taken. I thought he might decide to give it a miss, but he could have rung to let me know.'

'Could he have overslept or forgotten?'

'I've rung Peregrine Cottage. Miranda said she'd heard him going out at about seven-twenty. She was in her bedroom and they didn't speak. She's no idea where he was going. He didn't say anything to her yesterday night about coming to give blood.'

'Is he with Tremlett?'

'Tremlett's already at Peregrine Cottage. He arrived to catch up with some work soon after eight. He says he hasn't set eyes on Oliver since yesterday. Of course, Oliver may have left early with the idea of taking a walk before coming to the surgery but, if so, why hasn't he arrived? And he's had no proper breakfast. Miranda says he made himself tea – the pot was still warm when she went into the kitchen – but all he'd eaten was a banana. He may just be playing up for the hell of it, but Miranda's worried.'

So the foreboding had been justified. Here was more trouble. It was unlikely that Oliver had come to harm. If he had merely decided to cause inconvenience by missing the appointment and had gone for a walk instead, to organise a search party would be an added irritation. And with reason; it was part of the ethos of the island that visitors were left in peace. But he was no longer a young man. He had been gone now without explanation for nearly two hours. Suppose he was lying somewhere struck down by a stroke or a heart attack, how would he, as the man in charge, be able to justify inaction?

He said, 'We'd better start looking. Tell Guy, will you. I'll phone people and get them to meet here. You'd better stay in the surgery and let me know if he turns up.'

He put down the receiver and turned to Boyde. 'Oliver's gone missing. He should've been at the surgery at nine o'clock to give blood but didn't turn up.'

Boyde said, 'Miranda will be worried. I can call there and then go on to search the north-east of the island.'

'Do that, will you, Adrian? And if you see him, play down the fuss. If he's panicked about giving blood the last thing he'll want is a search party.'

Five minutes later a little group, summoned by telephone, had formed in front of the house. Roughtwood, uncooperative as usual, had told Adrian that he was too busy to help, but Dr Staveley, Dan Padgett and Emily Holcombe were there, Emily Holcombe because she had arrived at the surgery at nine-fifteen for her annual anti-flu injection. Jago had been summoned from his cottage but had not yet appeared. The little party looked to Maycroft for instructions. He pulled himself together and began giving thought to their next step.

And then, as suddenly and capriciously as always on Combe, the mist came up, in parts no more than a delicate translucent veil, in others thickening into a damp occlusive fog, shrouding the blue of the sea, transforming the massive tower of the house into a looming presence, felt but not seen, and isolating the delicate red cupola at the top of the lighthouse so that it looked like some bizarre object floating in space.

As it thickened, Maycroft said, 'There's no point in going far until this lifts. We'll try the lighthouse, but that's all.'

They moved together, Maycroft in front. He heard muted voices behind him but one by one the figures disappeared into the obliterating mist and the voices faded and then died. Now, with disconcerting suddenness, the lighthouse was before him, the concave shaft stretching into nothingness. Looking up he felt a second of giddiness, but was afraid to press his hands for support against the glistening surface in case the whole edifice, unreal as a dream, shuddered and dissolved into the mist. The door was ajar and cautiously he pushed at the heavy oak and reached for the light switch. Without pausing, he climbed the first flight of stairs through the fuel room and halfway up the second flight, calling Oliver's name, at first quietly as if afraid to break the mist-shrouded silence. Resisting the futility of the half-hearted summons, he paused on the stairs and shouted loudly into the darkness. There was no reply and he could see no lights. Coming down, he stood in the doorway and called into the mist. 'He doesn't seem to be here. Stay where you are.'

There was still no answer. Without thinking and with no clear purpose he moved round the lighthouse to the seaward side and stood against the sea wall looking upwards, grateful for the strength of the hard granite in the small of his back.

And now, as mysteriously as it had risen, the mist began to lift. Frail and wispy veils drifted across the lighthouse, formed and dissolved. Gradually shapes and colours revealed themselves, the mysterious and intangible became familiar and real. And then he saw. His heart leaped and began a hard pounding which shook his body. He must have cried out, but he heard no sound except the wild shriek of a single gull. And gradually the horror was revealed, at first behind a thin drifting veil of mist and then with absolute clarity. Colours were restored, but brighter than he remembered them – the gleaming walls, the tall red lantern surrounded by white railing, the blue expanse of the sea, the sky as clear as on a summer day.

And high against the whiteness of the lighthouse a hanging body: the blue and red thread of the climbing rope taut to the railings, the neck mottled and stretched like the neck of a bald turkey, the head, grotesquely large, dropped to one side, the hands, palms outward, as if in a parody of benediction. The body was wearing shoes, and yet for one disorientated second he seemed to see the feet drooping side by side in a pathetic nakedness.

It seemed to him that minutes passed but he knew that time had been suspended. And then he heard a high continuous scream. Looking to the right he saw Jago and Millie. The girl was staring up at Oliver, her scream so continuous that she hardly drew breath.

And now round the curve of the lighthouse came the search party. He could distinguish no words but the air seemed to vibrate with a confused symphysis of moans, low cries, exclamations, groans and whimpers, a muted keening made terrible by Millie's screaming and the sudden wild screech of gulls.

BOOK TWO

Ashes in the Grate

I

It was shortly before one o'clock and Rupert Maycroft, Guy Staveley and Emily Holcombe were closeted together for the first time since the discovery of the body. It was at Maycroft's request that Emily had returned to the house from Atlantic Cottage. Earlier, finding that her attempts to comfort and console Millie had only exacerbated her noisy distress, she had announced that, as there was obviously nothing she could usefully do, she would go home and come back if and when they were wanted. Millie, who at every opportunity had been clinging hysterically to Jago, had been gently prised off and handed over to the more acceptable ministrations of Mrs Burbridge to be solaced with common-sense advice and hot tea. Gradually a spurious normality had been imposed. There had been orders to be given, telephone calls to be made, staff to be reassured. Maycroft knew that he had done those things, and with surprising calmness, but had no longer any clear memory of the words he had spoken or the sequence of events. Jago had returned to the harbour and Mrs Plunkett, having work to do, had gone off to prepare lunch and make sandwiches. Joanna Staveley was at Peregrine Cottage, but Guy, grey-faced, had kept to Maycroft's side, speaking and walking as if he were an automaton, giving no real support.

It seemed to Maycroft that time had become

disjointed and that he had experienced the last two hours less as a continuum than as a series of vivid scenes, unlinked, each as instantaneous and indelible as a photograph. Adrian Boyde standing beside the stretcher and looking down at Oliver's body, then slowly lifting his right hand as if it were weighted and making the sign of the cross. Himself with a silent Guy Staveley walking to Peregrine Cottage to break the news to Miranda and mentally rehearsing the words he would use. They had all seemed inadequate, banal, sentimental or brutally monosyllabic: hanged, rope, dead. Mrs Plunkett, grim-faced, pouring tea from a huge teapot he couldn't remember having seen before. Dan Padgett, who had acted sensibly at the scene, suddenly demanding reassurance that it wasn't his fault, that Mr Oliver hadn't killed himself because of the lost blood, and his own irritated response. 'Don't be ridiculous, Padgett. An intelligent man doesn't kill himself because he has to give blood a second time. It's hardly a major operation. Nothing you did or failed to do is that important.' Watching Padgett's face quiver into childish tears as he turned away. Standing beside the bed in the sickroom while Staveley drew the sheet more tightly over Oliver's body and noticing for the first time with a desperate intensity of gaze the pattern of the William Morris wallpaper. Most vivid of all, as if floodlit against the wall of the lighthouse, the dangling body, the stretched neck and the pathetically drooped naked feet – which his brain told him hadn't been naked. And this, he realised, was how Oliver's death would live in memory.

Now at last he had a chance to clear his mind and to discuss the arrival of the police with the people whom he felt had a right to be consulted. The choice of the sitting room of his private flat had arisen from an unspoken general agreement rather than from a specific decision. He had said, 'We have to talk now, before the police arrive. Let's go somewhere where we won't be disturbed. I'll leave Adrian in the office. He'll cope. We're not taking any incoming calls.' He had turned to Staveley. 'Your cottage or my flat, Guy?'

Staveley had said, 'Wouldn't it be better if we stayed in the house? That way we'll be here when the police arrive.'

Maycroft asked Boyde to telephone Mrs Plunkett and ask her to bring soup, sandwiches and coffee up to his flat, and they moved together to the lift. They were borne upwards to the top of the tower in silence.

Once in the sitting room Maycroft closed the door and they sat down, Emily Holcombe on the two-seater sofa with Staveley beside her. He turned one of the fireside chairs to face them. The movement, which, in this setting, would normally have been familiar and domestic, had become portentous. Even his sitting room, in which the three of them had so often been together, became for one disconcerting moment as unfamiliar and temporary as a hotel lounge. It was furnished entirely by familiar things he had brought from his wife's drawing room: the comfortable chintz-covered chairs and sofa, the matching curtains, the oval mahogany table with the silver-framed photographs of their wedding and that of their son, the delicate porcelain figures, the obviously amateur watercolours of the Lake District which her grandmother had painted. In bringing them with him he must have hoped to re-create the quiet evenings he and

Helen had shared. But now, with a shock, he realised how much he had always disliked every object of this feminine cluttered chintzy domesticity.

Looking across at his colleagues, he felt as graceless as a socially inept host. Guy Staveley was sitting rigidly upright like a stranger aware of the inconvenience of his visit. Emily, as always, looked comfortably at ease, one arm stretched along the back of the sofa. She was wearing black trousers, boots and a voluminous fawn jumper in fine wool and long amber earrings. Maycroft was surprised that she had taken the trouble to change but, after all, so had he and Staveley, he supposed from some vestigial notion that Saturday informality was inappropriate in the presence of death.

He said, detecting in his voice a note of forced bonhomie, 'What will you have? There's sherry, whisky, wine, the usual things.'

Why, he wondered, had he said that? They knew perfectly well what was on offer. Emily Holcombe asked for sherry, Staveley – surprisingly – for whisky. Maycroft had no water at hand and muttered apologies as he went to his small kitchen to fetch it. Returning, he poured the drinks and a glass of Merlot for himself. He said, 'There was a hot lunch at twelve-thirty in the staff dining room for anyone who was able to eat it, but I thought it better if we had something here. The sandwiches shouldn't be long.'

Mrs Plunkett had anticipated their need. Almost immediately there was a knock on the door and Staveley opened it. Mrs Plunkett came in pushing a trolley containing plates, cups and saucers, jugs and two large Thermos flasks and, on the bottom shelf, two plates covered with napkins. Maycroft said quietly, 'Thank you', and they watched as the food and crockery were laid out by Mrs Plunkett as reverently as if they were part of some religious ceremony. Maycroft almost expected her to drop a curtsey as she reached the door.

Going over to the table, he lifted the damp napkins from the plates. 'Mostly ham, apparently, but there's egg and cress if you don't feel like meat.'

Emily Holcombe said, 'I can't think of anything less appealing. Why does violent death make one so hungry? Perhaps hungry is the wrong word – in need of food but requiring something appetising. Sandwiches don't meet the need. What's in the thermoses? Soup, I suppose, or it could be the coffee.' She went over to one of the flasks, twisted the lid and sniffed. 'Chicken soup. Unimaginative but nourishing. However, it can wait. What we've got to do is to decide how we're going to play this. We haven't much time.'

'To play it?' The words *It isn't a game* hung on the air unspoken.

As if recognising that her phrase had been ill-judged, Emily said, 'To decide our response to Commander Dalgliesh and his team. I'm assuming there will be a team.'

Rupert said, 'I'm expecting three. The Metropolitan Police rang to say he's bringing a detective inspector and a sergeant, that's all.'

'But it's a pretty senior invasion, isn't it? A commander of the Metropolitan Police and a detective inspector. And why not the local force? Presumably they've been given some explanation.'

It was a question Rupert had been expecting and he

was prepared. 'I think it's because of the importance of the victim and the insistence of the Trustees on discretion and as much privacy as possible. Whatever Dalgliesh does, it's unlikely to cause the kind of upheaval or publicity which calling in the local force would inevitably produce.'

Emily said, 'But that isn't quite good enough, Rupert. How did the Metropolitan Police get to know that Oliver was dead? Presumably you telephoned them. Why not phone the Devon and Cornwall Constabulary?'

'Because, Emily, I have instructions to contact a London number if there's anything worryingly untoward on the island. My understanding is that that's always been the procedure.'

'Yes, but what number? Whose number?'

'I wasn't told whose. My instructions were to report and to say nothing further. I'm sorry, Emily, but that's in line with a long-standing arrangement and I intend to adhere to it. I have adhered to it.'

'Long-standing? It's the first I've heard of it.'

'Probably because no crisis of this magnitude has occurred before. It's a perfectly reasonable procedure. You know better than most how important some of our guests are. The procedure's intended to deal with any untoward event effectively, speedily and with the maximum of discretion.'

Emily said, 'I suppose Dalgliesh will want to question us together, I mean all of us, visitors and staff.'

Maycroft said, 'I've really no idea. Both together and then later separately, I imagine. I've been in touch with the staff and arranged for them to be available here in the house. That seemed advisable. The library will be the best room to use. The commander will need to question the guests as well, of course. I felt it wrong to disturb Miranda Oliver, and she and Dennis Tremlett are still in their cottage. She made it clear that she wanted to be alone.'

Emily said, 'Except presumably for Tremlett. Incidentally, how did Miranda take the news? I suppose you and Guy broke it to her, you as the person in charge here and Guy to deal with any physical reactions to the shock. Very appropriate.'

Was there, Maycroft thought, a tinge of irony in her voice? He glanced at Staveley but got no response. He said, 'Yes, we went together. It was less distressing than I feared. She was shocked, of course, but she didn't break down. She was perfectly calm – stoical even. Tremlett was the more affected. He pulled himself together but he looked devastated. I thought he was going to faint.'

Staveley said quietly, 'He was terrified.'

Maycroft went on, 'There was one rather odd thing. It looked to me as if Oliver had burnt some papers before he went out this morning. There was a heap of ash and some blackened remnants in the sitting-room grate.'

Emily said, 'Did Miranda or Tremlett mention it? Did you?'

'No, it didn't seem the right time, particularly as they said nothing.'

Emily said, 'I doubt whether the police will allow them to be so uncommunicative.'

Guy Staveley made no comment. After a few seconds, Maycroft spoke to Emily Holcombe. 'Miss

Oliver insisted on seeing the body. I tried to dissuade her but I didn't feel I had the right to forbid her. The three of us went to the sickroom together. Guy pulled back the covering sheet to just under the chin so that the mark of the rope was concealed. Miss Oliver insisted that he pull it down further. She looked at the marks intently and then said, "Thank you" and turned away. She didn't touch him. Guy covered him up again and we left.'

Emily said, 'The police may feel that you should have been firmer.'

'No doubt. They have authority I lack. I agree that it would have been better if I'd been able to dissuade her, but I don't see how. He looked . . . Well you know how he looked, Emily. You saw.'

'Only briefly, thank God. What I should like some advice on is how we respond to questioning. Obviously we tell the truth, but how much of the truth? For example, if Commander Dalgliesh asks whether Miranda Oliver's grief for her father is genuine, what do we reply?'

Here Maycroft felt he was on firmer ground. 'We can't speak for other people. Obviously he'll see her. He can make up his own mind, he's a detective.'

Emily said, 'Personally I don't see how it can be. The girl was a slave to her father – so was Tremlett, if you ask me, but the relationship there is somewhat more complex. He's supposed to be a copy-editor and personal assistant but I think he does a great deal more than copy-editing. His last novel, *The Gravedigger's Daughter*, was respectfully but unenthusiastically received. Hardly vintage Nathan Oliver. Wasn't that the book he finished while Tremlett was in hospital, when they were trying to do something about his leg? Incidentally, what's wrong with it?'

Staveley's voice was curt. 'Polio when he was a child. It left him lame.'

Maycroft turned to Emily Holcombe. 'You're not suggesting that Tremlett writes the novels?'

'Of course he doesn't write them. Nathan Oliver does. I'm suggesting that Tremlett fulfils a more important role in Oliver's life than copy-editing, however meticulously, that and dealing with his fan letters. Gossip has it that Oliver refused ever to be edited by his publishers. Did he need to be? He had Tremlett. And what about Oliver himself? Surely there's no point in pretending that he was a welcome or agreeable guest. I doubt whether there's anyone on the island who actually wishes he were still alive.'

Guy Staveley had been silent. Now he said, 'I think it would be sensible to defer discussion until Jo arrives. She shouldn't be long. Adrian will tell her we're meeting here.'

Emily Holcombe said, 'Why do we need her? This was supposed to be a meeting of the permanent residents other than supporting staff. Jo hardly qualifies as a full-time resident.'

Guy Staveley said quietly, 'She qualifies as my wife.'

'Also in a somewhat part-time capacity.'

Staveley's grey face suffused with scarlet. He shifted in his chair as if about to rise but, at an appealing glance from Maycroft, sank back.

Maycroft said quietly, 'We won't get anywhere if we're at each other's throats even before the police arrive. I asked Jo to be with us, Emily. We'll give her another five minutes.'

'Where is she?'

'At Peregrine Cottage. I know that Miranda said that she wanted to be left alone, but Guy and I both felt that she might like to have a woman with her. There could be delayed shock. After all, Jo is a trained nurse. She'll go straight back there after we've talked if she feels there's anything she can do to help. Miranda might like her to stay in the cottage tonight.'

'In Nathan's bed? I hardly think so!'

Maycroft persisted. 'Miranda ought not to be alone, Emily. I did suggest when Guy and I went to break the news that she might like to move into the house. We've got the two empty suites. She was vehemently against the idea. It's a problem. She may agree to let Jo stay. Jo has said she wouldn't mind spending the night in an armchair in the sitting room if it would help.'

Emily Holcombe held out her glass. Maycroft went over to the sherry decanter. 'I'm grateful you didn't think of calling on me to provide feminine consolation. Since I take the view that this island – which is my chief concern – will be happier without the periodic intrusion of Nathan Oliver, I would have found it difficult to voice the customary insincerities.'

Maycroft said, 'I hope you won't express that view so bluntly to Commander Dalgliesh.'

'If he's as clever as by reputation he's reported to be, I won't need to.'

It was then that they heard footsteps. The door opened and Joanna Staveley was with them. For Maycroft, as always, she brought with her an enlivening inrush of confident sexuality which he found more appealing than disturbing. The thick blonde hair with its narrow strip of darker roots was bound back with a blue silk scarf, giving the tanned face a look of naked guilelessness. Her strong thighs were tightly enclosed in blue jeans, her denim jacket was open over a tee-shirt enclosing unencumbered breasts. Beside her vitality her husband looked a discouraged, ageing man, and even the fine bones of Emily's handsome face looked as stripped and sharp as a death's head. Maycroft remembered something she had said when Jo returned to the island. 'It's a pity we don't go in for amateur theatricals. Jo is typecast as a blonde, golden-hearted barmaid.' But Jo Staveley did have a heart; he was less sure of Emily Holcombe.

Jo plonked herself down in the empty armchair and stretched out her legs with a sigh of relief. She said, 'Thank God that's over. The poor kid didn't really want me there, and why the hell should she? It's not as if we know each other. I've left two sleeping pills and told her to take them tonight with a warm milky drink. She won't leave the cottage, she was adamant about that. Is that bottle your usual Merlot, Rupert? Pour it for me, will you, ducky? Just what I need.'

Pouring a glass of the wine and handing it to her, Maycroft said, 'I've just been saying that I'm not happy for her to be alone in that cottage tonight.'

'She won't be. She says Dennis Tremlett will move in with her. She'll sleep in her father's bed and he'll have hers.'

Emily said, 'If that's what she wants, it's a solution. In the circumstances this is hardly a time for proprieties.'

Jo laughed. 'They're not worried about proprieties! They're having an affair. Don't ask me how they manage it, but they are.'

Staveley's voice sounded unnaturally sharp. 'Are you sure, Jo? Did they tell you?'

'They didn't need to. Five minutes in the same room with them and it was obvious. They're lovers.' She turned to Emily Holcombe. 'It's a pity you didn't go with the chaps to break the news, Emily. You'd have seen the situation quickly enough.'

Emily said dryly, 'Very likely. Old age has not entirely blunted my perceptions.'

Watching them, Maycroft caught the quick glance between them – one, he thought, of amused female complicity. The two women could hardly be more different. He had thought that if either had a strong feeling about the other, it would have been of dislike. Now he realised that if the four of them in the room should disagree, the two women would be allies. It was one of those moments of insight into the unexpected vagaries of personality to which he had rarely been sensitive before coming to the island, and which still had power to surprise him.

Emily said, 'It's a complication, of course, for them if not for us. I wonder if they told Oliver. If they did, it could be a motive.'

The silence that followed lasted only seconds but it was absolute. Jo Staveley's hand froze, the wine glass halfway to her lips. Then she replaced it on the table with careful deliberation, as if the slightest sound would be fatal.

Emily Holcombe seemed unaware of the effect of

that one unwelcome accusatory word. She said, 'A motive for Oliver's suicide. Jo told me about that extraordinary scene at dinner yesterday. It wasn't normal behaviour even for Nathan at his worst. Add to that the fact that his last novel was a disappointment and he's facing old age and the draining away of his talent, and one can understand why he felt it was time to make his quietus. It's obvious that he depended almost entirely on his daughter, and probably as much on Tremlett. If he had just learned that they proposed to desert him for more conventional satisfactions, it could have been the catalyst.'

Jo Staveley said, 'But if Tremlett married Miranda, Oliver wouldn't necessarily lose him.'

'Maybe not, but there might well be a change in Tremlett's priorities which I imagine could be unwelcome. Still, I agree that it isn't our business. If the police want to explore that fascinating bypath, let them discover it for themselves.'

Staveley spoke slowly, as if to himself. 'There are contra-indications to suicide.'

Again there was silence. Maycroft resolved that it was time to put an end to speculation. The talk was becoming dangerously out of control. He said, 'I think we should leave all this to the police. It's their job to investigate the facts, ours to cooperate in every way we can.'

Jo said, 'To the extent of telling them that two of their suspects are having an affair?'

Maycroft said, 'Jo, no one is a suspect. We don't yet know how Oliver died. We must avoid that kind of talk. It's inappropriate and irresponsible.'

Jo was unrepentant. 'Sorry, but if this was murder – it has to be a possibility, Guy has more or less said so – surely we're all suspects. I'm just asking how much we should volunteer. I mean, do we tell this commander that the deceased won't be universally mourned, that as far as we're concerned he was a pain in the butt? Do we let on that he was threatening to move in permanently and make all our lives hell? More to the point, do we tell him about Adrian Boyde?'

Maycroft's voice was unusually firm. 'We answer his questions and do so truthfully. We speak for ourselves and not for others, and that includes Adrian. If anyone feels that they're at risk of being compromised they have the right to refuse to answer any further questions except in the presence of a lawyer.'

Jo said, 'Which I take it can't be you.'

'Obviously not. If this is a suspicious death I shall be as much a suspect as anyone. You'd have to send for a solicitor from the mainland. Let's hope it doesn't come to that.'

'And what about the other two guests, Dr Yelland and Dr Speidel? Have they been told that Oliver's dead?'

'We've still not been able to contact them. When they learn the news they may want to leave. I don't think in the normal course of things that Commander Dalgliesh can prevent them. After all, the island will hardly be a haven of peace and solitude with the police milling round. I suppose he'll need to question them before they leave. One of them may have seen Oliver going into the lighthouse.'

Emily Holcombe said, 'And are this commander and his officers proposing to stay on the island? Are we expected to offer hospitality? Presumably they won't be bringing their own rations. Are we expected to feed them and at the Trust's expense? Who are they?'

'As I've said, only the three. Commander Dalgliesh, a woman detective inspector, Kate Miskin, and a sergeant, Francis Benton-Smith. I've consulted Mrs Burbridge and Mrs Plunkett. We thought we could accommodate the two subordinates in the stable block and give Commander Dalgliesh Seal Cottage. They'll be treated as any other residents. Breakfast and lunch will be provided in their quarters, and they can join us in the dining room for dinner or have it in their quarters, as they prefer. I take it that's acceptable?'

Emily said, 'And the weekly staff? Have they been warned off?'

'I managed to reach them by telephone. I told them to take a week's paid leave. No boat will go to Pentworthy on Monday morning.'

Emily said, 'Acting under instructions from London no doubt. And how did you explain this sudden and atypical beneficence?'

'I didn't. I told them that with only two guests they wouldn't be needed. The news of Oliver's death will be given tonight, probably too late for the Sunday papers. Miss Oliver has agreed the timing and that we don't want the local media to get in first.'

Emily Holcombe moved to the table. 'Murder or no murder, I shall need the launch on Monday morning. I've a dental appointment in Newquay at eleven-thirty.'

Maycroft frowned. 'It will be inconvenient, Emily. The media may be waiting.'

'Hardly in Newquay. They'll be on the quay at

Pentworthy harbour if they're anywhere. And I can assure you that I'm more than competent to deal with the media, local or national.'

Maycroft made no further objection. He felt that, on the whole, he had handled the meeting more effectively than he had feared. Guy had been little help. The man seemed to be emotionally distancing himself from the tragedy. Perhaps it wasn't surprising; having escaped from the responsibilities of general practice he was probably determined to avoid any others. But this dissociation was worrying. He had rather depended on Guy's support.

Emily said, 'If any of you want to eat, you'd better grab a sandwich now. The police should be here soon. Then I'll go back to Atlantic Cottage if that's all right by you, Rupert. I suggest we leave this to the men, Jo. A reception committee of two is adequate. We don't want to encourage our visitors' self-importance. They're hardly the most distinguished people we've welcomed to Combe. And you can count me out of the group in the library. If the commander wants to see me he can make an appointment.'

The door opened and Adrian Boyde came in. A pair of binoculars was slung round his neck. He said, 'I've just sighted the helicopter. The police are on their way.'

2

The Twin Squirrel helicopter rattled over southern England, its shadow printed on the autumnal fields like an ominous ever-present harbinger of potential disaster. The uncertain and unseasonable weather of the past week was continuing. From time to time the black clouds curdled above them, then dropped their load with such concentrated force that the helicopter seemed to be bumping through a wall of water. Then suddenly the clouds would pass and the rain-washed fields lay beneath them bathed in sunshine as mellow as midsummer. The unfolding landscape had the neatness of a needlework collage, the clusters of woodland worked in knots of dark green wool, the linen fields, some in muted colours of brown, pale gold and green, and the winding side roads and the rivers laid out in strips of glistening silk. The small towns with their square church towers were miracles of meticulous embroidery. Glancing at his companion, Dalgliesh saw Benton-Smith's eyes fixed in fascination on the moving panorama and wondered whether he saw it similarly patterned and contrived, or whether in imagination he was passing over a wide, less verdant and less precisely domesticated landscape.

Dalgliesh had no regrets about his choice of Benton-Smith for the Squad, judging that he brought with him the qualities Dalgliesh valued in a detective: intelligence, courage and common sense. They were not often found together. He hoped that Benton-Smith also had sensitivity but that was a quality less easy to assess; time, no doubt, would tell. A minor worry was how well Kate and Benton-Smith would work as a team now that Piers Tarrant had left. He didn't need them to like each other; he did require them to respect each other, to cooperate as colleagues. But Kate was intelligent too. She knew how destructive open antagonism could be to the success of an investigation. He could safely leave it in her hands.

He saw that she was reading a slim paperback, *The No. 1 Ladies' Detective Agency,* with a resolute intensity which he understood. Kate disliked helicopters. A winged fuselage at least gave one the subconscious reassurance that this birdlike machine was designed to fly. Now they were tightly encased in a noisy contraption which looked less designed than put together in a mad attempt to defy gravity. She was keeping her eyes on the book, but only occasionally turning a page, her mind less occupied with the exploits of Alexander McCall Smith's gentle and engaging Botswanan detective than with the accessibility of her life jacket and its certain ineffectiveness. If the engine failed, Kate expected the helicopter to drop like a stone.

Now, in this noisy interlude between summons and arrival, Dalgliesh closed his mind to professional problems and confronted a personal and more intractable fear. He had first told Emma Lavenham of his love, not by mouth but by letter. Hadn't that been an expedient of cowardice, the wish not to see rejection in her eyes? There had been no rejection. Their time together, contrived from their separated and over-busy lives, was a concentrated and almost frightening happiness: the sexual intensity; the varied and uncomplicated mutual passion; the carefully planned hours spent with no other company needed in restaurant, theatre, gallery or concert; the informal meals in his flat, standing together on that narrow balcony, drinks in hand, with the Thames lapping the walls fifty feet below; the talks and the silences which were more than the absence of words. This was the weekend they should be having now. But this disappointment wasn't the first time that his job had demanded priority. They were inured to the occasional mischance, which only increased the triumph of the next meeting.

But he knew that this weekend-dominated life wasn't living together, and his unspoken fear was that Emma found it enough for her. His letter had been a clear proposal of marriage, not an invitation to a love affair. She had, he thought, accepted, but marriage had never afterwards been mentioned between them. He tried to decide why it was so important to him. Was it the fear of losing her? But if their love couldn't survive without the tie of a legal commitment, what future had it? What right had he even to attempt to bind her? He hadn't found the courage to mention marriage, excusing cowardice with the thought that it was her prerogative to set the date. But he knew the words he dreaded to hear. 'But darling, what's the hurry? Do we have to decide now? Aren't we perfectly happy as we are?'

He forced his mind back to the present and, looking down, experienced the familiar illusion of an urban landscape rising up to meet them. They cushioned down gently at the Newquay heliport and, when the blades came to rest, unbuckled their seat belts in the expectation of a few minutes' delay in which to stretch their legs. The hope was frustrated. Almost immediately Dr Glenister emerged from the departure lounge and strode vigorously towards them, a handbag slung over her shoulder and carrying a brown Gladstone bag. She was wearing black trousers tucked into high leather boots and a closely fitted tweed jacket. As she approached and looked up, Dalgliesh saw a pale, finely lined and delicately boned face almost eclipsed by a black wide-brimmed trilby worn with a certain rakishness. She climbed aboard, refusing Benton-Smith's attempt to stow her bags, and Dalgliesh made the introductions.

She said to the pilot, 'Spare me the regulation safety spiel. I seem to spend my life in these contraptions and confidently expect to die in one.'

She had a remarkable voice, one of the most beautiful Dalgliesh had ever heard. It would be a potent weapon in the witness box. He had not infrequently sat in court watching the faces of juries being seduced into bemused acquiescence by the beauty of a human voice. The miscellaneous scraps of disjointed information about her which, unsought, had come his way over the years – mostly after she had featured in a particularly notorious case – had been intriguing and surprisingly detailed. She was married to a senior Civil Servant who had long since taken his retirement, solaced with the customary honour, and, after a lucrative period as a non-executive director in the City, now spent his days sailing and bird-watching on the Orwell. His wife had never taken his name or used his title. Why indeed should she?

But the fact that the marriage had produced four sons, all successful in their various spheres, suggested that a marriage seen as semi-detached had had its moments of intimacy.

One thing she and Dalgliesh had in common: although her textbook on forensic pathology had been widely acclaimed, she never allowed her photograph to be used on a book-jacket, nor did she cooperate in any publicity. Neither did Dalgliesh – initially to his publishers' chagrin. Herne & Illingworth, fair but rigorous where their authors' contracts were concerned and notably hard-nosed in business, were in other matters disarmingly naïve and unworldly. His response to their pressure for photographs, signing sessions, poetry readings and other public appearances had in his view been inspirational: not only would it jeopardise the confidentiality of his job at the Yard, but it could expose him to revenge from the murderers he had arrested, the most notorious of which were soon to be released on parole. His publishers had nodded in knowing compliance and no more had been said.

They travelled in silence, spared the need to initiate conversation by the noise of the engines and the shortness of the journey. It was only minutes before they were passing over the crinkled blue of the Bristol Channel and almost at once Combe Island lay beneath them, as unexpectedly as if it had risen from the waves, multicoloured and as sharply defined as a coloured photograph, its silver granite cliffs towering from a white boiling of foam. Dalgliesh reflected that it was impossible to view an offshore island from the air without a quickening of the spirit. Bathed in autumnal sunshine there stretched a sea-estranged other world, deceptively calm but rekindling boyhood memories of fictional mystery, excitement and danger. Every island to a child is a treasure island. Even to an adult mind Combe, like every small island, sent out a paradoxical message: the contrast between its calm isolation and the latent power of the sea which both protected and threatened its self-contained alluring peace.

Dalgliesh turned to Dr Glenister. 'Have you been on the island before?'

'Never, although I know something about it. All visitors are prohibited from landing except where the visit is necessary. There is a modern, automatic light-house on the north-west tip, which means that Trinity House, the body responsible for lighthouses, has to come from time to time. Our visit will be among their more unwelcome necessities.'

As they began their descent, Dalgliesh fixed the main features in his mind. If distances became important, no doubt a map would be provided, but now was the chance to fix the topography. The island lay roughly north-east to south-west, some twelve miles from the mainland, the easterly side slightly concave. There was only one large building and it dominated the south-west tip of the island. Combe, like other large houses seen from the air, had the precisely ordered perfection of an architect's model. It was an eccentric stone-built house with two wings and a ponderous central tower, so like a battlement that the absence of turrets seemed an architectural aberration. On the seaward façade four long curved windows glittered in the sun and to the rear were parallel stone buildings which looked like stable blocks. Some fifty yards beyond them was the helicopter pad marked with a cross. On a spur of rock to the west of the house stood a lighthouse, its elegant white-painted shaft topped with a red lantern.

Dalgliesh managed to make his voice heard. 'Would you make a fairly low circuit of the island before we land? I'd like to get an overall view.'

The pilot nodded. The helicopter rose, veered away from the house and then descended to rattle over the north-east coastline. There were eight stone cottages irregularly spaced, four on the north-west cliffs and four on the south-east. The middle of the island was a multicoloured scrubland with clutches of bushes and a few copses of spindly trees crossed by tracks so faint that they looked like the spoor of animals. The island did indeed look inviolate; no beaches, no receding lace of foam. The cliffs were taller and more impressive in the north-west where a spur of jagged rocks running out to sea like broken teeth rose from a turmoil of crashing waves. Dalgliesh saw that a low and narrower strip of cliff ran round the whole southerly part of the island, broken only by the narrow harbour mouth. Looking down at this neat toy-town inlet, it was difficult to imagine the agonised terror of those captured slaves landing in this place of horror.

And here for the first time was evidence of life. A stocky dark-haired man wearing sea boots and a roll-neck jersey appeared from a stone cottage on the quay. He stood shading his eyes and looking up at them for a moment before, disconcertingly dismissive of their arrival, he quickly turned to re-enter the cottage.

They saw no other sign of life, but when the circuit

was completed and they were hovering above the landing-circle, three figures emerged from the house and walked towards them with the orderly precision of men on parade. The two in front were more formally suited than was surely customary for the island, their shirt collars immaculate and both wearing ties. Dalgliesh wondered if they had changed before his arrival, whether this careful conformity conveyed a subtle message: he was being officially welcomed not to a scene of crime but to a house in mourning. Apart from the three male figures there was no one else in sight. The rear of the house behind them was plain-fronted with a wide stone courtyard between the parallel sets of coach-houses, which, from the curtained windows, looked as if they had been converted into dwellings.

They ducked under the slowing blades of the helicopter and moved towards the waiting party. It was obvious which of the three was in charge. He stepped forward. 'Commander Dalgliesh, I'm Rupert Maycroft, the secretary here. This is my colleague and resident physician, Guy Staveley, and this is Dan Padgett.' He paused as if uncertain how to classify Padgett, then said, 'He'll look after your bags.'

Padgett was a lanky young man, his face paler than one would expect in an islander, his hair closely cropped to show the bones of a slightly domed head. He was wearing dark blue jeans and a white tee-shirt. Despite his apparent frailty his long arms were muscular and his hands large. He nodded but didn't speak.

Dalgliesh made the introductions and there was a formal shaking of hands. Professor Glenister resolutely declined to part with her bags. Dalgliesh and Kate kept their murder cases but Padgett hoisted the rest of their luggage easily on to his shoulders, picked up Benton's holdall and strode off to a waiting buggy. Maycroft made a gesture towards the side of the house and was obviously inviting them to follow him, but his voice was drowned by the renewed noise of the helicopter. They watched as it gently lifted, circled in what could have been a gesture of goodbye, and veered away over the sea.

Maycroft said, 'I take it you'll want to go first to the body.'

Dr Glenister said, 'I'd like to complete my examination before Commander Dalgliesh hears anything about the circumstances of the death. Has the body been moved?'

'To one of our two sickrooms. I hope we didn't do wrong. We let him down and it felt – well – inhuman to leave him alone at the foot of the tower, even covered by a sheet. It seemed natural to put him on a stretcher and bring him into the house. We've left the rope in the lighthouse.'

Dalgliesh asked, 'Unguarded? I mean, is the lighthouse locked?'

'No. It can't be because we no longer have a key. One was provided when the lighthouse was restored – at least I'm told it was – but it's been missing for years. It was never thought necessary to replace it. We have no children on the island and we don't admit casual visitors so there was no reason why the lighthouse should be kept locked. There is a bolt on the inside. The visitor who paid for the restoration, who was an enthusiast for lighthouses, used to sit on the platform beneath the lantern and know he couldn't be disturbed. We've never bothered to remove the bolt but I doubt that it's ever used.'

He had been leading the way, not to the rear door of the house, but round the left-hand wing and to a pillared front entrance. The central block with its two long curved windows on the first and second floors under the massive square tower, reared above them, more intimidatingly impressive than when seen from the air. Almost involuntarily, Dalgliesh came to a stop and looked up.

As if taking this as an invitation to break what had become an uncomfortable silence, Maycroft said, 'Remarkable, isn't it? The architect was a pupil of Leonard Stokes, and after Stokes died, modelled it on the house he built for Lady Digby at Minterne Magna in Dorset. The main façade there is at the rear and the house is entered that way, but Holcombe wanted both the principal rooms with the long curved windows and the front door to face the sea. Our visitors, those who know something about architecture, are fond of pointing out that design has been sacrificed to pretension and that Combe has none of the brilliant co-ordination of styles which Stokes achieved at Minterne. The substitution of four curved windows instead of two, and the design of the entrance, make the tower look too bulky. I don't know Minterne but I expect they're right. This house looks impressive enough for me. I suppose I've got used to it.'

The front door, dark oak heavily encrusted with ironwork, stood open. They passed into a square hall with a tiled floor in a formal but intricate design. At the rear a wide staircase branched to left and right, giving access to a minstrels' gallery dominated by a large stained-glass window showing a romanticised King Arthur and the Knights of the Round Table. The hall was sparsely furnished in ornate oak, a style which suggested that the original owner was aiming at baronial ostentation rather than comfort. It was difficult to imagine anyone sitting in those ponderous chairs or on the long settle with its high, intricately carved back.

Maycroft said, 'We have a lift. Through this door.'

The room they entered was obviously used partly as a business room and partly as a cloakroom and storeroom. There was a desk which showed signs of use, a row of pegs holding waterproofs and a low shelf for boots. Since their arrival there had been no sign of life. Dalgliesh asked, 'Where are they all now, the visitors and resident staff?'

Maycroft replied, 'The staff have been warned that they'll be needed for questioning. They're waiting in the house or in their quarters. I've asked them to congregate later in the library. We only have two visitors now in addition to Oliver's daughter, Miranda, and his copy-editor, Dennis Tremlett. The other two can't be contacted. Of course, one wouldn't expect them to be inside on a day like this. They could be anywhere on the island, but we should be able to reach them by telephone when the light fades. Neither has booked in for dinner.'

Dalgliesh said, 'I may need to see them before then. Haven't you some way of getting in touch?'

'Only by sending out a search party, and I decided against it. I thought it better to keep people together in the house. It's the custom here never to disturb or contact visitors unless absolutely necessary.'

Dalgliesh was tempted to reply that murder imposes its own necessity, but stayed silent. The two visitors would have to be questioned but they could wait. It was now more important to have the residents together.

Maycroft said, 'The two sickrooms are in the tower immediately under my apartment. Perhaps not very practical but the surgery is on that floor and it's peaceful. We can just get a stretcher into this lift but it's never before been necessary. We replaced the lift three years ago. About time too.'

Dalgliesh asked, 'You found no note from Mr Oliver in the lighthouse or elsewhere?'

Maycroft said, 'Not in the lighthouse, but we didn't think to search. We didn't look in his pockets, for example. Frankly it didn't occur to us. It would have seemed crassly inappropriate.'

'And Miss Oliver hasn't mentioned any note left in the cottage?'

'No, and it's not a question I'd have liked to ask. I'd gone to tell her that her father was dead. I was there as a friend, not as a policeman.'

The words, although quietly spoken, held a sting and, glancing at Maycroft, Dalgliesh saw that his face had flushed. He didn't reply. Maycroft had been the first to see Oliver's body; in the circumstances he was coping well.

Surprisingly it was Dr Glenister who spoke. She said dryly, 'Let's hope that the rest of your colleagues appreciate the difference.'

The lift, clad in carved wood and with a padded

leather seat along the back, was commodious. Two of the walls were mirrored. Seeing the faces of Maycroft and Staveley reflected into infinity as they were borne upwards, Dalgliesh was struck by their dissimilarity. Maycroft looked younger than he had expected. Hadn't the man come to Combe Island after retirement? Either he had retired young or the years had dealt kindly with him. And why not? The life of a country solicitor would hardly expose a man to a higher than usual risk of a coronary. His hair, a silky light brown, was beginning to thin but showed no sign of greying. His eyes, under level brows, were a clear grey and his skin almost unlined except for three parallel shallow clefts along the brow. But he had none of the vigour of youth. The impression Dalgliesh gained was of a conscientious man who was settling into middle-age with his battles avoided rather than won; the family solicitor you could safely consult if seeking a compromise, not one suited to the rigours of a fight.

Guy Staveley, surely the younger man, looked ten years older than his colleague. His hair was fading into a dull grey with a tonsure-like patch of baldness on the crown. He was tall, Dalgliesh judged over six feet, and he walked without confidence, his bony shoulders bent, his jaw jutting, as if ready to encounter once again the injustices of life. Dalgliesh recalled Harkness's easy words. *Staveley made a wrong diagnosis and the child died. So he's got himself a job where the worst that can happen is someone falling off a cliff, and he can't be blamed for that.* Dalgliesh knew that there were things which happened to a man that marked him irrevocably in body and mind, things that could never be forgotten, argued away, made less painful by reason or even by remorse. He had seen on the faces of the chronically ill Staveley's look of patient endurance unlit by hope.

3

The lift stopped without a jerk and the group followed Maycroft down a corridor, cream-walled and with a tiled floor, to a door on the right.

Maycroft took a key with a name tab from his pocket. He said, 'This is the only room we can lock and luckily we haven't lost the key. I thought you'd want to be assured that the body hadn't been disturbed.'

He stood aside to let them in, and he and Dr Staveley stationed themselves just inside the door.

The room was unexpectedly large with two high windows overlooking the sea. The top of one was open and the delicate cream curtains drawn across it fluttered erratically like a labouring breath. The furnishings were a compromise between domestic comfort and utility. The William Morris wallpaper, two button-backed Victorian armchairs and a Regency desk set under the window were appropriate to the unthreatening informality of a guestroom, while the surgical trolley, over-bed table and the single bed with its levers and backrest held something of the bleak impersonality of a hospital suite. The bed was placed at right angles to the windows. At this height a patient would see only the sky, but presumably even this restricted view provided a comforting reminder that there was a world outside this isolated sickroom. Despite the breeze from the open window and the constant pulse of the sea, the air seemed to Dalgliesh sour smelling, the room as claustrophobic as a cell.

The bed pillows had been removed and placed on one of the two easy chairs and the corpse, covered with a sheet, lay outlined beneath it as if awaiting the attention of an undertaker. Professor Glenister placed her Gladstone bag on the over-bed table and took out a plastic coat, packaged gloves and a magnifying glass. No one spoke as she put on the coat and drew the thin latex over her long fingers. Approaching the bed, she gave a nod to Benton-Smith who removed the sheet by meticulously folding it from top to bottom and then side to side, before carrying the square of linen, as carefully as if he were taking part in a religious ceremony, and placing it on top of the pillows. Then, unasked, he switched on the single light over the bed.

Professor Glenister turned to the two figures standing beside the door. 'I shan't need you any more, thank you. A special helicopter for the transport of the dead will be coming in due course. I'll go with the body. Perhaps you could wait for Mr Dalgliesh and his team in your office.'

Maycroft handed the key to Dalgliesh. He said, 'It's on the second floor opposite the library. The lift stops in the hallway between the two.'

He hesitated for a moment and gave a last long look at the body almost as if he thought some final gesture of respect were required, if only a bend of the head. Then without another word he and Staveley left.

Oliver's face was not unfamiliar to Dalgliesh; he had seen it photographed often enough over the years and the carefully chosen images had made their statement, imposing on the fine features the lineaments of intellectual power, even of nobility. Now all that was changed. The glazed eyes were half-open, giving him a look of sly malevolence, and there was a faint stink of urine from a stain on the trouser front, the final humiliation of sudden and violent death. The jaw had fallen and the upper lip, drawn back from the teeth, was set in a snarl. A thin thread of blood had oozed from the left nostril and dried black so that it looked like an emerging insect. The thick hair, iron grey and streaked with silver, waved back from a high forehead; the silver threads, even in death, glittered in the light from the window and would have looked artificial had not the eyebrows shown the same discordant mixture of colours.

He was short, Dalgliesh judged no more than five foot four, the head disproportionately large compared with the delicate bones of the wrists and fingers. He was wearing what looked like a Victorian shooting jacket in heavy blue and grey tweed, belted and with four patch pockets with the flaps buttoned down, an open-necked grey shirt and grey corduroy trousers. His brown brogues, brightly polished, looked incongruously heavy for so slight a frame.

Professor Glenister stood for a moment silently contemplating the corpse, then gently she touched the muscles of the face and neck and moved to test the joints of each of the fingers curved over the lower sheet as if half-clutching it in death.

She bent her head close to the corpse, then straightened up and said, 'Rigor is well established. I would assess the time of death as between seven-thirty and nine o'clock this morning, probably closer to the former. With this degree of rigor there's little point in attempting to undress him. If I can later get a more accurate assessment I will, but I doubt I shall get closer than that, even assuming there are contents in the stomach.'

The mark of the ligature was so vivid on the white scrawniness of the neck that it looked artificial, a simulation of death, not death itself. Under the right ear the bruise, obviously caused by the knot, was extensive; Dalgliesh estimated that it must measure some five centimetres square. The circular mark of the rope, high under the chin, stood out as clearly as a tattoo. Professor Glenister peered at it, then handed the magnifying glass to Dalgliesh.

'The question is: is this death by hanging or by manual strangulation? We'll get nothing useful from the right-hand knot on the neck. The bruise is extensive, suggesting a large, fairly rigid knot. The interesting side of his neck is here on the left, where we have two distinct circular bruises, probably both from fingers. I would expect a thumb mark on the right, but that's obscured by the mark of the knot. The assumption is that the assailant is right-handed. As for the cause of death, you hardly need my opinion, Commander. He was strangled. The hanging came later. There's a distinct surface mark from the ligature itself which looks like a regular and repeated pattern. It's more precise and different than I would expect from an ordinary rope. It could be a rope with a strong core, probably of nylon, and a patterned outer cover. A climbing rope for example.'

She spoke without glancing at Dalgliesh. He thought,

She must know that I've been told how he died, but she won't ask. Nor does she need to, given this island and its cliffs. Even so, the deduction had been surprisingly quick.

Looking down at Professor Glenister's gloved hands as they moved about the body, Dalgliesh's mind obeyed its own compulsions, even as he responded to the imperatives of the present. He was struck, as he had been as a young detective constable on his first murder case, by the absoluteness of death. Once the body was cold and rigor mortis had started its inevitable and predictable progress, it was almost impossible to believe that this stiffening encumbrance of flesh, bone and muscle had ever been alive. No animal was ever as dead as was a man. Was it that so much more had been lost with that final stiffening, not only the animal passions and the urges of the flesh, but the whole encompassing life of the human mind? This body had at least left a memorial to its existence, but even that rich legacy of imagination and verbal felicities seemed a childish bagatelle in the face of this ultimate negativity.

Professor Glenister turned to Benton-Smith, who was standing silently a little apart. 'This can't be your first murder case, Sergeant?'

'No, ma'am. It's my first by manual strangulation.'

'Then you'd better take a longer look.'

She handed him the glass. Benton-Smith took his time, then returned it without speaking. Dalgliesh remembered that Edith Glenister had been a notable teacher. Now that she had a pupil to hand, the temptation to assume her previous role of pedagogue was proving irresistible. So far from resenting this instruction of his subordinate, Dalgliesh found it rather endearing.

Professor Glenister continued to address Benton-Smith.

'Manual strangulation is one of the most interesting aspects in forensic medicine. It can't, of course, be self-inflicted – unconsciousness would intervene and the grip would relax. That means strangling is always assumed to be homicidal unless there is convincing evidence to the contrary. Most strangulation is manual and we expect to find the marks of the grip on the neck. Sometimes there's scratching or the impression of a fingernail made when the victim is trying to loosen the assailant's grip. There's no evidence of that here. The two almost identical bruises on the left side of the neck over the cornu of the thyroid suggest strongly that this was strangulation by a right-handed adult and that one hand only was used. The pressure between the thumb and finger means that the voice-box is squeezed, and there may be bruising behind it. In elderly persons, such as this victim, there can be a fracture of the superior cornu of the thyroid at its base. It is only where the grip has been very violent that more extensive fractures are likely. Death can occur with very little violence and may indeed not be intended. A strong grip of this kind may cause death from vagal inhibition or cerebral anaemia, not asphyxia. Do you understand the terms I've used?'

'Yes, ma'am. May I ask a question?'

'Of course, Sergeant.'

'Is it possible to give an opinion on the size of the hand, whether it's male or female, and whether there's any abnormality?'

'Occasionally, but with reservations, particularly when it comes to an abnormality of the hand. If there are distinct thumb and finger bruises, an estimate of the spread is possible, but only an estimate. One should beware of asserting too forcibly what is or isn't possible. Ask the Commander to tell you about the case of Harold Loughans in 1943.'

The glance she gave Dalgliesh was faintly challenging. This time he decided not to let her get away with it. He said, 'Harold Loughans strangled a pub landlady, Rose Robinson, and stole the evening's takings. The suspect had no fingers on his right hand, but the forensic pathologist, Keith Simpson, gave evidence that strangulation would be possible if Loughans sat astride his victim so that the weight of his body pressed down with his hand. This explained why there was no finger bruising. Loughans pleaded not guilty and Bernard Spilsbury appeared for the defence. The jury believed his evidence that Loughans was incapable of strangling Mrs Robinson and he was acquitted. He later confessed."

Professor Glenister said, 'The case is a warning to all expert witnesses and to juries who succumb to the cult of celebrity. Bernard Spilsbury was regarded as infallible, largely because he was a superb witness. This was not the only case in which he was later proved wrong.' She turned to Dalgliesh. 'I think that's all I need to do or see here. I hope to do the autopsy tomorrow morning and should be able to let you have a preliminary verbal report by midday.'

Dalgliesh said, 'I've got my laptop with me and there'll be a telephone in the cottage where I'm staying. That should be secure.'

'Then I'll phone you at midday tomorrow to give you the gist.'

As Benton-Smith replaced the sheet over the body, Dalgliesh said, 'Isn't there work being done on obtaining fingerprints from skin?'

'It's fraught with difficulties. I had a talk recently with one of the scientists involved in the experiments, but the only success so far has been in America where it's possible that a higher humidity caused more sweat to be deposited. The neck area is too soft to receive a detectable impression and it's unlikely you'd get the necessary ridge detail. Another possibility is to swab the bruised area and try for DNA, but I doubt whether this would stand up in court given the possibility of con-tamination by a third person or by the victim's own body fluids at the post mortem. This method of DNA analysis is particularly sensitive. Of course, if the killer had attempted to move the body and had handled the corpse by any other area of bare skin, it could provide a better surface for fingerprints or DNA than the neck. If the perpetrator had oil or grease on his hands, this would also increase the chance of finding fingerprints. I don't think in this case there's a hope. The victim was obviously fully clothed and I doubt whether you'll get any contact traces on his jacket.'

Kate spoke for the first time. 'Suppose this was suicide but he wanted it to look like murder. Could Oliver have made those finger marks on his own neck?'

'Judging by the pressure necessary to produce those marks I'd say it was impossible. In my opinion Oliver was dead when he was pushed over the railings. But I'll learn more when I open the neck.'

She collected her instruments, clicked shut the Gladstone bag. She said, 'I suppose you won't want to call the helicopter until you've been to the scene of crime. There may be exhibits you'll want taking to the laboratory. So this is an opportunity for me to take a walk. I'll be back in forty minutes. If you want me before then I'll be on the north-west cliff path.'

Then she was gone without a backward glance at the body. Dalgliesh went to his murder case and took out his gloves, then insinuated his fingers into Oliver's jacket pockets. He found nothing except one clean and folded handkerchief in the bottom left-hand pocket and a rigid spectacle case containing a pair of half-moon reading glasses in the right. Without much hope that they would yield useful information, he placed them in a separate bag and returned it to the body. Both of the trouser pockets were empty except for a small curiously shaped stone which, from the fluff adhering to it, had probably been there for some time. The clothes and shoes would be removed in the autopsy room and sent to the laboratory.

Kate said, 'It's a bit surprising that he didn't even carry a wallet but I suppose on the island he didn't need one.'

Dalgliesh said, 'No suicide note. Of course he could have left one in the cottage, but if he had, surely his daughter would have said so by now.'

Kate said, 'He might have put it in his desk drawer or half-hidden it. He wouldn't have wanted people to come after him before he had a chance to get to the lighthouse.'

Benton was replacing the sheet. He said, 'But do we really believe that this was suicide, sir? Surely he couldn't have made those bruises himself.'

'No, I don't think he did, Sergeant. But we'd better not begin theorising until we get the autopsy report.'

They were ready to leave. The enclosing sheet seemed to have softened, defining rather than obliterating the sharp point of the nose and the bones of the quiescent arms. And now, thought Dalgliesh, the room will take possession of the dead. It seemed to him, as it always did, that the air was imbued with the finality and the mystery of death; the patterned wallpaper, the carefully positioned chairs, the Regency desk, all mocking with their normality and permanence the transience of human life.

4

Dr Staveley followed them into the office. Maycroft said, 'I'd like Guy to be here. Effectively he's my deputy, although that has never been formalised. There may be details he can add to what I say.'

Dalgliesh knew that the proposal was less to assist him than to protect Maycroft. Here was a lawyer anxious to have a witness to anything said between them. He could see no valid reason for objection and made none.

Dalgliesh's first impression on entering the office was of a comfortably furnished sitting room not altogether successfully adapted as a place dedicated to official business. The great curved window was so dominant that the eye took in belatedly the room's peculiar dichotomy. Two panes were wide open to a glittering expanse of sea which, even as Dalgliesh looked, was deepening from pale to a deeper blue. From here the crash of the surf was muted but the air hummed with a deep plangent moan. The untameable for a while looked tranquil and dormant and the room in its comfortable conformity held inviolate a calm invulnerability.

Dalgliesh's eye was practised in taking in swiftly and without apparent curiosity what a room betrayed about its occupier. Here the message was ambiguous, a room inherited rather than personally arranged. A mahogany desk and round-backed chair stood facing the window and set against the far wall were a smaller desk and chair and a rectangular table holding a computer, printer and fax-machine. Next to this was a large black safe with a combination lock. Four grey filing cabinets stood against the wall opposite the window, their modernity contrasting with the low glass-fronted bookcases each side of the ornate marble fireplace. The shelves held an incongruous mixture of leather-bound volumes and more utilitarian books. Dalgliesh could see the red-jacketed *Who's Who*, *The Shorter Oxford English Dictionary* and an atlas lodged between rows of box-files. There were a number of small oil paintings but only the one over the fireplace made any impact: a group portrait with a house as the background and the owner, his wife and children carefully posed before it. It showed three sons, two of them in uniform and the other standing a little apart from his brothers and holding the bridle of a horse. It was meticulously over-painted but the statement it made about the family was unambiguous. No doubt it had remained in place over the decades, justifying its place less by artistic merit than by its scrupulous delineation of family piety and a nostalgic reminder of a lost generation.

As if feeling the room required some explanation, Maycroft said, 'I took the office over from the previous Secretary, Colonel Royde-Matthews. The furniture and the pictures belong to the house. I put most of my own things in store when I took the job.'

So he had come to the island unencumbered. What else, Dalgliesh wondered, had he left behind?

He said, 'You'd like to sit down. Perhaps if we moved one of the desk chairs to the fireplace with the four armchairs we'd be more comfortable.'

Benton-Smith did so. They sat in a semicircle in front of the ornate over-mantel and the empty grate, rather, Dalgliesh felt, like a prayer meeting uncertain who would utter the first petition. Benton-Smith had placed his desk chair a little away from the armchairs and now unobtrusively took out his notebook.

Maycroft said, 'I don't need to tell you how anxious we all are to cooperate with your inquiry. Oliver's death, and particularly the horror of the way he died, has shocked the whole island. We've a violent history, but that's long in the past. There's been no unnatural death – indeed no death – on this island since the end of the last war except for Mrs Padgett and that was two weeks ago. The cremation took place on the mainland last Friday. Her son is still with us but is expected to leave shortly.'

Dalgliesh said, 'I shall, of course, need to speak with everyone individually, apart from meeting them all in the library. I was told something of the history of the island including the setting up of the Trust. I also know a little about the people living here. What I need to know is how Nathan Oliver fitted in and the relations between him and your staff and visitors. I'm not in the business of exaggerating personal proclivities or of ascribing motives where they don't exist, but I do need frankness.'

The warning was unambiguous. There was the slightest trace of resentment in Maycroft's voice. 'You shall have it. I'm not going to pretend that relations with Oliver were harmonious. He came regularly, every quarter, and in my time – and I think in my predecessor's – his arrival wasn't greeted with pleasure. Frankly he was a difficult man, demanding, critical, not always civil to the staff and liable to nurse a grievance, genuine or otherwise. The Trust deed states that anyone born on the island can't be refused admission, but is not specific on how often or how long visits can be. Oliver is – was – the only living person who was born on the island and we couldn't refuse him, though frankly I wonder whether his behaviour wouldn't have justified it. He was becoming more difficult with advancing age and no doubt he had his problems. The last novel wasn't as well received as the previous ones and he may have felt that his talent was declining. His daughter and his copy-editor-cum-secretary may be able to tell you more about that. My main problem was that he wanted Emily Holcombe's cottage, that's Atlantic Cottage. You'll see from the map that it's the closest to the cliff and has wonderful views. Miss Holcombe is the last surviving member of the family, and although she resigned some years ago from being a Trustee, she has the right under the terms of the Trust to live on the island for the rest of her life. She has no intention of leaving Atlantic Cottage and I have no intention of asking her to move.'

'Had Mr Oliver been particularly difficult during the last few days? Yesterday, for example?'

Maycroft glanced across at Dr Staveley. The doctor said, 'Yesterday was probably the unhappiest day Oliver had spent on the island. He had a blood test on Thursday, the blood taken by my wife who's a nurse. He asked for it to be done because he was complaining of being over-tired and thought he might be anaemic. It seemed a reasonable precaution and I decided to ask for a number of tests on the sample. We use a private pathology service attached to the hospital at Newquay. The sample was lost overboard by Dan Padgett, who was taking some of his mother's clothes to the Oxfam shop there. It was obviously an accident, but Oliver reacted violently. At dinner he was engaged in a furious argument with one of our visitors, Dr Mark Yelland, Director of the Hayes-Skolling Laboratory, about his research work with animals. I doubt whether I have sat through a more uncomfortable and embarrassing meal. Oliver left the dining room before the meal was over, saying that he wanted the launch this afternoon. He didn't say definitely that he intended to leave, but the implication was clear. That was the last time I saw him alive.'

'Who began the argument at dinner, Oliver or Dr Yelland?'

Maycroft appeared to be thinking before he spoke, then he said, 'I think it was Dr Yelland but you'd better ask him when you see him. My memory isn't clear. It could have been either of them.'

Dalgliesh wasn't inclined to make too much of Maycroft's reluctance. An eminent scientist didn't resort to murder because of a quarrel over dinner. He knew something of Mark Yelland's reputation. Here was a man who was used to violent controversy about his chosen profession and no doubt had developed strategies for coping with it. It was unlikely that they included murder.

He asked, 'Did you think Mr Oliver was irrational to the point where he was mentally unstable?'

There was a pause, then Staveley said, 'I'm not competent to give an opinion but I doubt whether a psychiatrist would go that far. His behaviour at dinner was antagonistic but not irrational. Oliver struck me as a deeply unhappy man. It wouldn't surprise me if he had decided to end it all.'

Dalgliesh said, 'Even so spectacularly?'

It was Maycroft who spoke. 'I don't think any of us really understood him.'

Dr Staveley seemed to regret his last statement. Now he said, 'As I said, I'm not competent to give an opinion on Oliver's state of mind. When I said that suicide wouldn't surprise me, I suppose it was because he was obviously unhappy and anything else is inconceivable.'

'And what happened about Dan Padgett?'

Maycroft said, 'I spoke to him, of course. Oliver wanted him dismissed but there was no question of that. As I've said, it was an accident. It wasn't a sacking offence and there would've been no point. I steeled myself to suggest that he might be happier if he found a job on the mainland. He said he'd already planned to leave now that his mother had died. He'd decided to go to London and enrol for a degree at one of the newer universities. He'd already written for particulars and apparently they weren't much worried that he hadn't any good A-levels. I told him he'd made a wise decision to leave Combe and make a new start. He'd come to the office expecting a reprimand but he left more cheerful than I've ever seen him. Perhaps cheerful is the wrong word – he was elated.'

'And there's no one on the island who can be described as Oliver's enemy? No one who might hate him enough to wish him dead?'

'No. I still can't believe this is murder. I feel there

must be some other explanation, and I hope you'll succeed in finding it. In the meantime I suppose you want everyone to stay on the island. I think I can promise that the staff will be cooperative, but I have no control over our visitors, Dr Raimund Speidel, a German diplomat and ex-Ambassador to Beijing, and Dr Yelland, nor, of course, over Miss Oliver and Tremlett.'

Dalgliesh said, 'I've no power at present to prevent anyone leaving, but obviously I hope they won't. If anyone does, they'll still need to be interviewed but with less convenience and more publicity than if they'd stayed.'

Maycroft said, 'Miss Holcombe has a dental appointment in Newquay on Monday morning. Apart from that the launch will remain in harbour.'

Dalgliesh said, 'How certain can you be that no one can land here unseen?'

'No one ever has in living memory. The harbour is the only safe landing place by sea. There are enough people in and around the house to keep a continual if not organised watch. As you'll have seen, the entrance to the harbour is very narrow and we have light sensors on each side. If a boat comes into harbour by night the lights come on. Jago's cottage is on the quay. He sleeps with his curtains drawn back and he'd wake up immediately. It's never happened. I suppose there are about two places where someone could get ashore at low tide by swimming from an offshore boat, but I can't see how he'd get up the cliff without an accomplice on the island, and they'd both need to be experienced climbers.'

'And who on the island is an experienced climber?'

It was obvious that Maycroft spoke with some

reluctance. 'Jago. He's a qualified climbing instructor and occasionally visitors he considers competent can climb with him. I think you can dismiss any suggestion that we have been harbouring an unwelcome visitor. It's a comforting thought but it isn't feasible.'

And it wasn't only the problem of getting ashore. If Oliver had been lured to the lighthouse by someone who had gained access and perhaps hidden overnight, the killer would have had to have known that the lighthouse would be unlocked and where to find the climbing ropes. Dalgliesh had no doubt that the assumed murderer was one of the people on Combe, but the question of access had to be asked. It would certainly be raised by the defence if someone were brought to trial.

He said, 'I'll need a map of the island showing the cottages and their present occupants.'

Maycroft went over to the desk drawer. He said, 'We've a number. Obviously visitors need them to find their way about. I think these will give sufficient details both of the buildings and the terrain.'

He handed the folded maps to Dalgliesh, Kate and Benton-Smith. Dalgliesh moved over to the desk, opened his map and Kate and Benton joined him to study it.

Maycroft said, 'I've marked the present occupants. The island is four-and-a-half miles long and lies north-east to south-west. You'll see from the map that it's widest – about two miles – in the middle and tapers to the north and south. I have a flat here in the house and so do the housekeeper, Mrs Burbridge, and the cook, Mrs Plunkett. Millie Tranter, who helps Mrs Burbridge, has accommodation in the converted stables, and so does Dennis Tremlett, Mr Oliver's copy-editor and secretary. Any temporary staff employed on a weekly basis from the mainland also stay there. There are none at present. There are two flats in the house for visitors who prefer not to occupy the cottages, but they're usually empty, as they are now. Jago Tamlyn, who's our boatman and looks after the generator, is in Harbour Cottage at the harbour. Moving east we have Peregrine Cottage with Miss Oliver at present in it. Then about three hundred yards further is Seal Cottage, which is at present empty and which you yourself might wish to take. Beyond that is Chapel Cottage with Adrian Boyde, my secretary. It's named after the square chapel which is about fifty yards to the north. The farthest south-east cottage is Murrelet, which Dr Yelland at present occupies. He arrived on Thursday.

'Moving to the western shore, the most northerly cottage is Shearwater, where Dr Speidel, who arrived last Wednesday, is staying. About a quarter of a mile south is Atlantic Cottage with Miss Emily Holcombe. Hers is the largest cottage and is semi-detached. Her butler, Arthur Roughtwood, lives in the smaller part. Then there's Puffin Cottage, where Martha Padgett lived until her death two weeks ago. It's one-bedded, so Dan had an apartment in the stable block. After his mother's death he moved into the cottage to clear up her possessions. Finally there's Dolphin Cottage just north-west of the lighthouse.' He looked at his colleague. 'That's occupied by Guy and his wife Joanna. Jo's a nurse and she and Guy looked after Martha Padgett until she died.'

Dalgliesh said, 'You have at present six staff excluding Dr Staveley. Surely that can't be adequate when all the cottages are full.'

'We employ temporary staff from the mainland, mostly for cleaning. They come a week at a time. All have been with us for years and are reliable and, of course, discreet. They don't usually work weekends but we're cutting down on visitors now because of keeping ready for the VIPs we're told we should expect. You probably know more about that than do I.'

Was there a trace of resentment in his voice? Ignoring it, Dalgliesh went on, 'I'd better have the names and addresses of the temporary workers but it seems unlikely that they'll be able to help.'

'I'm sure they won't. They hardly ever saw the visitors let alone spoke to them. I'll look up the records but I think only two were ever here when Oliver was in his cottage. I doubt they set eyes on him.'

Dalgliesh said, 'Tell me what you know about the people here.'

There was a pause. Maycroft said, 'I'm in some difficulty. If there's any suggestion that one of us is suspected of homicide, I ought to advise that he or she phones for a lawyer. I can't act for them.' He paused and said, 'Or, of course, for myself. My own position is invidious. The situation is difficult, unique.'

Dalgliesh said, 'For both of us. Until I get the autopsy report I can't be sure what I'm investigating. I expect to hear from Dr Glenister sometime tomorrow. Until she reports, I'm assuming that this is a suspicious death. Whatever the outcome, it has to be investigated and the sooner we get an answer the better for everyone.

The bruise on Oliver's neck, who first noticed it?'

The two men looked at each other. Guy Staveley said, 'I think I did. I can't be sure. I remember that when I first saw it I looked up at Rupert and our eyes met. I got the impression we were thinking the same thing, but neither of us spoke of it until we had taken the body into the sickroom and were alone. But anyone who saw the body could have noticed the bruising. Miss Oliver must have done. She insisted on seeing her father's body and made me fold back the covering sheet.'

'And neither of you mentioned it to anyone else?'

Maycroft said, 'I thought it important to discourage speculation until the police arrived. Naturally I expected that there would be an investigation of some kind. I went at once to the office and phoned the number I'd been given. They told me to close down the island and wait for further instructions. Twenty minutes later they said you'd be on your way.'

He paused, then went on, 'I know the people on this island. I know I've only been here for eighteen months but it's long enough to understand the essentials about them. The idea that any one of them could have murdered Oliver is bizarre. There has to be another explanation, however implausible it may seem.'

'So tell me what you know about them.'

'Mrs Burbridge, the housekeeper, is the widow of a clergyman and has been here for six years, Lily Plunkett, the cook, for twelve. As far as I know, neither had any particular cause to dislike Oliver. Adrian Boyde, my secretary, is an ex-priest. He'd been away on leave and returned just before I arrived. I doubt whether he's capable of killing a living creature. I expect you know about Emily Holcombe. As the only living member of her family she has a right to stay here under the provision of the Trust, and she brought her manservant, Arthur Roughtwood, with her. Then there's Jago Tamlyn, the boatman and electrician. His grandfather once worked as boatman here on Combe.'

Kate asked, 'And Millie Tranter?'

'Millie's the only young person on our staff and I think she enjoys the distinction. She's only eighteen. She helps Mrs Plunkett in the kitchen, waits at table and makes herself generally useful to Mrs Burbridge.'

Dalgliesh said, 'I must see Miss Oliver, if she's feeling well enough to talk. Is anyone with her now?'

'Only Dennis Tremlett, Oliver's copy-editor. Guy and I went together to break the news of Oliver's death. Jo called in later to see if there was anything she could do. Dennis Tremlett is still there, so Miranda's not alone.'

Dalgliesh said, 'I'd like you both to come with me to the lighthouse. Perhaps you would ring the library and let the people waiting know that I'll be with them as soon as possible. Or you might prefer to release them to get on with what they were doing and call them together when I'm ready.'

Maycroft said, 'I think they'd prefer to wait. Before we leave here, is there anything else you need?'

'It will be helpful if we could have the use of the safe. There may be exhibits requiring safekeeping until they can be sent to the lab. I'm afraid it will mean changing the combination. Will that be an inconvenience for you?'

'Not at all. The Trust deed and other important

papers are not on the island. Information about our past visitors is, of course, confidential but those papers will be as secure in the filing cabinets as they are in the safe. It should be large enough for your needs. I sometimes wonder if it was built to hold a body.'

He flushed as if suddenly aware that the remark had been singularly inappropriate. To cover the moment of embarrassment, he said, 'To the lighthouse.'

Benton opened his mouth to comment, then closed it promptly. Probably he had been about to make reference to Virginia Woolf but thought better of it. Glancing at Kate's face, Dalgliesh felt that he had been wise.

5

Dalgliesh, his two colleagues, Maycroft and Staveley left the house by the front door and took the narrow path along the cliff edge. Dalgliesh saw that about fifteen feet below was the lower cliff he had first seen from the air. Viewed from above, the narrow plateau looked as foliate as a planned garden. The patches of grass between the rocks were bright green, the huge boulders with their planes of silvery granite looked carefully placed and there hung from the crevices a profusion of yellow and white spongy-leaved flowers. More prosaically, Dalgliesh noted that the under-cliff offered a concealed route to the lighthouse for anyone agile enough to clamber down.

Maycroft, walking between Dalgliesh and Kate, gave an account of the restoration of the lighthouse. Dalgliesh wondered whether this volubility was a defence against embarrassment or whether Maycroft was attempting to impose some normality on their walk as if speaking to more conventional and less threatening visitors.

'The lighthouse was modelled on the famous one by Smeaton which was taken down in 1881 and rebuilt on Plymouth Hoe as a monument to him. This is just as elegant and almost as high. It was neglected after the modern lighthouse was built on the north-west tip of the island, and during the last war, when the island was evacuated, it suffered a fire that destroyed the three upper storeys. After that it was left derelict. It was one of our visitors, an enthusiast for lighthouses, who gave the money for its restoration. The work has been done with remarkable attention to detail and, as far as possible, is a model of the lighthouse as last used. The working lighthouse is run by Trinity House and is automatic. The Trinity House boat arrives to inspect it from time to time.'

And now they had left the path and were walking up an encircling grassy mound and then descending to the lighthouse door. It was of stout oak with an ornamental knob almost too high to reach, an iron latch and a keyhole. Dalgliesh noted, as he knew would both Kate and Benton-Smith, that the door would not be visible beyond the grassy mound. The lighthouse was even more impressive seen now than from a distance. The slightly concave and glistening walls, as bright as if newly painted, rose some fifty feet to the elegant super-structure containing the light, its sectioned walls rising to a roof shaped like a mandarin's hat topped with a bobble and weather vane. The whole top edifice, which looked eccentrically naïve and childlike, was painted red and surrounded by a railed platform. There were four narrow paned windows high above the door, the top two so small and distant that they looked like peepholes.

Pushing open the heavy oak door, Maycroft stood aside and let Dalgliesh and the rest of the party enter first. The circular ground-floor chamber was obviously used as a storeroom. There were half a dozen folding chairs stacked to one side and a row of pegs from which hung oilskin jackets and waders. To the right of the door was a heavy chest and, above it, six hooks holding climbing ropes, five of which had been meticulously coiled. The sixth on the final peg hung loosely, its dangling end twisted into a loop no more than six inches wide. The knot was a bowline with above it two half-hitches, an odd combination. Surely anyone capable of tying a bowline would have had confidence in its ability not to slip. And why not initially make the noose using a single slipknot at one end of the rope? The complicated method used suggested either someone inexperienced in handling a rope or so confused or agitated that he wasn't thinking coherently.

Dalgliesh said, 'Do this loop and knot look as they did when you first saw them after the body had been taken down?'

It was Staveley who replied. 'Exactly the same. I remember that it looked clumsy and I was surprised Oliver knew how to tie a bowline.'

'Who rewound the rope and replaced it on the hook?'

Maycroft said, 'Jago Tamlyn did. As we started to wheel the stretcher back to the house. I called back to tell him to see to the rope. I told him to put it back on its hook with the others.'

And with the door unlocked the rope would be accessible to anyone who needed to tamper with it. It would be sent to the laboratory in the hope, if not of prints, of DNA from sweaty hands. But any such evidence, even if decipherable, was already compromised.

He said, 'We'll go up to the gallery. I'd like to hear exactly what happened from the moment Oliver went missing.'

They began toiling in single file up the circular wooden staircase which lined the walls. Room succeeded room, each smaller in size, each meticulously restored. May-croft, seeing Benton's obvious interest, gave a brief description as they ascended.

'The ground floor, as you saw, is mostly used now for storing Jago's climbing equipment. The chest holds climbing boots, gloves, the slings, karabiner, clips and harnesses, and so on. Originally the room would've held water which had to be pumped up and heated on a stove if the keeper wanted a bath.

'Now we're entering the room where the electricity was generated and the tools kept. Next we have the fuel room for the storing of oil, and up through a storeroom where the tinned food was kept. Today light-houses have refrigerators and freezers but in earlier times keepers would have relied on tins. We're passing through the winch room now and on to the battery room. Batteries are used to supply power for the lantern if the generators should fail. Little to see here, but I think the living room is more interesting. Keepers used to cook and eat their meals here using a coal stove or an oven fuelled by bottled gas.'

No one else spoke as they ascended. And now they were in the bedroom. The circular room had only space enough for two narrow bunk beds with storage beneath, the beds covered by identical plaid blankets. Lifting the edge of one, Dalgliesh saw that beneath it was only a hard mattress. The blankets, stretched tightly over the beds, looked undisturbed. In an attempt to re-create an atmosphere of domesticity, the restorer had added photographs of the keeper's family and two small circular porcelain plaques with religious texts – *Bless This House* and *Peace, Be Still*. This was the only room which gave Dalgliesh a sense of how these long-dead lives must have been lived.

And now they were passing up the curved and narrow steps from the service room, which was fitted with a model of a radiotelephone, a barometer, a thermometer and a large chart of the British Isles fixed to the wall. Stacked against the wall was a folding chair.

Maycroft said, 'Some of our more energetic visitors like to carry a chair on to the platform round the lantern. They not only get the best view on the island, but can read in absolute privacy. We get to the lantern by these steps and through a door on to the gallery.'

None of the windows to any of the rooms had been opened and the air, although not tainted, had been stale, the gradually decreasing space unpleasantly claustrophobic. Now Dalgliesh breathed in a sweet sea-laden air, so fresh that he felt like a liberated prisoner. The view was spectacular: the island lay below, the muted greens and browns of the central scrubland a sober contrast to the glitter of the granite cliffs and the shining sea. They moved round to the seaward side. The sharp-edged waves were flecked to the horizon as if a giant hand had flicked a brush of white paint over the immensity of blue. They were met by an erratic breeze which, at this height, had the occasional force of a strong wind, and instinctively all five clutched at the rails. Watching Kate, he saw her gulp in the fresh air as if she too had been long confined. Then the breeze died and it seemed to Dalgliesh that even in that moment the white-flecked restless sea became calmer.

Looking down, he saw there was nothing beneath them on the seaward side but a few yards of paved stone bounded by a rough dry-stone wall and beyond it the sheer rock sandwiched in polished layers and slicing down to the sea. He leaned over the rail and felt a second of disorientating dizziness. In what extremity of despair or with what annihilating exultation would a man hurl himself into this infinity? And why would a suicide choose the degrading horror of hanging? Why not fling himself into the void?

He said, 'Where exactly was the rope fixed?'

Again it was Maycroft who took the initiative. 'I think he fell from about this spot here. He was dangling some twelve or fourteen feet down, I can't be more precise than that. He had fixed the rope to the railings by threading it in and out of the spurs and then over the top. The rest of the rope lay just loose here on the floor.'

Dalgliesh didn't comment. Any discussion with his colleagues was inhibited by the presence of Maycroft and Staveley and would have to wait. He wished he could have seen exactly how the rope had been secured to the rail. That must have taken time and the perpetrator, whether Oliver or another, would have had to judge the length of the drop. He turned to Staveley. 'Is that your memory too, Doctor?'

'Yes. Normally we might have been too shocked to notice details, but of course we had to unravel the rope from the railings before we could let the body down, and that took a little time. We tried to force it through coiled, but in the end had to take the end and laboriously unthread it.'

'Were you the only two up here at the lantern?'

'Jago had followed us up. The three of us began to pull the body up. We stopped almost at once. It seemed terrible to be stretching the neck still further. I don't know why we decided on that course of action. I suppose it was just that the body was so much closer to the lantern than it was to the ground.'

Maycroft said, 'It's distressing even to think of it. I had a moment of panic when I actually thought we might tear the head from the body. The right and only thing seemed to be to let him gently down. We unwound the rope and then Jago threaded it under one spur to act as a kind of brake. Guy and I could then manage perfectly well between us with the rope twisted over the rail, so I told Jago to go down to receive the body.'

Dalgliesh asked, 'Who else was there at the time?'

'Just Dan Padgett. Miss Holcombe and Millie had gone.'

'And the rest of the staff and your visitors?'

'I didn't phone Mrs Burbridge or Mrs Plunkett to let them know that Oliver was missing, so they didn't join the search. I could only have got in touch with Dr Speidel and Dr Yelland if they'd been in their cottages, but obviously I didn't try. As visitors they're not responsible for Oliver's safety. There was, in any case, no point in disturbing them unnecessarily. Later, when I'd spoken to London and we learnt you were on your way, I did phone the cottages, but neither man answered. They were probably walking somewhere in the north-west part of the island. I expect they still are.'

'So the search party consisted of you two, Jago, Miss Holcombe, Dan Padgett and Millie Tranter?'

'I hadn't asked Miss Holcombe or Millie to help. Millie came later with Jago and Miss Holcombe had been in the surgery when Jo phoned me. She had an appointment for her annual anti-flu injection. Adrian Boyde and Dennis Tremlett had gone to search the eastern side of the island and Roughtwood said he was too busy to help. Actually the search didn't really get underway. We were together outside the house when the mist came down and there seemed little point in going further than the lighthouse until it lifted. It usually does on Combe, and quite quickly.'

'And you were the first actually to see the body?'

'Yes, with Dan Padgett right behind me.'

'What made you think Oliver might be in or near the lighthouse? Was this a place he normally came to?'

'I don't think so. But of course the whole point of the island is that people have privacy. We don't keep a watch on our visitors. But we were close to the lighthouse and it occurred to me to look there first. The door wasn't bolted so I went up one storey and called up the stairs. I thought he'd have heard me if he'd been there. I'm not sure why I then decided to walk round the lighthouse. It seemed the natural thing to do at the time. Anyway, the mist was now fairly thick and it seemed pointless to go on with the search. It was when I was on the seaward side that it suddenly began to clear and I saw the body. Millie and Jago were coming round the house from the harbour. She began screaming, and then Guy and Miss Holcombe appeared.'

'And the rope?'

It was Staveley who answered. 'When we saw that Jago had caught the body and laid it on the path, we both went down immediately. Dan was standing and Jago was kneeling by the body. He said, "He's gone, sir. No point in trying resuscitation." He'd loosened the rope round Oliver's neck and drawn the noose over his head.'

Maycroft said, 'I sent Jago and Dan to get the stretcher and a sheet. Guy and I waited without speaking. I think we turned away from Oliver and looked out to sea, at least I did. We had nothing to cover him with and it seemed – well – indecent to be staring down at that distorted face. It seemed a long time before Jago and Dan came back and by that time Roughtwood had arrived. Miss Holcombe must have sent him. He helped Dan and Jago lift the body on to the stretcher. We started off for the house, Dan and Roughtwood wheeling the stretcher, Guy and myself walking at either side. I called back to Jago: "Pick up the rope and put it back in the lighthouse, will you? Don't touch the knot or the noose. There'll be an inquest and the rope may be part of the evidence."'

Dalgliesh said, 'It didn't occur to you to take the rope with you?'

'There would've been no point. We all thought we were dealing with a suicide. The rope would have been too cumbersome for my desk drawer and it was as safe in the lighthouse as anywhere. Frankly it never occurred to me that it wouldn't be. What else could I reasonably have done with it? It had become an object of horror. It was best out of public sight.'

But it hadn't been out of public reach. With the unlocked door, anyone on the island could have had access to it. The more people who had handled the rope and the knot, the more difficult it would be to discover who had first tied the bowline and made doubly sure with the two half-hitches. He needed to talk to Jago Tamlyn. Assuming this was murder, Jago was the only one who could say when and how the rope had been replaced. It would have been useful to have had Jago with them, but Dalgliesh had been anxious not to have more people than necessary at the scene of crime, or to complicate the inquiry at this stage by revealing, however indirectly, his train of thought.

He said, 'I think that's as far as we can go at present. Thank you.'

They descended in silence, Guy Staveley as carefully as if he were an old man. Now they were again in the entrance chamber. The loosely coiled blue-and-red-veined rope, the small dangling noose, seemed to Dalgliesh's eyes to have subtly changed into an object portentous with latent power. This was a reaction he had experienced before when contemplating a murder weapon: the ordinariness of steel, wood and rope and their terrible power. As if by common agreement they contemplated the rope in silence.

Dalgliesh turned to Maycroft. 'I'd like a word with Jago Tamlyn before I see the residents together. Can he be reached quickly?'

Maycroft and Staveley looked at each other. Staveley said, 'He may have gone over to the house. Most people will probably be in the library by now, but he won't want to hang about waiting. He could still be on the launch. If he is, I'll give him a wave.'

Dalgliesh turned to Benton-Smith. 'Find him, will you, Sergeant?'

Dalgliesh didn't miss the quick flush to Staveley's face. He could guess his train of thought. Was Dalgliesh ensuring that he had no time to warn or brief Jago before his first encounter?

Benton-Smith said, 'Yes, sir', and moved quickly round the lighthouse and out of sight. He would be walking round the cliff edge towards the harbour. The wait seemed interminable but it must have been less than five minutes before they heard footfalls on the stone and the two figures appeared round the curve of the lighthouse.

And now, coming towards them was the watcher on the quay they had seen from the helicopter. Dalgliesh's first impression was of a confident masculine handsomeness. Jago Tamlyn was short, Dalgliesh judged under five foot six, and was powerfully built, his stockiness emphasised by the thick dark-blue fisherman's jersey, intricately patterned. Beneath it he wore corduroy trousers tucked into black rubber sea-boots. He was very dark with a long, strong-featured face, curly dishevelled hair and short beard, his eyes narrow under a creased brow, the irises a clear sapphire blue against the sun-burnt skin. He regarded Dalgliesh with a fixed look, wary and speculative, which, under Dalgliesh's gaze, quickly changed to the passionless acquiescence of a private on a charge. It was a face which gave nothing away.

Maycroft introduced Dalgliesh and Kate, using their ranks and full names with a careful formality which suggested that they were expected to shake hands. No one did. Jago nodded and was silent. Dalgliesh led the group round to the seaward side of the lighthouse. He spoke without preliminaries. 'I want you to tell me exactly what happened from the time you were called to join the search party.'

Jago was silent for about five seconds. Dalgliesh thought it unlikely that he needed the time to refresh his memory. When he spoke, the account came fluently and without hesitation.

'Mr Boyde phoned me from the office to say Mr Oliver hadn't turned up at the surgery as expected and asking me to come and help look for him. The fog was coming up by then and I couldn't see the sense of searching, but I went up the path from the harbour none the less. Millie Tranter was in the cottage and ran after me. When we got in sight of the lighthouse, the fog suddenly cleared and we saw the body. Mr Maycroft was there with Dan Padgett. Dan was shaking and moaning. Millie started screaming and then Dr Staveley and Miss Holcombe came round the lighthouse. Mr Maycroft, Dr Staveley and I went inside and up to the gallery. We began pulling the body up, then Dr Staveley said we should let it down instead. We wound the rope round the top railing so as to control the drop. Mr Maycroft told me to go back down to catch the body and that's what I did. When I'd got hold of him Mr Maycroft and Dr Staveley let the rope drop down.'

He was silent. After a pause Dalgliesh asked, 'Did you lay the body on the ground unaided?'

'Yes sir. Dan came to help but it wasn't needed. Mr Oliver wasn't that heavy.'

Again a pause. It was apparent that Jago had decided not to volunteer any information, but only to respond to questions.

Dalgliesh said, 'Who was with you when you laid him on the ground?'

'Only Dan Padgett. Miss Holcombe had taken the lass away, as was right.'

'Who loosened and removed the rope?'

The pause was longer now. 'I think I did.'

'Was there any doubt about it? We're talking about this morning. It wasn't a moment anyone would forget.'

'I did. I think Dan helped. I mean, I got hold of the knot and he started pushing the rope through. We'd just got it over the head when Mr Maycroft and Dr Staveley arrived.'

'So you both took part in taking it off?'

'I reckon so.'

'Why did you do that?'

And now Jago looked straight at Dalgliesh. He said, 'It seemed natural. The rope had bitten deep into his neck. We couldn't leave him like that. It wasn't decent.'

'And then?'

'Mr Maycroft told Dan and me to get the stretcher. Mr Roughtwood – Miss Holcombe's butler – was here when we got back.'

'Was that the first time you saw Mr Roughtwood at the scene?'

'I told you, sir. After Millie and Mrs Holcombe had gone, it was just the three of us here and Dan. Roughtwood arrived while we were fetching the stretcher.'

'What happened to the rope?'

'Mr Maycroft called back for me to put it with the others, so I wound it up and put it back on the hook.'

'You wound it just loosely? The others are more carefully coiled.'

'I look after all the climbing equipment. The ropes are my responsibility. They're always kept like that. This one was different. No point in coiling it like the others, I wasn't going to use it again. That rope's unlucky now. I wouldn't trust my life to it, or any other life. Mr Maycroft said not to touch the knot. There'd have to be an inquest and maybe the coroner might want to see the rope.'

'But of course you had already touched it, and you say Dan Padgett had also touched it.'

'Could be. I grasped it so as to loosen the noose and draw it over his head. I knew he was dead and past help, but it wasn't proper leaving him like that. I reckon Dan felt the same.'

'He was able to help despite his distress? What state was he in when he first arrived?'

Kate could see the question was unwelcome. Jago replied quickly. 'He was upset, like you said. Better ask him, sir, about his feelings. Much the same as mine, I guess. It was a shock.'

Dalgliesh said, 'Thank you, Mr Tamlyn. You've been very clear. I'd like you to look at the knot carefully.'

Jago did so, but didn't speak. Kate knew that Dalgliesh could be patient when patience could best get results. He waited, then Jago said, 'Mr Oliver could tie a bowline, but seemingly he had no faith in it. There's two half-hitches above. Clumsy.'

'Do you know whether Mr Oliver would know that a bowline was a safe knot to use?'

'I reckon he could tie a bowline, sir. His father was boatman here and brought him up after his ma died. He lived on Combe until he was evacuated with the others when the war started. Afterwards he lived here with his father until he was sixteen and took off. His dad would've taught him to tie a bowline.'

'And the rope? Are you able to say whether it looks the same now as it did after you'd hung it up?'

Jago looked at the rope. His face was expressionless. He said, 'Much the same.'

'Not much the same – does it look the same, Mr Tamlyn, as far as you can remember?'

'Hard one to answer. I took no great notice of how it looked. I just coiled it and hung it up. It's what I said, sir. Seems much the same as I left it.'

Dalgliesh said, 'That's all for now. Thank you, Mr Tamlyn.'

Maycroft gave a dismissive nod. Jago turned to him in a gesture which could have been intended to convey his dismissal of Dalgliesh and all his doings. 'No point in going back to the launch now, sir. No need I reckon. The engine's running sweetly enough now. I'll be in the library with the others.'

They watched as he strode vigorously over the bank and disappeared. Dalgliesh nodded to Kate. Opening her murder case she put on her latex gloves, drew out a large exhibit bag and, carefully lifting the rope from the hook, dropped it inside and sealed the bag. Taking a pen from her pocket, she glanced at her watch then wrote the time and the bag contents on the label. Benton-Smith added his name. Maycroft and Staveley watched in silence, not meeting each other's eyes, but Dalgliesh sensed a small tremor of unease as if only now were they realising the full implications of why he and his colleagues were on the island.

Suddenly Staveley said, 'I'd better get back to the house and make sure everyone's in the library. Emily won't come but the rest should be there.'

Without waiting for a reply he hurried out of the door and loped clumsily over the ridge with surprising speed. For a moment no one spoke. Then Dalgliesh turned to Rupert Maycroft. 'I need the lighthouse to be locked. Is there a chance of finding the key?'

Maycroft was still staring after Staveley. He gave a start. 'I could try. Up till now, of course, no one has bothered. I haven't much hope. The key could have been lost years ago. Either Dan Padgett or Jago could probably replace the whole lock but I doubt whether we've got one on the island strong enough for this door. It would take time. Failing that they could fix strong external bolts but that, of course, wouldn't prevent people getting in.'

Dalgliesh turned to Benton. 'Will you see to that, Sergeant, as soon as we've finished in the library? If we have to rely on bolts they'll need to be taped. That too won't prevent entry but we'll know if someone has broken in.'

'Yes sir.'

For the moment they had finished with the lighthouse. It was time to make acquaintance with the residents of Combe.

6

They crossed a wide hall to the library door. Before
opening it, Maycroft said, 'Most of the present residents
should be here except for Miss Oliver and Mr Tremlett.
Obviously I haven't bothered them. Miss Holcombe
and Roughtwood are in Atlantic Cottage but will be
available for interview later. When you've finished here
I'll try again to contact Dr Speidel and Mark Yelland.'

They entered a room identical in shape and size to
Maycroft's office. Here again was the great curved
window and the unrestricted view of sky and sea. But
the room was unmistakably a library with mahogany
glass-fronted bookcases lining the other walls from the
floor almost to the ceiling. To the right of the door the
bookcase had been adapted to provide shelving for a
collection of CDs. There were two high-backed leather
chairs before the fireplace and others ranged around
a large oblong table in the middle of the room. Here
the company had seated itself, except for two women
who had taken the armchairs and a younger, strongly
built blonde who was standing looking out of the
window. Guy Staveley was at her side. She turned as
Dalgliesh and the little group entered, and fixed on
him a frankly appraising look from remarkable eyes, the
irises as richly brown as treacle.

Without waiting for an introduction, she said, 'I'm
Joanna Staveley. Guy deals with illness, I provide

sticking plasters, laxatives and placebos. The surgery's on the same floor as the sickroom if you need us.'

No one spoke. There was a low shuffle as the men at the table shifted their chairs as if to rise, then thought better of it. The heavy mahogany door had been too solid to allow any murmur of voices to reach the little group in the hall, but now the silence was complete and it was difficult to believe that it had ever been broken. All but one of the windows were closed and once again Dalgliesh was consciously aware of the pounding of the sea.

Maycroft had obviously mentally rehearsed what he had to say and, although not totally at ease, he made the introductions with quiet confidence and more authority than Dalgliesh had expected. 'This is Commander Dalgliesh from New Scotland Yard, and his colleagues Detective Inspector Miskin and Detective Sergeant Benton-Smith. They are here to investigate the circumstances of Mr Oliver's tragic death and I have given Commander Dalgliesh an assurance that all of us will cooperate fully in helping him to establish the truth.' He turned to Dalgliesh. 'And now I'd like to introduce my colleagues.' He nodded towards the two seated women. 'Mrs Burbridge is our housekeeper in charge of all domestic arrangements, and Mrs Plunkett is our cook.'

Mrs Plunkett was a solid plump-cheeked woman with a plain but pleasant face. She was wearing a white coat tightly buttoned over her broad frame. It was rigidly starched and Dalgliesh wondered if she had put it on to proclaim unambiguously her place in the island hierarchy. Her dark hair with only the first flecks of grey lay in strong waves held back by a slide, a style Dalgliesh had seen pictured in photographs of the 1930s. She sat in apparently untroubled calm, her strong hands – the fingers round as sausages, the skin slightly red – resting in her capacious lap. Her eyes were small and very bright – but not, he thought, unfriendly – and were fixed on him with the experienced scrutiny of a cook assessing the potential merits and inadequacies of a prospective kitchen maid.

Mrs Burbridge looked very much the doyenne of the house. She sat upright in her chair as still as if posing for a portrait. She had a short compact body with a high full bust and delicate wrists and ankles. Her hands, pale and with the nails short and unpainted, lay unclasped, revealing no sign of strain. The steel-grey hair was neatly plaited and twisted into a bun at the top of her head, the sharp eyes fixed on Dalgliesh from behind silver-rimmed spectacles were more questioning than speculative. Her mouth was generous and firm and he sensed that she held her authority lightly: one of those women who gained their own way less by insisting on it than by never imagining that it could ever be questioned.

The two women remained seated but their faces creased briefly into considered and conditional smiles.

Maycroft turned his attention to the group at the table. 'You've already met Jago Tamlyn. Jago acts not only as waterman responsible for the launch, but is a qualified electrician and maintains our generator, without which we should be cut off from the mainland with no light and no power. Next to Jago we have Adrian Boyde, my personal assistant, then Dan Padgett, the gardener and general handyman, and at the end Millie

Tranter. Millie helps with the linen and in the kitchen.'

Dalgliesh didn't intend the occasion to be portentous but he had no illusions. He knew that he couldn't put them at ease and that any attempt could only be derisory. He didn't come as a friend and no formal regrets at Oliver's death, no platitudes about regretting the inconvenience could disguise this uncomfortable truth. It was during the later individual interviews that he expected to learn most, but if anyone had seen Oliver that morning, particularly if he had been making his way to the lighthouse, the sooner he was told the better. And there was another advantage in this group questioning. Statements openly made could be immediately queried or challenged, by look if not by word. His suspects might be more confiding later in private, but it was here together that their relationships were most likely to be revealed. And he needed to know, if possible, the precise time of death. He was confident that Dr Glenister's preliminary assessment would be proved accurate: Oliver had died at about eight o'clock that morning. But an interval of ten minutes could make the difference between an alibi that stood firm and one that could be challenged, between doubt and certainty, between innocence and guilt.

He said, 'I or one of my officers will see you individually some time later today or tomorrow. Perhaps you would let Mr Maycroft know if you intend to leave this house or your quarters. But now that we're together, I'm asking if anyone saw Mr Oliver either after he left the dining room at about nine-fifteen last night, or at any time this morning.'

There was a silence. Their eyes slewed round the

group but at first no one spoke. Then Mrs Plunkett broke the silence. 'I saw him at dinner. He left when I went into the dining room to start clearing the main course. I served coffee as usual at nine-thirty here in the library, but he didn't return. Dinner was the last I saw of him. This morning I've been busy in my kitchen getting Mr Maycroft's breakfast and preparing lunch.' She paused, then added, 'No one wanted it, which was a pity because it was salmon-en-croute. No point in trying to heat that up later. Bit of a waste really. Sorry I can't help.'

She glanced at Mrs Burbridge as if conveying a signal. Mrs Burbridge followed. 'I had dinner in my own flat and then read until ten-fifteen when I went to get a last breath of fresh air. I saw no one. The wind had got up and was gusting harder than I'd expected so I didn't stay out for more than fifteen minutes. This morning I was in my flat, mostly in my sewing room, until Mr Maycroft telephoned to tell me that Mr Oliver had been found hanged.'

Kate asked, 'Last night you went in which direction?'

'To the lighthouse and back, along the top cliff. It's a walk I often take before bed. As I said, I saw no one.'

Adrian Boyde was sitting in disciplined calm, his shoulders slightly hunched, his hands under the table. Of the four seated with him he, who had been spared the sight of Oliver's hanging body, looked the most distressed. His face, drained of colour, glistened with sweat, the single strand of very dark hair plastered damply across his forehead looked as theatrically black as if it had been dyed. He had been staring down at his hands but now raised his eyes and gazed fixedly at Dalgliesh.

'I ate supper alone in my cottage and I didn't go out afterwards. This morning I left early for work – just before eight – and walked across the island but I didn't see anyone until Mr Maycroft arrived and joined me in the office at about twenty-past nine.'

Now they looked at Dan Padgett. His pale fear-filled eyes flickered round as if seeking assurance that it was his time to speak. He sucked in his lips. The others waited. The words, when they came, were brief and spoken with a forced bravado that sounded embarrassingly hostile. Dalgliesh was too experienced to assume that fear implied guilt; it was often the most innocent who were the most terrified by a murder inquiry. But he was interested in the reason for it. He had already sensed that the general dislike of Oliver had a deeper cause than his disagreeable personality or arguments about accommodation. Miss Emily Holcombe, with the prestige of her name, could no doubt stand up to Oliver. He was looking forward to interviewing Miss Holcombe. Had Padgett perhaps been a more vulnerable victim?

Now Padgett said, 'I had a walk before supper but I was in my cottage by eight o'clock and I didn't go out again. I didn't see Mr Oliver last night or this morning.'

Millie said, 'Nor me neither', and looked across at Kate as if challenging her to say otherwise. Dalgliesh thought it surprising that someone who looked hardly older than a child should choose or have been chosen to work on Combe. Surely this small, isolated and sedulously controlled island would be anathema to most teenagers. She was wearing a very short jacket in faded blue denim much ornamented with badges, and constantly fidgeted in her chair so that from time to time he could glimpse a narrow strip of delicate young flesh between the jacket hem and the top of her jeans. Her fair hair was combed back into a ponytail and strands from an undisciplined fringe half obscured a sharp-featured face and small restless eyes. There was no sign of her recent distress and the small mouth was fixed in an expression of sulky belligerency. He judged that now was not the most propitious time to question Millie further, but with tactful handling and in private she might prove more informative than her elders.

Their eyes turned to Jago. He said, 'Seeing as Mr Oliver was alive and well at dinner you'll not be interested in Friday afternoon. I had supper in my cottage. Sausages and mash, if you're interested. This morning I took the launch out for forty minutes or so to test the engine. She's been giving a bit of trouble. That took from seven-forty-five until twenty-past eight, near enough.'

Kate asked, 'Where did you go? I mean, in which direction?'

Jago looked at her as if the question had been incomprehensible. 'Straight out and straight back, miss. It wasn't a pleasure cruise.'

Kate kept her temper. 'Did you go past the light-house?'

'I wouldn't, would I, not going straight out to sea and back?'

'But you could see the lighthouse?'

'I would've done if I'd been looking that way, but I wasn't.'

'It's hardly inconspicuous, is it?'

'I was busy with the launch. I saw nothing and

nobody. I was back in my cottage alone until Millie arrived at about half-past nine. The next excitement was Mr Boyde ringing to tell me that Mr Oliver was missing and asking me to join the search. I've told you the rest.'

Millie broke in. 'You said you weren't going out to test the launch until half-past nine. You promised to take me with you.'

'Well I changed my mind. And it wasn't a promise, Millie.'

'You didn't even want me to go with you on the search. You told me to stay in the cottage. I don't know what made you so angry.' She looked close to tears.

Neither Staveley nor his wife had chosen to sit. Watching them still standing together at the window, Dalgliesh was struck by their disparity. The impression Guy Staveley gave of an internal tension, disciplined by a cultivated ordinariness, emphasised his wife's flamboyant vitality. She was only an inch shorter than her husband, full-breasted with long legs. Her blonde hair, dark at the roots, as thick as his was sparse, was caught up in two red combs. Some yellow strands lay curled across her forehead and framed a face on which the first ravages of time emphasised rather than diminished her assured femininity. It would be easy to see her as a type, the handsome sexually demanding woman dominating a weaker and ineffectual husband. Dalgliesh, always wary of stereotypes, thought that the reality might be subtler and more interesting. It might also be more dangerous. Of all the people in the room she was the most at ease. She had changed for this encounter into something more formal than she would surely normally choose to wear on a working day. The cream quilted jacket worn above narrowly cut black trousers held the sheen of silk. She wore it open to reveal a black tee-shirt, the neck low enough to show the cleavage of her breasts.

She said, 'You've met my husband, of course, when you went to the scene of crime. Or isn't suicide a crime any more? Assisted suicide is though, isn't it? I don't suppose Oliver needed any assistance. That's one thing he had to do for himself.'

Kate said, 'Could you answer the question, Mrs Staveley?'

'I was with my husband at dinner here last night. Both of us stayed for coffee in the library. We went back to Dolphin Cottage and we were together until we went to bed just before eleven. Neither of us left our cottage. I don't share this passion for fresh air before bed. We breakfasted together in the cottage – grapefruit, toast and coffee – and then I came out to the surgery to wait for Oliver. He was due to give blood at nine. When he hadn't arrived by nine-twenty, I began ringing round to find out what was keeping him. He was an obsessive and, despite his dislike of the needle, I expected him either to phone and cancel or to be punctual. I didn't join in the search but my husband did. The first I knew what had happened was when Guy came back to tell me. But you know all about that.'

Dalgliesh said, 'It's helpful to hear it from you.'

She smiled. 'My account would hardly differ from my husband's. We had plenty of time before you arrived if we wanted to fabricate an alibi.'

It was obvious that her frankness had embarrassed the company. In the silence that followed a small tremor of shock was almost audible. They were careful not to meet each other's eyes.

Then Mrs Burbridge spoke. 'But surely we aren't here to provide each other with alibis? You don't need an alibi for a suicide.'

Jago broke in. 'And you don't get a top copper from the Met Police arriving by chopper either. What's wrong with the Cornish police? I reckon they're competent to investigate a suicide.' He paused, then added, 'Or murder too for that matter.'

All eyes turned to Dalgliesh. He said, 'No one is questioning local competence. I'm here with the agreement of the Cornish Constabulary. They're hard-pressed, as almost all police forces are. And it's important to clear this matter up as quickly as possible with the minimum of publicity. At present what I'm investigating is a suspicious death.'

Mrs Burbridge said gently, 'But Mr Oliver was an important man, a famous author. People talk of his getting the Nobel Prize. You can't hide death, not this death.'

Dalgliesh said, 'We're not hiding it, only attempting to explain it. The news has already been communicated to Mr Oliver's publishers and will probably be on tonight's TV and radio news and perhaps in tomorrow's papers. No journalist will be allowed to land on the island and inquiries will be dealt with by the Metropolitan Police public relations branch.'

Maycroft looked at Dalgliesh, then as if on cue said, 'There is bound to be speculation but I hope none of you will add to it by communicating with the outside world. Men and women with great responsibilities come here to find solitude and peace. The Trustees want to ensure that they can still find that solitude and that peace. The island has fulfilled what the original donor intended, but only because the people who work here – all of you – are dedicated, loyal and completely discreet. I'm asking you to continue that loyalty and that discretion and help Mr Dalgliesh to get to the truth of Mr Oliver's death as soon as possible.'

It was then that the door opened. All eyes turned to the new-comer. He walked with quiet confidence and took one of the empty chairs at the table.

Dalgliesh was surprised, as he often was when meeting a distinguished scientist, at how young Yelland looked. He was tall – over six feet – with fair curly hair whose length and unruliness emphasised the appearance of youth. A handsome face was saved from the insipidity of conventional good looks by the jutting jaw and the firm set of the thin-lipped mouth. Dalgliesh had seldom seen a face so ravaged by exhaustion or so stamped with the prolonged endurance of responsibility and overwork. But there was no mistaking the man's authority.

He said, 'Mark Yelland. I only got the answer-phone message about Oliver's death when I returned to Murrelet Cottage for lunch. I take it that the purpose of this meeting is to try to fix the time of death.'

Dalgliesh said, 'I'm asking if you saw Mr Oliver after dinner last night or at any time this morning.'

Yelland's voice was surprising, a little harsh and with a trace of an east London accent. 'You'll have been told of our altercation at the dinner table. I didn't see anyone, dead or alive, this morning until I came into this room. I can't be more helpful about timing than that.'

There was a silence. Maycroft looked at Dalgliesh. 'Is that all for now, Commander? Then thank you everyone for coming. Please make sure that I or one of Mr Dalgliesh's team know where we can find you when you're wanted.'

The company, all but Mrs Burbridge, got up and began to file out with the dispirited air of a group of mature students after a particularly unsuccessful seminar. Mrs Burbridge rose briskly, glanced at her watch and delivered a parting shot at Maycroft as she passed him at the door.

'You handled that very competently I thought, Rupert, but your admonition to be loyal and discreet was hardly necessary. When has anyone on this island been other than loyal and discreet during the time we've been here?'

Dalgliesh spoke quietly to Yelland as the latter reached the door. 'Could you wait please, Dr Yelland?' When Benton-Smith had closed the door on the last of the departing residents, Dalgliesh said, 'I asked you to stay because you didn't reply when I asked whether you had spoken to Mr Oliver after nine-thirty last night. I would still like an answer to that question.'

Yelland looked at him steadily. Dalgliesh was struck again by the power of the man.

Yelland said, 'I don't enjoy being interrogated, particularly in public. That's why I took my time coming. I didn't see or speak to Oliver this morning, which would surely be the relevant time unless he chose late at night to launch himself into the final darkness. But I did see him after dinner. When he left I followed him out.'

And that, thought Dalgliesh, was a fact that neither Maycroft nor Staveley had thought worth telling him.

'I followed him because we had had an argument which had been more acrimonious than illuminating. I only booked in for dinner because I'd checked that Oliver would be there. I wanted to challenge him about his new book, to make him justify what he'd written. But I realised that I'd been directing at him anger that had its cause elsewhere. I found there were still things I needed to say to him. With some people I wouldn't have bothered. I'm inured to ignorance and malice – well, not inured perhaps, but for most of the time psychologically I can cope. With Oliver it was different. He's the only modern novelist I read, partly because I haven't much time for recreational reading, but mainly because time spent in reading him isn't wasted. He doesn't deal in trivialities. I suppose he provides what Henry James said was the purpose of a novel: to help the heart of man to know itself. A bit pretentious but, if you need the sophistry of fiction, there's some truth in it. I wasn't setting out to justify what I do – the only person I need to convince in the end is myself – but I did want him to understand, or at least part of me did. I was very tired and I had drunk too much wine at dinner. I wasn't drunk but I wasn't thinking clearly. I seem to have had two opposing motives – to make some kind of peace with a man whose total dedication to his craft I understood and admired and to warn him that if he interfered again with my staff or my laboratory I would apply for an injunction. I wouldn't, of course. That would have provided the very publicity we have to avoid. But I was still angry. He stopped walking when

I drew up and at least turned in the darkness to listen.'

There was a pause. Dalgliesh waited. Yelland went on, 'I pointed out that I might use – and the word is appropriate – five primates in the course of a particular experiment. They would be well looked after, properly fed, exercised, played with – loved even. Their deaths would be easier than any death in nature, and those deaths could help eventually alleviate, perhaps cure, the pain of hundreds of thousands of human beings, could put an end to some of the most distressing and intractable diseases known to man. Doesn't there have to be an arithmetic of suffering? I wanted to ask him one question: if the use of my five animals could save the lifetime suffering, or even the lives, of fifty thousand other *animals* – not humans – wouldn't he see the loss of those five as justifiable, in reason and in humanity? So why not humans? He said, "I'm not interested in the suffering of others, human or animal. I was engaging in an argument." I said, "But you're a great humane novelist. You understand suffering." I remember clearly what he replied. "I write about it; I don't understand it. I can't vicariously feel it. If I could feel it, I couldn't write about it. You're wasting your time, Dr Yelland. We both do what we have to do. There's no choice for either of us. But it does have an end. For me the end is very close." He spoke with an intense weariness as if he had passed beyond caring.

'I turned away and left him. I believed I had spoken to a man who was at the limit of his endurance. He was as caged as one of my animals. I don't care what contra-indications to suicide there may be; I am convinced Nathan Oliver killed himself.'

Dalgliesh said quietly, 'Thank you. And that was the end of the conversation and the last time you saw or spoke to him?'

'Yes, the last time. Perhaps the last time anyone did.' He paused and then added, 'Unless, of course, this is murder. But I'm being naïve. I'm probably attaching too much importance to Oliver's last words. The Met wouldn't send their formidable poet-detective to investigate a putative suicide on a small offshore island.'

If the words weren't meant as a taunt they succeeded in sounding like one. Kate was standing next to Benton and she thought she detected a low growl like an angry puppy. The sound was so ridiculous that she had to restrain a smile.

Yelland went on, 'Perhaps I should say that I had never met Nathan Oliver until dinner last night and our encounter afterwards. I respected him as a novelist but I didn't like him. And now, if you've nothing else to ask, I'd like to get back to Murrelet Cottage.'

He left as quickly as he had arrived.

Benton said, 'That was a rum do, sir. First he admits that he only booked in for dinner to provoke a row with Oliver, then he follows him out either to propitiate him or threaten him further. He doesn't seem sure which, and he's a scientist.'

Dalgliesh said, 'Even scientists are capable of irrationality. He lives and works under a constant threat to himself and his family. The Hayes-Skolling lab is one the animal liberation people have particularly targeted.'

Benton said, 'So he comes to Combe and leaves the wife and family unprotected.'

Kate broke in. 'We can't know that, but one thing's

certain, sir. Given Dr Yelland's evidence, no one would be convinced that this is murder. He was pretty determined to persuade us that Oliver killed himself.'

Benton said, 'Perhaps because he genuinely believes it. After all, he hasn't seen those marks on Oliver's neck.'

'No, but he's a scientist. If he made them he must know that they would be there.'

7

Miranda Oliver said on the telephone that she was ready to be interviewed if Commander Dalgliesh would come now. Since he would be interviewing a presumably grieving daughter, Dalgliesh thought it would be tactful to take only Kate with him. There were things he needed Benton to do – the distances between the cottages and the lighthouse to be checked and photographs taken of the lower cliff, particularly of places where it would be comparatively easy for people to climb or slither down. The lower cliff was always going to present a problem. Overhung as it was with bushes, there seemed little doubt that people living in the cottages on the western coast of the island could walk the final quarter mile or so to the lighthouse unseen.

Peregrine Cottage was larger than it had seemed from the air when it had been dwarfed by Combe House, and even by its neighbour, Seal Cottage. It lay in a shallow hollow, half-hidden from the path, and was farther from the cliff edge than the other cottages. It was built to the same pattern, stone walled with a porch, two ground-floor windows and two above under a slate roof, but there was something slightly desolate, even forbidding, about its stark conformity. Perhaps it was the distance from the cliff and the seclusion of the hollow ground which gave an impression of deliberate isolation, of a cottage designed to be less attractive than its neighbours.

The curtains were drawn across the lower windows. There was a plain iron knocker and the door opened almost at once to Kate's gentle knock. Miranda Oliver stood aside and, with a stiff gesture, motioned them in.

Dalgliesh had taken half a minute to check the salient facts about Nathan Oliver from *Who's Who* before leaving his office and knew that he had married in 1970 and had been thirty-six when his daughter was born. But the young woman who now looked at him composedly appeared older than her thirty-two years. She was high busted and with the beginning of a matronly stateliness. He saw little resemblance to her father except for the strong nose and high forehead from which copious light brown hair was drawn back and pulled through a woollen loop at the nape of her neck. Her mouth was small but firm between slightly marsupial cheeks. Her most remarkable features were the grey-green eyes which now calmly appraised him. They showed no signs of recent weeping.

Dalgliesh made the introductions. This was a moment he had experienced many times during his career as a detective and he had never found it easy, nor indeed did any other officer he had known. Formal words of condolence had to be spoken but to his ears they always sounded insincere at best and mawkishly inappropriate at worst. But this time he was forestalled.

Miranda Oliver said, 'Of course my loss is the greatest. After all, I am his daughter and I've been his close working companion for most of my adult life. But my father's death is also a loss to literature and to the world.' She paused. 'Is there anything I can offer you? Coffee? Tea?'

The moment seemed to Dalgliesh almost bizarre. He

said, 'Nothing, thank you. I'm sorry to have to disturb you at a time like this but I'm sure you'll understand the need.' Since no offer of a chair had been made, he added, 'Shall we sit down?'

The room stretched the length of the cottage, the dining area near a door leading to what Dalgliesh presumed was the kitchen and with Oliver's study at the far end. There was a heavy oak desk in front of the window which looked out seaward, a square table beside it with a computer and copier, and oak shelves ranged along two of the walls. The dining area also served as a small sitting room with two upright chairs on each side of the stone fireplace and a sofa set under the window. The general impression was of comfortless austerity. There was no detectable smell of burning but the grate was filled with blackened paper and white ash.

They seated themselves at the dining table, Miranda Oliver as composedly as if this were a social call. It was then that they heard laborious footsteps coming slowly down the stairs and a young man appeared. He must have heard their knock, must have known they had arrived, but his eyes moved from Dalgliesh to Kate as if startled by their presence. He was wearing blue jeans and above them a dark blue Guernsey sweater, its chunkiness emphasising his fragility. Unlike Miranda Oliver he looked devastated, either with grief or fear, or perhaps with both. He had a youthful, vulnerable-looking face, the skin of his lips almost colourless. His brown hair was cut in a regular and very short fringe above deep-set eyes, giving him the appearance of a novice monk. Dalgliesh almost expected to see a tonsure.

Miranda Oliver said, 'This is Dennis Tremlett. He was my father's copy-editor and secretary. I think I should tell you that Dennis and I are engaged to be married – but maybe my father mentioned it at dinner last night.'

'No', said Dalgliesh, 'we haven't been told.' He wondered whether he should congratulate the couple. Instead he said, 'Will you please join us, Mr Tremlett?'

Tremlett walked to the table. Dalgliesh saw that he had a slight limp. After a moment's hesitation he took a chair next to Miranda. She gave him a look, possessive, a little minatory, and stretched her hand towards his. He seemed uncertain whether to take it but their fingers briefly touched before he placed both hands under the table.

Dalgliesh asked, 'Was your engagement recent?'

'We knew that we were in love during Daddy's last visit to the States. It was in Los Angeles actually. We didn't become formally engaged until yesterday and I told my father yesterday evening.'

'How did he take the news?'

'He said that he'd suspected for some time that we were growing fond of each other, so it wasn't a surprise to him. He was happy for us and I spoke briefly about our future plans, how we could live in the London flat he bought for Dennis's use, at least until we had a home of our own, and that we would ensure that he was looked after and that Dennis and I still saw him every day. He knew he couldn't manage without us and we were going to make sure that he didn't have to, but of course it would mean some change in his life. We've been wondering since whether he was only pretending to be pleased for us, that he was more worried than we realised about the prospect of living alone. He wouldn't have had to, of course. We were going to find a reliable housekeeper and we'd be there during the day, but the news might have been more of a shock than I realised at the time.'

Kate said, 'So it was you who broke the news. You didn't confront your father together?'

The verb was perhaps unfortunate. Miranda Oliver's face reddened and she snapped out her reply through tight lips. 'I didn't confront him. I'm his daughter. There was no confrontation. I told him my news and he was happy about it, at least I thought so.'

Kate turned to Dennis Tremlett. 'Did you speak to Mr Oliver at any time after your fiancée had given him the news?'

Tremlett was blinking as if trying to hold back his tears and it was obviously with an effort that his eyes met hers. 'No, there wasn't a chance. He had dinner at the house and came home after I'd left. When I arrived this morning he'd already gone out. I didn't see him again.'

His voice shook. Kate turned to Miranda Oliver. 'How has your father been since you arrived on the island? Did he seem distressed, worried, in any way not himself?'

'He was very quiet. I know he was worried about growing old, worried that his talent might be fading. He didn't say so but we were very close. I sensed that he was unhappy.' She turned to Tremlett. 'You felt that, didn't you, darling?'

The endearment, almost shocking in its unexpectedness, was brought out self-consciously, a word newly acquired and not yet familiar, less a caress on the tongue than a small note of defiance. Tremlett seemed not to notice.

He turned to Dalgliesh and said, 'He didn't confide in me very much; we weren't really on those terms. I was just his copy-editor and secretary. I know that he was concerned that the last book wasn't as well received as the previous ones. Of course he's become part of the canon now; reviewers are always respectful. But he himself wasn't satisfied. The writing was taking longer and the words didn't come as easily. But he was still a wonderful writer.' His voice broke.

Miranda Oliver said, 'I expect Mr Maycroft and Dr Staveley and the others will tell you that my father was difficult. He had every right to be difficult. He was born here and under the Trust deed they couldn't stop him visiting whenever he liked. He should have had Atlantic Cottage. He needed it for his work and he had a right to it. Emily Holcombe could easily have moved but she wouldn't. And then at first there was a difficulty because Daddy insisted that Dennis and I should be here with him. Visitors are supposed to come on their own. Father took the view that if Emily Holcombe could have Roughtwood, he could bring Dennis and me. He had to anyway; he needed us. Mr Maycroft and Emily Holcombe run this place between them. They don't seem to understand that Daddy is – was – a great novelist. Silly rules didn't apply to him.'

Dalgliesh said, 'Did you feel that he was depressed enough to take his own life? I'm sorry but this is something I have to ask.'

Miranda glanced at Dennis Tremlett, as if this were a

question more appropriately asked of him than of her. He was sitting rigidly looking down at his clasped hands and didn't meet her eyes. She said, 'That's a terrible suggestion, Commander. My father wasn't the kind of man who kills himself and if he had been he wouldn't have done it that horrible way. He was repelled by ugliness and hanging is ugly. He had everything to live for. He had fame, security, and his talent. He had me. I loved him.'

It was Kate who broke in. She was never unfeeling and only rarely tactless, but she was never inhibited by over-sensitivity from asking a direct question. She said, 'Perhaps he was more upset by your decision to marry than he let on. After all, it would have meant a major disruption to his life. If he had other worries that he didn't confide to you, this may have seemed the last straw.'

Miranda turned to her, her face flushed. When she spoke her voice was barely under control. 'That's a horrible thing to say. What you are implying is that Dennis and I were responsible for Daddy's death. That's cruel, and it's also ridiculous. Do you think I didn't know my father? We've lived together since I left school and I've looked after him, made his life comfortable for him, served his talent.'

Dalgliesh said gently, 'That's what Inspector Miskin had in mind. You and Mr Tremlett were obviously determined that your father shouldn't suffer, that you would go on taking responsibility for his care and that Mr Tremlett would continue as his secretary. But your father may not have realised how much thought you'd given to it. Inspector Miskin was asking a reasonable question which was neither cruel nor insensitive. We have evidence that the evening after you had broken the news your father dined in the main house – which was unusual – and was certainly upset. He also ordered the launch for this afternoon. He didn't actually say he proposed to leave the island, but that was implied. Did he tell either of you that he intended to leave?'

This time they looked at each other. Dalgliesh could see that the question was both unexpected and unwelcome. There was a pause. Dennis Tremlett said, 'He did say something to me earlier in the week about going to the mainland for the day. He didn't say why. I had a feeling it was something to do with research.'

Kate said, 'To order the launch after lunch wouldn't give him a full day on the mainland. Did he ever leave the island once he'd arrived?'

Again there was a pause. If either Tremlett or Miss Oliver were tempted to lie, a moment's thought would warn them that the police could check anything they said with Jago Tamlyn. At last Tremlett said, 'He did occasionally but not often. I can't remember the last time.'

Dalgliesh could sense a change, subtle but unmistakable, in the tenor of the questions and in their response. He changed tack. 'Did your father tell you about his will? Are there any organisations, for example, which will benefit by his death?'

This question, he saw, was more easily dealt with. Miranda said, 'I'm his only child and naturally the main beneficiary. He told me that some years ago. He may have left something to Dennis as a way of thanking him for his services over the last twelve years, and I think he did mention that. He also told me that he was leaving two million pounds to the Combe Island Trust, to be used in part to have another cottage built and named after him. I don't know whether he's altered his will recently. If he has, he didn't tell me. I know that he was increasingly unhappy that the Trust wouldn't put Atlantic Cottage at his disposal. I expect they were acting on the advice of Mr Maycroft. No one here has any idea what that cottage meant to Daddy. Where he works is important to him and this place isn't really suitable. I know it has two bedrooms, which most of the cottages haven't got, but he never felt at home here. Mr Maycroft and Emily Holcombe never seemed to realise that my father was one of England's greatest novelists and there are things he needed for his work – the right place, the right view, enough room as well as privacy. He wanted Atlantic Cottage and it could perfectly well have been arranged. If he has cut the Trust out of his will I'll be glad.'

Kate asked, 'When exactly did you break the news to your father about your engagement?'

'At about five o'clock yesterday, perhaps a little later. Dennis and I had been for a walk along the cliff and I came back alone. Daddy was here reading, and I made tea for him and told him then. He was very sweet about it, but he didn't say very much except that he was glad for us and he'd seen it coming. Then he said he would have dinner in the big house, so would I ring Mrs Burbridge and let her know there'd be one extra. He said there would be a guest there he wanted particularly to meet. It must have been Dr Speidel or Dr Yelland because they're the only other visitors.'

'Did he tell you what it was about?'

'No he didn't. He said he was going to his room to rest until it was time to change for dinner. I didn't see him again until he came down just before half-past seven and left for Combe House. All he said was that he wouldn't be late.'

Dalgliesh turned to Tremlett. 'And when did you see him last?'

'Just before one o'clock. I went back to my rooms in the stable block for lunch as usual. He said he wouldn't need me in the afternoon – he doesn't usually on a Friday – so that's when I decided on the walk. I told Miranda where I was going and I knew she'd come to meet me so that we could talk about our plans. Afterwards she agreed she'd speak to her father and I went back to my room in the stable block. I came back at eight o'clock expecting him to be here for dinner with the two of us, and Miranda told me that he'd gone to the big house. I didn't see him again.'

This time the words came quickly and more easily. Had they, perhaps, been rehearsed?

Kate looked at Miranda. She said, 'He must have come in very late.'

'He came back later than I expected but I heard the door and looked at my bedside clock. It was just after eleven. He didn't come to say goodnight. He usually does but not always. I expect he didn't want to disturb me. I saw him leave from my window at twenty-past seven this morning. I'd just come out of the shower and was dressing at the time. When I came down I saw that he'd made tea and eaten a banana. I thought that he'd gone for an early walk and would be back for his usual cooked breakfast.'

There had been no mention of the pile of charred paper in the grate. Dalgliesh was a little surprised that it hadn't been cleared away, but perhaps Miranda Oliver and Tremlett had realised that this would be pointless since Maycroft and Staveley would almost certainly have reported what they'd had seen.

He said, 'Some paper has been burned. Can you tell me about that?'

Tremlett swallowed but didn't reply. He glanced appealingly at Miranda but she was prepared. 'They were the proofs of my father's last book. He'd been working on them, making important alterations. My father wouldn't have done this. Someone must have got into the cottage during the night.'

'But wasn't the door locked?'

'No. It very rarely is because there's no need on the island. When he returned late last night he would normally have locked the door just as a matter of habit, but he might easily have forgotten or not bothered. It wasn't locked when I got up this morning, but then it wouldn't have been. Daddy would have left it unlocked when he left.'

'But surely he would have seen the destruction. It must have horrified him. Wouldn't it have been natural to wake you and ask how it happened?'

'Perhaps, but he didn't.'

'Don't you find that rather surprising?'

And now he was facing frankly antagonistic eyes. 'Everything that's happened since yesterday is surprising. It's surprising that my father's dead. He might not have noticed or, if he did, might not have wanted to disturb me.'

Dalgliesh turned to Dennis Tremlett. 'How important is the loss? If those were galleys, presumably there's a second set here and more at his publishers.'

Tremlett found his voice. 'They were very important. He would never have burned them. He always insisted on having galley proofs so that he could do the editing at that stage rather than on the manuscript. It made things very difficult for his publishers, of course, and more expensive for him, but he never revised until he got the proofs. And he did a lot of editing. That's how he liked to work. Sometimes he even made alterations between printings. He could never quite believe a novel was perfect. And he wouldn't have a publisher's editor. We did it together. He would write his alterations in pencil and I would copy them in ink on my copy of the proofs. That copy is missing as well as his.'

'And they were kept where?'

'In the top drawer of his desk. They weren't locked up. It wouldn't have occurred to him that that was necessary.'

Dalgliesh wanted to talk to Tremlett alone but it wasn't going to be easy. He turned to Miranda. 'I think I'll change my mind about the tea or coffee. Perhaps some coffee, if it won't be too much trouble.'

If the request was unwelcome she concealed her irritation well and without a word left the sitting room. He saw with relief that she closed the door after her. He wondered whether coffee had been the right choice. If Oliver had been particular, she would probably have to grind the beans and that would take time, but if she had no intention of going to any trouble he couldn't rely on more than a few minutes of privacy.

Without preamble he said to Tremlett, 'What was Mr Oliver like to work for?'

Tremlett looked up. And now he seemed almost anxious to speak. 'He wasn't easy, but then why should he be? I mean, he didn't make a confidant of me and he could be impatient at times, but I didn't mind. I owe him everything. I've worked for him for twelve years and they've been the best years of my life. I was a freelance copy-editor when he took me on and I mostly worked for his publisher. I'd been ill a lot so it was difficult to get a more regular job. He saw that I was meticulous, so after I'd copy-edited one of his books he took me on full-time. He paid for me to go to evening classes to learn computer skills. It was just a privilege to work for him, to be there day by day. There're some words I read by T. S. Eliot which seemed to be absolutely right for him. *Leaving one still with the intolerable wrestle with words and meanings.* People spoke of him as the modern Henry James but he wasn't really. There were the long complicated sentences but with James I always thought they obscured truth. With Nathan Oliver they illuminated it. I'll never forget what I've learnt from him. I can't imagine life without him.'

He was close to tears. Dalgliesh asked gently, 'How much did you help him? I mean, did he ever discuss progress with you, what he was trying to do?'

'He didn't need my help. He was a genius. But he did sometimes say – perhaps about a piece of action – do you believe that? Does it seem reasonable to you? And I would tell him. I don't think he much enjoyed plotting.'

Oliver had been fortunate to find an acolyte with a genuine love of literature and a sensibility to match his own, someone perhaps happy to undervalue his minor talent in the service of the greater. But his grief was genuine and it was difficult to see him as Oliver's murderer. But Dalgliesh had known killers with equal acting ability. Grief, even if genuine, could be the most duplicitous of emotions and was seldom uncomplicated. It was possible to mourn the death of a man's talent while rejoicing in the death of the man. But the burning of the proofs was surely different. That showed hatred for the work itself and a pettiness of mind which he hadn't detected in Tremlett. What was it that the man was grieving for, a mentor horribly done to death or a heap of blackened paper with the careful pencilled notes of a great writer? He couldn't share the grief but he did share the outrage.

And now Miranda came in. Kate got up to help her with the tray. The coffee, which Miranda poured and which he hadn't needed, was excellent. After the coffee, which Dalgliesh and Kate drank quickly, the interview seemed to have come to a natural conclusion. Tremlett got to his feet and stumbled out of the room and Miranda saw Dalgliesh and Kate to the door, carefully closing it behind them.

They walked towards Seal Cottage. After a moment's silence Dalgliesh said, 'Miss Oliver left her options carefully open, didn't she? Adamant that her father couldn't possibly have killed himself while previously enumerating the reasons why he might have done just that. Tremlett's distressed and terrified while she has herself well under control. It's easy to see who's the dominant partner there. Did you think Tremlett was lying?'

'No, sir, but I thought she might be. I mean, all that stuff about the engagement – Daddy loves me, Daddy would like his little girl to be happy – does that sound like the Nathan Oliver we know?'

'Not that we know, Kate. Only what others have told us.'

'And the whole business of the engagement initially struck me as odd. At first I kept wondering why they didn't see Oliver together, why Tremlett took such care to keep out of his way after the news was broken. Then I thought that maybe it wasn't so strange. Miranda might have wanted to tell her father alone, explain her feelings, set out their plans for the future. And if he cut up rough she might not have told Tremlett. She might have lied to him, told him that Oliver was happy about the marriage.' She thought for a moment, then added, 'But there wouldn't be much point in that. He'd have known the truth soon enough when he came in to work this morning. Daddy would have told him.'

Dalgliesh said, 'Yes, he would. Unless, of course, Miranda could be confident that next morning Daddy wouldn't be there to tell.'

8

By four o'clock Dalgliesh and the team had been given their keys, including one to the side entrance of Combe House, and had settled themselves into their accommodation, Dalgliesh in Seal Cottage and Kate and Benton in adjoining apartments in the stable block. Dalgliesh decided to let Kate and Benton interview Emily Holcombe, at least in the first instance. As the last of her family and the longest-standing resident, she could probably tell him more about the islanders than anyone else and, apart from that, he looked forward to talking to her. But the interview could wait and he, not she, would control it. It was important that all the suspects realised that Kate and Benton were part of his team.

Returning to the office to settle some administrative details he was a little surprised at Maycroft's apparent lack of concern at Dr Speidel's non-appearance, but presumably this arose from the long-standing policy of leaving visitors undisturbed. Dr Speidel had been on the island at the time of the murder; sooner or later his self-imposed solitude would have to be broken.

Maycroft was alone in the office when he arrived, but almost immediately Adrian Boyde put his head round the door. 'Dr Speidel is here. He was asleep, not out walking, when you rang earlier and didn't get the message until after three.'

'Show him up, please, Adrian. Does he know about Nathan Oliver?'

'I don't think so. I met him coming in at the back door. I didn't tell him.'

'Good. Ask Mrs Plunkett to send in some tea, will you. We'll have it in about ten minutes. Where's Dr Speidel now?'

'Inside the entrance hall, sitting on the oak settle. He doesn't look at all well.'

'We could have gone to him if only he'd let us know. Why didn't he ring for the buggy? It's a longish walk from Shearwater Cottage.'

'I asked that. He said he thought the walk would do him good.'

'Tell him I'd be grateful if he could spare a moment. It shouldn't take long.' He looked at Dalgliesh. 'He only arrived on Wednesday and this is his first visit. I doubt whether he'll have anything useful to tell you.'

Boyde disappeared. They waited in silence. The door opened and Boyde said, as if formally introducing an important visitor, 'Dr Speidel.'

Dalgliesh and Maycroft stood up. Dr Speidel, glancing at Dalgliesh, seemed for a moment disorientated, as if wondering whether this was someone he ought to recognise. Maycroft deferred any introduction. Perhaps feeling that his stance behind the desk conveyed an inappropriate, even slightly intimidating formality, he motioned Speidel to one of the easy chairs before the empty fireplace, then seated himself opposite. The man did indeed look ill. His handsome face with its unmistakable patina of power was flushed and sweaty and beads of sweat stood out like pustules on his brow.

Perhaps he was over-clad for a mild day. The heavy trousers, roll-necked jersey in thick wool, leather jacket and scarf were more suitable for winter than this mild autumn afternoon. Dalgliesh swung his chair round but waited for an introduction before seating himself.

Maycroft said, 'This is Commander Dalgliesh, a police officer from New Scotland Yard. He's here because we have a tragedy. That's why I found it necessary to disturb you. I'm sorry to have to tell you that Nathan Oliver is dead. We discovered his body at ten o'clock this morning hanging from the railing at the top of the lighthouse.'

Disconcertingly, Speidel's response was to rise from his chair and shake Dalgliesh's hand. Despite his flushed face, his hand was unexpectedly cold and clammy. Seating himself again and slowly unwinding his scarf, he appeared to be contemplating the most appropriate response. Finally he said, with only the faintest trace of a German accent, 'This is a tragedy for his family, his friends and for literature. He was highly regarded in Germany, especially the novels of his middle period. Are you saying that his death was suicide?'

Maycroft glanced at Dalgliesh and left him to reply. 'Apparently so, but there are some contra-indications. Obviously it's desirable to clear them up and, if possible, before the news breaks nationally.'

Maycroft broke in. 'There's no question of concealment. Such a death must attract international interest and sorrow. The Trust hopes that, if the full facts can be known quickly, then the life of this island won't be too long disrupted.' He paused and seemed for a moment to regret his words. 'Of course, the tragedy will disrupt far more than the peace of Combe, but it is in everyone's interest, including Mr Oliver's family, that the facts are known as quickly as possible and rumour and speculation prevented.'

Dalgliesh said, 'I'm asking everyone here whether they saw Mr Oliver at any time after dinner last night and particularly early this morning. It would be helpful to have some idea of the state of his mind in the hours preceding his death and, if possible, when that death occurred.'

Speidel's reply was interrupted by a fit of harsh coughing. Then he looked down at his clasped hands in his lap and seemed for some seconds lost in contemplation. The silence seemed inordinately prolonged. It could hardly, thought Dalgliesh, be a response to grief for a man he had not claimed personally to know. His first reaction to the news had been words of conventional condolence, spoken unemotionally. Nor did it seem feasible that Dalgliesh's single question required much thought. He wondered if the man were seriously ill. The cough had obviously been painful. He coughed again into his handkerchief, and this time it was more prolonged. Perhaps the silence had been no more than an attempt to suppress it.

Finally he looked up and said, 'Please excuse me, the cough is troublesome. I began to feel unwell on the boat coming here, but not enough to cancel my visit. It is nothing that rest and good air will not cure. I should regret being a nuisance by bringing influenza to the island.'

Dalgliesh said, 'If you'd rather talk to me later . . .'

'No, no. It is important to speak now. I think I can assist with the time of death. As for his state of mind, of that I have no knowledge. Nathan Oliver was not known to me personally and I would not presume to understand the man except insofar as I can understand the writer. As to the time of death, there I can be helpful. I made an appointment to meet him in the lighthouse at eight o'clock this morning. I had a restless night with some fever and was a little late in starting out. It was six minutes past eight when I arrived at the lighthouse. I was unable to gain entry. The door was locked.'

'How did you get to the lighthouse, Dr Speidel? Did you order the buggy?'

'No, I walked. After I had passed the cottage nearer to me – Atlantic I think it is called – I clambered down and took the under-cliff path until it became impassable some twenty metres from the lighthouse. I was hoping to be unobserved.'

'Did you see anyone?'

'No one, either on that walk or on my return.'

There was a silence. Without being prompted, Speidel went on, 'I looked at my watch when I arrived at the lighthouse door. Despite my being six minutes late I expected that Mr Oliver would have waited for me, either outside the door or in the lighthouse. However, as I have said, the door was locked.'

Maycroft looked at Dalgliesh. 'It would've been bolted from the inside. As I've explained to Mr Dalgliesh, there was a key but it's been missing for some years.'

Dalgliesh asked, 'Did you hear the bolts being shot home?'

'I heard nothing. I knocked on the door as loudly as I could, but there was no response.'

'Did you walk round the lighthouse?'

'It did not occur to me to do that. There would have been no point in it, surely. My first thought was that Mr Oliver had arrived to find the lighthouse locked and had gone to get the key. Other possibilities were that he had had no intention of meeting me, or that my message had not reached him.'

Dalgliesh asked, 'How was the assignation arranged?'

'Had I been well enough to be at dinner I would have spoken to Mr Oliver. I was informed he was expected to be present. Instead I wrote a note. When the young woman came with my soup and whisky, I gave it to her and asked her to deliver it. She was driving the buggy and as I was at the door I saw her put it in the leather pouch marked *Post* attached to the dashboard. She said she would deliver it to Mr Oliver personally at Peregrine Cottage.'

Dalgliesh didn't say that no note had been found on the body. He asked, 'Did you say in the note that the assignation should be kept secret?'

Speidel managed a wry smile interrupted by another but shorter bout of coughing. He said, 'I did not add "burn this or eat it after reading". There were no school-boy histrionics. I wrote simply that there was a private matter important to us both that I wished to discuss.'

Dalgliesh said, 'Can you remember your exact words?'

'Of course. I wrote it yesterday before the young woman – Millie, isn't it? – arrived with the provisions I had requested. That is less than twenty-four hours ago. I used a sheet of plain white paper and headed the message with the name and the telephone number of my cottage, and the time and date. I wrote that I was sorry to disturb his solitude but that there was a matter of great importance to me, and one of interest also to him, that I wished to discuss with him privately. Could he please meet me at the lighthouse at eight o'clock the next morning. If that were inconvenient, I would be grateful if he would telephone Shearwater Cottage so that we could arrange another time.'

'Was the time – eight o'clock – written in words or in numerals?'

'In words. When I found the lighthouse locked, it occurred to me that the young woman might have forgotten to deliver the note, but I was not particularly concerned. Mr Oliver and I were both on the island. He could hardly escape me.'

The phrase, spoken almost casually, was still unexpected and, thought Dalgliesh, perhaps significant. There was a silence. He asked, 'Was the envelope sealed?'

'No, it was not sealed but the flap was tucked in. I would not normally close an envelope that was being delivered by hand. Is that not also your custom? It could of course have been read, but it never occurred to me that anyone would do that. It was the matter I wished to discuss that was confidential, not the fact of our meeting.'

'And after that?' Dalgliesh spoke as gently as if he had been interrogating a vulnerable child.

'I then decided to see if Mr Oliver was at his cottage. I had enquired of the housekeeper where he was staying when I arrived. I began to walk there and then thought better of it. I was not feeling well and decided that, perhaps, it might be advisable to postpone a meeting which could have been painful until I felt stronger. There was no urgency. As I have said, he could hardly avoid an encounter. But I decided to walk back to my own cottage by way of the lighthouse and make one last check. This time the door was ajar. I pushed it open and went up the first two flights, calling out. There was no reply.'

'You didn't go to the top of the lighthouse?'

'There was little point, and I had become tired. My cough was beginning to trouble me. I realised I had already walked too far.'

Now, thought Dalgliesh, for the vital question. He thought carefully about the words he would use. It would be futile to ask Speidel if he had noticed anything different on the ground floor since this was the first time he had entered it. At the risk of it being a leading question, it had to be asked direct. 'Did you notice the coils of climbing ropes hung on the wall just inside the door?'

Speidel said, 'Yes, I noticed them. There was a wooden chest underneath. I assumed it held other climbing equipment.'

'Did you notice how many ropes were hanging there?'

Speidel said, 'There were five. There was no rope on the hook furthest from the door.'

'You're certain about that, Dr Speidel?'

'I am certain. I tend to notice such details. Also I have done some rock climbing in my youth and was interested to see that there were facilities for climbing on this island. After that I closed the door and made my way back to my cottage across the scrubland, which of course was the easier route, avoiding the clamber down to the lower plateau.'

'So you didn't walk round the lighthouse?'

Dr Speidel's cough and obvious temperature had not robbed him of his intelligence. He said with a hint of asperity, 'If I had, Commander, I think I would have noticed a hanging body, even in the morning mist. I did not circle the lighthouse, I did not look up and I did not see him.'

Dalgliesh asked quietly, 'What was it you wished to discuss with Mr Oliver in private? I'm sorry if the question seems intrusive but I'm sure you will realise that I need to know.'

Again there was a silence, then Speidel said, 'A purely family matter. It could have no possible bearing on his death, I can assure you of that, Commander.'

With any other suspect – and Speidel was a suspect, as was everyone else on the island – Dalgliesh would have pointed out the imperatives of a murder investigation, but Speidel would need no reminding. He waited as the man wiped his forehead and seemed to be summoning strength. Dalgliesh glanced at Maycroft, then said, 'If you feel unable to continue we can speak later. You look as if you have a fever. As you know, there is a doctor on the island. Perhaps you should see Guy Staveley.'

He did not add that there was no urgency about a further interview. There *was* urgency, and the more so if Dr Speidel was likely to be confined in the sickroom. On the other hand, apart from his reluctance to worry a sick man, there could be danger in continuing if Speidel were unfit.

There was a touch of impatience in Speidel's voice. 'I'm all right. This is no more than a cough and a slight temperature. I would rather we got on with it. One question first, if you please. Do I take it that this inquiry has now become a murder investigation?'

Dalgliesh said, 'That was always a possibility. Until I get the pathologist's report I'm treating it as a suspicious death.'

'Then I had better answer your question. Could I have some water, please?'

Maycroft was moving over to a carafe on the side table when there was a knock on the door followed immediately by Mrs Plunkett, wheeling a small trolley with three cups, a teapot, milk jug and sugar bowl.

Maycroft said, 'Thank you. I think we would also like some fresh water. As cold as possible, please.'

While they waited Maycroft poured the tea. Speidel shook his head, as did Dalgliesh. The wait was not long before Mrs Plunkett returned with a jug and a glass. She said, 'It's very cold. Shall I pour it for you?'

Speidel had got up and she handed him the glass. They nodded briefly, then she placed the jug on the trolley. She said, 'You don't look too good, Doctor. I think bed would be the best place for you.'

Speidel seated himself again, drank thirstily and said, 'That is better. My story will not take long.' He waited until Mrs Plunkett had left then put down his glass. 'As I have said, it is a family matter, and one I had hoped to keep private. My father died on this island under circumstances into which the family have never fully inquired. The reason is that my parents' marriage had begun to fail even before I was born. Mother was from a distinguished military Prussian family and her marriage to my father was regarded as a misalliance. During the war he was stationed with the occupying force on Guernsey in the Channel Islands. That itself was no matter of pride to my mother's family who would have preferred a more distinguished regiment, a more important role. The rumour was that, with two fellow officers, he made an excursion here after the island was known to have been evacuated. I had no knowledge why this happened or whether it was with his commanding officer's authority. I suspected not. None of the three returned. After an investigation which revealed the escapade, it was assumed that they had been lost at sea. The family were thankful that the marriage had ended, at least not in ignominy or divorce, which they strongly opposed, but by a convenient death on active service, if not with the glory traditional in the family.

'I was told very little about my father during my childhood and gained the impression, as children do, that questions would be unwelcome. I married again after the death of my first wife and I now have a twelve-year-old son. He asks questions about his grandfather and I think very much resents the fact that the details of his life are unrecorded and unspoken of, as if they are somehow disgraceful. I told him that I would try to discover what had happened. I got little help from official sources. Records show that the three young men had gone absent without leave, taking a thirty-foot sailing boat with an engine. They never returned and were posted as missing believed drowned. I was more fortunate when I managed to track down a fellow officer in whom my father had confided under the seal of secrecy. He said his comrades intended to raise the German flag on a small island off the Cornish coast, probably to show that it could be done. Combe was the only possible island and my first choice for investigation. I came to Cornwall last year, but not to Combe Island. I met a retired fisherman, well over eighty, who was able to give me some information, but it was not easy. People were suspicious, as if we were still at war. With your national obsession about our recent history, particularly the Hitler era, I sometimes feel that we could be.' There was a trace of bitterness in his voice.

Maycroft said, 'You wouldn't get much out of the natives if you asked about Combe Island. This place has a long and unhappy history. There's a folk memory about its past, not helped by the fact that it's privately owned and no tourists are allowed.'

Speidel said, 'I got enough to make a visit here worthwhile. I knew that Nathan Oliver had been born here and that he visited quarterly. He revealed that in a newspaper article in April 2003. Much was made then in the press about his Cornish boyhood.'

Maycroft said, 'But he was only a child when the war broke out. How could he help?'

'He was four in 1940. He might remember. And if not, his father could have told him something of what went on here during the evacuation. My informant told me that Oliver was one of the last to leave.'

Dalgliesh said, 'Why choose to meet in the light-house? Surely there's privacy almost anywhere on the island. Why not your own cottage?'

And now he sensed a change, subtle but unmistakable, in Dr Speidel's response. The question had been unwelcome.

'I have always had an interest in lighthouses. It's something of a hobby of mine. I thought Mr Oliver would be helpful in showing this one to me.'

Dalgliesh thought, *Why not Maycroft or Jago*? He said, 'So you know its history, that it's a copy of an earlier and more famous lighthouse by the same builder, John Wilkes, who built Eddystone?'

'Yes, I know that.'

Speidel's voice had suddenly become weaker and the beads of moisture on his brow coalesced, the sweat running so freely that the flushed face looked as if it were melting.

Dalgliesh said, 'You've been very helpful, particularly in placing the time of death. Can we please get the timings absolutely clear. You first arrived at the lighthouse when?'

'As I have said, a little late. I looked at my watch. It was six minutes past eight.'

'And the door was bolted?'

'Presumably so. I couldn't get in or make anyone hear.'

'And you later returned when?'

'About twenty minutes later. It would have taken me about that time but I did not look at my watch.'

'So at about eight-thirty the door was open?'

'Ajar, yes.'

'And during all this time did you see anyone either at the lighthouse or when you were walking?'

'I saw no one.' He put his hand to his head and closed his eyes.

Dalgliesh said, 'Thank you, we'll stop now.'

Maycroft said, 'I think it would be wise to let Dr Staveley have a look at you. The sickroom here might be a better place for you at present than Shearwater Cottage.'

As if to refute what he heard, Speidel got to his feet. He tottered and Dalgliesh, hurrying over, managed to support him and help him back into the chair.

Speidel said, 'I'm all right. It's just a cough and a slight fever. I have a tendency to chest infections. I would prefer to return now to my cottage. If I could have the use of the buggy perhaps Commander Dalgliesh could drive me there.'

The request was unexpected; Dalgliesh could see that it had surprised Maycroft. It surprised him too, but he said, 'I'll be glad to.' He looked at Maycroft. 'Is the buggy outside?'

'By the back door. Are you fit to walk, Dr Speidel?'

'Perfectly fit, thank you.'

He seemed indeed to have regained his strength and he and Dalgliesh took the lift down together. In the confined space Speidel's breath came to him sour and warm. The buggy was parked on the rear forecourt and they drove together in silence, at first on the rough road and then bumping gently over the scrubland. There were questions Dalgliesh wanted to ask, but instinct told him the moment was not propitious.

At Shearwater Cottage he helped Speidel into the sitting room and supported him while he sank into a chair. He said, 'Are you quite sure you're all right?'

'Perfectly, thank you. Thank you for your help, Commander. There are two questions I want to ask you. The first is this. Did Nathan Oliver leave a note?'

'None that we've found. And your second question?'

'Do you believe that his death was murder?'

'Yes,' said Dalgliesh, 'I believe that.'

'Thank you. That was all I wanted to know.'

He rose. Dalgliesh moved to help him up the stairs but Speidel grasped the rail refusing the offer. 'I can manage, thank you. This is nothing a night's sleep cannot cure.'

Dalgliesh waited until Speidel was safely in his bedroom, then shut the door of the cottage and drove back to Combe House.

Back in the office he accepted a cup of tea and took it over to a fireside chair. He said, 'Speidel knows nothing about lighthouses. I invented the name John Wilkes. He didn't build your lighthouse or Eddystone.'

Maycroft seated himself in the chair opposite, cup in hand. He stirred his tea thoughtfully, then said without looking at Dalgliesh. 'I realise you only allowed me to be present because Dr Speidel is a guest and I'm responsible on behalf of the Trust for his well-being. I also realise that if this is murder, I'm as much a suspect as anyone else. I don't expect you to tell me anything, but there is something I'd like to tell you. I thought he was speaking the truth.'

'If he wasn't, the fact that I questioned him when he could argue that he was not physically fit to be interrogated could be a problem.'

'But he insisted on going on. We both asked him if that was what he wanted. He was not coerced. How could it be a problem?'

Dalgliesh said, 'For the prosecution. The defence

could argue that he was too ill to be questioned or to know what he was saying.'

'But he said nothing to throw any light on Oliver's death. It was all about the past, the old unhappy far-off things, and battles long ago.'

Dalgliesh didn't reply. It was a pity that Maycroft had been present during the interview. It would have been difficult to banish him from his own office or to request an obviously sick man to move to Seal Cottage. But if Speidel was speaking the truth, they now had vital confirmation about the time of death which he would prefer to have kept to himself and the team. Oliver had died between seven forty-five that morning and quarter past eight. By the time Speidel had first arrived at the lighthouse Oliver's killer was somewhere behind that bolted door and the body could already have been slowly swinging against the seaward wall.

9

Dalgliesh asked Maycroft for the continued use of his office to interview Millie. It might, he thought, be less intimidating for her than asking her to come to Seal Cottage and it would certainly be quicker. Maycroft agreed, adding, 'I'd like to be present unless you object. Perhaps Mrs Burbridge could join us. She's the one with the most influence over Millie. It might be helpful to have a woman present, I mean other than a police officer.'

Dalgliesh said, 'Millie's eighteen, isn't she? She's not a juvenile, but if you feel she needs protection . . .'

Maycroft said hastily, 'It's not that. It's just that I feel responsible for taking her on here. It was probably a mistake at the time but she's here now and she's got herself involved in this mess, and of course she's had the shock of actually seeing Oliver's body. I can't help thinking of her as a child.'

Dalgliesh could hardly forbid Maycroft access to his office. He doubted whether Mrs Burbridge would be welcomed by Millie, but the housekeeper seemed a sensible woman and, he hoped, would know when to keep silent. Dalgliesh summoned Kate and Benton-Smith by radio. With Maycroft and Mrs Burbridge present, Millie would be faced with five people; more than was desirable, but he had no intention of excluding Kate and Benton. Millie's evidence promised to be vital.

He said, 'Then please phone Mrs Burbridge and ask her if she would be good enough to find Millie and bring her here.'

Maycroft looked disconcerted at having so easily got his own way. He lifted the receiver and made the call. Then he surveyed the office with a frown and began arranging the upright chairs in a half-circle to join the two button-backed ones in front of the fireplace. The intention was obviously to create an atmosphere of unthreatening informality but, since there was no fire in the grate, the arrangement looked incongruous.

It was ten minutes before Mrs Burbridge and Millie arrived. Dalgliesh wondered if they had had an altercation on the way. Mrs Burbridge's lips were compressed and there were two red blotches on her cheeks. Millie's mood was even easier to read. It passed from surprise at the appearance of the office to truculence and finally to a sly wariness with the versatility of an actor auditioning for a soap opera. Dalgliesh gave her one of the easy chairs and placed Kate immediately opposite her on the other, with himself on Kate's right. Mrs Burbridge seated herself next to Millie, and Benton and Maycroft took the other two chairs.

Dalgliesh began without preamble. 'Millie, Dr Speidel tells us that yesterday afternoon he gave you an envelope to take to Mr Oliver. Is that right?'

'He might've done.'

Mrs Burbridge broke in. 'Millie, don't be ridiculous. And don't waste time. Either he did or he didn't.'

'Yeah, OK. He gave me a note.' Then she burst out, 'Why do I have to have Mr Maycroft and Mrs Burbridge here? I'm not a juvenile now!'

So Millie wasn't unfamiliar with the juvenile criminal justice system. Dalgliesh wasn't surprised but had no wish to pursue past and probably minor delinquencies. He said, 'Millie, we're not accusing you of anything. There's no suggestion that you've done anything wrong. But we need to know exactly what happened on the day before Mr Oliver died. Do you remember what time Dr Speidel gave you the note?'

'Like you said, in the afternoon.' She paused, then added, 'Before tea.'

Mrs Burbridge said, 'I think I can help here. Dr Speidel phoned to say that he wouldn't take dinner but would be grateful for some soup to heat up and some whisky. He said he wasn't feeling well. Millie was helping in the kitchen when I went to speak to Mrs Plunkett about the soup. She nearly always has soup available. Yesterday it was chicken, home-made of course, and very nourishing. Millie offered to take it to Shearwater Cottage in the buggy. She likes driving the buggy. She left at about three o'clock.'

Dalgliesh turned to Millie. 'So you delivered the soup and whisky, and then what happened?'

'Dr Speidel give me a note, didn't he? He said would I take it to Mr Oliver and I said, OK I would.'

'And what did you do then?'

'Put it in the postbag, didn't I?'

Mrs Burbridge explained. 'It's a letter pouch marked *Post* attached to the buggy's dashboard. Dan Padgett delivers any post to the cottages and collects letters for Jago to take to the mainland.'

And now it was Kate who took over the questioning. 'And after that, Millie? Did you go straight to Peregrine

Cottage? And don't say you may have done. Did you?'

'No I didn't. Dr Speidel never told me it was urgent. He never said to take it to Mr Oliver straight away. He just told me to deliver it.' She added grumpily, 'Anyway, I forgot.'

'How did you forget?'

'I just forgot. Anyway, I had to go back to my room. I wanted to go to the loo and I thought I'd change my top and my jeans. Nothing wrong in that I suppose?'

'Of course not, Millie. Where was the buggy when you were in your room?'

'I left it outside, didn't I?'

'Was the note from Dr Speidel still in the pouch?'

'Must've been, mustn't it? Otherwise I couldn't have delivered it.'

'And when was that?'

Millie didn't answer. Kate went on, 'What happened after you changed your clothes? Where did you go next?'

'All right, I went down to see Jago. I knew he was taking the boat out this morning to test the engine and I wanted to go with him. So I went down to Harbour Cottage. He gave me a mug of tea and some cake.'

'Still in the buggy?'

'Yeah, that's right. I went down in the buggy and I left it outside on the quay when I was talking to Jago in his cottage.'

Mrs Burbridge said, 'Didn't it occur to you, Millie, that the envelope might have contained something urgent and that Dr Speidel must have expected you to deliver it on your way back to the house?'

'Well he never said anything about it being urgent,

and it wasn't urgent, was it? The meeting wasn't till eight o'clock this morning.' There was a silence. Millie said, 'Oh shit!'

Kate said, 'So you did read it.'

'I may've done. OK, I read it. I mean, it was open. Why did he leave it open if he didn't want people to read it? You can't take people to court for reading notes.'

Dalgliesh said, 'No, Millie, but Mr Oliver's death may end in a trial and if it does you could be one of the witnesses. You know how important it will be to tell the truth in court. You'll be on oath. If you lie to us now, you may be in very great difficulties later. So you read the note?'

'Yeah, like I said, I read it.'

'Did you tell Mr Tamlyn that you'd read it? Did you tell him about the meeting at the lighthouse between Mr Oliver and Dr Speidel?'

There was a long pause, then Millie said, 'Yeah, I told him.'

'And what did he say?'

'He didn't say nothing. I mean, he didn't say nothing about the meeting. He told me I'd better go and take the note to Mr Oliver straight away.'

'And then?'

'So I got into the buggy, didn't I, and went up to Peregrine Cottage. I didn't see no one, so I put the note in the post box in the porch. If he didn't get it I daresay it's still there. I could hear Miss Oliver talking to someone in the sitting room but I didn't want to give it to her. She's a snooty stuck-up bitch and the note wasn't for her anyway. Dr Speidel said to give it to Mr Oliver and I would've done if I'd seen him. So I put it in the box in the porch. And then I got into the buggy and came back to the house to help Mrs Plunkett with the dinner.'

Dalgliesh said, 'Thank you Millie. You've been very helpful. Are you quite sure there's nothing else we should know? Anything else you did or said, or was said to you?'

Suddenly Millie was shouting. 'I wish I'd never taken that f— – that bloody note. I wish I'd torn it up!' She turned on Mrs Burbridge. 'And you aren't sorry he's dead. None of you! You all wanted him off the island, anyone could see that. But I liked him. He was all right to me. We used to meet up and go for walks. We was . . .' Her voice dropped to a sullen whisper. 'We were friends.'

In the silence that followed Dalgliesh said gently, 'When did the friendship start, Millie?'

'When he was here last time – July, wasn't it? It was soon after Jago brought me here anyway. That's when we met.'

In the pause that followed Dalgliesh saw Millie's calculating eyes shifting from face to face. She had thrown her verbal bombshell and was gratified, and perhaps a little scared, at the extent of the fall-out. She could sense their reaction in the momentary silence and in Mrs Burbridge's worried frown.

Mrs Burbridge said with a note of severity, 'So that's what you were doing on those mornings when I wanted you to check the linen. You told me you were out walking. I thought you were at Harbour Cottage with Jago.'

'Yeah, well sometimes I was, wasn't I? Other times I was seeing Mr Oliver. I said I was out walking and I was out walking. I was walking with him. Nothing wrong in that.'

'But Millie, I told you when you arrived here that you mustn't bother the guests. They come here to be private, Mr Oliver particularly.'

'Who said I was bothering him? He didn't have to meet me. It was his idea. He liked seeing me. He said so.'

Dalgliesh didn't interrupt Mrs Burbridge. So far she was doing his job for him rather well. There were again two unbecoming splodges of red on her cheeks but her voice was resolute. 'Millie, did he want – well – want to make love to you?'

The response was dramatic. Millie shouted her outrage. 'That's disgusting! Course he didn't. He's old. He's older than Mr Maycroft. It's gross. It wasn't like that. He never touched me. You saying he was a perv or something? You saying he was a paedo?'

Surprisingly Benton broke in. His youthful voice held a note of amused common sense. 'He couldn't be a paedophile, Millie, you're not a child. But some older men do fall in love with young girls. Remember that rich old American in the papers last week? He married four of them, they all divorced him and became very rich and now he's married to a fifth.'

'Yeah, I read. I think it's gross. Mr Oliver wasn't like that.'

Dalgliesh said, 'Millie, we're sure he wasn't but we're interested in anything you can tell us about him. When people die mysteriously, it's helpful to know what they were feeling, whether they were worried or upset, whether they were afraid of anyone. It seems you may have known Mr Oliver better than anyone else on Combe, except his daughter and Mr Tremlett.'

'So why not ask them about him?'

'We have. Now we're asking you.'

'Even if it's private?'

'Even if it's private. You liked Mr Oliver. He was your friend. I'm sure you want to help us discover why he died. So go back to your first meeting and tell us how the friendship started.'

Mrs Burbridge met Dalgliesh's glance and bit back her comments. All their attention now was on Millie. Dalgliesh could see that she was beginning to enjoy the unaccustomed notoriety. He only hoped she would resist the temptation to make the most of it.

She leaned forward, her eyes bright, and looked from face to face. 'I was sunbathing on the top of the cliff further on from the chapel. There's a hollow in the grass and some bushes, so it's private. Anyway, no one goes there. If they did, it wouldn't worry me. Like I say, I was sunbathing. Nothing wrong in that.'

Mrs Burbridge said, 'In your swimsuit?'

'What swimsuit? In nothing. I was lying on a towel. So there I was, lying in the sun. It was my afternoon off so it must have been a Thursday. I wanted to go to Pentworthy and Jago wouldn't take the launch. Anyway, I was just lying there when suddenly I heard this noise. It was a sort of cry – well more like a groan. I thought it was some kind of animal. I opened my eyes and there he was standing over me. I shrieked and pulled at the towel and wrapped it round me. He looked terrible. I thought he was going to faint he was so white. I never saw a grown man look that scared. He said he was sorry and asked if I was all right. Well I was all right. I wasn't really scared, not like he was. So I said he'd better sit down and he'd feel better, and he did. It was really weird. Then he said he was sorry he'd frightened me and that he thought I was someone else, a girl he'd once known and she'd been lying on a beach in the sun like me. And I said, "Did you fancy her?" and he said something really weird about it being in a different country and the girl was dead, only he didn't say girl.'

Dalgliesh realised that Millie was the perfect witness, one of those rare people with almost total recall. He said, '*But that was in another country: and besides, the wench is dead.*'

'Yeah, that's right. Funny you know that. Weird, wasn't it? I thought he'd made it up.'

'No, Millie, the man who made it up has been dead for over four hundred years.'

Millie paused, frowningly contemplating the weirdness of it. Dalgliesh prompted her gently. 'Then?'

'I said how did he know she was dead and he said if she wasn't dead he wouldn't be dreaming about her. He said the living never came to him in dreams, only the dead. I asked what she was called and he said he didn't remember and perhaps she never told him. He said the name didn't matter. He called her Donna, but that was in a book.'

'And after that?'

'Well we got talking. Mostly about me – how I came to be on the island. He had a notebook and sometimes, when I said things, he'd write them down.' She glared angrily at Mrs Burbridge. 'I'd put my clothes on by then.'

Mrs Burbridge looked as if she would have liked to

say that it was a pity they had ever been taken off, but she stayed silent.

Millie went on. 'So after that we got up and I went back to the house. But he said perhaps we could meet and talk again. And we did. He used to ring me early in the morning and say when we'd meet. I liked him. He told me some of the things he'd done when he was travelling. He'd been all over the world. He said he was meeting people and learning how to be a writer. Sometimes he didn't say much so we just walked.'

Dalgliesh asked, 'When was the last time you saw him, Millie?'

'Thursday. It was Thursday afternoon.'

'And how did he seem then?'

'Like he always was.'

'What did he talk about?'

'He asked me if I was happy. And I said I was all right except when I was unhappy, like when they took Gran away to the home and when Slipper my cat died – she had white paws – and when Jago won't take me out in the launch and Mrs Burbridge is going on at me about the linen. Things like that. He said for him it was the other way round. He was unhappy most of the time. He asked about Gran and when she started getting Alzheimer's, so I told him. He said that everybody who was old dreaded Alzheimer's. It took away the greatest power human beings have. He said it's a power as great as any tyrant's or any god's. We can be our own executioner.'

The silence was total. Dalgliesh said, 'You've been very helpful. Is there anything else you can tell us, Millie, about Mr Oliver?'

'No there isn't.' Millie's voice was suddenly belliger-ent. 'I wouldn't have told you that if you hadn't made me. I liked him. He was my friend. I'm the only one who cares that he's dead. I'm not staying here any longer.'

Her eyes brimmed with tears. She got up and Mrs Burbridge rose too, looking back at Dalgliesh accusingly as she edged Millie gently from the room.

Maycroft spoke for the first time. He said, 'This changes things, surely. It must have been suicide. There has to be a way of explaining those marks on the neck. Either he made them himself or someone else did after death, someone who wanted this to look like murder.'

Dalgliesh said nothing.

'But his unhappiness, the burning of the proofs . . .'

Dalgliesh said, 'I shall have confirmation tomorrow but I don't think you can take comfort from Millie's evidence.'

Maycroft began putting back the chairs. He said, 'Oliver was using her, of course. He wouldn't have spent time with Millie for the pleasure of her conversation.'

But that, thought Dalgliesh, was precisely what he had wanted: her conversation. If he were planning to create a fictional Millie for his next novel he would know her character better than he knew himself. He would know what she felt and what she thought. What he needed to know was how she would put those thoughts into words.

They were inside the lift before Kate spoke. 'So from the time Millie arrived back at her room until she put the note in the box at Peregrine Cottage, anyone could have had access to it.'

Benton said, 'But ma'am, how would they know it

was there? Would anyone open the mail pouch just out of curiosity? They couldn't hope to find anything valuable.'

Dalgliesh said, 'It has to be a possibility. We now know that Jago was certainly aware of the eight o'clock assignation and that Miranda and Tremlett may well have known too, as could anyone who saw the buggy while it was unattended. I can understand why Jago kept quiet – he was shielding Millie. But if the other two found the note and read it, why have they said nothing? It's possible that Oliver didn't check the post box until he was leaving the cottage this morning. He might have set out on an early walk because he wanted to avoid seeing his daughter. After reading Speidel's note he saw a reason to change his plans and decided to go to the lighthouse early.'

They waited until they were back in Seal Cottage before phoning Peregrine Cottage. Miranda Oliver answered. She said that she hadn't heard the buggy arrive yesterday evening, but as it was never driven up to the door because the path was too narrow, she wouldn't have expected to hear it. Neither she nor Mr Tremlett had checked the post box and neither would have opened any letter addressed to her father.

Kate and Benton went down to interview Jago in the cottage. They found him stripping the dead leaves from the geraniums in the six terracotta pots outside Harbour Cottage. The plants had grown high and straggly, the stems woody, but most of the foliage was still green and there were a few small flowers on the etiolated shoots to give the illusion of summer.

Faced with Millie's admission, he said, 'She did tell

me about the note and I said she'd better take it to Peregrine Cottage straight away. I never saw it or read it. I wasn't that interested.' His tone suggested that he wasn't interested now.

Kate said, 'Maybe not at the time, but after Mr Oliver's death surely you realised that this was vital information. Withholding it was close to an offence, obstructing the police in their investigation. You're not stupid. You must know how it looks.'

'I thought Dr Speidel would tell you himself when he turned up. And he did, didn't he? What the visitors do, who they meet and where, is none of my business.'

Benton said, 'You said nothing earlier this afternoon when you were all being questioned as a group. You could have spoken then, or come to see us in private.'

'You asked me if I'd seen Mr Oliver either the previous night or this morning. I hadn't seen him and neither had Millie.'

Kate said, 'You know perfectly well it was information you should have passed on at once. So why didn't you?'

'I didn't want anyone getting at Millie. She hasn't done anything wrong. Life on Combe isn't altogether easy for the kid. And it would have been pointing the finger at Dr Speidel, wouldn't it?'

'And you didn't want to do that?'

Jago said, 'Not in front of the whole lot of them, not without him being there. I don't care who killed Nathan Oliver, if he was killed. And I reckon you wouldn't be here if he topped himself. It's your job to find out who strung him up. You're paid to do it. I'll not lie, but I'm not in the business of helping you either, not by pointing the finger at other people and landing them in the shit.'

Benton said, 'You hated Mr Oliver that much?'

'You could say so. Nathan Oliver may have been born on this island but both his mum and dad were incomers. None of them were Cornish, not Nathan nor his parents, whatever he may have chosen to say. Maybe he didn't realise that we have long memories in these parts. But I'm not a murderer.'

He seemed about to say something more but, instead, bent again to his flowerpots. Kate glanced at Benton. There was nothing else to be heard from Jago at present. She thanked him, not without irony, and they left him to his pruning.

10

Maycroft had offered Dalgliesh the use of bicycles while the team was on the island. There were four of them kept ready for the use of visitors but Kate, although she knew that they were working against time, said that she and Benton-Smith would walk to Atlantic Cottage. There was something almost risible in the thought of the two of them pedalling away down the lane to interview a murder suspect. Dalgliesh, she knew, was unlikely to be worried about losing face and would probably have been amused by the unorthodox method of transport. Kate, while regretting that she hadn't his self-confidence, preferred to walk. It was after all, only about half a mile. The exercise would do them good.

For the first hundred yards the path was close to the cliff edge and from time to time they would pause briefly to gaze down on the cracked and layered granite, the jagged teeth of the rocks and the sluicing tide. Then the path swerved to the right and they were walking down a grassy lane bounded on the right by rising ground and protected by a low hedge of brambles and hawthorn. They walked without speaking. If Kate had been accompanied by Piers Tarrant they would, she knew, have been discussing the case – their first reactions to the people, the curious knot on the noose – but now she preferred not to speculate aloud until Dalgliesh held his usual get-together which could be last thing tonight.

And by midday tomorrow Dalgliesh would have received Dr Glenister's report and with luck they would know with certainty that they were investigating a murder. She knew that already Dalgliesh had no doubt, and neither had she. She supposed that Benton felt the same, but some inhibition, not altogether related to her seniority, held her back from asking his opinion. She accepted that they would have to work closely together. With only three of them on the island and no immediate prospect of the usual paraphernalia of a murder investigation – photographers, fingerprint experts, scene of crime officers – it would be ludicrous to be punctilious about status or the division of tasks. Her problem was that their relationship, however apparently formal, had to be harmonious; the difficulty was that there was no relationship. He had worked with her as a member of the team only on one previous occasion. Then he had been efficient, not afraid to speak his mind, bringing an obvious intelligence to bear on the case. But she simply hadn't begun to know him or to understand him. He seemed to be surrounded by some self-erected palisade with *Keep Out* notices hung on the wire.

And now Atlantic Cottage was in view. She had observed from the air that it was the largest of the stone cottages and the one closest to the cliff edge. Now she saw that there were two cottages, the larger to the right with a tiled porch, two bay windows either side and two above under a stone roof. The smaller was flat-fronted and low roofed with four smaller windows. In front of both ran a flowerbed some three feet wide bounded by a stone wall. Small red flowers and trailing plants drooped from the crevices and a tall fuchsia bush was flourishing to the right of the porch, its petals littering the pathway like specks of blood.

Roughtwood opened the door to Kate's knock. He was of medium height but broad shouldered with a square, somewhat intimidating face, full lipped, the blue-grey eyes deep set, their paleness in contrast to the fading but still remarkable yellow hair and eyelashes, a colour Kate had seldom seen on a man. He was wearing a formal black suit, a sober striped tie and a high collar, which gave him a look of an undertaker's assistant. Was this, she wondered, his usual garb in the early evening, or had he changed into what he considered a more appropriate suit for an island in mourning? But was it in mourning?

They moved into a small square hall. The door opening to the left gave a glimpse of the kitchen and the room on the right was obviously the dining room. Beyond the gleaming top of an oblong table, Kate saw a whole wall patterned with the spines of leather books.

Roughtwood opened the door at the end of the hall, and said, 'The police have arrived, madam. They're six minutes early.'

Miss Holcombe's voice, strong, authoritative and upper class, came to them clearly. 'Then show them in, Roughtwood. We would not wish to be accused of non-cooperation.'

Roughtwood stood aside and announced with formality, 'Inspector Miskin and Sergeant Benton-Smith, madam.'

The room was larger than a first sight of the cottage would suggest. In front of them were four windows and a glass-topped door to the terrace. The fireplace was on the left with a small table set before it and two chairs. A Scrabble game was obviously in progress. Kate, resisting the temptation to display any unseemly curiosity by letting her eyes wander, had an impression of rich deep colours, polished wood, rugs on the stone floor, oil paintings and one wall which, like that in the dining room, held leather-bound volumes from ceiling to floor. A wood fire was burning in the grate, filling the room with its pungent autumnal smell.

Miss Holcombe did not rise from her seat in front of the Scrabble board. She looked younger than Kate had expected: the strong-boned face was almost unlined and the immense grey eyes were still unclouded by age under the curved brows. The steel-grey hair with strands of silver was brushed back and intricately wound into a heavy bun above the nape of the neck. She was wearing a flared skirt in black, grey and white tartan and a turtleneck white jumper, with a heavy amber necklace, the stones as large as marbles. Her long-lobed ears were studded with intricately wrought amber earrings. She made a slight motion towards Roughtwood, who seated himself opposite her, then looked at him fixedly for a moment as if anxious to reassure herself that he wouldn't move. She turned to Kate.

'As you will see, Inspector, we're just finishing our Saturday game of Scrabble. It's my turn to play and I have seven letters left. My opponent has – how many have you to play, Roughtwood?'

'Four, madam.'

'And the bag is empty, so we shan't be delaying you for long. Please sit down. I've a feeling that there's a seven-letter word on my rack but I can't get it. Too

246

many vowels. An O, two Is, and an E. M is the only consonant except for two Ss. It's unusual to have them left at the end of a game, but I've only just picked one up.'

There was a pause while Miss Holcombe studied her tiles and began rearranging them on the rack. The joints of her slender fingers were distorted with arthritis and on the back of her hands the veins stuck out like purple cords.

Benton-Smith said quietly, 'MEIOSIS, madam. The third line from the top on the right.'

She turned towards him. Taking her interrogatory lift of the eyebrows as an invitation, he moved over to study the board. 'If you place it so that the second S is on the double over LACK, you get another twenty-two points for SLACK. Then the M is on the double letter square for six, and the seven-letter word is also on a double.'

Miss Holcombe made the calculations with surprising speed. 'Ninety-six in total, plus my two hundred and fifty-three.' She turned to Roughtwood. 'I think that puts the result beyond cavil. You take the score for your four away, Roughtwood, and what does that leave you with?'

'Two hundred and thirty-nine, madam, but I register an objection. We have never said that help is permissible.'

'We've never said it isn't. We play by our own rules. Whatever is not forbidden is allowable. That is in accordance with the sound principle of English law that everything is permissible unless legally prohibited, compared with the practice in mainland Europe where nothing is permitted unless legally sanctioned.'

'In my view, madam, the sergeant has no status in the game. No one asked him to interfere.'

Miss Holcombe obviously recognised that the conversation was veering towards an uncomfortable confrontation. Beginning to gather up the tiles and replace them in the bag, she said, 'All right, we'll take the last score. That still leaves me the winner.'

'I'd prefer, madam, for the game to be declared null and void and not recorded in the monthly total.'

'All right, since you're being difficult. You don't seem to consider whether I might not very well have found the word myself if the sergeant hadn't interfered. I was close to it.'

Roughtwood's silence was eloquent. He reiterated, 'The sergeant had no right to interfere. We should make a new rule. No help.'

Benton-Smith spoke to Miss Holcombe. 'I'm sorry, but you know how it is with Scrabble. If you spot a seven-letter word it's impossible to keep quiet about it.'

Miss Holcombe had decided to make a common cause with her butler. 'When it's not your game, a more disciplined mind would attempt to. Well, it's certainly brought the contest to a swift conclusion, which is no doubt what you intended. We usually have a glass of wine after Scrabble. I suppose it's no use offering you one. Isn't there some rule about not compromising yourselves by drinking with suspects? If Mr Dalgliesh is over-punctilious about this he is likely to have an uncomfortable stay on Combe Island: we pride ourselves on our cellar. But I don't suppose either of you will be suborned by a cup of coffee.'

Kate accepted the offer. Now that there was a hope of

getting on with the interview she was in no hurry. Miss Holcombe could hardly suggest that they had outstayed their welcome when they were drinking her coffee, and at their own pace.

Roughtwood went out showing no apparent resentment. When the door had closed behind him, Miss Holcombe said, 'As Roughtwood and I are likely to provide each other with alibis, we'd better defer any questions until he returns. That way we'll all save time. While you're waiting for the coffee you might like to go outside on the terrace. The view is spectacular.'

She continued to gather up the Scrabble tiles, making no movement to show them out. They got up and moved together to the terrace door. The top half was glass-panelled but the door was heavy, the glass obviously thick, and it took Benton some strength to pull it open. The door itself had clasps fitted for shutters and Kate saw that there were wooden shutters fitted to each of the four windows. The edge of the cliff was less than five feet away, bounded by a waist-high stone wall. The roar of the ocean pounded in their ears. Instinctively Kate recoiled a step before moving to gaze over the wall. Far below them the spray rose in a white mist as the waves broke in thunderous explosions against the cliff face.

Benton-Smith moved beside her. He shouted against the roar, 'It's wonderful. Nothing between us and America. No wonder Oliver wanted this place.'

Kate heard the awe in his voice but didn't reply. Her thoughts went to that distant London river beneath her windows, the strong brown pulsating Thames, pricked and dazzled with the lights of the city. The tide seemed at times to move as sluggishly as a muddy pond but, gazing out at the water, she would give a shiver of apprehension and would picture its latent power suddenly surging into life to sweep away the city, and bear on its turbulent surface the debris of her flat. It wasn't a fanciful imagining. If the ice-cap melted not much of riverside London would remain. But to think of her flat was to remember Piers, the bed warmed by his body, his hand reaching for her in the morning. What, she wondered, was he doing now? How much of that night together had he intended? Was she as much in his mind as he was in hers? Did he regret what had happened or was it, for him, the last in a line of easy conquests? Resolutely she put that uncomfortable thought out of mind. Here, where the cottage itself seemed to have grown out of the granite cliff, was a different power, infinitely stronger, potentially far more dangerous than the Thames. How odd that the river and this ocean shared the same element, the same salt taste on the tongue, the same tangy smell. A small splash of spume alighted on her cheek and dried before she could raise a hand to wipe it away.

Minutes passed, then, as if simultaneously realising that they were here for a purpose, they re-entered the cottage. The turbulence of wind and ocean was instantly muted. They re-entered peaceful domesticity to the smell of freshly brewed coffee. The Scrabble table had been folded away. Roughtwood moved to station himself beside the door leading to the terrace as if to prevent any further explorations and Miss Holcombe was seated in the same chair, but now turned towards them.

She said, 'I think you'll find that sofa comfortable. I

don't think this will take more than a few minutes. I assume you'd like to know what we were doing at the time Nathan Oliver was presumed to have died. What time is that?'

Kate said, 'We can't be sure, but we're told he was seen leaving Peregrine Cottage at about seven-twenty this morning. He had an appointment to give blood in the surgery at nine o'clock but didn't turn up. I expect you've been told all that. We need to know where everyone was between the time of his last sighting yesterday night and ten o'clock this morning when the body was found.'

'That's easily answered as far as we're concerned. I dined here so I didn't see him last night. Roughtwood brought me early-morning tea at six-thirty and served breakfast an hour later. I didn't see him again until he came into the cottage to collect the breakfast things and my silver for cleaning. He does that next door in his own cottage as I detest the smell of the polish.'

The ornaments on the small round table to the right of the fireplace were certainly gleaming, but that didn't necessarily mean that they had recently been cleaned. Kate suspected that they were usually pristine; probably only a rub with a soft cloth would have brought up the shine.

'And that was when, Miss Holcombe?'

'I can't be precise about the time. As I couldn't foresee being part of a murder investigation I wasn't keeping a record. I think it was some time between eight-fifteen and eight-thirty. I was on the terrace at the time with the sitting-room door open. I heard him but didn't see him.'

Kate turned to Roughtwood. 'Can you be more precise, Mr Roughtwood?'

'I'd put it closer to eight-fifteen, Inspector, but, like Madam, I was not keeping note of the time.'

Miss Holcombe went on, 'I didn't see him again until about nine o'clock when I looked in on my way up to the surgery to have my anti-flu jab.'

Kate said, 'And neither of you went out this morning until you, Miss Holcombe, left for the surgery?'

'I certainly didn't, except on to the terrace. You'd better answer for yourself, Roughtwood.'

'I remained in my cottage, madam, in the kitchen cleaning the silver. My telephone rang a little time after Madam had left. It was Mr Boyde telling me that Mr Oliver was missing and asking me to join the search.'

Benton-Smith said, 'But you didn't in fact go?'

'No. I wanted to finish the job I was doing, and I reckoned there was no great hurry. Enough people would be looking for Mr Oliver. Visitors to the island like taking long walks and they don't expect people to go chasing after them. I couldn't see why there was such a panic. Anyway I work for Madam, not for Mr Boyde or the big house.'

Kate said, 'But later you did go to the lighthouse?'

'I did when Madam returned and told me Mr Oliver had been found dead. Madam asked me to go to the lighthouse to see if there was anything I could do. I got there in time to help with the stretcher.'

Kate said, 'Would either of you have known if the other had left their cottage this morning?'

'Not necessarily. We lead largely independent lives. You say Oliver was seen leaving Peregrine Cottage at about seven-twenty. It could have taken him about fifteen minutes to get to the lighthouse. If Roughtwood had been in the lighthouse at eight o'clock murdering him – which I take it is what you're suggesting – he would hardly have been back here by eight-thirty at the latest estimate, when he came in to collect the silver. As you've probably discovered, we're half a mile from the big house and only a little less from the lighthouse.'

Benton-Smith said, 'Surely Mr Roughtwood has a bike?'

'So now the suggestion is that he cycled to and from the lighthouse? Are you also suggesting that he carried me perched on the bicycle basket?'

Kate said, 'No suggestions are being made, Miss Holcombe. We're asking, as we have to, where you were between those hours, and at present this is a suspicious death. No one has mentioned murder.'

'I'm sure you're being very careful not to, but no one on this island is a fool. A commander, a detective inspector and a detective sergeant of the Metropolitan Police are unlikely to be arriving by helicopter to investigate either a suicide or an accidental death. All right, you needn't provide explanations; I know I'm not going to get them. If any more information is required, I prefer to give it to Commander Dalgliesh. There's only a limited number of suspects on the island so he can hardly claim he's overworked.'

Kate said, 'He asked me to explain that he would be seeing you later.'

'Please give him my compliments. If he feels I can help him further, perhaps he would care to telephone and fix a time convenient to us both. Monday morning will not be possible for me as I have a dentist appointment in Newquay. In the meantime, Roughtwood will no doubt be happy to show you his bicycle. And now, Inspector, I would be grateful to have my sitting room to myself.'

The machine was in a small stone annexe to Roughtwood's cottage. It must previously have been a washhouse and the copper, encased in its stone surround, was still in place. One wall was hung with tools and garden implements – more, Kate thought, than a small strip of cultivated soil in front of both cottages would warrant. Everything was very clean and meticulously arranged. The bike, an old and heavy Raleigh with a large wicker basket fitted on the front, was leaning against another wall. The front tyre was flat.

Benton-Smith knelt to examine the tyre. He said, 'There's a sharp tear, ma'am, about half an inch long.'

Kate crouched beside him. It was hard to believe that this single precise slash could have been made by a stone, a nail or anything other than a knife, but she didn't comment. She said to Roughtwood, 'When did this happen?'

'Two days ago, Inspector, when I was cycling to the house to collect some cleaning materials.'

'Did you see what caused it?'

'There was nothing stuck in the tyre. I reckoned I had struck a sharp piece of flint.'

Kate wondered for a moment whether it would be advisable to take the bike away now as a possible exhibit, but decided against it. It was hardly likely to disappear and at this stage of the investigation Roughtwood – or indeed anyone else – was not a prime suspect. She could imagine the reaction on the island if Benton-Smith wheeled the machine away. *They've taken poor Roughtwood's old bike now. God knows what they'll be up to next.* Briefly she thanked Roughtwood for his cooperation, and they left.

They walked for some minutes in silence, then Kate said, 'I didn't know you were an expert at Scrabble. You should have put it on your CV. Are there any other talents you haven't told us about?'

His voice was expressionless. 'I can't immediately think of any, ma'am. I used to play Scrabble as a boy with my grandmother. The English one.'

'Oh well, it's as well you couldn't resist showing off. At least it put an end to the game. She didn't take us seriously and neither did he, and they didn't mind showing it. It was play-acting. Still, we got the information we were asked to get, where they were from seven-thirty this morning. Mr Dalgliesh will get anything else that he needs. They won't play-act with him. What did you think of her?'

'As a suspect?'

'Why else were we there? It wasn't a social visit.'

So they were to discuss the case as colleagues. There was a pause, then Benton said, 'I think if she decided to murder someone she would be pretty ruthless about it. And I don't think she would be much troubled afterwards by guilt. But where's the motive?'

'According to Miranda Oliver, her father was dead set on getting her out of her cottage.'

'There's no reason to suppose he'd succeed. She's a Holcombe, the Trustees would be on her side. And isn't she eighty? She could probably manage the lighthouse stairs all right and she seemed pretty tough for her age, but I can't see her having the strength to heave Oliver's body over that railing or carrying it up from the floor beneath. I'm assuming that's where he died. Whoever lured him to the lighthouse wouldn't plan to kill him on the lantern level. There would always be a risk of being seen.'

Kate said, 'Unlikely on the seaward side. And it would be easier than lugging a dead weight up those last stairs and on to the platform. She could have suggested that they talk in the open air. And he wasn't a big man. I think she could have pushed him over the railings. But it would have meant lifting him. It wouldn't have been easy.'

Benton-Smith said, 'Do you think Roughtwood would kill for her, or help her?'

'How do I know, Sergeant? There's little point in speculating about motive or collusion before we've checked alibis, if any, and know if anyone is definitely in the clear. What we need are facts. Assuming he used a bike, what was the risk of being seen?'

'Not much, ma'am, not while he was in the lane anyway. It's sunken enough to keep him hidden if he kept his head well down. And that rip in the tyre could have been made with a knife. Look at this path: rough grass, sandy earth, smooth pebbles except for one or two. Or he could have cycled along the lower cliff. That way he'd probably be guaranteed to get a puncture. A sharp flint would make a gash very like a knife. But I'd guess the slit was deliberate however it was made.'

'That needn't point to guilt necessarily. He might

have done it with the idea of putting himself in the clear, hoping we'd leave them both alone.'

Benton-Smith said, 'Then why not do it more convincingly?'

'No time. The idea might only have occurred to him a short time before our arrival. There were tools and a pair of shears in the shed. Anything sharp would have done.'

'But ma'am, if the murder and the alibi were pre-meditated, wouldn't he have disabled the bike earlier?'

'There is that, Sergeant.'

They walked the rest of the way back to the house without speaking but Kate felt that the silence was companionable, that one small section of the palisade had been cautiously opened up.

II

It was interesting, Dalgliesh thought, how different, at least externally, were the cottages he had seen. It was as if the architect, given a simple plan, had been anxious to avoid any impression of institutional conformity. Seal Cottage promised to be one of the pleasantest. It had been built only thirty feet from the edge of the cliff and although simple in design, had an attractive symmetry in the arrangement of windows and in the proportion between the stone walls and the roof. It had only two main rooms, a large bedroom and modern shower upstairs, and a sitting room and kitchen on the ground floor. There were windows on two aspects, so that the cottage was full of light. Everything had been done for his comfort, he assumed by Mrs Burbridge. The wide stone fireplace with a wooden trug of logs and smoke-free nuggets in the hearth was already laid with kindling. In the recess to the left he saw the iron door of a bread oven and, opening it, found that it contained additional kindling. The furniture was minimal but well designed. Two easy chairs flanked the fireplace and a simple table with two upright chairs stood in the middle of the room. There was a functional modern desk beneath one of the windows overlooking the sea. The kitchen was little more than a galley but well equipped with a small electric cooker and a microwave. There was a generous supply of oranges and an electric juicer and the refrigerator held milk, half a dozen eggs, four rashers of bacon – not cellophane-packed but in a plastic container – crème brûlée and a loaf of obviously home-baked bread. On a shelf in the cupboard were small packets of breakfast cereals and a screw jar of muesli. Another cupboard held crockery and cutlery for three people and glasses, including three wine glasses. There were also six bottles of wine, three of a New Zealand Sauvignon Blanc and three of Chateau Batailley '94, a quality too good for casual tippling. He wondered who would pay for them or whether the ungenerous might regard wine either as an inducement or a deliberate temptation to insobriety. How long, he wondered were the bottles supposed to last? Did they represent Mrs Burbridge's nicely judged calculation of the quantity three police officers might be expected to drink in a couple of days, would they be replaced when empty?

And there were other indications of Mrs Burbridge's concern for his comfort that amused him since they seemed to indicate some thought to his personality and taste. There were fitted bookshelves in the recesses each side of the fireplace, presumably kept empty so that visitors could shelve the volumes they had brought. Mrs Burbridge had made a choice for him from the library: *Middlemarch*, that safe stand-by for desert-island choice, and four volumes of poetry, Browning, Housman, Eliot and Larkin. Although there was no television, the sitting room had been fitted with modern stereo equipment and on another shelf Mrs Burbridge had made a selection of CDs, or had she, perhaps, taken them from the shelf at random? There was enough variety to satisfy, at least temporarily, an uncapricious taste: Bach's Mass in

B Minor and his Cello Suites with Paul Tortelier playing, songs by Finzi, James Bowman singing Handel and Vivaldi, Beethoven's Ninth Symphony and Mozart's *Marriage of Figaro*. His pleasure in jazz was apparently not to be accommodated.

Dalgliesh had not suggested that the team should eat dinner together to discuss the case. Going through the ritual of serving up the food, coping with an unfamiliar kitchen and finally washing up would be a time-wasting postponement to serious discussion. He judged too that Kate and Benton would prefer to eat in their own apartments, either separately or together as Kate decided – although 'apartments' seemed too spacious a word for the staff accommodation in the stable block. He wondered how they were getting on when they were alone together. Kate would have no difficulty in coping with a male subordinate who was obviously highly intelligent and physically attractive, but he had worked with her long enough to sense that Benton's Oxford education combined with unconcealed ambition made her uneasy. Benton would be scrupulously correct, but Kate would detect that a readiness to judge his superiors and a careful calculation of chance might lie behind those dark and watchful eyes.

Mrs Burbridge had obviously envisaged that they would eat separately. No additional china or cutlery had been provided, only the two extra wine glasses and mugs suggested that she accepted they might at least drink together. A handwritten notice lying on the cupboard shelf read: *Please telephone for anything extra you need.* Dalgliesh resolved to keep requests to a minimum. If he and his colleagues wanted to take a meal together, anything needed could be carried up from the stable block.

Dinner had been left in a metal container placed on a shelf in the porch under a wooden box labelled *Letters*. A note on the larger can read: *Please reheat osso bucco and baked potatoes for thirty minutes in oven at 160 degrees. Crème brûlée in refrigerator.*

Following instructions and laying the table, he reflected wryly on the oddity of his situation. In the years since, as a sergeant, he had first entered the CID he had looked back on a series of meals on duty, hurried or more leisurely, indoors or out, alone or with colleagues, pleasurable or almost inedible. Most had been long forgotten, but some from his days as a young detective constable could still twitch the cord of memory: the brutal murder of a child forever incongruously associated with cheese sandwiches made with ferocious energy by the mother, the unwanted squares piling higher and higher until, with a scream, she took the knife in both hands and drove it into the board, then collapsed howling into a disintegrating mountain of cheese and bread. Sheltering with his detective sergeant under a railway bridge in sleeting rain while they waited for the forensic pathologist, Nobby Clark had taken two Cornish pasties from his murder case. 'Get this inside you, lad. Made by my wife. They'll put some life into you.' He could still recall the comfort of the still warm pasty enclosed in his frozen hands; none since had tasted so good. But the meals on Combe Island were likely to be among the strangest. Were he and his colleagues to be fed in the next few days by the charity of a killer? No doubt the police would eventually pay – some official at the Yard would have the job of negotiating how much – and presumably up at the house anxious consultations between Maycroft and Mrs Burbridge had already taken place about the domestic upheaval of their arrival. They were apparently to be treated as ordinary visitors. Did that mean that they could eat dinner in the main house if they gave notice? At least he could spare Maycroft that embarrassment. But he was grateful that tonight Mrs Burbridge or Mrs Plunkett had decided that after a sandwich lunch they were entitled to a hot dinner.

But when the osso bucco was ready, his appetite, so far from being stimulated by the evocative smell of onions, tomatoes and garlic which permeated the kitchen, had mysteriously waned. After a few mouthfuls of the veal, so tender that it fell from the bone, he realised that he was becoming too tired to eat. Clearing the table, he told himself that this wasn't surprising: he had been overworking for weeks before the case broke and even in his few solitary moments he found Combe Island strangely disturbing. Was its peace evading him because he had lost his own? His mind was a vortex of hope, longing and despair. He thought back to the women whom he had liked, respected and enjoyed as companions and lovers, affairs with no commitment beyond discretion and no expectations except the giving and receiving of pleasure. The women he had liked – fastidious and intelligent – had not been looking for permanency. They had prestigious jobs, incomes larger than his own, their own houses. An hour with the children of their friends had reinforced their view that motherhood was a life sentence for which, thankfully, they were psychologically unsuited. They admitted to

selfishness without compunction and if they later regret-
ted it, they didn't inflict their pain on him. The affairs
usually ended because of the demands of his job, and if
there had been hurt on either side, pride dictated that it
should be concealed. But now, in love and it seemed to
him for the first time since the death in childbirth of his
young wife, he wanted unattainable assurances, not
least that love could last. How odd that sex should be so
simple and love such a complication.

He disciplined his mind to throw off images of the
past and the personal preoccupations of the present.
There was a job to be done and Kate and Benton would
be with him in five minutes. Returning to the kitchen
he brewed strong coffee, uncorked a bottle of the red
and opened the cottage door to the mild, sweet-smelling
night made luminous under the glittering canopy of
stars.

Kate and Benton-Smith had dinner in their own rooms, collecting their metal containers from the kitchen of the main house when Mrs Plunkett phoned. Kate reflected that if she'd been with Piers Tarrant they would have eaten together, rivalries temporarily forgotten, discussed and argued over the case. But with Benton-Smith it was different, and not because he was junior in rank; that never worried her when she liked a colleague. But AD, as always, would ask for the junior's views first and if Benton were set to show off his intelligence she had no wish to provide a dress rehearsal. They had been given two adjacent apartments in the stable block. She had briefly inspected both before making her choice and knew that his was a mirror image of her own. The rooms were sparsely furnished; like her, Benton had a sitting room some twelve feet by eight, a galley kitchen adequate for the heating of meals and the making of hot drinks, and upstairs a single bedroom with an adjacent shower room.

She guessed that both apartments were usually occupied by overnight and weekly staff. Although Mrs Burbridge, presumably helped by Millie, had prepared the room for this unexpected and hardly welcome guest – the bed freshly made up, the kitchen immaculate and with food and milk in the refrigerator – there was still evidence of the previous occupier. A print of Raphael's

Madonna and Child hung to the right of the bed and to the left a family photograph framed in oak. There they were, immobilised in sepia, carefully posed against the railings of a seaside pier, the grandparents – the man in a wheelchair – smiling broadly, the parents in their summer holiday clothes and three young children, moon-faced with identical fringes, staring stolidly into the camera lens. Presumably one of them was the usual occupant of the room. Her pink chenille dressing-gown had hung in the single cupboard, her slippers placed ready beneath it, her paperback copies of Catherine Cookson on the shelf. In taking down the dressing-gown and hanging up her own, Kate felt like an intruder.

She showered, changed her shirt and vigorously brushed and replaited her hair, then knocked at Benton's door to signal she was ready. He came out immediately and she saw that he had changed into a Nehru-style suit in a green so dark that it looked black. It gave him a look, hieratic, distinguished and alien, but he wore it unself-consciously as if he had changed into something familiar and comfortable merely to please himself. Perhaps he had. She was tempted to say, *Why change? We're not in London and this isn't a social occasion,* but knew that the comment would be revealingly petty. Besides, hadn't she too taken trouble?

They walked across the headland path to Seal Cottage without speaking. Behind them the lit windows of the great house and the distant pinpoints of light from the cottages only intensified the silence. With the setting of the sun the illusion of summer was erased. This was the air of late October, still unseasonably mild but with the first chill of autumn, the air faintly scented, as if the dying light had drawn up from the headland the concentrated sweetness of the day. The darkness would have been absolute but for the stars. Never had they seemed to Kate more multitudinous, more glittering or so close. They made of the furry darkness a mysterious luminosity so that, looking down, she could see the narrow path as a faintly gleaming ribbon in which individual blades of grass glittered like small spears, silvered with light.

The open door of Seal Cottage was at the side facing north and light spilled out from it over a stone patio. Kate saw Dalgliesh had recently lit the fire. The kindling was still crackling and the few pellets of smokeless fuel were as yet untouched. On the table was an open bottle of wine and three glasses and there was the smell of coffee. Kate and Benton decided on the wine and as AD poured it, Benton drew up the desk chair to the table.

This was the part of the investigation Kate most enjoyed and looked forward to, the quiet moments, usually at the end of every day, when progress was assessed and future plans laid out. This hour of talk and silence with the cottage door still open to the night, the dancing gules of light from the fire on the stone floor and the smell of the wine and coffee was as close as she would ever get to that comfortable, unthreatening domesticity she had never known as a child, and which she imagined must be at the heart of family life.

AD had spread on the table his map of the island. He said, 'We can, of course, take it that we are investigating murder. I'm reluctant to use that word to anyone on Combe until we get confirmation from Dr Glenister. With luck that should be by midday tomorrow. Let's state the facts as we know them so far, but first we'd better find a name for our presumed murderer. Any suggestions?'

Kate knew the chief's invariable practice. He had an abhorrence for 'chummy' or other soubriquets currently being used. She should have been prepared, but she found herself without an idea.

Benton said, 'We could call him Smeaton, sir, after the designer of the lighthouse at Plymouth Hoe. The one here is a copy.'

'That seems tough on a brilliant engineer.'

Benton said, 'Or there's Calcraft, the nineteenth-century hangman.'

'Then Calcraft it is. Right Benton, what do we know?'

Benton pushed his wine glass a little to one side. His eyes met Dalgliesh's. 'The victim, Nathan Oliver, came to Combe Island regularly each quarter, always for two weeks. On this occasion he arrived on Monday with his daughter Miranda and secretary Dennis Tremlett. This was usual. Some of the facts we know depend on information which may or may not be accurate, but his daughter says that he left Peregrine Cottage at about seven-twenty this morning and without his usual cooked breakfast. The body was discovered at ten a.m. by Rupert Maycroft, who was quickly joined by Daniel Padgett, Guy Staveley, Jago Tamlyn, Millie Tranter and Emily Holcombe. The apparent cause of death is strangulation, either in the room under the lantern of the lighthouse or on the circular platform above. Calcraft then fetched the climbing rope, knotted it round Oliver's neck, tied the rope to the railings and heaved the body over. Calcraft must therefore have sufficient strength, if not to carry Oliver's dead weight up one short flight of stairs, at least to push him over the railings.

'Dr Speidel's evidence, you said, sir, struck you as being less than complete. He wrote a note requesting a meeting in the lighthouse at eight o'clock this morning. This note was given to Millie Tranter who says she delivered it by putting it in the letterbox at Peregrine Cottage. She admits that she told Jago about the assignation. Miranda Oliver and Tremlett could have read the note, as could anyone who had access to the buggy. Did Oliver ever receive it? If not, why did he go to the lighthouse? If the meeting was to be at eight o'clock, why was he on his way as early as seven-twenty? Was the time on the note altered, and if so by whom? Eight couldn't easily be changed to seven-thirty except by crossing out and writing the revised time above. But surely that would be ludicrous. It would only give Calcraft thirty minutes to meet Oliver, get to the top of the lighthouse, do his killing and get away, and that's assuming Oliver arrived on time. Of course, Calcraft could have destroyed the original note and substituted another. But it would still be ridiculous to alter the time of assignation by only thirty minutes.

'Then there's the evidence of the lighthouse door. Speidel says it was locked when he arrived. That means someone was inside – Oliver, his murderer, or both. When he returned about twenty-five minutes later the door was open and he noticed that the rope was missing. He heard nothing, but then would he, some hundred feet down from a killing chamber? But Speidel could have been lying. We've only his word that the lighthouse was locked and that he never met Oliver. Oliver could have been waiting for him as planned and Speidel could have killed him. And we've only Speidel's evidence confirming the time of death. But why choose the lighthouse for the assignation? We know he lied to Mr Dalgliesh about lighthouses being his hobby.'

Kate said, 'You were supposed to be giving us the facts. You've strayed into supposition. There are other things we definitely know. Oliver was always a difficult visitor, but this time he seems to have been more unreasonable than usual. There was the scene at the harbour when he learned that his blood sample had been lost, his subsequent complaint to Maycroft, his reiterated demand to have Emily Holcombe turned out of Atlantic Cottage and the scene during dinner on Friday. And then there's Miranda's engagement to Tremlett. The behaviour of all three of them was pretty odd, wasn't it? Oliver returns home late after dinner when Miranda is in bed, and leaves before she gets up. It looks as if he was determined not to see her. And why did he order the launch for that afternoon? Who was that for? Do we believe Miranda's story that he was reconciled to the marriage? Does it seem a likely reaction in a man so selfishly devoted to his work that nothing was allowed to interfere with his convenience? Or does the motive lie much further back in the past?'

Dalgliesh said, 'If it does, then why did Calcraft wait for this weekend? Oliver came regularly to the island. Most of our suspects had ample time and opportunity to take revenge before now. And revenge for what? It's an unpropitious weekend to choose with only two other guests, part-time staff on the mainland, all possible suspects reduced to a total of thirteen. Fifteen, if we add Mrs Plunkett and Mrs Burbridge.'

Benton said, 'But it could work both ways, sir. Fewer people to become suspects but a better chance of moving about unseen.'

Kate said, 'But it does look as if Calcraft may have had to act this weekend. So what's changed since Oliver's previous visit? Two people have arrived who weren't here when Oliver last visited three months ago, Dr Speidel and Dr Yelland. There's the incident of the lost blood which led to Oliver threatening to live here full-time. And then there's the engagement between Tremlett and Miranda. It's difficult to see her as a murderess but she might have planned it with Tremlett. It's obvious she's the stronger of the two.'

Dalgliesh said, 'Let's look at the map. Calcraft could have gone to the lighthouse either because he'd made a separate appointment with Oliver – which seems an unlikely coincidence although we've known more unbelievable ones – or because he read the note and changed the time, or because, fortuitously, he saw Oliver on his way and followed him. The obvious route is by the lower cliff. The people who could most conveniently use that are those in the house or in the cottages on the south-west side of the island: the Staveleys, Dan Padgett, Roughtwood and Miss Holcombe. There's also an under-cliff on the east side extending beyond Chapel Cottage, but it's broken by the harbour. We have to remember that the note was delivered the previous night. Calcraft could have gone to the lighthouse on Friday night under cover of darkness and been there waiting early on Saturday morning.

There's also the possibility that he didn't worry about being seen since at that time his intention wasn't murderous. The killing could have been unpremeditated, manslaughter rather than murder. At present we're working largely in the dark. We need Dr Glenister's report on the autopsy and we have to interview Dr Speidel again. Let's hope he'll be well enough.'

An hour later it was time for speculation to stop. Tomorrow would be a busy day. Dalgliesh got to his feet and Kate and Benton followed. He said, 'I'll see you after breakfast to set out the programme. No, leave the glasses, Benton. I'll see to them. Sleep well.'

13

The wine glasses had been washed and put away and the fire was dying. He would listen to some Mozart before bed. He chose Act Two of *The Marriage of Figaro* and Kiri Te Kanawa's voice, controlled, strong and heart-stoppingly lovely, filled the cottage. It was a CD he and Emma had listened to in his flat above the Thames. The stone walls of the cottage were too enclosing to contain such beauty and he again opened the door to the headland and let the Countess's yearning for her husband swell out under the stars. There was a seat against the cottage wall and he sat listening. He waited until the act was finished before returning to switch off the CD player, then went out for a final look at the night sky.

A woman was walking across the headland from Adrian Boyde's cottage. She saw him and paused. He had known immediately from the confident stride and the transient glint of starlight on the fair hair that it was Jo Staveley and now, after a moment's hesitation, she came towards him.

He said, smiling, 'So you do occasionally walk out at night.'

'Only when I have a purpose. I thought Adrian ought not to be left alone. This has been a pretty ghastly day for all of us, but for him it's been hellish, so I went to share the osso bucco. Unfortunately he's teetotal. I could do with a glass of wine if it's not too much trouble. Guy will be in bed and I don't like drinking alone.'

'No trouble at all.'

She followed him into the cottage. Dalgliesh opened the second bottle of red and brought it to the table with two glasses. She was wearing a red jacket, the collar upturned to frame her face, and now she slipped it off and hung it on the back of her chair. They sat opposite each other, neither speaking. Dalgliesh poured the wine. At first she gulped it as thirstily as if it were water, then replaced her glass on the table, stretched her legs and sighed her satisfaction. The fire was dying with one frail wisp of smoke curling from the last blackened log. Relishing the quietude, Dalgliesh wondered if visitors occasionally found the silence and solitude too much for them and returned promptly to the seductive glamour of their testosterone-fuelled lives. He put the question.

She laughed. 'It's been known, or so I'm told, but it's rare. They know what they're in for before they come. It's the silence they're paying for, and believe me it doesn't come cheap. Don't you ever feel that if you have to answer another question, hear another phone ring or see another face you'll go screaming mad? And then there's the security. What with terrorists and the threat of kidnapping it must be bliss to know you can sleep with doors and windows open and no security guard or police watching your every move.'

Dalgliesh said, 'Won't Oliver's death put an end to that illusion?'

'I doubt it. Combe will recover. The island has forgotten worse horrors than putting an end to Nathan Oliver.'

He said, 'The general dislike of Oliver seems to have been caused by something more serious than his uncooperative behaviour as a guest. Did something happen between him and Adrian Boyde?'

'Why ask me?'

'Because Mr Boyde is your friend. You probably understand him better than do the other residents. That means you're the one most likely to know the truth.'

'And the one most likely to tell you?'

'Perhaps.'

'Have you asked him? Have you spoken to Adrian?' She was drinking the wine more slowly now and with obvious appreciation.

'No, not yet.'

'Then don't. Look, no one – not even you – really believes that Adrian had anything to do with Oliver's death. He's no more capable of murder than you and I are, probably a bloody sight less. So why cause him pain? Why stir up the past when it's got nothing to do with Oliver's death, nothing to do with why you're here or your job?'

'I'm afraid stirring up the past is part of my job.'

'You're an experienced detective. We know about you. So don't tell me that you see Adrian as a serious suspect. Aren't you just grubbing out the dirt for the fun of it – the power, if you like? I mean, it must give you some satisfaction, this asking questions which we have to answer. If we don't, we look guilty; if we do, someone's privacy is violated. And for what? Don't tell me it's all in the cause of justice or truth. *What is truth? said jesting Pilate; and would not stay for an answer.* He knew a thing or two, did Pilate.'

The quotation surprised him, but why should he assume that she hadn't read Bacon? He was surprised too that she could be so passionate and yet, despite the vehemence of her words, he felt no personal antagonism. He was merely a substitute. The real enemy had passed for ever beyond the reach of her hatred.

He said gently, 'I haven't time for a quasi-philosophical discussion about justice and truth. I can respect confidences but only up to a point. Murder destroys privacy – the privacy of the suspects, of the victim's family, of everyone who comes into contact with the death. I'm getting rather tired of telling people this, but it has to be accepted. Most of all, murder destroys the privacy of the victim. You feel you have a right to protect your friend; Nathan Oliver is beyond anyone's protection.'

'If I tell you, will you accept what I say is the truth and leave Adrian alone?'

'I can't promise that. I can say that if I know the facts it will be easier for me to question him without causing unnecessary distress. We're not in the business of causing pain.'

'Aren't you? OK, OK, I accept that it's not deliberate. God knows what you'd be like if it were.'

He resisted the temptation to retort, and it wasn't difficult. He recalled what he had been told in that high room at New Scotland Yard. Her husband had caused the death of an eight-year-old boy. It had been clinical error, but local police may have been marginally involved. It would have needed only one over-zealous officer to account for her bitter resentment.

She pushed her empty glass towards him and he

poured the wine. He said, 'Is Adrian Boyde an alcoholic?'

'How did you know?'

'I didn't. Tell me what happened.'

'He was administering at some important service, Holy Communion. Anyway, he dropped the chalice then fell down dead drunk. Or he fell down dead drunk, dropping the chalice. He'd taken over at the church where Mrs Burbridge's husband was previously the vicar and one of the churchwardens knew that Mrs Burbridge had moved here and had probably been told something about Combe. He wrote to our previous secretary and suggested he should give Adrian a job. Adrian's perfectly competent. He already knew how to use a computer and he's numerate. At first it went well. He'd been here, perfectly sober, for more than a year and we'd hoped he could stay sober. And that's when it happened. Nathan Oliver came for his quarterly visit. He asked Adrian to supper one night and gave him wine. That was fatal of course. All that Adrian had achieved here was undone in one night.'

'Did Oliver know that Boyde was an alcoholic?'

'Of course he knew. That's why he invited him. It was all planned. He was writing a book with a character who was a drunkard and he wanted to witness exactly what happened when you feed wine to an alcoholic.'

Dalgliesh asked, 'But why here? He could witness descent into a drunken stupor in a dozen London clubs I could name. It's not exactly uncommon.'

She said, 'Or on the streets any Saturday night. Oh but that wouldn't be the same, would it? He needed someone who was trying to fight his demons. He wanted time and privacy to control the situation and watch every minute of it. And I suppose it was important to have his victim available at short notice when he'd reached that stage in his novel.'

Dalgliesh saw that she was shaking. She emanated a moral outrage so powerful that he felt it as a physical force bouncing against the unyielding stone walls and recoiling to fill the room with concentrated hate. He waited for a moment, then said, 'What happened next?'

'Someone – either Oliver with that copy-editor of his or the daughter – must have carried Adrian to his cottage. It took a couple of days for him to sober up. We didn't even know what had happened, only that he had been drinking. It was thought that somehow he'd got hold of some wine in the house, but we couldn't see how. Two days later he went with Jago to get the weekly supplies, and disappeared. I went to my London flat later that month, and one night I found him on the doorstep, paralytic. I took him in and looked after him for a few weeks. Then I brought him back here. End of story. While we were together he told me what had happened.'

'It can't have been easy for you.'

'Or for him. I'm not everyone's idea of an ideal flatmate, especially when I'm on the wagon. I realised that London would be impossible, so I took an isolated cottage near Bodmin Moor. The season hadn't started so it wasn't difficult to find something cheap. We stayed there for six weeks.'

'Did anyone here know what was happening?'

'I phoned Guy and Rupert to say I was all right and that Adrian was with me. I didn't tell them where I was but I did tell Jago. He used to come over and relieve me when he had a weekend off. I couldn't have done it without him. One or other of us didn't let Adrian out of our sight. God, it was boring at the time but funnily enough, looking back on it, I seem to have been happy, happier perhaps than I'd been for years. We walked, talked, cooked, played cards, spent hours in front of the TV looking at the videos of old ITV serials, some of them – like *The Jewel in the Crown* – used to go on for weeks. And, of course, we had books. He was easy to be with. He's kind, intelligent, sensitive and amusing. He doesn't whine. When he felt the time was right we came back here. No one asked any questions. That's how they live here. They don't ask questions.'

'Was it the alcoholism that made him leave the Church? Did he confide in you about that?'

'Yes, as far as we could communicate at that level. I don't understand religion. Partly it was the alcoholism, but mainly because he'd lost faith in some of the dogma. I can't understand why that worried him. I thought that that was the thing about the dear old C of E; you can believe more or less what you like. Anyway, he came to believe that God couldn't be both good and all-powerful; life's a struggle between the two forces – good and evil, God and the devil. That's some kind of heresy – a long word beginning with M.'

Dalgliesh said, 'Manichaeanism.'

'That sounds like it. It seems sensible to me. At least it explains the suffering of the innocent, which otherwise takes some sophistry to make sense of. If I had a religion, that's what I'd choose. I suppose I became a manichaean – if that's the word – without knowing it the first time

I watched a child dying of cancer. But apparently you're not supposed to believe it if you're a Christian and I suppose particularly not if you're a priest. Adrian is a good man. I may not be good myself but I can recognise it. Oliver was evil; Adrian is good.'

Dalgliesh said, 'If it were as simple as that, my job would be easy. Thank you for telling me.'

'And you won't question Adrian about his alcoholism? That was our bargain.'

'There was no bargain, but I won't mention it to him at present. It may never be necessary.'

'I'll tell him you know, that seems only fair. He may choose to tell you himself. Thank you for the wine. I'll say goodnight. You know where to find me.'

Dalgliesh watched her until she was out of sight, moving confidently under the stars, then rinsed the two wine glasses and locked the cottage door. So there were three people who could have had a motive: Adrian Boyde, Jo Staveley and probably Jago who had given up his free weekends to relieving Jo, a generosity which suggested that he shared her disgust at Oliver's cruelty. But would Jo Staveley have been so confiding if she'd known, or even suspected, that one of the other two was guilty? Probably, if she'd realised that, sooner or later, he would inevitably have discovered the truth. None of the three seemed a likely killer, but that could be said of everyone on Combe Island. He knew that it was dangerous to concentrate on motive to the neglect of *modus operandi* and means, but it seemed to him that here motive was at the heart of the case. Old Nobby Clark had told him that the letter L could cover all motives for murder: Lust, Lucre, Loathing and Love. It was sound enough as far as it went. But motives were extraordinarily varied and some of the most atrocious murderers had killed for no reason explicable to a rational mind. Some words came into his mind, he thought by George Orwell. *Murder, the unique crime, should arise only from strong emotions.* And of course it always did.

BOOK THREE

Voices from the Past

I

On Sunday morning Dalgliesh woke just before dawn. From boyhood his waking had been sudden with no discernible moments between oblivion and consciousness, his mind instantly alert to the sights and sounds of the new day, his body impatient to throw off the enclosing sheets. But this morning he lay in a somnolent peace, prolonging each gentle step of a slow awakening. The two large windows, panes wide open, became palely visible and the bedroom slowly revealed itself in shape and colour. Last night the sea had been a soothing accompaniment to his last subliminal waking moments, but now it seemed quieter, more a gentle throbbing of the air than a consciously heard sound.

He showered, dressed and went downstairs. He made himself fresh orange juice, decided against a cooked breakfast and walked round the sitting room with his bowl of muesli, assessing this unusual stone-built operations room with a more leisurely appreciation than had been possible the previous day, then moved out of the cottage into the soft sea-smelling air of the morning. The day was calm, patches of pale blue were appearing over low streaks of cloud, the pale grey tinged with pink. The sea was a pointillist picture pricked in silver light to the horizon. He stood very still looking towards the east – towards Emma. Even when he was on a case, how quickly she took possession of his mind. Last night it had been almost a torment to picture her in his arms; now she was a less troubling presence, moving up quietly beside him, her dark hair tumbled from sleep. Suddenly he longed to hear her voice but he knew that, whatever the day brought, she wouldn't phone. Was this silence when he was on a job her way of affirming his right to be undisturbed, a recognition of the separateness of their working lives? The wife or lover ringing at the most inconvenient or embarrassing time was one of the stock situations of comedy. He could phone now – her working day had surely not yet begun – but he knew that he wouldn't. There seemed to be some unspoken pact which separated in her mind the lover who was a detective and the lover who was a poet. The former disappeared periodically into alien and uncharted territory, which she had no wish – or perhaps felt she had no right – to question or explore. Or was it that she knew as well as did he that his job fuelled the poetry, that the best of his verse had its roots in the pain, horror and pathetic detritus of the tragic and broken lives which made up his working life? Was it this knowledge that kept her silent and distanced when he was working? For him as a poet, beauty in nature, in human faces, had never been enough. He had always needed Yeats's foul rag-and-bone shop of the heart. He wondered, too, whether Emma sensed his uncomfortable half-shameful acknowledgement that he who so guarded his privacy had chosen a job that permitted – indeed required – him to violate the privacy of others, the dead as well as the living.

But now, glancing northwards towards the square stone bulk of the chapel, he saw a woman walking with the remembered purposeful tread of one of his father's parishioners who, conscious of duty done and spiritual hunger satisfied, was making for the secular satisfaction of a hot breakfast. It took only a second to recognise her as Mrs Burbridge, but it was a Mrs Burbridge transformed. She was wearing a blue and fawn tweed coat of a rigidly old-fashioned cut, a blue felt trilby with a jaunty feather, and her gloved hand was holding what must surely be a prayer book. She must have attended some form of service in the chapel. That meant that Boyde should by now be free and in his cottage.

There was no hurry and he decided to walk first past the cottage to the chapel some fifty yards beyond. It was more crudely built than the cottages, an uncompromising building no more than fifteen feet square. There was a latched half door like a stable door and, opening it, he was met by a cooler damp-smelling air. The floor was paved with broken slabs and a single high window, with a pane so grubby that little light filtered through, gave only a smeared view of the sky. Placed precisely beneath the window was a heavy boulder, flat-topped, which was obviously being used as an altar, although it was uncovered and bare except for two stubby silver candlesticks and a small wooden cross. The candles were almost burnt out but he thought he could detect the lingering acridity of smoke. He wondered how the boulder had got there. It must have taken half a dozen strong men to move it into place. There were no benches or seats except for two wooden folding chairs leaning against the wall, one presumably provided for the use of Mrs Burbridge who must have been the only worshipper expected. Only a small stone cross stuck rather crookedly at the apex of the roof had suggested that the building had ever been consecrated and he thought it more likely to have been built as a shelter for animals and only some generations later used as a place of prayer. He felt none of that numinous awe born of emptiness and the echo of plainsong on the silent air that ancient churches could evoke. Nevertheless he found himself closing the door more quietly than he would have done, and marvelled, as he often did, how deep-seated and lasting were the influences of his childhood when, for a priest's son, the year had been divided not by school terms, holidays or months, but by the church calendar: Advent, Christmas, Pentecost, the seemingly interminable Sundays after Trinity.

The door to Chapel Cottage was open and Dalgliesh's tall figure momentarily eclipsing the light made a knock unnecessary. Boyde was sitting in front of the window at a table which served as a desk, and turned at once to greet him. The room was filled with light. A centre door with windows on either side led out to the stone patio at the edge of the cliff. To the left was a large stone grate with what looked like a bread oven, and a pile of kindling on one side and small logs on the other. Before it were two high-backed armchairs, one with a reading table beside it and a modern angled light. There was a greasy plate on the desk and a smell of bacon.

Dalgliesh said, 'I hope I'm not interrupting you. I did see Mrs Burbridge leaving the chapel so I thought it might be a convenient time to call.'

Boyde said, 'Yes, she usually comes to seven o'clock Mass on Sundays.'

'But no one else?'

'No. I don't think it would occur to them. Perhaps not even to those who were once churchgoers. They probably think that a priest who has stopped working – I mean, one who hasn't a parish – is no longer a priest. I don't advertise the service. It's really a private devotion but Mrs Burbridge found out about it when she and I helped care for Dan Padgett's mother.' He smiled. 'Now I'm Rupert Maycroft's secretary. Perhaps it's just as well. I might find the job of unofficial chaplain of the island more than I could cope with.'

Dalgliesh said, 'Particularly if they all decided to use you as their father confessor.'

The remark had been light-hearted. He had briefly indulged the risible image of Combe residents pouring into Boyde's ears their uncharitable thoughts about each other or the visitors, particularly Oliver. But he was surprised at Boyde's reaction. There was a second when Dalgliesh could almost believe that he had been guilty of a lapse of taste except that Boyde had not struck him as a man who looked for causes of offence.

Now he smiled again and said, 'I'd be tempted to change my churchmanship, become firmly evangelical and refer them all to Father Michael at Pentworthy. But I'm being inhospitable. Please sit down. I'm making some coffee. Would you like some?'

'Thank you, yes I would.'

Dalgliesh reflected that one of the minor hazards of a murder investigation was the inordinate quantity of caffeine he was expected to consume. But he wanted the interview to be as informal as possible and food or drink always helped.

Boyde disappeared into the kitchen leaving the

door ajar. There were the familiar kitchen sounds, the hiss of a kettle being filled, the metallic rattle of coffee beans being ground, the tinkle of cups and saucers. Dalgliesh settled himself in one of the chairs before the fire and contemplated the oil painting above the empty mantelpiece. Could it be a Corot? It was a French scene, a straight road between lines of poplars, the roofs of a distant village, a church spire shimmering beneath a summer sun.

Boyde came in carrying a tray. The smell of sea and wood fire was overlaid with the smell of coffee and hot milk. He nudged a small table between the chairs and set down the tray.

Dalgliesh said, 'I've been admiring your oil.'

'It was a bequest from my grandmother. She was French. It's an early Corot, painted in 1830 near Fontainebleau. It's the only valuable thing I own. One of the compensations of being on Combe is that I can hang it knowing that it won't be stolen or vandalised. I've never been able to afford to insure it. I like it because of the trees. I miss trees, there are so few here on the island. We even import the logs we burn.'

They drank their coffee in silence. Dalgliesh felt a curious peace, something that was very rare when he was in the company of a suspect. *Here*, he thought, *is a man I could have talked with, one I would have liked.* But he sensed that, despite Boyde's comfortable hospitality, there was no confidence between them.

After a minute he put down his cup and said, 'When I met you all together in the library and questioned you about yesterday morning, you were the only one who said he had been walking on the headland before breakfast. I have to ask you again whether you saw anyone on that walk.'

Without meeting Dalgliesh's eye, Boyde said quietly, 'I saw no one.'

'And you went where exactly?'

'I walked across the headland as far as Atlantic Cottage and then back here. It was just before eight o'clock.'

Again there was silence. Boyde picked up the tray and took it into the kitchen. It was three minutes before he returned to his seat and he seemed to be considering his words.

'Would you agree that we ought not to pass on suspicions which might only confuse or mislead and do great damage to the person concerned?'

Dalgliesh said, 'Suspicion usually has a basis in fact. I need to be told those facts. It's for me to decide their significance, if any.' He looked at Boyde and asked bluntly, 'Father, do you know who killed Nathan Oliver?'

Addressing Boyde as a priest had been involuntary and the word surprised him even as he heard himself speak it. It took him some seconds to realise the significance of what seemed no more than a slip of the tongue. The effect on Boyde was immediate. He looked at Dalgliesh with pain-filled eyes which seemed to hold an entreaty.

'I swear I don't know. I also swear that I saw no one on the headland.'

Dalgliesh believed him. He knew there was no more he could learn now and perhaps there was nothing else that he could learn. Five minutes later, after periods of commonplace chat but longer ones of silence, he left the cottage dissatisfied. He would leave the interview to do its work but he would have to see Boyde again.

It was now quarter-past nine and, arriving at the door of Seal Cottage, Dalgliesh could see Kate and Benton making their way over the scrubland. He went to meet them and they walked back together.

As they entered the telephone rang. Guy Staveley was on the line. 'Mr Dalgliesh? I'm ringing to tell you that it won't be possible for you to interview Dr Speidel again, not at present anyway. His condition worsened in the night. We've transferred him to the sickroom.'

2

It was just before eleven o'clock. Dalgliesh had decided to take Kate with him to interview Mrs Plunkett, but when she rang to make the appointment, she was asked by the cook whether they would mind coming to the kitchen. Dalgliesh readily agreed. It would be more convenient and time-saving for Mrs Plunkett and she was, he thought, more likely to be communicative in her working environment than in Seal Cottage. Five minutes later he and Kate were sitting side by side at the long kitchen table while Mrs Plunkett on the opposite side was busy at the Aga.

The kitchen reminded Dalgliesh of his childhood: the same stove only more modern, the scrubbed wooden table and Windsor chairs and a long oak dresser with a miscellany of plates, mugs and cups. One end of the room was obviously Mrs Plunkett's sanctum. There was a bentwood rocking chair, a low table and a desk topped with a row of cookbooks. This kitchen, like the one in the rectory, was an amalgam of smells – fresh baked bread, ground coffee beans, fried bacon – all redolent with anticipatory promise which the food never quite achieved. He remembered the family cook, the fourteen-stone, incongruously named Mrs Lightfoot, a woman of few words who had always been ready to welcome him into the rectory kitchen, allowing him to scrape out the bowl of cake mixture, giving him small lumps of dough to model into gingerbread men, listening to his endless questions. Sometimes she would reply, 'You'd better ask His Reverence about that.' She invariably referred to the rector as His Reverence. His father's study had always been open to him but for the young Adam that warm stone-flagged kitchen had been the heart of the house.

He left most of the questioning to Kate. Mrs Plunkett continued working. She was trimming fat from pork chops, dipping both sides of the meat in seasoned flour, then browning and turning them in a frying pan of hot fat. He watched as she lifted the chops from the pan and placed them in a casserole and then came to sit opposite them at the table where she began peeling and slicing onions and de-seeding some green peppers.

Kate, who had been unwilling to speak to Mrs Plunkett's back, now said, 'How long have you worked here, Mrs Plunkett?'

'Twelve years last Christmas. The previous cook was Miss Dewberry. She was one of those lady cooks with a cordon bleu diploma and everything "very nicely thank you" about her. Well, she was a good cook, I'll not deny that. Sauces. She was very particular about sauces, was Miss Dewberry. I learnt a lot from her about sauces. I used to come over during the week when she was extra busy to act as her kitchen maid. Not that she was ever that busy – you can't be with only six guests at most and the staff mostly looking after themselves. Still, she was used to having help in the smart restaurants where she worked, and I was a widow with no kids and time on my hands. I was always a good cook, still am. I got it from my mother. There was nothing she couldn't put her hand to in the kitchen. When Miss Dewberry retired she suggested I might take over. She knew by then what I was capable of. I had two weeks' probation and that was that. It suited both parties. I'm cheaper than Miss Dewberry was and I can do without a full-time kitchen maid, thank you very much. I like to be alone in my kitchen. Anyway, the girls today are more trouble than they're worth. If they go in for cooking at all it's because they see themselves on the telly with one of those celebrity chefs. I won't say I'm not glad to have Millie's help occasionally but she spends more time chasing after Jago than she does in my kitchen.'

She was working as she spoke, then got up and went back to the stove, quietly and methodically moving about her kitchen with the confidence of any craftsman in his familiar habitat. But it seemed to Dalgliesh that there was no link between those familiar actions and her thoughts, that she was employing a comforting and undemanding routine and her chat about Miss Dewberry's idiosyncrasies to avoid the more direct confrontation of again sitting opposite himself and Kate at the scrubbed wooden table and meeting their eyes. The air of the kitchen became savoury and he could detect the faint hiss of the hot fat.

Kate said, 'That smells good. What are you cooking?'

'Pork chops with tomato and green pepper sauce. For dinner tonight, but I thought I'd get on with them now. I like a nap in the afternoon. A bit heavy, maybe, now that the weather has changed but Dr Staveley likes pork occasionally and they'll be needing something hot. People have got to keep their strength up when there's been a bereavement. Not that anyone except Miss Oliver will feel much grief, but the poor man must have been terribly unhappy to do something dreadful like that.'

Dalgliesh said, 'In a case like this we need to know as much as possible about the person who has died. I'm told Mr Oliver came here regularly, every three months throughout the year. I expect you got to know him.'

'Not really. We aren't encouraged to talk to the visitors unless it's what they want. It's nothing to do with not being friendly or us being staff. Nothing snobbish like that. Mr Maycroft and Dr Staveley hardly see them either. They're here for silence and solitude and security. They come here to be alone. Mind you, we had a prime minister here for two weeks. A lot of fuss that was over security, but he did leave his protection officers behind him. He had to or he wouldn't have been allowed to come. He spent a lot of time sitting at that table just watching me work. Didn't chat much. I suppose he found it restful. Once I said, "If you've nothing better to do, sir, you might as well whisk those eggs." He did.'

Dalgliesh would like to have asked which prime minister and from which country, but knew that the question would have been crass and that he wouldn't get an answer. He said, 'If visitors spend their time alone, what about meals? When are they fed?'

'The cottages all have a fridge and a microwave. Well, you'll have seen that for yourself. The guests see to their own breakfast and midday meal. Dan Padgett drives the van and he delivers what they need for breakfast and lunch the night before. They get eggs fresh from our own hens, bread I bake myself, and bacon. We've a butcher on the mainland who cures his own – none of that milky fluid that seeps out of packet bacon. For lunch they mostly get salad or roast vegetables in winter, and a pie or cold meats. Then there's dinner here at eight o'clock for anyone who wants it. Always three courses.'

Kate said, 'Mr Oliver was at dinner on Friday. Was that usual?'

'No, it wasn't. He's only done that about three times before in all the years he's been coming here. He liked to eat in his cottage. Miss Oliver did the cooking for him and she'd give me orders the day before.'

Dalgliesh said, 'Did he seem his usual self at dinner? It was probably the last time he was seen alive except by his family. Anything unusual that happened might give us a pointer to his mental state.'

She had turned her face away from him towards the stove, but not quickly enough. He thought he detected the quick look of relief. She said, 'I wouldn't say he was behaving – well, what you might call normally, but I don't know what was normal for him. As I've said, we don't usually get to know the visitors. But it's usual for people to be fairly quiet at dinner. It's understood they don't talk about their work or why they're here. And you don't expect raised voices. Dr Staveley and Mr Maycroft were there, so you'd do better asking them.'

Kate said, 'Of course. But now we're asking for your impression.'

'Well, I wasn't in the dining room for much of the time, I never am. We began with melon balls with orange and I'd arranged that on the plates before I banged the dinner gong, so I wasn't in the room until Millie and I went in with the guinea fowl and the vegetables and to take away the first-course plates. I could see that Dr Yelland and Mr Oliver were beginning to argue. I think it was something to do with Dr Yelland's laboratory. The other three looked embarrassed.'

Kate asked, 'Mr Maycroft, and Dr and Mrs Staveley?'

'That's right, just the three. Miss Holcombe and Mrs Burbridge don't usually take dinner in the house. I expect Dr Yelland will tell you about it himself. Do you think it showed that Mr Oliver wasn't himself on Friday, that something else had upset him?'

Dalgliesh said, 'It certainly seems possible.'

'Come to think of it, I suppose I do get to know some of the visitors better than most, seeing that I wait at dinner. Better than Dr Staveley and Mr Maycroft if truth be told. Not that I could give you their names and I wouldn't if I could. There was a gentleman – I think they called him a captain of industry – he liked his bread and dripping. If we had roast beef – we did more often then, especially in winter – he'd whisper to me before he left the dining room, "Mrs P, I'll be round to the kitchen just before bed." I would've done my cleaning up before that and be having a quiet cup of tea before the fire. He loved his bread and dripping. He told me that he'd had it as a boy. He talked a lot about the cook his family had. You never forget the people who were kind to you in childhood, do you sir?'

'No', said Dalgliesh. 'You never do.'

Kate said, 'It's a pity, Mrs Plunkett, that Mr Oliver wasn't as friendly and confiding. We were hoping you'd be able to tell us something about him, help us to understand why he died as he did.'

'Truth to say I hardly set eyes on him. Can't imagine him coming into my kitchen for a chat and bread and dripping.'

Kate asked, 'How did he get on with other people on the island? I mean, staff and the permanent residents.'

'As I say, I hardly set eyes on him and I don't suppose the staff did much. I did hear a rumour that he was planning to move here permanently. I expect Mr Maycroft will have told you about that. It wouldn't have been popular with the staff and I don't expect Miss Holcombe would have been any too pleased. Of course we all knew he couldn't get on with Dan Padgett. Not that he saw him all that often, but Dan takes the meals round and does any odd jobs that need doing in the cottages, so I suppose they came into contact more than most of the people here. Dan couldn't do anything right as far as Mr Oliver was concerned. He or Miss Oliver would ring me with complaints that Dan hadn't delivered what they'd ordered or that it wasn't fresh enough – which couldn't be true. No food goes out of this kitchen that isn't fresh. Seems like Mr Oliver had to pick a quarrel with someone and I suppose Dan was the easiest person.'

Kate said, 'And then there was trouble about the blood sample lost overboard.'

'Yes, I did hear about that. Well of course Mr Oliver had a right to be annoyed. It meant he had to give another sample and no one enjoys having a needle stuck in them. Not that he did give another sample, as it turned out. Still, he probably had it hanging over him. And it was careless of Dan, no denying.'

Kate said, 'You don't think he could have done it on purpose to get his own back on Mr Oliver for picking on him?'

'No, I can't see that. I'd say he was too frightened of Mr Oliver to do something daft like that. Still, it was an odd accident. Dan didn't like the sea so why hang over the edge of the boat? More likely he'd be sitting in the cabin, I'd have thought. That's where he sat the odd times I've been in the launch with him. Proper scared he was.'

Kate asked, 'Did he ever talk to you about how he came to be here – Dan Padgett, I mean.'

Mrs Plunkett seemed to be considering how and whether to reply. Then she said, 'Well, you'll be asking him, I daresay, and no doubt he'll tell you.'

Dalgliesh said, 'I expect he will, Mrs Plunkett, but it's always useful to get two opinions about people when we're investigating a suspicious death.'

'But Mr Oliver committed suicide. I mean, he was found hanging. I don't see that it's anything to do with anyone except him and maybe his daughter.'

'Perhaps not, but his state of mind must have been influenced by other people, what they said, what they did. And we can't be certain yet that it was suicide.'

'You mean it could've been murder?'

'It could have been, Mrs Plunkett.'

'And if it was, you can put Dan Padgett out of mind. That boy hasn't got the guts to kill a chicken – not that he's a boy, of course. He could be nearing thirty now for all he looks young. But I always think of him as a boy.'

Kate said, 'We were wondering if he ever confided in you, Mrs Plunkett. Most of us need to talk to someone about our lives, our problems. I get the impression that Dan wasn't really at home on Combe.'

'Well, that's true enough, he wasn't. It was his mother who was dead keen on coming here. He told me that his mum and her parents used to stay in Pentworthy for two weeks every August when she was a child. Of course, you couldn't visit the island even then, but she longed to see it. It became a kind of romantic dream for her. When she got so ill and knew she was dying, she longed to come here. Maybe she'd come to believe that the island could cure her. Dan didn't like to refuse, seeing how ill she was. They were both very wrong not telling Mr Maycroft that she was so ill when they applied for the jobs. It wasn't fair on him – or on any of us, come to that. Mrs Staveley was in London but she came back towards the end and took over the nursing. Mr Boyde was there a bit too, but I suppose that was because he used to be a clergyman. Most of us women helped with the nursing and Dan didn't do much of his own work during that last month. I think he resented his mother at the end. I was in the cottage cleaning up after Mrs Padgett had died. Mrs Staveley had laid her out and she was on the bed waiting to be taken down to the harbour. Dan said that he'd like a lock of hair, so I went to find an envelope for him to put it in. He fairly tugged it out and I could see the look on his face, which wasn't really what you'd call loving.

'I think he resented both his parents, which is sad really. He told me they should've been quite well off.

His dad had a small business – printing, I think he said – which he had inherited from his own father. But he wasn't much of a businessman. He took on a partner who cheated him, so the business went bankrupt. And then he got cancer – just like Dan's mother only his was in the lungs – and died, and they found he hadn't even bothered to insure himself. Dan was only three so he doesn't really remember his dad. So Dan and his mother went to live with her older sister and her husband. They had no children of their own so you'd think they might have taken to the boy, but they never did. They belonged to one of those puritanical sects which think everything you enjoy is a sin. They even made him change his name. He was christened Wayne, Daniel is actually his second name. He had a horrible childhood and nothing seemed to go right for him after that. His uncle did teach him carpentry and decorating – he's really very good with his hands, is Dan. Still, he never was an islander and never will be. Of course he didn't tell me all this about his childhood at once. It came out bit by bit over the months. It's like you said, we all need someone to talk to.'

Dalgliesh said, 'But now that his mother is dead, why does he stay?'

'Oh, he's not going to. His mother's left him a bit of money she saved and he plans to go to London and take some kind of training. I think he's applied for a degree course at one of the new universities there. He can't wait to get away. To tell you the truth, I don't think our previous secretary would have taken him on. But Mr Maycroft was new and he did have two vacancies, one for a general handyman and the other to give Mrs

Burbridge a bit of help. He'll have another vacancy when Dan leaves – that's if the island carries on.'

'Has there been any talk that it might not?'

'Well, a bit. Suicide does put people off, doesn't it? Murder too, of course. But you don't murder people just because they're irritating occasionally. Anyway, Mr Oliver only ever stayed two weeks so he'd have been gone in less than a fortnight. And if he was murdered, someone must've got on the island unseen, which we've always thought wasn't possible. And how did he get off again? I suppose he could be still here, hidden some-where. Not a nice thought, is it?'

'And there's Millie. Mr Maycroft appointed her too, didn't he?'

'Yes, he did, but I can't see that he had much choice. Jago Tamlyn found her begging on the streets of Pentworthy and took pity on the girl. He's got a soft heart, has Jago, especially for the young. He had a sister and she hanged herself after she was seduced and made pregnant by a married man. That was six years or so ago, but I don't think he's ever got over it. Maybe Millie looked a bit like her. So he rang Mr Maycroft and asked if he could bring her to the island and find a room and a job for her until he could settle what best to do. It was either that or the police. So Mr Maycroft found a job for her as assistant to Mrs Burbridge with the linen and to help me in the kitchen. There's not much wrong with Millie. She's a good little worker when the mood takes her and I've no complaints. Still, the island's not really a suitable place for a young girl. She needs her own kind and a proper job. Millie does more in the sewing line than she does for me and I know Mrs Burbridge worries about her. Not that it isn't nice to have a bit of young life on Combe.'

Kate asked bluntly, 'How did you get on with Miranda Oliver, Mrs Plunkett? Is she as difficult as her father?'

'I'll not say she's an easy woman. More likely to give criticism than thanks. Still, she hasn't had an easy life, poor girl, tied to an ageing father, always at his beck and call. Mrs Burbridge tells me that she's engaged to that secretary who worked for her father. Dennis Tremlett. You'll have met him, of course. If that's what she wants I'm sure I hope they'll be happy. There'll be no shortage of money I suppose, and that always helps.'

Kate said: 'Did the engagement surprise you?'

'I never heard about it until this morning. I didn't see enough of either of them to have an opinion one way or the other. As I said, we're supposed to leave the visitors in peace and that's what I do. If they care to come into the kitchen, that's another matter, but I don't go looking for them. I haven't the time anyway. I wouldn't get much done if people were always in and out of the kitchen.'

It was said easily with no apparent intention of conveying a hint, but Kate glanced at Dalgliesh. He nodded. It was an appropriate time to leave. ·

Kate had things to do. She left to join Benton, and Dalgliesh walked back to Seal Cottage to await the call from Dr Glenister. Mrs Plunkett had been more informative than she, perhaps, had realised. It was the first he had heard of Oliver's proposal to move to Combe permanently. The other permanent residents would be more likely to see this as a disaster rather than an inconvenience, particularly Emily Holcombe. And there was something else. He was irked by a nagging conviction that somewhere enmeshed in Mrs Plunkett's domestic chat she had told him something of crucial importance. The thought lay like an irritating thread of cotton in his mind; if he could only grasp the end it would unravel and lead him to the truth. Mentally he reviewed their conversation: Dan Padgett's deprived childhood, Millie begging on the streets of Pentworthy, the captain of industry and his bread and dripping, Oliver's quarrel with Mark Yelland. The thread lay in none of these. He decided to put the problem firmly out of his mind for the present in the hope that, sooner or later, his mind would become clearer.

At midday precisely the telephone rang. Dr Glenister's voice came over strong, calm, authoritative and as unhesitatingly as if she were reading from a script. 'Nathan Oliver died of asphyxiation caused by manual strangulation. The internal damage is considerable. The full autopsy report isn't yet typed but I'll let you have it by e-mail when it is. Some of the internal organs are being analysed but there's little else of importance. Physically he was in pretty good shape for a sixty-eight-year-old. There's evidence of extensive arthritis in the right hand, which must have caused some inconvenience if he wrote by hand – which from the evidence of a slight callus on the forefinger he did. The cartilages were calcified, as is not uncommon with the elderly, and there was a fracture of the superior cornu of the thyroid. This localised fracture is invariably caused by local pressure where a sharp grip has been applied. In this case great violence wouldn't have been necessary. Oliver was frailer than he looked and his neck, as you saw, was comparatively narrow. There is also a small bruise at the back of the neck where his head was forced back against something hard. Given the findings, there is no possibility that he bruised his own neck in an attempt to make suicide look like murder, if that fanciful possibility has been put forward. Oliver's clothes are with the lab, but as you'll know, with strangulation of this kind where the head is driven back against a hard object, there may be no physical contact between the assailant and the victim. But that's your concern, not mine. One fact is interesting though: I had to phone the lab this morning about a different case and they'd had a preliminary look at the rope. They won't get anything useful there, I'm afraid. An attempt had been made to wipe the rope clean along its whole length. They might get some evidence of the material used to clean it, but it's unlikely on that surface.'

Dalgliesh said, 'Including the knot?'

'Apparently. They'll e-mail you when they've got anything to report but I said I'd tell you about the rope. Ring me if there's anything else I can help with. Goodbye, Commander.'

'Goodbye, and thank you.'

The receiver was replaced. Dr Glenister had done her job; she had no intention of wasting her time by discussing his.

Dalgliesh summoned Kate and Benton back to Seal Cottage and gave them the news.

Kate said, 'So we're unlikely to get anything useful from the rope except that Calcraft must have thought that the lab could raise fingerprints from the surface so he isn't ignorant of forensics. He might even have known that sweat can provide DNA. Jago and Padgett both handled the rope after the body was taken down so would they have needed to wipe it clean? After the rope was replaced in the unlocked lighthouse anyone could've had access to it.'

Benton said, 'It could have been wiped, not by the killer, but by someone who was trying to protect him.'

Settling round the table, Dalgliesh set out the programme for the rest of the day. There were distances to be measured, the possibility of Padgett from Puffin Cottage seeing Oliver walking to the lighthouse and the time it would have taken him to get to the lighthouse on the lower cliff to be checked, the whole of the lighthouse to be meticulously examined for possible clues and the suspects individually questioned. It was always possible that after a night's reflection something new would be learnt.

Now that Dr Glenister had officially confirmed that the case was murder, it was time to phone Geoffrey Harkness at the Yard. He didn't expect the Assistant Commissioner to be pleased with the verdict, and nor was he.

He said, 'You're going to need technical back-up now, SOCOs and the fingerprint experts. The reasonable course would be to hand the case over to Devon and Cornwall, but that won't be popular with certain people in London, and of course there's a case for your carrying on now you're there. What's the possibility that you'll get a result, say within the next two days?'

'That's impossible to say.'

'But you've no doubt that your man is on the island?'

'I think we can be reasonably sure of that.'

'Then the job shouldn't take long with a restricted number of suspects. As I've said, the feeling in London will be that you ought to carry on, but I'll let you know as soon as we have a decision. In the meantime, good luck.'

3

Mrs Burbridge's office was a small room on the first floor of the west wing, but her private apartment was one floor above. Since the lift only served the tower, it was reached either by the stairs from the ground floor rear entrance or by the lift outside Maycroft's office and then by way of the library. The shining white-painted door had a brass nameplate and bell push affirming the housekeeper's status and acknowledging her right to privacy. Dalgliesh had made an appointment and Mrs Burbridge came promptly to his almost inaudible buzz and greeted Kate and himself as if they were expected guests, but not ones whom she was particularly anxious to see. But she was not ungracious. The demands of hospitality must be met.

The hall into which she ushered them was unexpectedly wide and even before the door was closed behind them Dalgliesh felt he had entered a more personal domain than any he had expected to find on Combe. In coming to the island, Mrs Burbridge had brought with her the accumulated relics of generations: family mementoes of transitory or more lasting enthusiasms, carefully preserved furniture typical of its age, retained less because it fitted her new home than through family piety. A bow-fronted mahogany desk held a collection of Staffordshire figures discordant in size and subject. John Wesley exhorted from his pulpit next to a large portrait of Shakespeare, legs elegantly crossed, one hand supporting an impressive brow, the other resting on a pile of bound volumes. Dick Turpin's legs dangled from a diminutive horse towered over by a two-foot-high Queen Victoria in the regalia of Empress of India. Beyond, a row of chairs – two elegant, the others monstrous in size and shape – were ranged in an uninviting row. Above them the faded wallpaper was almost obliterated with pictures: undistinguished watercolours, small oils in pretentious frames, a few sepia photographs, prints of Victorian rural life which none of the villagers of that age would have recognised, a pair of delicate oils of prancing nymphs in gilt oval frames.

Despite this superfluity, Dalgliesh had no sense of entering an antique shop, perhaps because the objects were set out with no regard either to intrinsic attractiveness or seductive commercial advantage. In the few seconds negotiating the hall behind Mrs Burbridge and Kate, he thought, *Our parents' generation carried the past memorialised in paint, porcelain and wood; we cast it off. Even our national history is taught or remembered in terms of the worst we did, not the best.* His mind went to his own sparsely furnished flat high above the Thames with something too close to irrational guilt to be comfortable. The family pictures and furniture he had selected to keep and use were the ones he personally liked and wished to rest his eyes on. The family silver was in a bank vault; he neither needed it nor had time to polish it. His mother's pictures and his father's theological library had been given to their friends. And what, he wondered, would those friends' children eventually do with their unwanted legacy? To the young the past was always an encumbrance. What, if anything, would Emma want to bring to their life together? And then the same insidious doubt intruded. Would they have a life together?

Mrs Burbridge was saying, 'I was just finishing some tidying up in my sewing room. Perhaps you won't mind joining me there for a few minutes, then we could go into my sitting room, which you'll find more comfortable.'

She was leading them into a room at the end of the passage so different from the over-crowded hall that Dalgliesh had difficulty in not showing his surprise. It was elegantly proportioned and very light, with two large windows looking westwards. It was obvious at first glance that Mrs Burbridge was a highly talented embroideress. The room was given over to her craft. Apart from two wooden tables set at right angles and covered with a white cloth, one wall was lined with boxes through whose cellophane front panels could be glimpsed the sheen of reels of coloured silk thread. Against another wall a large chest held rolls of silk cloth. Next to it a notice-board was covered with small samples and patterned with coloured photographs of altar fronts and embroidered copes and stoles. There were about two dozen designs for crosses, symbols of the four evangelists and various saints, and drawings of doves descending or ascending. At the far end of the room was a tailor's dummy on which had been draped an embroidered cope in a rich green silk, the panels embroidered with twin designs of delicate foliage and spring flowers.

Sitting at the table nearest the door at work on a

cream stole was Millie. Dalgliesh and Kate saw a very different girl from the one they had interviewed yesterday. She was wearing a spotless white overall, her hair was tied back with a white band and with very clean hands she was delicately stabbing a fine needle into the edge of an appliquéd design in silk. She barely glanced at Dalgliesh and Kate before bending again to her task. The sharp-featured childish face was so transformed by serious intent that she looked almost beautiful as well as very young.

Mrs Burbridge went over to her and looked down at the stitching which to Dalgliesh's eye was invisible. Her voice was a soft hiss of approval. 'Yes, yes, Millie. That's very good. Well done. You can leave it for now. Come back this afternoon if you feel like it.'

Millie had become truculent. 'Maybe I will, maybe I won't. I've got other things to do.'

The stole had rested on a small sheet of white cotton. Millie slid her needle into a corner, folded the sheet over her work, then divested herself of overall and headband and hung them in a wardrobe beside the door. She was ready with her parting shot.

'I don't think the cops ought to come bothering us when we're working.'

Mrs Burbridge said quietly, 'They're here by my invitation, Millie.'

'Nobody asked me. I work here too. I had enough of the cops yesterday.' And Millie was gone.

Mrs Burbridge said, 'She'll be back this afternoon. She loves sewing and she's become a really clever embroideress in the short time she's been here. Her granny taught her and I find that's usually the way with the young. I'm trying to persuade her to take a City and Guilds course but it's difficult. And, of course, there would be the problem of where she'd live if she left the island.'

Dalgliesh and Kate sat at the long table while Mrs Burbridge moved about the room, rolling up a transparent pattern for what was obviously a design for an altar frontal, placing the reels of silk in their boxes according to colour and replacing the bales of silk in the cupboard.

Watching her, Dalgliesh said, 'The cope is beautiful. Do you do the design as well as the actual embroidery?'

'Yes, that's almost the more exciting part. There have been great changes in church embroidery since the last war. You probably remember that altar frontals were usually just two bands of braid to cover the seams with a standard central motif, nothing original or new. It was in the nineteen-fifties that there was a movement to be more imaginative and to reflect the design of the mid-twentieth century. I was doing my City and Guilds exam at the time and was very excited by what I saw. But I'm only an amateur. I only embroider in silk. There are people doing far more original and complicated work. I started when the altar frontal in my husband's church began to fall apart at the seams and the vicar's warden suggested that I might take on the job of making a new one. I mostly work for friends although, of course, they do pay for the material and help towards the money I give to Millie. The cope is a retirement present for a bishop. Green, of course, is the liturgical colour for Epiphany and Trinity, but I thought he would prefer the spring flowers.'

Kate said, 'The vestments when finished must be heavy and valuable. How do you get them to the recipients?'

'Adrian Boyde used to take them. It gave him an opportunity – rare, but I think welcome – of leaving the island. In a week I hope he'll be able to deliver this cope. I think we can risk it.'

The last words were spoken very softly. Dalgliesh waited. Suddenly she said, 'I've finished here now. Perhaps you'd like to come to the sitting room.'

She led them into a smaller room almost as over-furnished as the hall but surprisingly welcoming and comfortable. Dalgliesh and Kate were settled beside the fire in two low Victorian chairs with velvet covers and button backs. Mrs Burbridge drew up a stool and perched herself opposite them. She made the expected offer of coffee, which they declined with thanks. Dalgliesh was in no hurry to broach the subject of Oliver's death but he was confident that something useful would be learnt from Mrs Burbridge. She was a discreet woman but she could probably tell him more about the island and the residents than could the more recently arrived Rupert Maycroft.

She said, 'Millie was brought here by Jago at the end of May. He was taking a day off from the island and visiting a friend in Pentworthy. Returning from the pub they saw Millie begging on the sea front. She looked hungry and Jago spoke to her. He's always been sympathetic to the young. Anyway, he and his friend took Millie to a fish-and-chip shop – she was ravenous apparently – and she poured out her story. It's the usual one, I'm afraid. Her father walked out when she was very young and she's never got on with her mother or her mother's succession of boyfriends. She left Peckham and went to live with her paternal grandmother in a village outside Plymouth. That worked well but after two years the old lady sank into Alzheimer's and was taken off to a home, and Millie was homeless. I think she told the social services that she was going back home to Peckham, but no one checked. After all, she was no longer a juvenile and I suppose they were too busy. There was no chance of staying in the house. The landlord had always wanted them out and she had no way of paying the rent. She lived rough for a time until the money ran out and that's when she met Jago. He rang Mr Maycroft from Pentworthy and asked if he could bring Millie here temporarily. One of the rooms in the stable block was vacant and Mrs Plunkett did need some help in the kitchen. It would have been difficult for Mr Maycroft to say no. Apart from natural human- ity, Jago is indispensable to Combe, and there could be no possibility of having any sexual interest in the girl.'

Suddenly she said, 'But of course, you're not here to talk about Millie. You want to question me again about Oliver's death. I'm sorry if I was a little sharp yesterday, but his exploitation of Millie was absolutely typical. He was using her, of course.'

'Can you be sure that of that?'

'Oh yes, Mr Dalgliesh. That's how he worked, that's how he lived. He watched other people and made use of them. If he wanted to see someone descending into their particular hell he'd make sure he saw it. It's all in his novels. And if he couldn't find someone else to experiment on, he might experiment on himself. That's how I think he died. If he wanted to write about someone who was hanged, or perhaps planning to die in that way, he would need to get as close as possible to the deed. He might even have gone as far as putting the rope round his neck and stepping over the rail. There's about eight inches or more of space, and of course he'd have the rail to hold on to. I know it sounds foolish but I've been thinking about it very carefully, we all have, and I believe that's the explanation. It was an experiment.'

Dalgliesh could have pointed out that this would be a remarkably foolish experiment but he didn't need to. She went on with something like eagerness in her eyes, as if anxious to convince him. 'He'd have held on firmly to the rail. It could have been a moment's impulse climbing over, the need to feel death touching your cheek, but believing at the same time that you're in charge. Isn't that the satisfaction of all the really dangerous games that men play?'

The idea was not altogether fanciful. Dalgliesh could imagine the mixture of terror and exhilaration with which Oliver could have stood on that narrow strip of stone with only his hand on the rail to prevent his falling. But he hadn't made those marks on his neck. He had been dead before he was launched into that immensity.

Mrs Burbridge sat in silence for a moment and seemed to be making up her mind. Then she looked him full in the face and said with some passion. 'No one on this island will say that they liked Nathan Oliver, no one. But most of the things he did to upset people were minor really – bad temper, ungraciousness, complaints about Dan Padgett's inefficiency, late delivery of his food, the fact that the boat wasn't always available when he wanted a trip round the island, that sort of thing. But one thing he did was evil. That's a word people don't use here, Commander, but I use it.'

Dalglesh said, 'I think I know what you mean, Mrs Burbridge. Mrs Staveley has spoken to me.'

'It's easy to criticise Jo Staveley, but I never do. Adrian could have died except for her. Now he's trying to put it behind him, and naturally we never mention it. I'm sure you won't either. It hasn't anything to do with Oliver's death but no one will forget what he did. And now, if you'll excuse me, I have things I need to get on with. I'm sorry I've not been very helpful.'

Dalgliesh said, 'You have been very helpful, Mrs Burbridge. Thank you.'

Passing through the library, Kate said, 'She thinks Jo Staveley did it. Mrs Staveley certainly feels strongly about what happened to Adrian Boyde but she's a nurse. Why kill in that way? She could have given Oliver a lethal injection when she took his blood. That's ridiculous, of course. She'd be the first suspect.'

Dalgliesh said, 'And wouldn't that be against her every instinct? And we have to remember that the killing could have been impulsive rather than premeditated. But she's certainly strong enough to heave Oliver's body over the railings and she could easily get to the lighthouse from Dolphin Cottage by the lower cliff. Somehow I can't see Jo Staveley as a murderess. But then I don't think we've ever been faced with a more unlikely set of suspects.'

4

As Mrs Burbridge had expected, Millie returned in mid-afternoon, but not to work on the stole. Instead they spent an hour arranging the skeins of coloured silk in their boxes in a more logical order and packing the cope in a long cardboard box, folding it with anxious care in tissue paper. Most of this was carried out in silence. Then they took off their white overalls and went together into Mrs Burbridge's immaculate kitchen while she boiled the kettle for tea. They drank it sitting at the kitchen table.

Millie's violent distress at Oliver's death had subsided and now, after her questioning by Dalgliesh, she was in a mood of sulky acquiescence. But there were things Mrs Burbridge knew she had to say. Sitting opposite Millie she steeled herself to say them.

'Millie, you did tell the truth to Commander Dalgliesh, didn't you, about what happened to Dr Speidel's note? I'm not saying you've been dishonest but sometimes we forget important details and sometimes we don't tell everything because we're trying to protect someone else.'

'Course I told the truth. Who's been saying I was lying?'

'No one has, Millie. I just wanted to be sure.'

'Well now you are sure. Why d'you all keep on

nagging me about it – you or Mr Maycroft or the police or anyone else?'

'I'm not nagging you. If you tell me you were being truthful that's all I need to know.'

'Well I was, wasn't I?'

Mrs Burbridge made herself go on. 'It's just that I worry about you sometimes, Millie. We like having you here but it isn't really a suitable home for someone young. You have your whole life before you. You need to be with other young people, to have a proper job.'

'I'll get a proper job when I want one. Anyway, I've got a proper job, I'm working for you and Mrs Plunkett.'

'And we're glad to have you. But there isn't much prospect for you here, is there Millie? I sometimes wonder if you might be staying here because you're fond of Jago.'

'He's all right. He's my friend.'

'Of course he is, but he can't be more than that, can he? I mean, he does have someone in Pentworthy he visits, doesn't he? The friend he was with when you first met him.'

'Yeah, Jake. He's a physio at the hospital. He's cool.'

'So there isn't really any hope of Jago falling in love with you, is there?'

'I dunno. There could be. He could swing both ways.'

Mrs Burbridge nearly asked, *And you're hoping he'll swing in your direction?*, but stopped herself in time. She was regretting ever beginning this dangerous conversation. She said weakly, 'It's just that you ought to meet other people, Millie, have more of a life than you have here. Make friends.'

'I've got friends, haven't I? You're my friend. I've got you and you've got me.'

The words stabbed her with a shaft of joy so overwhelming that for a few seconds she was unable to speak. She made herself look directly at Millie. The girl's hands were clasped round her teacup and she was looking down. And then Mrs Burbridge saw the childish mouth stretch into a smile wholly adult in its mixture of amusement and – yes – of disdain. They were just words like most of Millie's words: spoken in passing, holding nothing but the meaning of the moment. She dropped her own eyes and, steadying her hands around the cup, raised it carefully to her lips.

5

Clara Beckwith was Emma Lavenham's closest friend. They had first met when they were both freshers at Cambridge and she was the only one in whom Emma confided. They could not have been more different; the one heterosexual and burdened by her dark beauty, the other stocky, her hair close-cropped above a chubby spectacled face and with – in Emma's eyes – the gallant sturdiness of a pit pony. She wasn't sure what Clara valued in her, half suspecting, as she always did, that it was largely physical. In her friend she relied on her honesty, common sense and an unsentimental acceptance of the vagaries of life, love and desire. She knew that Clara was sexually attracted both to men and women, but had for five years been happily settled with the gentle-faced Annie who was as frail and vulnerable as Clara was strong. Clara's ambivalence about Emma's relationship with Dalgliesh might have produced complications if Emma had suspected that it was grounded in jealousy rather than in her friend's instinctive suspicions of the motives of men. The two had never met. Neither had yet suggested that they should.

Clara had been awarded a starred First in Mathematics at Cambridge and worked in the City as a highly successful fund manager, but she still lived with her partner in the Putney flat she had bought when leaving university and spent little on clothes, her only extravagances, her

Porsche and the holidays they took together. Emma suspected that a sizable proportion of her earnings went on charity and that Clara was saving for some future enterprise with her lover, as yet unplanned. The City job was intended to be temporary; Clara had no wish to be sucked into that seductive world of over-dependence on treacherous and precarious wealth.

They had been to an evening concert at the Royal Festival Hall. It had ended early and by eight-fifteen they had struggled through the cloakroom queue and joined the crowd making its way along the Thames to Hungerford Bridge. As was their custom, they would discuss the music later. Now, with it echoing in their minds, they walked in silence, their eyes on the glitter of the lights strung like a necklace on the opposite bank. Before reaching the bridge they paused and both leaned on the stone parapet to gaze down on the dark pulsating river, its surface as supple and rippling as the hide of an animal.

Emma gave herself up to London. She loved the city, not with Dalgliesh's passionate commitment, he who knew both the best and the worst of his chosen territory, but with a steady affection, as strong as that she felt for Cambridge, her native city, but different in kind. London withheld some part of her mystery even from those who loved her. London was history solidified in brick and stone, illuminated in stained glass, celebrated in monument and statue, and yet to Emma it was more a spirit than a place, a vagrant air which breathed down the hidden alleyways, possessed the silence of empty city churches, and lay dormant under her most raucous streets. She gazed across the river at the moon of Big Ben and the illuminated Palace of Westminster, its flagstaff unadorned, the light on the clock tower switched off. It was Saturday night; the House was not sitting. High above a plane was descending slowly, its wing-lights like moving stars. The passengers would be craning down at the black curving river, its fairy-tale bridges painted in coloured light.

She wondered what Dalgliesh was doing. Still working, sleeping or walking out on that unnamed island to look at the night sky? In London the stars were eclipsed by the city's glare, but on an isolated island the dark would be luminous under a canopy of stars. Suddenly the longing for him was so intense and so physical that she felt a rush of blood to her face. She longed to be returning to that flat high above the river at Queenhithe, to his bed, to his arms. Tonight she and Clara would take the District Line from Embankment station to Putney Bridge and Clara's riverside flat. So why not to Queenhithe, which was almost within walking distance? It had never occurred to her to invite Clara there, nor did her friend seem to expect it. Queenhithe was for her and Adam. To let anyone else in would be to let them in on his private life, his and hers. But was she at home there?

She remembered a moment in the early days of their love when Adam, coming out of his shower room, had said, 'I've left my spare toothbrush in your bathroom. Is it all right if I get it?'

Laughing, she had replied, 'Of course, darling. I live here now – at least for part of the time.'

He had come up behind her chair, his dark head bent, his arms encircling her. 'So you do, my love, and that's the wonder of it.'

She was aware that Clara had been looking at her. Her friend said, 'I know you're thinking of your Commander. I'm glad the poetry isn't a substitute for performance. What's that quotation from Blake about the lineaments of gratified desire? That's you all right. But I'm happy you're coming back to Putney tonight. Annie will be pleased to see you.' There was a pause, then she said, 'Is anything wrong?'

'Not wrong. The times we have together are so short, but they're wonderful, perfect. But you can't live for ever at that intensity. Clara, I do want to marry him. I'm not sure why I feel it so strongly. We couldn't be happier than we are, or more committed. I couldn't be more certain. So why do I want a legal tie? It isn't rational.'

'Well, he proposed to you, on paper too, and before you went to bed together. That suggests a sexual confidence amounting to arrogance. Doesn't he still want to marry you?'

'I'm not sure. He may feel that living and working apart as we do, coming together so wonderfully but briefly, is all either of us needs.'

Clara said, 'You heterosexuals make life so complicated for yourselves. You speak to each other don't you? I mean, you do communicate? He proposed to you. Tell him it's time to set a date.'

'I'm not sure I know how.'

'I can suggest a number of alternatives. You could say, "I'll be busy in December once the interviews begin for next year's intake. If you're thinking of a honeymoon as opposed to just a weekend in the flat, the best time is the New Year." Or you could take your Commander to be introduced to your father. I take it he's been spared that traditional ordeal. Then get the Prof to ask him what his intentions are. That has an original old-fashioned touch which might appeal to him.'

'I doubt whether it would appeal to my father – that is if he took his attention away from his books long enough to understand what Adam was saying. And I wish you'd stop calling him my Commander.'

'The last and only time we spoke I remember calling him a bastard. I think we've got some way to go before we're on first-name terms. If you don't want to throw him unprepared to the Prof, what about a spot of black-mail? "No more weekends until the ring's on my finger. I've developed moral scruples." That's been remarkably efficacious over the centuries. No point in rejecting it just because it's been used before.'

Emma laughed. 'I'm not sure I could carry it off. I'm not a masochist. I could probably hold out no longer than two weeks.'

'Well, settle the method for yourself, but stop agonis-ing. You're not really afraid of rejection?'

'No, not that. It's just that at heart he may not want marriage, and I do.'

They were crossing the bridge home. After a silence, Clara said, 'If he were ill – sweaty, smelling horrible, vomiting, a mess – would you be able to clean him up, comfort him?'

'Of course.'

'Suppose you were the one who was sick. What then?'

Emma didn't reply. Clara said, 'I've diagnosed the problem for you. You're afraid he loves you because

323

you're beautiful. You can't bear the thought he might see you when you're less than beautiful.'

'But isn't that important, at the beginning anyway? Wasn't it like that with you and Annie? Isn't that how love starts, with physical attraction?'

'Of course. But if that's all you have, then you're in trouble.'

'It isn't all we have. I'm sure of that.'

But in some corner of her mind she knew that the treacherous thought had taken hold. She said, 'It's nothing to do with his job. I know we have to be apart when we don't want to be. I know he had to go away this weekend. Only this time it feels different. I'm afraid he may not come back, that he's going to die on that island.'

'But that's ridiculous. Why should he? He's not there to confront terrorists. I thought his speciality was upmarket murder, cases too sensitive for the local PC Plod to plant his boots on. He's probably in no more danger than we will be on the Tube to Putney.'

'I know it's irrational, but I can't shake it off.'

'Then let's go home.'

Emma thought, *And that's a word she can use. So when I'm with Adam, why can't I?*

6

Rupert Maycroft had explained to the team that after the death of Padgett's mother Dan had moved from the stable block to the one-bedded Puffin Cottage, between Dolphin and Atlantic Cottages on the north-west coast. Kate had phoned him early on the Monday morning and arranged to see him at midday. He opened the door immediately to their knock and, without speaking, stood aside.

Benton's first reaction was to wonder how Padgett occupied himself when he was at home. The sitting room bore no sign of interests – or indeed of any activity – and except for a few paperback books on the top shelf of an oak bookcase and a row of china figurines on the mantelpiece, was bare of everything but the furniture. Most of that was of heavy oak, a table set in the middle of the room with bulbous legs and two leaves which could be drawn out, six dining-chairs of similar design and a heavy matching sideboard with its doors and top panel intricately carved. The only other furniture was a divan set under the window and covered with a patchwork quilt. Benton wondered if Mrs Padgett had been nursed here when she was bedridden, leaving the one bedroom for whoever was caring for her during the night hours. Although there was no tincture of sickness in the room, it still smelled stale, perhaps because all three windows were closely shut.

Padgett drew out three of the chairs and they sat down facing him. To Benton's relief Padgett made no offer of tea or coffee but sat, his hands under the table, like an obedient child, his eyes blinking. His thin neck rose from a heavy jersey in an intricate cable-stitch design which emphasised the pallor of his face and the delicate bones of the high domed skull visible through cropped hair.

Kate said, 'We're here to go over again what you told us on Saturday in the library. Perhaps it would be easier if you went through your routine on Saturday morning from the moment of getting up.'

Padgett began a recital which sounded like a statement learnt by rote. 'I have the job of taking round any food ordered by phone by the visitors the previous evening, and I did that at seven o'clock. The only one who wanted supplies was Dr Yelland in Murrelet Cottage. He wanted a cold lunch, some milk and eggs and a selection of CDs from the music library. His cottage has a porch like most of the others so I left the food there. That's what I'm instructed to do. I didn't see Dr Yelland and I was back at the house with the buggy by seven forty-five. I left it in its usual place in the courtyard and came back here. I've applied for a place at a university in London to take a course in psychology and the tutor's asked me to write a paper explaining my choice. I haven't got good A-levels but that doesn't seem to matter. I was here in the cottage working until Mr Maycroft phoned just after nine-thirty to say that Mr Oliver was missing and he wanted me for the search party. It was beginning to get misty by then, but of course I went. I joined the group in the courtyard in front of the house. I was just behind Mr Maycroft at the lighthouse when the mist suddenly lifted and we saw the body. Then we heard Millie screaming.'

Kate said, 'And you're quite certain that you saw no one, either Mr Oliver or anyone else, until you joined the search party?'

'I've told you. I saw no one.'

It was then that the phone rang. Padgett got up quickly. He said, 'I have to answer that. The phone's in the kitchen. We had it moved so that mother wouldn't be disturbed.'

He went out of the door, closing it behind him. Kate said, 'If that's Mrs Burbridge trying to get hold of him he shouldn't be long.'

He didn't come back. Kate and Benton got up and Kate moved over to the bookcase. She said, 'Obviously his mother's paperbacks, mostly popular romantic fiction. There's one Nathan Oliver though, *The Sands of Trouville*. Looks as if it's been read, but not often.'

Benton said, 'It sounds like the title of a block-buster. Not his usual style.' He was examining the china figurines on the mantelpiece. 'These too presumably belonged to Mother, so why are they still here? Surely these were candidates for the trip to the charity shop in Newquay, unless Padgett is keeping them out of sentiment.'

Kate joined him. 'You'd think these would be the first objects to go overboard.'

He was pensively turning one of the pieces in his hand, a crinolined woman wearing a beribboned bonnet languidly weeding a garden path with a slender hoe.

Kate said, 'Hardly dressed for the job, is she? Those

shoes wouldn't last five minutes outside the bedroom and her hat will blow off with the first puff of wind. What's on your mind?'

Benton said, 'Just the usual question, I suppose. Why do I despise it? Isn't it a kind of cultural snobbery? I mean, do I dislike it because I've been trained to make that kind of value judgement? After all, it's well made. It's sentimental, but you can call some good art sentimental.'

'What art?'

'Well, Watteau for one. *The Old Curiosity Shop* if you're thinking of literature.'

Kate said, 'You'd better put that down or you'll break it. But you're right about cultural snobbery.'

Benton replaced the figurine and they returned to the table. The door opened and Padgett joined them. He said, 'I'm sorry about that. It was the college. I'm trying to persuade them to take me early. The new academic year's begun, but only just and they might make an exception. But I suppose it depends on how long you expect to be here.'

Benton knew that Kate could have pointed out that the police at present had no power to detain Padgett on the island, but didn't. She said. 'You'll have to speak to Commander Dalgliesh about that. Obviously if we had to interview you in London, perhaps at the college, it would be more inconvenient for you, and probably for them, than seeing us here.'

It was a bit disingenuous, thought Benton, but probably justified. They went through the details of all that had happened after the finding of the body, and Padgett's account agreed with that given by Maycroft and Staveley. He had helped Jago remove the rope from Oliver's neck and heard Maycroft tell Jago to put it back on its peg, but he hadn't seen or touched it subsequently. He had no idea who, if anyone, had re-entered the lighthouse.

Finally Kate said, 'We know that Mr Oliver was angry with you about dropping his blood sample overboard and we've been told that he was critical of you generally. Was that true?'

'I couldn't do anything right for him. Of course we didn't come into contact all that much. We're not supposed to speak to the visitors unless that's what they want. And he was a visitor, although he always acted as if he belonged here, had some kind of right to be on the island. But if he did speak to me it was usually to complain. Sometimes he, or Miss Oliver, was unhappy with the provisions I'd brought, or he'd say I'd got the order wrong. I just sensed that he didn't like me. He's . . . he was the kind of man who has to have someone to pick on. But I didn't kill him. I couldn't kill even an animal, let alone a man. I know some people here would like me to be guilty because I've never really settled here, that's what they mean by saying I'm not really an islander. I've never wanted to be an islander. I came here because my mother was set on it and I'll be glad to get away, start a new life, get qualified for a proper job. I'm worth something better than being an odd-job man.'

The mixture of self-pity and truculence was unattractive; Benton had to remind himself that it didn't make Padgett a killer. He said, 'And there's nothing else you want to tell us?'

Padgett gazed down at the table top then looked up and said, 'Only the smoke.'

'What smoke?'

'Well someone must have been up and about in Peregrine Cottage. They'd lit a fire. I was in the bedroom and looked out of the window, and I saw the smoke.'

Kate's voice was carefully controlled. 'At what time was this? Try to be accurate.'

'It was soon after I got back. Just before eight anyway. I know that because I usually listen to the eight o'clock news if I'm here.'

'Why didn't you mention this before?'

'You mean when we were together in the library? It didn't seem important. I thought it would make me look a fool. I mean, why shouldn't Miss Oliver light a fire?'

It was time to bring the interview to an end and return to Seal Cottage to report to Dalgliesh. They walked in silence for a time, then Kate said, 'I don't think anyone's told him about the burning of the proofs. We'll have to check that. But I wonder why not. Perhaps he's right, they don't see him as an islander. He doesn't get told anything because he's never been one of them. But if Padgett saw smoke rising from Peregrine Cottage just before eight o'clock, then he's in the clear.'

7

After breakfast on Monday morning Dalgliesh telephoned Murrelet Cottage and told Mark Yelland that he wished to see him. Yelland said he was setting out for a walk but if there was no urgency he would call in at Seal Cottage shortly before midday. Dalgliesh had expected to go to Murrelet Cottage but decided that, as Yelland probably preferred his privacy to be undisturbed, there was no point in objecting. He had had a restless night, alternately throwing off the bedclothes because he was uncomfortably hot and then waking an hour later shivering with cold. He overslept, waking finally just after eight with the beginning of a headache and heavy limbs. Like many healthy people, he regarded illness as a personal insult best countered by refusing to accept its reality. There was little a good walk in the fresh air couldn't alleviate. But this morning he wasn't sorry to let Yelland do the walking.

Yelland arrived promptly. He was wearing stout walking shoes, jeans and a denim jacket and was carrying a rucksack. Dalgliesh made no apology for disturbing his morning since none was necessary or justified. He left the cottage door open, letting in a shaft of sunlight. Yelland dumped his rucksack on the table but didn't sit.

Without preamble Dalgliesh said, 'Someone burnt the proofs of Oliver's new novel sometime on Saturday morning. I have to ask if it was you.'

Yelland took the question easily. 'No, it wasn't. I'm capable of anger, resentment, vengefulness and no doubt most other human iniquities, but I'm not childish and I'm not stupid. Burning the proofs couldn't prevent the novel being published. It probably wouldn't even cause more than the minimum inconvenience or delay.'

Dalgliesh said, 'Dennis Tremlett says that Oliver made important changes to the galleys. Those have now been lost.'

'That's unfortunate for literature and for his devotees, but I doubt whether it's of earth-shattering importance. Burning the galleys was obviously an act of personal spite, but not on my part. I was in Murrelet Cottage on Saturday until I left for a walk at about eight-thirty. I had other things on my mind than Oliver or his novel. I didn't know that he had the proofs with him, but I suppose you could say that that would be a natural assumption.'

'And there's nothing else that happened since you arrived on Combe, however small and apparently unimportant, which you feel I should know?'

'I've told you about the altercation at dinner on Friday. But as you're interested in details, I did see someone visiting Emily Holcombe on Thursday night, shortly after ten. I was coming back from walking round the island. It was dark, of course, and I only saw his figure when Roughtwood opened the door. It wasn't one of the permanent residents so I assume it was Dr Speidel. I can't think that it has any relevance to your inquiry but it's the only other incident I can recall. I've been told that Dr Speidel is now in the sickroom but I expect he'll be well enough to confirm what I said. Is that all?'

Dalgliesh said that it was, adding a customary 'for the present'.

At the door Yelland paused. 'I didn't kill Nathan Oliver. I can't be expected to feel grief at his death. I find we truly grieve for very few people. And for me he certainly isn't one. But I do regret his death. I hope you find out who strung him up. You know where I am if there's anything else you want to say.'

And he was gone.

The telephone rang as Kate and Benton arrived. Dalgliesh lifted the receiver and heard Rupert Maycroft's voice.

'I'm afraid it won't be possible for you to speak again to Dr Speidel, and probably not for some time. His temperature rose alarmingly during the night and Guy is having him transferred to a hospital in Plymouth. We have no facilities here for nursing the seriously ill. We're expecting the helicopter any minute now.'

Dalgliesh put down the receiver. Even as he did so he heard the distant rattle. Walking out again into the air, he saw Kate and Benton gazing up at the helicopter, like a noisome black beetle against the delicate blue of the morning sky.

Kate said, 'I thought that helicopter was only for emergencies. We haven't asked for reinforcements.'

Dalgliesh said, 'It is an emergency. Dr Speidel is worse. Dr Staveley thinks he needs more care than he can be given here. It's unfortunate for us, but worse, one assumes, for him.'

Speidel must have been brought out with surprising

speed and it seemed only minutes after the helicopter had landed before they were watching in silence as it rose and wheeled low above them.

'There,' said Kate, 'goes one of our suspects.'

Dalgliesh thought, *Hardly the prime suspect, but certainly the one whose evidence about the time of death is vital. The one, too, who hasn't told me all he knows.* They turned back to the cottage as the noise died away.

8

Dalgliesh's appointment to see Emily Holcombe was for eight o'clock and at seven-thirty he put out the lights in Seal Cottage and closed the door behind him. Brought up in a Norfolk rectory, he had never felt alien under starless skies, but he had seldom known blackness like this. There were no lights in the windows of Chapel Cottage; Adrian Boyde had probably left for dinner at the house. He saw no pinpricks from the distant cottages to reassure him that he was walking in the right direction. Pausing for a moment to orientate himself, he switched on his torch and set off into the darkness. The aching in his limbs had persisted all day and it occurred to him that he might be infectious and, if so, whether it was fair to call on Miss Holcombe. But he wasn't either sneezing or coughing. He would keep his distance as far as possible and, after all, if Yelland was right, she had already received Speidel in Atlantic Cottage.

Because of the rising ground which protected Atlantic Cottage on the inland side, he was almost at the door before he saw the lights in the lower windows. Roughtwood showed him into the sitting room with the condescension of a valued retainer receiving a dependant of the house come to pay his rent. The room was lit only by firelight and a single table-lamp. Miss Holcombe was sitting beside the fire, her hands resting in her lap. The firelight gleamed on the dull silk of her high-necked blouse and the black woollen skirt which fell in folds to her ankles. As Dalgliesh quietly entered, she seemed to break from a reverie and, holding out her hand, briefly touched his, then motioned him to the fireside chair opposite her own.

If Dalgliesh could imagine Emily Holcombe being solicitous, he would have detected it in her keen glance and her immediate careful thought for his comfort. The warmth of the wood-burning fire, the muted crash of the waves and the cushioned support of the high-backed armchair revived him and he leaned back in it with relief. He was offered wine, coffee or camomile tea and accepted the last gratefully. He had drunk enough coffee for one day.

Once the camomile tea had been brought in by Roughtwood, Miss Holcombe said, 'I'm sorry this is so late. Partly but not wholly it was at my convenience. I had a dental appointment which I was reluctant to cancel. Some people on this island, if they speak frankly – which they seldom do – will tell you that I am a selfish old woman. That at least I have in common with Nathan Oliver.'

'You disliked him?'

'He wasn't a man who could tolerate being liked. I have never believed that genius excuses bad behaviour. He was an iconoclast. He arrived every three months with daughter and copy-editor, stayed for two weeks, created a disturbance and succeeded in reminding us that we permanent residents are a coterie of irrelevant escapees from reality; that, like the old lighthouse, we are merely symbols, relics of the past. He punctured our complacency. To that extent he served his purpose. You could call him a necessary evil.'

Dalgliesh said, 'Wouldn't he be escaping from reality if he moved here permanently?'

'So you've been told that? I don't think he would have put it that way. In his case he would claim that he needed the solitude to fulfil his purpose as a writer. He was desperate to produce a novel as good as the one before last, despite the knowledge that his talent was fading.'

'Did he feel that?'

'Oh yes. That and a terror of death were his two great fears. And, of course, guilt. If you decide to do without a personal god it's illogical to saddle yourself with a legacy of Judeo-Christian sin. That way you suffer the psychological inconveniences of guilt without the consolation of absolution. Oliver had plenty to feel guilty about, as indeed have we all.'

There was a pause. Putting down her glass, she gazed into the dying fire. She said, 'Nathan Oliver was defined by his talent – his genius, if that's the more appropriate word. If he lost that he would become a shell. So he feared a double death. I've seen it before in brilliant and highly successful men I've known – still know. Women seem to face the inevitable with more stoicism. You can't miss it. I go to London for three weeks once a year to visit those of my friends who are still alive and to remind myself what I'm escaping from. Oliver was frightened and insecure but he didn't kill himself. We've all been confused about his death, we still are. Whatever the evidence to the contrary, suicide still seems the only possible explanation. But I can't believe it. And he wouldn't have chosen that way – the ugliness, the horror, the degradation of it; a method of self-extinction which mirrors all those pathetic victims twisting from their gibbets down the centuries. Executioners using the victim's own body to choke out life – is that why we find it so abhorrent? No, Nathan Oliver wouldn't have throttled himself. His method would be mine: drink and drugs, a comfortable bed, an appropriately worded goodbye if the mood took him. He'd have gone gentle into that good night.'

There was silence, then she said, 'I was there, as you know. Not when he died, of course, but when he was cut down. Only it wasn't a cutting down. Rupert and Guy couldn't decide whether to lower him or pull him up. For minutes that seemed to stretch interminably he was a human yo-yo. It was then I left. I have my share of curiosity but I discovered in myself an atavistic repugnance to seeing a corpse mishandled. Death imposes certain conventions. You, of course, get used to it.'

Dalgliesh said, 'No, Miss Holcombe, we don't get used to it.'

'My dislike of him was more personal than general disapproval of his character defects. He wanted to get me out of this cottage. Under the Trust deed I have a right to residence here, but the deed doesn't specify what accommodation I should be offered, whether I have a choice, whether I can bring my servant with me. To that extent I suppose it's arguable he had a slight cause for resentment, although he always came with his own appendages. Rupert will have told you that he couldn't really be turned away, certainly not on the grounds that he was obnoxious. The Trust deed says that no one shall be refused admission if he or she was born on the island. It's a safe enough provision. No one has been born here since the eighteenth century except Nathan Oliver and he only qualified because his mother mistook her labour pains for indigestion and he was born two weeks prematurely and, I gather, in something of a rush. He was particularly persistent this visit. Oliver's proposal was that I move into Puffin Cottage, making this one available to him. It sounds all very reasonable, but I had – still have – no intention of moving.'

None of this was new, and it was not for this that Dalgliesh had come to Atlantic Cottage. He sensed that she knew why he was here. She bent to put another small log on the fire but he forestalled her and edged it gently on to the flames. Blue tongues licked the dry wood and the firelight strengthened, burnishing the polished mahogany and casting its glow over the spines of the leather books, the stone floor and the richly coloured rugs. Emily Holcombe leant forwards and held out her long heavily ringed fingers to the flames. He saw her face in profile, the fine features etched against the flames like a cameo. She sat in silence for a minute. Dalgliesh, resting his head against the back of the chair, felt the ache in his legs and arms gently ease. He knew that soon she would have to speak and he must be ready to listen, missing nothing of the story she was at last prepared to tell. He wished that his head didn't feel so heavy, that he could overcome this urge to shut his eyes and give himself over to the quietude and the comfort.

Then she said, 'I'm ready for some more wine', and passed over her glass. He half filled it and poured himself a second cup of tea. It tasted of nothing, but the hot liquid was comforting.

She said, 'I've put off making this appointment to see you because there were two people I needed first to consult. Now that Raimund Speidel has been taken to hospital I've decided to take his permission for granted. In doing that I'm assuming that you won't give the story more weight than it can bear. It's an old story and most of it known only to me. It can throw no light on Nathan Oliver's death, but in the end it must be for you to decide.'

Dalgliesh said, 'I spoke to Dr Speidel on Saturday afternoon. He didn't mention that he'd already spoken to you. He gave the impression of a man who was still seeking the truth rather than one who'd found it, but I don't think he was being completely candid. Of course, he wasn't well at the time. He may have thought it was prudent to await events.'

She said, 'And now, with Dr Speidel seriously ill and safely out of your reach, you'd like the truth, the whole truth and nothing but the truth. That must be the most futile oath anyone ever swears. I don't know the whole truth, but I can tell you what I do know.'

She leaned back in the chair and gazed into the fire. Dalgliesh kept his eyes on her face.

'I'm sure you've been told something of the history of Combe Island. It was acquired by my family in the sixteenth century. By then it was already a place of ill repute and half-superstitious horror. In the sixteenth century it had been taken over by pirates from the Mediterranean who preyed on the coasts of southern England, captured young men and women and sold them into slavery. Thousands were taken in this way and the island was dreaded as a place of imprisonment, rape and torture. To this day it's unpopular with local people and we used to have some difficulty finding temporary staff. The ones we have are all loyal and reliable, and are mostly incomers untroubled by folk history. My family were also untroubled by it during the years when we owned Combe. It was my grandfather who built the house and I came here every year as a child, and later as an adolescent. Nathan Oliver's father, Saul, was the boatman and general factotum. He was a fine sailor but a difficult man, given to violence fuelled by drink. After the death of his wife he was left to bring up the boy. I used to see Nathan when he was a young boy and I in my teens. He was an odd, very self-contained child, uncommunicative but strong willed. Strangely enough I got on rather well with his father, although in those days anything approaching real friendship between myself and one of the servants would have been discouraged, indeed unthinkable.'

She paused, holding out her glass as he poured the wine. She took a few sips before resuming her story. 'When war broke out it was decided that the island must be evacuated. It wasn't regarded as particularly vulnerable to attack but there wasn't fuel for the launch. We stayed on for the year of the phoney war, but by October 1940, after the fall of France and the death at Dunkirk of my brother, my parents decided it would be wisest to leave. We retreated to the main house near Exmoor, and the next year I was due to go to Oxford. The evacuation of the few staff we still had was managed by the then steward and Saul Oliver. After Oliver had landed the last of the staff on the mainland, he and the boy came back because he said he had some final tasks and was worried that the house wasn't as secure as it could be. He proposed to stay for one extra night. He came in his own sailing boat, not the motor launch we then had.'

She paused, and Dalgliesh said, 'Do you remember what date that was?'

'Tenth of October 1940. From now on I'm recounting what was told to me years later by Saul Oliver when hardly coherent and within two weeks of his death. I don't know whether he wanted to confess or boast – perhaps both – or why he chose me. I had lost touch with him during and after the war. I cut my university career short and went to London to drive an ambulance, then returned to Oxford and only rarely came back to the West Country. Nathan had long since left Combe and embarked on his self-imposed task of making himself into a writer. I don't think he ever saw his father again. Saul's story wasn't altogether new to me. There had been rumours, there always are. But I think I got as much of the truth as he was prepared to tell.

'During the night of tenth October three Germans from the occupied Channel Islands landed on Combe. Until this week I knew the names of none of them. It was an extraordinarily risky journey, probably a venture by bored young officers either making a reconnaissance or planning some private enterprise. Either they knew that the island had been evacuated or they found it by chance. Speidel thinks they may have planned to plant the German flag on the top of the disused lighthouse. It would certainly have caused some consternation. Some time after first light they went to the top of the lighthouse, presumably to spy out the land. While they were there, Saul Oliver discovered their boat and guessed where they were. The ground floor of the lighthouse was then used to house fodder for the animals and was packed with dry straw. He set this alight and the flames and smoke billowed up into the top chamber. Soon the whole interior was in flames. They couldn't escape on to the lantern. The railings had become unsafe and the door had long since been nailed up to prevent accidents. All three Germans died, probably by suffocation. Saul waited until the fire was burnt out, discovered the bodies halfway up the tower and carried them back to their boat. He then took it out with the dinghy from the sailing boat and scuttled it in deep water.'

Dalgliesh asked, 'Was there any evidence for this story?'

'Only the trophies he kept: a revolver, a pair of binoculars and a compass. As far as I know, no other boat landed during the war and after the war no inquiries were made. The three young officers – I assume they were officers since they were able to take the boat – were probably listed as missing, presumed drowned. The arrival of Dr Speidel last week was the first confirmation of the truth of the story other than the souvenirs that Saul gave me before he died.'

'What did you do with them?'

'I threw them into the sea. I regarded his action as murder and I had no wish to be reminded of something I wished I hadn't been told. I saw no point in getting in touch with the German authorities. The men's families – if there were families – could have received no comfort from the story. The soldiers had died horribly and to no purpose.'

Dalgliesh said, 'But it isn't the whole story, is it? Saul Oliver wasn't old and presumably he was strong, but even if he could carry three young men one by one down all those stairs and to the harbour, how did he manage to scuttle the boat and row back in the darkness unaided? Wasn't there someone on the island with him?'

Miss Holcombe picked up the brass poker and levered it under the log. The fire leapt into life. She said, 'He had taken the child Nathan with him and another man, Tom Tamlyn, Jago's grandfather.'

Dalgliesh said, 'Has Nathan Oliver ever spoken of this?'

'Not to me and, as far as I know, not to anyone. If he had remembered what happened I think that, somehow, he would have made use of it. After the boat had been scuttled and most of the evidence destroyed Saul and Tom returned to Combe and later, with the child, set out for the mainland. By then it was dark. Tom Tamlyn never reached shore. It was a stormy night and a bad journey. A lesser sailor than Saul wouldn't have made it. His story was that Tamlyn, helping to control the boat, fell overboard. The body was washed up six weeks later further down the coast. There wasn't enough of it to yield much information, but the back of the skull had been smashed. Saul claimed that this happened during the accident, but the coroner returned an open verdict and the Tamlyns have always believed that Tom was murdered by Oliver. The motive, of course, was to conceal what had happened on the island.'

Dalgliesh said, 'But at the time it could have seemed a

justifiable act of war, particularly if Saul had alleged that he was threatened by the Germans. They were, after all, armed. If Tamlyn was murdered, there must have been a stronger reason. I wonder why Saul Oliver insisted in the first place on being last on the island. Surely the steward would have ensured that the house was secure. And what did they do with the boy, a four-year-old, while they were disposing of bodies? They could hardly have left him to roam about unattended.'

Miss Holcombe said, 'Saul told me that they locked him in my nursery at the top of the house. They left milk and some food. There was a small bed there and plenty of toys. Saul lifted him on to my old rocking horse. I remember that horse. I loved Pegasus. It was immense, a magical beast. But it went with much else to be sold. There would be no more Holcombe children. I'm the last of my family.'

Was there a note of regret in her voice? Dalgliesh thought not, but it was difficult to tell. She gazed into the fire for a moment, then went on. 'When they returned the boy had slipped off it and had crawled over to the window. They found him fast asleep, or perhaps unconscious. He was kept below in the cabin during the voyage back to the mainland. According to his father, he remembered nothing.'

Dalgliesh said, 'There's still a difficulty about motive. Did Saul Oliver confess to you that he had murdered Tamlyn?'

'No. He wasn't drunk enough for that. He stuck to the story of the accident.'

'But he did tell you something else?'

And now she looked him full in the face. 'He told me

that it was the boy who set the straw alight. He was playing with a box of matches he'd found in the house. Afterwards, of course, he panicked and denied he'd been near the lighthouse but Saul told me he'd seen him.'

'And you believed him?'

Again she paused. 'I did at the time. Now I'm not so sure. But true or not, surely it's irrelevant to Nathan Oliver's death. Raimund Speidel is a civilised, humane and intelligent man. He wouldn't take revenge on a child. Jago Tamlyn has made no secret of his dislike of Nathan Oliver, but if he wanted to murder him he's had plenty of opportunity over the last few years. That's if Oliver was murdered, and I suppose you know by now, don't you?'

'Yes,' said Dalgliesh. 'We know.'

'Then the reason may lay in the past, but not in this past.'

The recital had tired her. She leaned back again in her chair and sat in silence.

Dalgliesh said, 'Thank you. It explains why Speidel wanted to meet Nathan Oliver in the lighthouse. That puzzled me. After all, it isn't the only secluded place on Combe. Did you tell Dr Speidel everything you have told me?'

'Everything. Like you, he couldn't believe that Saul Oliver had acted alone.'

'He knew that Oliver claimed that his son had lit the fire?'

'Yes, I passed on everything Saul had told me. I thought Dr Speidel had a right to know.'

'And the rest of the island? How much of this is known to others on Combe?'

'None of it, unless Jago has spoken, which I think unlikely. How could he know? Nathan Oliver was told nothing by his father and has never spoken about his life on Combe until seven years ago when he suddenly decided, apparently, that a comparatively deprived and motherless childhood on an island would be an interesting addition to the little he allowed to be known about his life. It was then that he began taking advantage of the clause in the Trust deed which allowed him to come here whenever he wished. He respected the convention that those who come here never reveal the existence of Combe until April 2003 when he was interviewed by a journalist from one of the Sunday broadsheets. Unhappily the story was taken up by the tabloid press. They didn't make much of it, but it was an irritating breach of confidence and certainly didn't add to Oliver's popularity here.'

And now it was time to go. Rising from the chair, Dalgliesh was for a second overcome with weakness, but he grasped the back of the chair and the moment passed. The ache in his arms and legs was worse and he wondered whether he would be able to make it to the door. Suddenly he was aware that Roughtwood was standing in the doorway, Dalgliesh's coat over his arm. He put out a hand and switched on a light. In the harsh brightness Dalgliesh felt for a second dazzled. Then their eyes met. Roughtwood was looking at him with no attempt to conceal his resentment. He escorted Dalgliesh to the door of the cottage as if he were a prisoner under escort, and his 'Goodnight, sir', sounded in Dalgliesh's ears as menacing as a challenge.

9

He had no memory of walking back across the scrubland. It seemed that his body had been transported, mysteriously and instantaneously, from Emily Holcombe's fire-lit sitting room to this stone-walled monastic emptiness. He moved over to the fireplace, holding chair backs for support, and knelt and put a match to the kindling. There was a puff of pungent smoke and then the fire took hold. Blue and red flames flared from the crackling wood. He had been overheated in Atlantic Cottage; now his forehead was wet with globules of cold sweat. With careful art he placed small twigs around the flames then built a pyramid of larger sticks. His hands seemed to have no relation to the rest of his body and when he held out his long fingers to the comfort of the strengthening fire, they glowed translucent red, frail disembodied images incapable of feeling heat.

After a few minutes he stood upright, glad that he was now firmer on his feet. Although his body was responding with painful clumsiness to his will, his mind was clear. He knew what was wrong: he must have caught Dr Speidel's influenza. He hoped that he hadn't infected Miss Holcombe. So far as he could remember he hadn't sneezed or coughed while in the cottage. He had touched her hand only briefly on arriving and had sat distanced from her. At eighty she must have built up a healthy resistance to most infections and she had been given her annual anti-flu injection. With luck she would be all right. He devoutly hoped so. But it would be sensible to call off the meeting with Kate and Benton, or at least keep away from them and make it short.

Because of his meeting with Miss Holcombe the nightly get-together had been arranged later than usual at ten o'clock. It must already be that now. Looking at his watch it showed nine-fifty. They would be coming across the scrubland. He opened the door and moved out into the darkness. There were no stars and the low cloud-base had hidden even the moon. Only the sea was visible, stretching faintly luminescent and peaceful under a black emptiness, more threatening and elemental than the absence of light. It would be easy to believe that even breathing could become difficult in this thickened air. There were no lights in Chapel Cottage, but Combe House showed pale rectangles like signals from a distant ship on an invisible ocean.

But then he saw a figure emerging like a wraith out of the darkness, making unerringly for the door of Chapel Cottage. It was Adrian Boyde coming home. He was carrying a long narrow box on his right shoulder. It looked like a coffin but no heavy object could be carried so lightly – almost, it seemed, with gaiety. And then Dalgliesh realised what it must be. He had seen it earlier in Mrs Burbridge's sewing room. This surely was the box with the embroidered cope. He watched while Boyde put it gently down and opened the door. Then he hesitated and after a moment picked up the box and made off towards the chapel.

And then Dalgliesh saw a different light, a small pool like a grounded moon which gently wavered towards him over the scrubland, was lost for a moment in a copse of trees and then reappeared. Kate and Benton were on time. He went back into the cottage and arranged three chairs – two at the table, his own against the wall. He placed a bottle of wine and two glasses on the table and waited. He would pass on to Kate and Benton what Miss Holcombe had told him and that would be all for today. After they'd gone he would have a hot shower, make a milk drink, take some soluble aspirins and sweat out the infection. He'd done it before. Kate and Benton could do the legwork but he had to stay well enough to direct the investigation. He *would* be well enough.

They came in peeling off their coats and dumping them in the porch. Looking at him, Kate said, 'Are you all right, sir?'

She was trying to keep the concern out of her voice. She knew how much he disliked being ill.

'Not entirely, Kate. I think I've caught Dr Speidel's flu. Take these two seats and don't come any closer. We can't all get sick. Benton, see to the wine will you, and put some more logs on the fire. I'll tell you what I've learnt from Miss Holcombe and then we'd better call it a day.'

They listened to him in silence. Sitting back, distanced, he saw them as if they were strangers or actors in a play, their contrived and deliberate scene carefully composed – Kate's fair hair and her face ruddied by the firelight; Benton's dark gravity as he poured the wine.

When he finished talking Kate said, 'It's interesting, sir, but it doesn't really get us much further except to strengthen Dr Speidel's motive. But I can't see him as Calcraft. He came to try and find out the truth of his father's death, not to wreak revenge for something a kid might or might not have done over sixty years before. It doesn't make sense.'

Benton said, 'It's strengthened Jago's motive. I suppose he must know the rumour that old man Oliver killed his grandfather on that trip together.'

Dalgliesh said, 'Oh yes, he knew it from childhood. Apparently most of the sailing fraternity in Pentworthy knew it or else suspected. They won't have forgotten.'

Benton went on, 'But if he was planning revenge, why wait until now? He could hardly have chosen a worse time with the island half empty. And why the lighthouse and that bizarre hanging? Why not just fake another accident when he'd got Oliver on the boat. There'd be a certain justice in that. We get back to that every time. Why now?'

Kate said, 'Isn't it a bit odd that Saul Oliver wanted to come back to the island? Do you think there was something valuable he wanted to steal or perhaps hide here until after the war when he'd retrieve it? Maybe he and Jago's granddad arranged it between them and Oliver killed him so that he wouldn't have to share the loot. Or am I being fanciful?'

Benton objected, 'But even if true that doesn't help us. We're not investigating the possible murder of Jago's granddad. Whatever happened on that last trip, we're not going to learn the truth of it now.'

Dalgliesh said, 'I think that this murder has its roots in the past, but not in the distant past. We have to ask ourselves the same question. Did something happen between Nathan Oliver's last visit in July of this year and his arrival last week? What caused one or more people on this island to decide that Oliver must die? I don't think we can get any further tonight. I want you to go and speak to Jago first thing tomorrow morning, then come and report to me. It may be distressing for him but I think we've got to learn the truth about the suicide of his sister. And there's another thing. Why was he so anxious that Millie shouldn't join in the search for Oliver? Why shouldn't she help? Was he trying to protect her from seeing that hanging body? When he was called to help search did he already know what they were going to find?'

BOOK FOUR

Under Cover of Darkness

I

Kate knew where to find Jago – in his boat. As she and Benton made their way down the steep pebbled path to the harbour shortly before eight o'clock on Tuesday morning, they could see his stocky figure moving about the launch. Beyond the calm of the harbour the sea was frisky. The wind was rising, bringing with it the compounded smells of the island: sea, earth, the first faint trace of autumn. Frail clouds moved like tattered paper across the morning sky.

Jago must have seen them coming, but he gave only one quick upward glance until they were on the quayside. By the time they were alongside the launch he had disappeared into the cabin. They waited until he chose to reappear, carrying a couple of cushions which he flung on the seat in the stern of the boat.

Kate said, 'Good morning. We'd like a word.'

'Then make it brief.' He added, 'No offence but I'm busy.'

'So are we. Shall we go to your cottage?'

'What's wrong with here?

'The cottage would be more private.'

'It's private enough here. People don't come messing about when I'm on the launch. Still, it's all the same to me.'

They followed him along the quay to Harbour Cottage. Kate wasn't sure why she preferred the interview

355

not to be on the launch. Perhaps it was because the boat was uniquely his place; the cottage, still his, but more like neutral ground. The door stood open. Sunlight laid patterns over the stone floor. Kate and Benton hadn't entered the cottage on their previous visit. Now, mysteriously, as if she had known it for years, the room imposed its atmosphere upon her; the bare scrubbed table and the two Windsor chairs, the open fireplace, the cork board almost covering one wall with a large-scale map of the island, the tide timetable, a poster of birdlife, a few notes stuck in with drawing pins, and beside it an enlarged sepia photograph, wooden-framed, of a bearded man. The resemblance to Jago was unmistakable. Father or grandfather? Probably the latter: the photograph looked old, the pose unrelaxed.

Jago made a movement towards the chairs and they sat down. This time Benton, after a glance at Kate, didn't take out his notebook.

Kate said, 'We want to talk about what happened in the lighthouse in the early months of the war. We know that three German soldiers died there and that their bodies and the boat they came in were dumped out to sea. We're told the person responsible was Nathan Oliver's father, Saul, and that Nathan Oliver himself was on the island at the time. He must have been four years old, little more than a toddler.'

She paused. Jago looked at her. 'You've been speaking to Emily Holcombe most likely.'

'Not only to her. Dr Speidel seems to have discovered much of the story.'

Kate glanced at Benton, who said, 'But Oliver's father couldn't have done that unaided surely. Three grown men to be carried down the lighthouse stairs and on to the boat, their bodies then weighted with rocks presumably, the boat to be scuppered. And then Saul Oliver's own boat would've had to be alongside to take him back to shore. Was there someone with him? Your grandfather?'

'That's right. Granddad was here. He and Saul Oliver were the last off Combe.'

'So what happened?'

'Why ask me? You got it from Miss Holcombe seemingly, and she must have got it from Saul. He was boatman here when she was a child. There's not much he wouldn't have told Miss Holcombe.'

'How did you know about all this?'

'Dad got to know when he grew up. He told me. Got most of it out of Saul Oliver when he was drunk. And there were one or two old 'uns in Pentworthy who knew about Saul Oliver. There were stories.'

Benton said, 'What stories?'

'Granddad never got back to Pentworthy alive. Saul Oliver killed him and threw his body overboard. He said it was an accident, but folk knew. My granddad wasn't a man to have an accident on board a boat. He was a better seaman than Oliver. Nothing was proved, of course. But that's what happened.'

Kate said, 'How long have you known these facts, if they are facts?'

'They're facts all right. Like I said, nothing could be proved at the time. A body with a smashed skull but no witnesses. The police did try to talk to the boy but he'd nothing to tell. Either that or he was in shock. But I don't need proof. Nathan Oliver's father killed my grandfather. It was well enough known in Pentworthy – still is by the few like Miss Holcombe who're still living.'

There was a silence, then Jago said, 'If you're thinking I had a motive for killing Nathan Oliver, you're right. I had a motive all right. I've had a motive since I was first told the tale. I was about eleven then, so if I wanted to avenge granddad I've had close on twenty-three years to do it. And I wouldn't have strung him up. I've had him on that launch alone often enough. That would've been the way to do it. Let him go overboard like granddad. And I wouldn't have chosen a time when the island was quarter empty.'

Kate said, 'We now know that Oliver must have died shortly after eight, when you say you were testing the launch. Tell us again which direction you took.'

'I went out to sea about half a mile. That was enough to test the engine.'

'From that distance you must have had a clear view of the lighthouse. The fog didn't come up thickly until shortly before ten. Surely you must have seen the body.'

'Might've done if I'd looked. I'd enough to do managing the boat without scanning the shore.' He got up. 'And now, if enough's been said, I'll get back to the boat. You know where to find me.'

Benton said, 'That isn't good enough, Tamlyn. Why did you try to stop Millie joining the search? Why order her to stay in the cottage? It doesn't make sense.'

Jago looked at him with hard eyes. 'And if I did see him dangling, what could I do about it? It was too late then to save him. He'd be found soon enough. I had my job to do.'

'So you admit you did see Mr Oliver's body hanging from the railings?'

'I'm admitting nothing. But there's one thing you'd best keep in mind. If I was in the launch at eight o'clock I couldn't be in the lighthouse stringing him up. And now I'd like to get back to the launch if you'll excuse me.'

Kate said as gently as she could, 'There's one other thing I have to ask. I'm sorry if it brings back distressing memories. Didn't your sister hang herself some years ago?'

Jago bent on her a look of such black intensity that for a second Kate thought he might strike her and Benton made a spontaneous movement, quickly checked. But Jago's voice was calm although his eyes never left Kate's.

'Yeah. Debbie. Six years ago. After she was raped. That was no seduction. It was rape.'

'And did you feel the need to take revenge?'

'I took it, didn't I? Got twelve months for GBH. Didn't anyone tell you that I'd got a record before you came here? I put him in hospital for three weeks, give or take a day. Worse for him, the local publicity didn't do his garage business much good and his wife left him. I couldn't bring Debbie back but by God I made him pay.'

'When did you attack him?'

'The day after Debbie told me. She was just sixteen. You can read about it in the local paper if you're interested. He called it seduction but he didn't deny it. Are you saying you thought it could've been Oliver? That's daft.'

'We needed to know the facts, Mr Tamlyn, that's all.'

Jago's laugh was hoarse. 'They say revenge is a dish

best served cold, but not that cold! If I wanted to kill Nathan Oliver he'd have been overboard years ago, same as my granddad was.'

He didn't wait for them to get up but strode at once to the door and disappeared. Moving into the sunshine they watched him leaping easily aboard the launch.

Kate said, 'He's right of course. If he wanted to kill Oliver why wait for over twenty years? Why choose the most unpropitious weekend, and why that method? He doesn't know the whole story about the lighthouse, does he? Either that or he's not saying. He didn't mention that the kid himself could have started that blaze.'

Benton said, 'But would that have worried him, ma'am? Would anyone take vengeance on an elderly man because of something he'd done as a four-year-old? If he hated Oliver – and I think he did – it must be for something more recent, perhaps something very recent, which gave him no choice but to act now.'

It was then that Kate's radio beeped. She listened to the message, then gazed at Benton. Her eyes must have told him all. She watched his face change, shock, disbelief and horror mirroring her own.

She said, 'That was AD. We've got another body.'

2

On the previous night, after Kate and Benton had gone, Dalgliesh locked the door, more from the habit of ensuring privacy and security than from any thought that there was danger. The fire was dying but he placed the guard in front of it. He washed the two wine glasses and replaced them in the kitchen cupboard then checked the cork on the wine bottle. It was half empty but they would finish the wine tomorrow. All these small actions took an inordinate time. He found himself standing in the kitchen trying to remember what he was there for. Of course, the hot drink. He decided against it, knowing that the smell of the heated milk would sicken him.

The stairs seemed to have become very steep and he grasped the rail and dragged himself painfully upstairs. The hot shower was an exhausting ordeal rather than a pleasure, but it was good to get rid of the sour smell of sweat. Lastly, he took two aspirin from the first-aid cupboard, drew back the curtains from the half-open window and climbed into bed. The sheets and pillowcases were comfortingly cool. Lying on his right side he stared into the darkness, seeing only the rectangle of the window printed palely against the blackness of the wall.

It was first light when he awoke, his hair and the pillow hot and dank with sweat. The aspirin had at least brought down his temperature. Perhaps all would be well. But the ache in his limbs was worse and he was possessed of a heavy weariness which made intolerable even the effort of getting out of bed. He closed his eyes. A dream remained, trailing faint tatters of memory, like soiled rags across his mind, half-dissolving but still clear enough to leave a legacy of unease.

He was marrying Emma, not in the college chapel, but in his father's Norfolk church. It was a blazing hot day in midsummer, but Emma was wearing a black dress, high-necked and long-sleeved, its heavy folds trailing behind her. He couldn't see her face because her head was covered with a thick patterned veil. His mother was there, plaintively complaining that Emma should be wearing her own wedding dress – she had saved it carefully for his bride. But Emma refused to change. The Commissioner and Harkness were there in formal uniform, braid glistening on their shoulders and caps. But he wasn't dressed. He was standing on the rectory lawn wearing only a singlet and underpants. No one seemed to think it remarkable. He couldn't find his clothes and the church bell was tolling and his father, fantastically robed in a green cope and mitre, was telling him that everyone was waiting. They were crossing the lawn to the church in droves – parishioners he had known from childhood, the people his father had buried, murderers he had helped to send to prison, Kate in bridesmaid's pink. He had to find his clothes. He had to get to the church. He had somehow to silence the sound of the bell.

And there was a bell. Suddenly wide awake, he realised that the phone was ringing.

He stumbled down the stairs and picked up the receiver. A voice said, 'Maycroft here. Is Adrian with you? I've been trying to reach him but there's no answer from the cottage. He wouldn't have left for work yet.'

The voice was insistent, unnaturally loud. Dalgliesh wouldn't have recognised it as Maycroft's. And then he recognised something else – the unmistakable urgency of fear.

He said, 'No, he's not here. I saw him coming home at about ten last night. Perhaps he's taking a morning walk.'

'He doesn't usually. He sometimes leaves his cottage by eight-thirty and takes his time arriving, but it's too early for that. I've some urgent and distressing news for you both. I need to speak to him.'

Dalgliesh said, 'Hold on, I'll take a look.'

He went to the door and looked out over the scrubland towards Chapel Cottage. There was no sign of life. He would have to go to the cottage and, perhaps look in the chapel, but both seemed mysteriously to have distanced themselves. His aching legs felt not to belong to him. It would take time. He went back to the telephone.

'I'll see if he's in his cottage or the chapel.' He added, 'It may take a little time. I'll ring back.'

His rainproof jacket was hanging in the porch. He tugged it on over his dressing-gown and urged his naked feet into outdoor shoes. A frail morning mist rose from the headland promising another fine day, and the air smelt sweetly damp. Its freshness revived him and he walked more steadily than he had thought possible. The door of Chapel Cottage wasn't locked. He opened it and gave a shout which made his throat ache, but it evoked no response. Crossing the sitting room, he clambered up the wooden stairs to check the bedroom. The counter-pane was stretched over the bed and, turning it back, he saw that the bed was made up.

He had no memory of crossing the fifty yards of stone-littered grass to the chapel. The half door was closed and, briefly, he leaned against it, glad of the support.

And then, raising his eyes, he saw the body. He had no doubt, even as he unlatched the door, that Boyde was dead. He was lying on the stone floor a foot from the improvised altar, his left hand protruding from the edge of the cope, the white fingers stiffly curved as if beckoning him forward. The cope had been thrown or placed over the whole of the rest of the body and through the green silk he could see the dark stains of blood. The folding chair had been opened and the long cardboard box rested on it, the tissue paper spilling out.

And now he was acting from instinct. He must touch nothing until he was wearing his gloves. Shock revitalised him and he found himself half-running, half-stumbling back to Seal Cottage, oblivious of pain. He paused for a few seconds to calm his breathing, then picked up the receiver.

'Maycroft, I'm afraid I have shocking news. We have another death. Boyde has been murdered. I've found his body in the chapel.'

There was a silence so absolute that he could almost believe the line was dead. He waited. Then Maycroft's voice again. 'You're sure? It's not an accident, it's not suicide?'

'I'm sure. This is murder. I shall need everyone on the island brought together as soon as possible.'

Maycroft said, 'Hold on, will you. I've got Guy here.'

Then there was Staveley's voice. He said, 'Rupert was ringing with a message for you both. I'm afraid it's going to make your job doubly difficult. Dr Speidel has SARS. I thought it was a possibility when I transferred him to Plymouth and the diagnosis has now been confirmed. I'm not sure that it will be possible for you to bring in reinforcements. The sensible thing would be for the island to be quarantined and I'm in touch with the authorities about this. Rupert and I are ringing everyone to let them know and later we'll get them together so that I can explain the medical implications. There's no need for anyone to panic. Your news turns a difficult situation into a tragedy. It will also make the medical situation much more difficult to manage.'

It sounded like an accusation, and perhaps it was. And Staveley's voice had changed too. Dalgliesh had never heard it so calmly and reassuringly authoritative. He stopped speaking but Dalgliesh could catch the mutter of voices. The two men were conferring. Staveley came back on the line. 'Are you all right, Commander? You must have inhaled Speidel's breath when you helped him after he collapsed and went with him back to his cottage. You, and Jo who nursed him, are the two most at risk.'

He didn't mention himself; he didn't need to. Dalgliesh asked quietly, 'What are the symptoms?'

'Initially much the same as flu – high temperature, aching limbs, loss of energy. There may not be a cough until later.'

Dalgliesh didn't reply but his silence was eloquent. Staveley's voice was more urgent. 'Rupert and I will bring up the buggy. Meanwhile, keep warm.'

Dalgliesh found his voice. 'I have to call my colleagues urgently. They'll need the buggy. I can walk.'

'Don't be ridiculous. We'll be on our way.'

The receiver was put down. All his limbs ached and he could feel the energy draining from his body as if even his blood were flowing sluggishly. He sat down and got Kate on her radio.

He said, 'Are you with Jago? Come here as quickly as you can. Commandeer the buggy and don't let Maycroft or Staveley stop you. Say nothing to Jago, of course. We have another body – Adrian Boyde.'

The pause was only momentary. Kate said, 'Yes, sir. We're on our way.'

He clicked open his case and put on his search gloves, then went back to the chapel, walking with his eyes on the ground, watching for unusual marks. There was small hope of identifiable footprints on the sandy turf and he saw none. Inside the chapel, crouching at the head of the body, he gently lifted the neck of the cope. The lower part of Boyde's face had been smashed to a pulp, the right eye invisible under a swollen carapace of congealing blood. The left had disappeared. The nose was a splinter of bones. Gently he felt the neck and then the outstretched fingers of the left hand. How could human flesh be so cold? The hand was rigid, as were the muscles of the neck. Rigor mortis was well established; Boyde must have died last night. The killer could have been waiting for him in the chapel, have been outside in the occlusive darkness, watching and listening, or could have seen Boyde leaving Combe House and followed him across the scrubland. One thought was particularly bitter for Dalgliesh. If he had only stood at the door of

Seal Cottage for a few more minutes last night watching Boyde arriving home, he might have seen a second figure emerging from the darkness. While he had been conferring with Kate and Benton the killer could already have been at work.

Painfully he got to his feet and stood at the foot of the body. The silence was numinous, broken only by the sound of the sea. He listened to it, not in the sense of being aware of the rhythmic crash of the waves against the unyielding granite, but letting the perpetual sound enter into some deeper level of consciousness so that it became an eternal lament for the unhealable anguish of the world. He supposed that if anyone had seen him so motionless, they would have thought that he was bending his head in reverence. And so in a sense he was. He was filled with a terrible sadness fused with the bitterness of failure, a burden which he knew he had to accept and live with. Boyde should not have died. It was no comfort to tell himself that there had been no evidence to suggest that after Oliver's death anyone else had been at risk, that he had no powers to detain a suspect on a vague suspicion that he could be guilty, no power even to prevent anyone leaving the island unless he had evidence to justify an arrest. He knew only one thing: Boyde should not have died. There were not two killers among the small company on Combe. If he had solved Oliver's murder in the past three days Adrian Boyde would still be alive.

And now his ears caught the sound of the approaching buggy. Benton was driving with Kate at his side, Maycroft and Staveley in the back seats. So they had got their way. The buggy stopped some thirty feet from the chapel. Kate and Benton got down and walked towards him.

Dalgliesh called to them, 'Don't come any closer. Kate, this means you'll have to take over.'

Their eyes met. Kate seemed to have difficulty speaking. Then she said calmly, 'Yes, sir, of course.'

Dalgliesh said, 'Boyde's been battered to death. The face has been destroyed. The weapon could be a stone. If so, Calcraft could have thrown it into the sea. The last sighting of Boyde was probably by me last night just before you arrived. You didn't see him when you were crossing the scrubland?'

Kate said, 'No, sir. It was pitch dark and we kept our eyes on the ground. We had a torch but I don't think he could've been carrying one. I think we'd have noticed a moving light.'

And now Maycroft and Staveley were coming purposefully towards him. They were without coats and had facemasks hanging round their necks. In the brightening light, which seemed to have grown unreal, the buggy looked as strange as a moon vehicle. He felt like an actor in some bizarre theatrical enterprise in which he was expected to play the lead without knowing the plot or having sight of the script.

He called in a voice he hardly recognised, 'I'll come, but I need to finish talking to my colleagues.'

They nodded without speaking and moved a little back.

Dalgliesh spoke to Kate. 'I'll try to telephone Mr Harkness and Dr Glenister when I get to the house. You'd better speak to them too. She should be able to examine and collect the body if she and the helicopter crew keep away from people. You'll have to leave it to her. The exhibits can go with her to the lab. If there's any chance of searching the foreshore safely for the weapon you may need Jago. I don't think he's our man. Don't climb, either of you, unless it's safe.' He took out his pocketbook and scribbled a note. 'Before the news breaks, could you phone Emma Lavenham on this number and try to reassure her? I'll try to speak to her from the house but it may not be possible. And Kate, don't let them move me from the island if you can help it.'

'No, sir, I won't.'

There was a pause, then he said, as if the words were difficult to form, 'Tell her ...', and stopped. Kate waited. Then he said, 'Give her my love.'

He walked as steadily as he could towards the buggy and the two figures raised their masks and moved towards him. He said, 'I don't want the buggy. I'm capable of walking.'

Neither man spoke, but the buggy wobbled into life and turned. Dalgliesh walked beside it for nearly thirty yards before Kate and Benton, rooted and watching, saw him stumble and be lifted aboard.

3

Kate and Benton watched the buggy trundle out of sight.

Kate said, 'We need gloves. We'll use Mr Dalgliesh's for now.'

The door of Seal Cottage was open and the murder case, also open, was on the table. They put on gloves and returned to the chapel. With Benton standing beside her, Kate squatted beside the body and lifted a corner of the cope. She studied the mess of congealed blood and smashed bones which had been Boyde's face, then gently touched the ice-cold fingers locked into rigor mortis. She felt herself shaking with emotions that she knew she must somehow control, a sick horror, anger and a pity which was more difficult to bear than either anger or revulsion. She was aware of Benton's breathing but did not look up to meet his eyes.

Waiting to control her voice, she said, 'He died here, and probably soon after he arrived home last night. Calcraft could have thrown the stone – or whatever it was – felled Boyde, and then decided to finish the job. This was hatred. Either that or he lost all control.'

She had seen it before: killers, often first-time murderers, possessed by horror and disbelief at the enormity of what they had done, striking out in a frenzy as if by destroying the face they could obliterate the deed itself.

Benton said, 'Boyde couldn't have been wearing the

cope. If he fell backwards it would have been under him. So it was probably Calcraft who took it from the box. Perhaps it was open when he came into the chapel. There's tissue paper here but no string. That's odd, surely, ma'am.'

Kate said, 'It's odd that the cope's here at all. Mrs Burbridge may be able to explain it. We'll have to get the residents together, reassure them as far as anyone can and make it plain that we're in charge. I'll need you with me but we can't leave the body unattended. We'll do what we need to do now at the scene then get the stretcher. We could lock him in Chapel Cottage but I'm not happy about that. It's too far from the house. Of course we could use the same sickroom where they put Oliver but that means he'll be next door to Mr Dalgliesh.'

Benton said, 'In the circumstances, ma'am, it's hardly likely to worry either of them.' As if regretting the crudity of his comment, he added quickly, 'But won't Dr Glenister want to examine the body *in situ*?'

'We're not even sure we can get her. It may have to be the local pathologist.'

Benton said, 'Why not move him to my apartment, ma'am? I've got a key and it will be handy when the helicopter arrives. He can stay on the stretcher until then.'

Kate wondered why she hadn't thought of this, why against all reason she had assumed that the tower sickroom was a destined morgue. She said, 'Good idea, Sergeant.'

Gently she replaced the edge of the cope, then got up and stood for a moment trying to discipline thought.

There was so much to be done, but in what order? Telephone calls to be made to London and the Devon and Cornwall force, photographs to be taken before the body was moved, residents to be seen together and later questioned separately, the scene to be examined, including Chapel Cottage and efforts made to recover the weapon, if that were possible. Almost certainly AD was right: the natural thing would have been for Calcraft to throw it over the cliff, and a smooth-surfaced stone was the most likely object. The sandy grass was littered with them.

She said, 'If it's in the sea then it's lost. It'll depend on the strength of the throw and whether he chucked it from the cliff edge or the lower cliff. Have you any idea about the tides?'

'I found a tide table in my sitting room, ma'am. I think we've got about a couple of hours before high tide.'

Kate said, 'I wonder what AD would do first.'

She was thinking aloud, not expecting a response, but after a pause Benton said, 'It isn't a question of what Mr Dalgliesh would do, ma'am, it's a question of what you decide to do.'

She looked at him and said, 'Get to your apartment as fast as you can and fetch your camera. You may as well bring my murder case with you. Use one of the bikes in the stable block. I'll ring Maycroft and ask for the stretcher to be brought here in twenty minutes. That'll give us time for the photographs. After we've moved him we'll see the residents. Then we'll come back here to see if there's a chance of getting down to the shore. And we'll need to examine Chapel Cottage.

Almost certainly Calcraft will have got blood on him, at least on his hands and arms. That's where he'll have washed.'

He sped off, running easily and very fast across the scrubland. Kate went back to Seal Cottage. There were two phone calls to be made, both of them difficult. The first was to Assistant Commissioner Harkness at the Yard. There was a delay in getting through to him but finally she heard his quick impatient voice. But the call proved less frustrating than Kate had expected. Admittedly Harkness gave the impression that the complication of SARS was a personal affront for which Kate was in some way responsible, but she sensed that he had at least the satisfaction of being the first to hear the news. So far it hadn't broken nationally. And when she had reported fully on the progress of the investigation his final decision, if not immediate, was at least clear.

'Investigating a double murder with only yourself and a sergeant is hardly ideal. I can't see why you can't call in technical backing from the local force. If the SOCOs and fingerprint people keep away from anyone who is infected, there shouldn't be a serious risk. It will be for the Home Office to authorise, of course.'

Kate said, 'Sergeant Benton-Smith and I don't yet know whether we are infected, sir.'

'There is that, I suppose. Anyway, the control of infection isn't our concern. The double murders are. I'll have a word with the CC at Exeter. At least they can cope with any exhibits. You'd better carry on with Benton-Smith, at least for the next three days. That will bring us to Friday. After that we'll see how things develop. Keep me informed, of course. How is Mr Dalgliesh, by the way?'

Kate said, 'I don't know, sir. I haven't liked to worry Dr Staveley with enquiries. I'm hoping I'll be able to speak to him and get some news later today.'

Harkness said, 'I'll ring Staveley myself and talk to Mr Dalgliesh if he's well enough.'

Kate thought, *You'll be lucky.* She had a feeling that Guy Staveley would be highly effective in protecting his patient.

After ringing off, she steeled herself to make the second more difficult call. She tried to rehearse what she would say to Emma Lavenham, but nothing seemed right. The words were either too frightening or too reassuring. There were two numbers on the paper AD had left, Emma's mobile and a landline; staring at them didn't make the choice any easier. In the end she decided to try the landline first. It was early, Emma might still be in her room at college. Perhaps AD had already spoken to her, but she thought that was unlikely. With no mobile, he would have to use the phone in the surgery and Dr Staveley would hardly see that as a priority.

After only five rings, Emma Lavenham's clear voice, confident and unconcerned, came on the line, bringing with it a confusion of memories and emotions. As soon as Kate announced herself the voice changed. 'It's Adam, isn't it?'

'I'm afraid it is. He's asked me to let you know that he's not well. He'll ring as soon as he can. He sends you his love.'

Emma was keeping herself under control but her

voice was edged with fear. 'How not well? Has he had an accident? Is it serious? Kate, please tell me.'

'Not an accident. You'll hear about it on the next radio news, I imagine. One of the visitors here arrived with SARS; Mr Dalgliesh caught it. He's in the sickroom.'

The silence seemed interminable and so absolute that Kate wondered whether the line was dead. Then Emma's voice. 'How bad is he? Please Kate, I have to be told.'

Kate said, 'It's only just happened. I don't really know very much myself. I hope to find out how he is when I go to the house later today. But I'm sure he'll be all right. He's in good hands. I mean, SARS isn't like that Asian bird flu.'

She was speaking from ignorance, trying to reassure, but careful not to lie. But how could she tell the truth when she didn't know it? She added, 'And he's very strong.'

Emma said with a heartbreaking lack of self-pity, 'He was tired when he took the case. I can't come to him, I know that. I can't even try to speak to him. I don't suppose they'd let me and he mustn't be worried about me and what I'm feeling. That's not important now. But I expect you'll be able to get a message to him. Tell him I'm thinking of him. Give him my love. And Kate – you will ring me, won't you? You will tell me the truth however bad. Nothing can be worse than what I'll be imagining.'

'Yes, Emma, I'll ring you and I'll always tell you as much as I know. Goodbye.'

Replacing the receiver, she thought, *Not, 'tell him that*

I love him', just 'give him my love'? That's the kind of message any friend would send. But what other words were there unless they could be spoken face to face? She thought, *We both want to say the same words. I've always known why I can't say them. But he loves her, so why can't she?*

She went back to the chapel and began to search, stepping carefully around the body, scrutinising the stone floor, moving slowly, eyes down. Then she went outside into the fresh morning air. Was it her imagination that it smelled sweeter? Surely it was too soon for even the first tentative but unmistakable stench of death. She tried to take in the implications of solving two murders with no resources but Benton and herself. For both of them the stakes were high but, whatever the outcome, the final responsibility would be hers. And the outside world, their world, would find no excuses for failure. Both murders were copybook killings: a small closed society, no access from outside, a limited number of suspects, even more limited now that Speidel had an alibi for Boyde's death. Only if she and Benton both fell victim to SARS would failure be excused. Both were at risk of infection. Both had sat closeted with Dalgliesh for an hour in his sitting room at Seal Cottage. Now they would be investigating murder under the threat of a dreaded disease. But she knew that the risk of catching SARS was far less onerous to her – as it would be to Benton – than the fear of public failure, of leaving Combe Island with the case unsolved.

And now she saw him in the distance, cycling vigorously, the camera strapped round his neck, one hand on the middle of the handlebars, the other holding her murder case. He flung the bike against the wall of

Seal Cottage and came towards her. She didn't speak about the phone call to Emma, but reported her conversation with Harkness.

Benton said, 'I'm surprised he didn't say that if the body count continues to go up, we'll soon solve the case by the process of elimination. What photographs do you want taken, ma'am?'

For the next quarter of an hour they worked together. Benton photographed the body with the cope in place and then the battered face, the chapel, the area round it, and the upper and lower cliff, focusing on a partly demolished dry stone wall. Then they moved to Chapel Cottage. How strange, thought Kate, that silence could be oppressive; that the dead Boyde was more vividly present to her in this emptiness than he had been in life.

She said, 'The bed's made up. He didn't sleep here last night. That means he died where we found him, in the chapel.'

They moved into the bathroom. The bath and basin were dry, the towels in place. Kate said, 'There may be prints on the showerhead or taps but that'll be for back-up if and when it's safe for them to come. Our job is to protect the evidence. That means locking and sealing the cottage. The best chance may be DNA on the towels, so they'd better go to the lab.'

And now, through the open door, they heard the rumble of the buggy. Looking out, Kate said, 'Rupert Maycroft on his own. He'd hardly bring Dr Staveley or Jo Staveley, they'll be in the sickroom. I'm glad it's only Maycroft. It's a pity he has to see the cope, but at least the face will be covered.'

The stretcher had been placed crossways in the back

of the buggy. Benton helped Maycroft unload it. Maycroft waited while he and Kate wheeled it into the chapel. A few minutes later the sad procession began its way over the scrubland, Maycroft driving the buggy in front, Kate and Benton behind, pushing and walking one on each side of the stretcher. To Kate the whole scene was unreal, a bizarre and alien rite of passage: the fitful sunlight less strong now and a lively breeze lifting Maycroft's hair, the bright green of the cope like a gaudy shroud, herself and Benton grave-faced mourners walking behind the lumbering buggy, the body jolting from time to time as the wheels hit a hummock, the silence broken only by the sound of their progress, by the ever-present murmur of the sea and the occasional almost human shrieking of a flock of gulls which followed them, wings beating, as if this strange cortège offered a hope of scraps of bread.

4

It was nearly nine-thirty. Kate and Benton had spent some twenty minutes with Maycroft discussing the logistics of this new situation and now it was time to face the rest of the company. At the door of the library Benton saw Kate hesitate and he heard her deep steadying breath and felt as if it were his own. He could see the tension in her shoulders and neck as she raised her head to face what lay beyond the smooth excluding mahogany. Looking back later, he was to be astonished at how many thoughts and fears had been crowded into those three seconds of time. He felt a spasm of pity for her; this case would be vital for her and she knew it. It could make or break him too, but it was she who was in charge. And could she ever bear to work for Dalgliesh again if she failed both herself and him? He had a sudden vivid image of Dalgliesh's final words to her outside the chapel, her face, her voice. He thought, *She's in love with him. She thinks he's going to die.* But the pause could only have lasted for a few seconds before, grasping the knob, she turned it firmly.

He closed the door behind them. The smell of fear met them, sour as a sickroom miasma. How could the air be so tainted? He told himself that he was being fanciful; it was just that all the windows were closed. They were breathing stale air, infecting each other with fear. The scene which met him was different from that first time in the library. Had it really been only three days ago? Then they had been sitting at the long rectangular table like obedient children awaiting the arrival of the headmaster. Then he had sensed shock and horror, but also excitement. Most in that room had had nothing to fear. For those on the margins of murder, involved but innocent, it could hold a terrible fascination. Now he sensed only fear.

As if unwilling to meet each other's eyes across the table, they had arranged themselves about the room. Only three were sitting together. Mrs Plunkett was sitting next to Millie Tranter, their hands on the table, the cook's large hand enclosing the girl's. Jago was on Millie's left and at the end of the table a white-faced Mrs Burbridge sat rigidly, the embodiment of horror and grief. Emily Holcombe had taken one of the high-backed leather chairs before the fireplace and Roughtwood stood behind her at attention, a guardian on duty. Mark Yelland sat opposite, his head leaning back, his arms held loosely on the rests as relaxed as if preparing to doze. Miranda Oliver and Dennis Tremlett had placed two of the smaller library chairs together in front of one of the bookcases and were seated side by side. Dan Padgett, also on one of the smaller chairs, sat alone, his arms hanging between his knees, his head bowed.

As they entered all eyes turned to them but at first no one moved. Maycroft, who had entered behind them, went over to the table and took one of the empty chairs. Kate said, 'Can we please have a window open?'

It was Jago who got up and moved from casement to casement. A chill breeze flowed in and they heard more clearly the pounding of the sea.

Miranda Oliver said, 'Not all the windows, Jago. Two are enough.'

There was a tinge of petulance in her voice. She looked round at the others as if seeking support, but no one spoke. Jago quietly closed all but two windows.

Kate waited, then she said, 'There are two reasons why we're all here together now, all except Dr Staveley and his wife and they will be joining us shortly. Mr Maycroft has told you that there has been a second death on the island. Commander Dalgliesh found the body of Adrian Boyde in the chapel at eight o'clock this morning. You will already know that Dr Speidel is being cared for in hospital and that he has SARS – Severe Acute Respiratory Syndrome. Unfortunately Mr Dalgliesh has also been taken ill. This means that I am now in charge, with Sergeant Benton-Smith. It also means that all of us here will be quarantined. Dr Staveley will explain how long that is likely to last. During that time my colleague and I will, of course, investigate both Mr Oliver's death and the murder of Adrian Boyde. In the meantime we think it would be wise as well as a convenience if those of you in the cottages moved to the stable block or to the house. Would you like now to say something, Mr Maycroft?'

Maycroft got to his feet. Before he could begin speaking Mark Yelland said, 'You used the word murder. Do we understand that this second death can't be either accident or suicide?'

Kate said, 'Mr Boyde was murdered. I'm not at this moment prepared to say more than that. Mr Maycroft?'

No one spoke. Benton had braced himself for a vocal reaction, disjointed muttering, exclamations of horror or surprise, but they seemed in shock. All he heard was a concerted intake of breath so low that it seemed no more than the susurration of the freshening breeze. All eyes turned to Maycroft. He got up and grasped the back of his chair, nudging Jago away, seeming unaware of his presence. His knuckles were white against the wood and his face, drained not only of colour but of all vitality, was the face of an old man. But when he spoke his voice was strong.

'Inspector Miskin has given you the facts. Guy and Jo Staveley are at present looking after Mr Dalgliesh, but Dr Staveley will be here shortly to talk to you about SARS. All I want to say is to express to the police on behalf of us all our shock and horror at the death of a good man who was part of our community and to say that we shall cooperate with Inspector Miskin's inquiry as we did with Mr Dalgliesh's. In the meantime I have discussed with her what domestic arrangements we are to make. With this new seemingly motiveless murder, all the innocent are in some danger. We may have been too ready to assume that our island is impregnable. We have been wrong. I have to emphasise that that is my opinion not that of the police, but they are anxious for us all to be together. There are two vacant guest suites here in the house and some accommodation in the stables. You all have keys and I suggest you lock your cottages and bring what you need here with you. The police may need access to the cottages to search for any intruder and I am providing Inspector Miskin with a set of keys. Has anyone any questions?'

Emily Holcombe's voice was firm and confident. Of all the people in the room it seemed to Benton that she was the least changed. She said, 'Roughtwood and I would prefer to stay in Atlantic Cottage. If I need protection he is perfectly able to provide it. We have locks to protect us from any night marauders. Since we can hardly imprison ourselves here in the house without inconvenience, those of us who feel adequately protected may as well stay where we are.'

Miranda Oliver broke in almost before she had finished. The eyes of the group, as if they were automata, turned to her. 'I want to stay where I am. Dennis has moved into my cottage so I'll be safe. I think it's common knowledge now that we're going to be married. It wouldn't be appropriate to announce it in the papers so soon after my father's death but we are engaged. Naturally I don't want to be parted from my fiancé at a time like this.'

Benton thought that the statement had been rehearsed in advance, but it still astounded him. Didn't she realise how inappropriate was the triumphant announcement of an engagement at such a moment? He sensed a general embarrassment. How odd that a social gaffe could actually disconcert people when they were faced with murder and the fear of death.

Emily Holcombe said, 'What about you, Dr Yelland? Your cottage is the most remote.'

'Oh, I shall move in here. There's only one person on this island who can feel safe from being murdered and that's the murderer himself. Since I'm not he, I would prefer to be here in the house rather than alone in Murrelet Cottage. It seems to me likely that the police are dealing with a psychologically disturbed killer who may not be rational in choosing another victim. I'd prefer one of the guest suites in the house rather than the stable block and, as I've brought work with me, I shall need a desk.'

Maycroft said, 'Jago will need to stay in his cottage to keep surveillance on the harbour. Are you happy with that, Jago?'

'Someone's got to be in that cottage, sir, and I wouldn't fancy it being anybody but me. I can look after myself.'

Since Maycroft had finished speaking, Millie had been unobtrusively sobbing, the sound as low and pathetic as a kitten's mewing. Mrs Plunkett from time to time tightened her grip on the small fist but made no other comforting move. No one else took any notice, but now Millie cried out, 'I don't want to move in here! I want to get off this island. I'm not staying where people get murdered! You can't make me stay!' She turned to Jago. 'Jago, you'll take me won't you? You'll take me in the launch? I can stay with Jake. I can go anywhere. You can't keep me here!'

Yelland said, 'I suppose she's technically right. We stay in quarantine voluntarily, surely. The appropriate authority, whichever one is responsible for the island, can't invoke compulsory measures unless we're actually suffering from an infectious disease. I'm perfectly prepared to stay, I'm just asking about the legal position.'

Now Maycroft's voice was more commanding than Benton had heard before. 'I'm ascertaining the position. If anyone did leave, I imagine they would be advised to stay at home and keep away from other people until the incubation period is past. I believe that to be ten days, but we shall know more from Dr Staveley. But the question is academic. No visitors' boats come to Combe, and certainly none will be allowed to land now.'

Emily said, 'So in fact we're prisoners?'

'Hardly more, Emily, than we are when there's thick fog or violent storms. The launch is under my control. I don't intend to make it available until the incubation period is over. Does anyone quarrel with that?'

No one did, but Millie's voice rose into a crescendo. 'I don't want to stay! You can't make me!'

Jago shifted his chair closer to her and whispered in her ear. No one heard what he said, but Millie gradually grew quiet, then she said querulously, 'Then why can't I be in Harbour Cottage with you?'

'Because you're going to be in the big house with Mrs Burbridge. No one's going to harm you. Be brave and sensible and you'll be a right heroine when this is over.'

During this time Mrs Burbridge hadn't spoken. Now she said, her voice breaking, 'Not one of you has said anything about Adrian Boyde. Not one. He's been brutally killed and all we're thinking about is our own safety, whether we'll be the next one, whether we'll get SARS, and he's in some morgue waiting to be cut up and labelled, an exhibit in a murder case.'

Maycroft said patiently, 'Evelyn, I said he was a good man, and he was. And you're quite right. I've been too preoccupied with the problem of coping with the double emergency to find the right words. But we shall find a time to grieve for him.'

'You didn't find a moment to grieve for my father!' Miranda was on her feet. 'You didn't care whether he was dead or alive. Some of you were glad he was dead. I know what you thought about him so don't think I'm going to stand up for two minutes' silence for Mr Boyde, if that's what you have in mind.' She turned to Kate, 'And don't forget Daddy died first. You're supposed to be investigating that too.'

'We are investigating it.'

Benton thought, *We need to keep them together. We can't protect them all and at the same time investigate a double murder. This is the only chance we'll have to exert our authority. If we don't take control now we never shall. We can't let Emily Holcombe take over.*

He glanced at Kate and somehow she grasped the force of his anxiety. She said, 'Have you anything to add, Sergeant?'

'Only this, ma'am.' He turned to the group then fixed his eyes on Emily Holcombe. 'We're not asking you to move from the cottages merely because you'll be safer. With Mr Dalgliesh ill we need to use effectively what manpower we have. It's sensible as well as prudent for all of you to be in one place. Those who don't cooperate will be seriously hampering the investigation.'

Was there, Benton wondered, a glimpse of grim amusement on Miss Holcombe's face? She said, 'If you put it like that, Sergeant, I suppose we have no choice. I've no wish to be used as a scapegoat for failure. I would like my parents' bedroom in the house. Roughtwood will be in the stable block. And you'd better join me in the house, Miranda. Mr Tremlett was perfectly comfortable before in the stable block. You should be able to tolerate a night or two apart.'

Before Miranda could reply, the door opened and Guy Staveley came in. Somehow Benton had been expecting him to be wearing a white coat, and now the brown corduroy trousers and tweed jacket in which he had started the day seemed incongruous. He came into the room quietly. His face was as grave as Maycroft's and before speaking he looked across at his colleague as if seeking reassurance, but his voice was steady and surprisingly authoritative. This was a different man from the Staveley Benton had first seen. All eyes were on him. Glancing from face to face, Benton saw hope, anxiety and the mute appeal he had seen in other eyes: the desperate need for the reassurance of an expert.

The chair at one end of the rectangular table was vacant and Staveley took it, facing Mrs Burbridge. Maycroft moved to his right and those of the company still standing, including Kate, found themselves seats. Only Benton remained standing. He moved over to the window, relishing the inrush of the sea-smelling breeze.

Staveley said, 'Inspector Miskin will have told you that we now know that Dr Speidel is suffering from SARS. He is in a special isolation unit in Plymouth and is being well cared for. His wife and some of his family are arriving from Germany and will, of course, only see him under controlled conditions. He's still seriously ill. I have also to tell you that Commander Dalgliesh has caught the infection and is at present in the sickroom here. Samples will be taken to confirm the diagnosis but I'm afraid there can be little doubt. If his condition worsens he too will be transferred by helicopter to Plymouth.

'First of all, I want to reassure you that the primary way that SARS spreads is by close person-to-person contact, perhaps by droplets when the infected person coughs or sneezes, or by someone touching the surface or object which has been contaminated by infected droplets and then carrying them to the nose, mouth or eyes. It's possible that SARS might be carried through the air by other means, but at present no one seems sure of that. We can take it that only those of you who came into close contact with either Dr Speidel or Mr Dalgliesh are seriously at risk. Nevertheless, it is right that everyone here on Combe should be in quarantine for about ten days. The Public Health Authority has powers to enforce quarantine on an infected person and in some cases on those at risk from infection. I don't know whether they would do so for those of you who have not been in close contact with Dr Speidel and Mr Dalgliesh, but I hope we can agree that the most sensible thing is for all of us to accept voluntary quarantine and to stay here on the island until we're advised that it's safe to leave. After all, we're not being quarantined away from home. Except for the police and our visitors, Combe is our home. We're only being asked to forgo our trips to the mainland until the danger of infection is over. If anyone objects to this, will you please let me know.'

No one spoke. Millie looked for a second rebellious, then subsided into glum resignation.

Then Padgett spoke, his voice high. 'It isn't convenient for me. Combe isn't my home – not now. I've got an interview in London for a university course. I'm leaving Combe now that Mother's dead, and it's impossible for me to stay on for ten days. If I miss the interview I may lose my chance of a place.'

It was Yelland who surprisingly replied. 'That's ridiculous. Of course they'll keep a place. They'd hardly welcome your appearance if they thought you'd been exposed to infection from SARS.'

'I haven't been. Dr Staveley's just explained.'

'Commander Dalgliesh interviewed you, didn't he? Either he or one of his colleagues, and they've been exposed to infection. Why not accept the inevitable and stop whining.'

Padgett flushed and seemed about to speak. Then Dr Staveley said, 'So, we agree to accept voluntary quarantine. I'll let the authorities know. Of course, while this is happening there'll be a great deal of international activity tracing visitors who flew from Beijing with Dr Speidel and the friend he stayed with in the South of France. That's not my responsibility, thank God. My wife and I are caring for Commander Dalgliesh at present, but I may have to transfer him to Plymouth later. In the meantime, if any of you fall ill, please come at once to the surgery. SARS usually begins with a fever and the symptoms associated with flu – headache, general feeling of being unwell, aches in the body. Some patients, but not all, have a cough at the very outset. I think that's all I have to tell you at present. The murder of Adrian Boyde, which normally would drive all other worries and considerations from our minds, is in the hands of Inspector Miskin and Sergeant Benton-Smith. I hope we shall all cooperate with them as we did with Commander Dalgliesh. Has anyone any questions?' He turned to Maycroft. 'Have you anything further to say, Rupert?'

'Only about publicity. This news will break on the one o'clock news bulletins on radio and on television. I'm afraid it will be the end of privacy on the island. We're doing all we can to cut the nuisance to a minimum. All the phones here are ex-directory, which doesn't mean some people won't discover the numbers. The public relations branch of New Scotland Yard are dealing with publicity about the murders. The line is that investigations are proceeding but it's very early days. The inquest on Mr Oliver has been postponed, and when it takes place is likely to be adjourned. Those of you who are interested in the publicity and want to share in the drama might be able to persuade Mrs Plunkett to let you watch her television. The newspapers, together with the necessary supplies, will be dropped by helicopter to-morrow. I can't say I'm looking forward to their arrival.'

Dr Yelland said, 'What about your temporary staff on the mainland, the ones who come over by the week? Won't they be harassed by journalists?'

'I don't think their names are generally known. If the press do get in touch, I doubt whether they'll get much help. There's no reasonable possibility of anyone landing on the island. The helicopter pad will be made unusable except when we know an air ambulance is arriving or supplies are being delivered. There'll probably be some noise nuisance from other helicopters circling but we'll have to put up with that. Have you anything more you want to say, Inspector?'

'Just one or two things to add to what I said earlier. People should stay together as much as they can. If you want exercise, take one or two companions and stay within sight of the house. You all have keys to your cottages or to your rooms in the house or the stable block and will probably prefer to keep them locked. Sergeant Benton-Smith and I would like your consent to search any of your rooms if it proves necessary. I'm anxious to save time. Has anyone any objection?' No one spoke. 'Then I'll take that as consent. Thank you. Before we disperse, I'd like you all to write down where you were and what you were doing between nine o'clock last night and eight this morning. Sergeant Benton-Smith will bring in the necessary paper and pens and collect your scripts.'

Emily Holcombe said, 'We'll look like a bunch of over-mature university students tackling their final exam papers. Will Sergeant Benton-Smith be invigilating?'

Kate said, 'No one will, Miss Holcombe. Are you proposing to cheat?' She turned to the rest of the company. 'That will be all for now. Thank you.'

The sheets of paper and pens had been placed ready on Maycroft's desk. Crossing the corridor to collect them, Benton reflected that Kate and his first encounter with the suspects as a duo hadn't gone badly. He sensed that they were now reverting to the comforting theory that, somehow, a stranger had managed to get on the island. If so, there was no point in disabusing them. The fear of a psychopathic murderer at large would at least keep them together. And there was another advantage: the murderer, feeling himself safer, would become more confident. It was when a murderer grew in confidence that he was most at risk. He glanced at his watch. It would be high tide in less than forty minutes. But first they must see Mrs Burbridge. Her evidence could make that dangerous climb unnecessary.

Unlike the others, she hadn't settled down to write her statement but had folded the sheet of paper and placed it carefully in her bag. Now, getting to her feet as if she had suddenly become an old woman, she was making for the door. Opening it for her Kate said, 'We'd like to have a word with you, Mrs Burbridge, and it is rather urgent. Shall we do that now?'

Without looking at them, Mrs Burbridge said, 'If you'll give me just five minutes. Please. Just five minutes.'

She was gone. Benton glanced at his watch. 'Let's hope it isn't more, ma'am.'

5

Mrs Burbridge received Kate and Benton at her door without speaking and, somewhat to Kate's surprise, led them not into the sitting room but into the sewing room. There she seated herself at the larger table. In the library Kate had been too preoccupied with finding the right words to concentrate on individual faces. Now she was looking at a woman so altered by grief that she was unrecognisable as the woman she had first seen after Oliver's murder. Her skin was a grey-green parchment creased with furrows, and the pain-filled eyes, swimming in a moist bed of unshed tears, had lost all colour. But Kate saw something more, a desolation of spirit which was beyond comfort. She had never felt more inadequate or more helpless. She wished passionately that AD were here. He would know what to say, he always did.

Fleetingly images of former bereavements passed through her mind in a moving collage of grief. There had been so many of them, so much bad news to break, since she had first become a WPC. A succession of doors that opened even before her ring or knock; wives, husbands, children, seeing the truth in her eyes before she had had time to speak; frantically rummaging in unfamiliar kitchens to make the traditional 'nice cup of tea', which was never nice and which the bereaved drank with heartrending courtesy.

But this distress was beyond the transitory comfort of hot sweet tea. Glancing round the sewing room as if seeing it for the first time, she was possessed by a confusing mixture of pity and anger; the bales of richly coloured silk, the corkboard patterned with cuttings, photographs, symbols and, in front of Mrs Burbridge, the small folded cloth enclosing the silk embroidered strip on which Millie had worked, all evidence of innocent and happy creativity which would now be forever tainted with horror and blood.

They could only have waited in silence for ten seconds but time seemed to have stopped, then the sad eyes looked into Kate's. 'It's the cope, isn't it? It's something to do with the cope. And I gave it to him.'

Kate said gently, 'It was placed over Mr Boyde's body but it wasn't used to kill him.' *Was that what Mrs Burbridge had been thinking?* Kate added, 'He wasn't suffocated. The cope was just laid over him.'

'And is it . . . Is it stained with his blood?'

'Yes, I'm afraid it is.'

Kate opened her mouth to say the words *But I think it can be cleaned,* then stopped herself. She had heard Benton's quick intake of breath. Did he too realise that she had saved herself from a folly as insulting as it was stupid? Mrs Burbridge wasn't grieving for the loss of an object she had lovingly created, nor for the waste of time and effort.

And now she too looked round the room as if it had become unfamiliar to her. She said, 'It's all pointless, isn't it? Nothing about it is real. It's just prettifying a fantasy. I gave him the cope. If I hadn't given it to him . . .' Her voice broke.

Kate said, 'It would have made no difference. Believe me, the murderer would've struck whether or not the cope was there. It had nothing to do with the cope.'

Then Kate heard Benton speaking and was surprised that his voice was so gentle.

'It was the killer who put the cope over him, but it was appropriate, wasn't it? Adrian was a priest. Perhaps the silk of the cope was the last thing he felt. Wouldn't that have been a comfort to him?'

She looked up at his face, then reached out a trembling hand and took his dark young hand in hers. 'Yes,' she said, 'it would. Thank you.'

Kate quietly moved a chair next to her and sat close. She said, 'We're going to catch this man but we need your help, particularly now Mr Dalgliesh is ill. We need to know what happened last night. You said you gave Mr Boyde the cope.'

Mrs Burbridge was calmer now. She said, 'He came to see me after dinner. I had my meal here as I usually do, but I knew he was coming. We'd arranged it earlier. I told him that the cope was finished and he wanted to see it. If things had been different, if it hadn't been for Mr Oliver's murder, Adrian was going to take it to the Bishop. He'd suggested it because for him it would have been a kind of test. I think he felt ready to leave the island, at least for a few days.'

Kate asked, 'So that was why the cope was packed in a box?'

'It was put in the box but not to be taken off the island. We knew that couldn't happen, not yet. It was just that I thought Adrian would like to wear it, perhaps when he was saying Evensong. He did most evenings.

He wouldn't wear it to celebrate Mass, that wouldn't have been suitable. I could see, when he was admiring it, that he would like to put it on, so I said it would be helpful to know how it sat, if it was comfortable. That was just an excuse really. I wanted him to have the pleasure of wearing it.'

Kate said, 'Do you remember at what time he left here carrying it?'

'He didn't stay long. I could sense that he wanted to get back to his cottage. After he left I put out the light here and went to listen to the radio in my sitting room. I remember looking at my watch because I didn't want to miss a programme. It was five to nine.'

Benton said, 'You sensed that he wanted to get back to his cottage. Is that usual? I mean, did he seem in more of a hurry than normal? Were you surprised that he didn't stay longer? Did he give you the impression that he might be calling on anyone on the way home?'

The question was important, the answer crucial, and Mrs Burbridge seemed to realise this. After a pause she said, 'It didn't seem unusual at the time. I thought that he had some work to do or a radio programme he wanted to listen to. It's true he usually didn't hurry away. But it wasn't exactly hurrying, was it? He was here for twenty-five minutes.'

Benton asked, 'What did you talk about?'

'The cope, the stole and other pieces I'd been working on. And he admired the altar fronts. It was just chat. We didn't mention Mr Oliver's murder, but I think he was preoccupied. He was deeply affected by Mr Oliver's death. Of course we all were, but with him it went deeper. But it would, wouldn't it? He understood about evil.'

Kate got up. She said, 'I don't want you to be alone in this flat, Mrs Burbridge. I know that everyone will be accommodated in the house, but even so I'd prefer you not to be alone in your flat at night.'

'Oh but I won't be. Mrs Plunkett doesn't want to be alone either and she suggested I move in with her. Jago and Dan are going to move my bed for me. She would come here I know, but she does like her television. I'm afraid neither of us will get much peace. People who aren't normally interested in television will want to watch the news now. Everything has changed, hasn't it?'

'Yes,' said Kate. 'I'm afraid it has.'

'You asked me to write down what we were doing last night. I brought the paper away with me but I haven't done anything with it. I couldn't bring myself to write down what happened. Does it matter?'

Kate said gently, 'Not now, Mrs Burbridge. You've told us what we needed to know. I'm afraid you may have to make a formal statement later but don't worry about that for now.'

They thanked her and left, and heard the door being locked behind them.

Benton said, 'So he took an hour to get home. That walk across the scrubland, even in the dark, couldn't have taken more than half an hour, probably less.'

'You'd better time it, preferably after dark. We can be reasonably certain Boyde didn't go for a stroll, not on a starless night and carrying a bulky package. He called on someone, and when we know who we'll have Calcraft.'

397

She looked at her watch. 'It's taken twenty minutes to get that information but we couldn't hurry her and it's important. I want to be on hand when Dr Glenister arrives. We'll have to keep well clear of her, but I think we should be there when they take the body away.'

They were entering Kate's apartment when the telephone rang. Dr Glenister was giving evidence at the Old Bailey and would be tied up for the next two days. There was a perfectly competent local man and she suggested that they use him. Any exhibits could be taken to the lab when the body was removed.

Replacing the receiver, Kate said, 'Perhaps it's just as well. We've got work to do at the scene ourselves and I want that stone if we can get it. If the tide's coming in we may have wasted too much time already.'

Benton said, 'Not wasted, ma'am. We had to see everyone on the island and ensure their safety. And we needed Mrs Burbridge's evidence. If Boyde had given her any clue about where he was going, the case could've been solved. There's a limit to what we can do with only the two of us. And we should be all right with the tide if it turned just before ten last night. That should give us roughly an hour before it's high again.'

'Well, let's hope you're right.'

After a moment's hesitation, she said, 'You did well in there, Sergeant. You knew what to say to Mrs Burbridge, what would comfort her.'

'I've had a religious education, ma'am. It comes in useful sometimes.'

She looked at his dark handsome face. It was as impassive as a mask. She said, 'And now to ring Jago and ask him to meet us with the buggy and the climbing equipment. We can't tackle that cliff without him. Someone – I suppose Maycroft – will have to relieve him at Harbour Cottage.'

6

To Benton it had seemed an unconscionable time before Maycroft managed to free himself from his other pre-occupations and went down to the harbour to take over from Jago and explain to him that he was wanted. Sensing that Maycroft would prefer to do this alone, they waited outside the lighthouse with the buggy, Benton resisting the temptation to keep gazing at his watch, an irritating obsession which only served to lengthen time.

On impulse he said, 'I suppose it's safe to use him.'

'As long as we don't let him see what, if anything, we manage to find.'

'I was thinking of the climb, ma'am.'

'We've no choice. AD said that he doesn't see Jago as our man and he hasn't yet been wrong.'

And now Jago was with them. He and Benton loaded the buggy with the climbing equipment and Kate took the wheel. They bumped over the headland without speaking. Benton knew that she would want to preserve the ground around the scene of crime, and when they were some twenty yards from the chapel she stopped the buggy.

She said to Jago, 'What we're looking for was probably thrown over the top or the lower cliff somewhere near the chapel. Either Sergeant Benton-Smith or I must abseil down to make a search. We'll need your help.'

Still Jago didn't speak. Kate slithered down between

bushes and jutting rocks to the lower cliff, then, with the others following, walked along the narrow plateau until, looking up, she assessed they were under the chapel. They moved to the edge and looked down. The layered granite, in parts fissured, in others smooth as polished silver, fell some eighty feet to the sea, broken only by jutting spurs like hanging baskets, the crevices festooned with foliage and clusters of small white flowers. At the foot of the cliff was a cove with no beach, heaped up to the rock face with stones and boulders. The tide was coming in fast.

Kate turned to Jago, 'Is it possible to get down? Do you see any problems?'

At last Jago spoke. 'Not getting down, I don't. How d'you intend to get back up? You need an experienced climber.'

Kate asked, 'Is there no other way of getting into the cove?'

Jago said, 'Walk further along and look for yourself, Inspector. It's always cut off, no matter what the tide.'

'And no chance of swimming round the headland?'

Jago's face was eloquent. He shrugged. 'Not unless you want to be cut to pieces. The underwater rocks are like razors.'

Benton said, 'My grandfather was a climber and he taught me. If you're willing to come down with me we should be able to get up, that is if there's a classified climb.'

'There's one about thirty yards south of the chapel. It's the only way up but it's not for a novice. What's the hardest climb you've done?'

'Tatra on the Dorset coast. It's near St Anselm's

head.' Benton thought, *And don't, for God's sake, ask me when that was.*

And now for the first time Jago looked him in the face, 'Are you Hugh Benton-Smith's grandson?'

'Yes.'

There was silence for a few seconds, then Jago said, 'OK, let's get on with it. You'd better give me a hand with the gear. We haven't much time.'

They left Kate on the edge of the cliff. Within minutes they were back. Jago led the way confidently, the ropes slung over his shoulder. Following him with the rest of the equipment, Benton thought, *He knows every inch of this cliff. He's done this climb before.*

Dropping the ropes, Jago said, 'You'd better take your jacket off. The shoes look all right. Try one of these helmets for fit. The one with the red badge is mine.'

The boulders here were larger and the under-cliff narrower than on any other part they'd seen. Jago put on his helmet, then quickly selected the rock he wanted and, with the other two watching, took three wide tapes, threaded them together and secured them round the boulder with a karabiner. Watching him screwing the heavy metal clip shut, Benton reflected that he hadn't thought of the word karabiner for over a decade. And the tapes were called slings. He must remember the names. Jago uncoiled the rope, threaded the middle through the karabiner and, stretching his arms in wide sweeps, re-coiled both halves of the rope and hurled them over the cliff. They fell, rhythmically uncoiling, patterned in blue and red on the shining air.

For Benton time stopped, and for one disorientating second spun out of control, then latched on to memory.

He was fourteen again, and standing with his grand-father on top of that cliff on the Dorset coast. His grandfather, whom he had always called Hugh, was a twice decorated fighter pilot in the Second World War and, after those tumultuous years, had never adjusted to an earthbound world in which the death of the best of his friends had left him a reluctant half-guilty survivor. Even in adolescence, Benton, loving him and desperately anxious to please, had sensed something of the loss and shame which lay behind his grand-father's brittle, half-mocking carapace. Hugh had been an obsessive amateur climber, seeing in that no-man's-land between air and rock something his grandson recognised as more than a sport. Francis – he was never called Benton by Hugh – had longed to share his passion, knowing even then that what his grandfather was teaching him was how to master fear.

In his first year at university, when Hugh had fallen to his death climbing in Nepal, his enthusiasm for the rock face dwindled. None of his friends climbed. His life was full of other more insistent interests. Now, in that second of memory he heard Hugh's voice. *The climb's a VS – Very Severe – but I think you're ready for it, Francis. Are you?*

Yes, Hugh. I'm ready.

But it was Jago's voice he was hearing. 'The climb's a VS, but as you've done Tatra you should be ready for it. OK?'

And this, he knew, was his last chance to withdraw. Soon he could be standing on that narrow fringe of stony sea-thrashed shore, facing a dangerous climb per-haps with a murderer. Mentally he spoke Kate's words.

'AD doesn't see Jago as our man. And he's never yet been wrong.'

He looked at Jago and said, 'I'm ready.'

He took off his jacket and felt through the fine woollen jersey the chill of the wind like a cold poultice on his back. Buckling on the harness with its waistband of karabiners, slings and nuts, he tried the two helmets, found one that fitted and strapped it on. He glanced at Kate. Her face was rigid with anxiety, but she didn't speak. He wondered if she wanted to say, *You don't have to do this, I'm not ordering you,* but knew that to put the onus on him would be an abdication of her responsibility. She could stop him but she couldn't order him to climb. He wondered why he was so glad of that. Now she took a plastic exhibit bag and a pair of search gloves from her case and handed them to him. Without speaking, he shoved them in his trouser pocket.

He watched while Jago satisfied himself that the slings round the boulder were secure, then clipped the rope through the karabiner at his waist. It came back to him so easily now, the rope over the right shoulder and round his back. No one spoke. He remembered that this routine preparation for a climb had always been done in silence, a formal, purposeful, putting on of courage and resolution, almost, he thought, as if his grandfather had been an ordained priest and he the acolyte, both performing some wordless but long familiar sacerdotal rite. Jago was an unlikely priest. Trying to relieve fear with sardonic humour, Benton told himself that he, Benton, was more likely to end as the sacrificial victim.

He walked to the very edge of the cliff, braced his feet and leaned backwards into space. This was the moment of commitment and it brought with it the remembered mixture of terror and exhilaration. If the belay didn't hold, he would plunge some eighty feet to his death. But the rope tightened and held. For a second, almost horizontal, he raised his eyes to the sky. The scudding clouds were racing in a vortex of white and pale blue and beneath him the sea thudded against the rock face in relentless waves of sound that he seemed to be hearing for the first time. But now all was easy and he felt, after more than a decade, some of that boyhood exhilaration in bouncing and sliding down the rock face, the left hand controlling the rope from behind, the right on the rope in front, feeling it slide through the karabiner, knowing that he was in control.

His feet struck ground. Quickly he released himself and shouted that he was down. Smoothing on his search gloves he surveyed the narrow strip of sea-smoothed rocks and pebbles, assessing where best to begin. The tide was coming in strongly, splurging over the smooth humps of the farthest outcrop, swirling into the deep rock pools, advancing and then briefly retreating to glitter the treacherous surfaces of rounded stones and the shards of broken granite. Time was against him. With every wave the field of search narrowed. Eyes down, he crouched forward yard by careful yard. He knew what he was looking for: a heavy stone but small enough to be held in the hand, a tool of death on which, with luck, there would still be some trace of blood. His heart grew more leaden with every yard. Even on this narrow fringe of shore the stones were piled in thousands, many of the right size and weight and most washed smooth by centuries of the sea. He was wasting time on a fruitless search and he still had that climb to face.

Minutes passed and his hopes were fading. The exhilaration of the abseil was forgotten. He pictured Kate waiting above for the call which would signal success. Now there would be only a single shout to let Jago know it was time for him to abseil down.

And then he saw, close to the edge of the cliff, something that should surely not be there on this untrodden shore: a pale flutter of litter. Going up to it he gazed down and for a second was tempted to fling his arms wide and give a shout of triumph. What he saw was an egg-shaped stone half enclosed in what was obviously the remnant of a surgical glove. Most of the thin latex must have been torn when it fell, rolled in the waves of the receding tide, and blown away, but one finger and a small part of the palm was still intact. Carefully he picked up the stone and examined the surface. The reddish stain, which didn't seem part of the natural stone, could surely only be blood. It must be blood. It had to be blood.

He put his trophy into the exhibit bag, closed it, and ran stumbling towards the abseil rope. He tied the bag to the end of it and, putting both hands to his mouth, gave a triumphant bellow. 'Got it! Heave it up.'

Looking up, he could glimpse Kate's face gazing down. She gave a wave of the hand and the rope with its package rose bumping gently against the rock face.

Almost immediately it was lowered again and Jago was coming down as quickly as if in free fall, the stocky body seeming to dance against the cliff. He released himself, gave a tug on the rope. It fell in coils at his feet.

He said, 'The climb's only thirty yards away, round this outcrop of rock. I'll fix the belay.'

The layered and fractured cliff towered above them. The surf was already breaking over their feet.

Jago said, 'You can lead. If you've done Tatra it shouldn't be too difficult. It's steep and exposed but well protected at the crucial moves. The crux is the roof at the top of that crack. There's a peg just before it right under the roof. Make sure you clip in. Don't worry, it's an overhang so if you lob, at least you'll fall clear of the rock.'

Benton hadn't expected to lead. He thought, *Jago planned this from the beginning, but then he's controlled every aspect of this climb.* He was too proud to argue about the order, but Jago would have depended on that too. He made a bowline at the end of the rope and attached it to his harness while Jago made a careful belay on a large boulder at the foot of the climb, then took hold of the rope and said, 'OK. If you're ready.'

And now, as if to emphasise the inevitability of the climb, a large wave thundered in almost sweeping them off balance. Benton began climbing. The first fifteen feet were not too difficult but he thought carefully about each hand and foot placement, feeling for the cracks in the rock, moving upward when he was confident he had a hold. After fifteen feet he took a nut from the rack at his waist and slid it into a crack, jiggling until it was firm. He attached a runner, clipped in the rope, then moved on with more confidence. The rock became steeper but was still firm and dry. He found another crack and threaded in another nut and runner.

He was some thirty feet above ground when –

suddenly and to his horror – he froze, all confidence gone. He had stretched his arms too widely to find a hold and found himself spread-eagled against the rock face, his shoulders so taut that they felt racked. He was terrified to try for another foothold in case he lost his precarious balance. His cheek was placed hard against the granite, which now felt wet and icy cold, and he realised that the rock face was damp with his sweat. There was no call from Jago but he remembered his grandfather's voice calling down to him on the fourth climb they'd done together. *This is classified VS so there'll be a hold. Take it slowly Francis. It isn't a race.* And now, after what seemed an eternity but must have been no more than half a minute, the tension in his shoulders eased. Tentatively he moved his right hand up and found a hold a few feet higher, then holds for his feet. The panic was over and he knew it wouldn't return.

Five minutes later his helmet bumped gently against the overhanging roof. This was the crux. It was a jutting shelf of splintered granite festooned with foliage. A gull had perched on the edge, bright beaked, motionless in its sleek white-and-grey perfection, dominating the cliff and seeming oblivious to the sweating invader only two feet below. Then it rose in a tumult of battered air and he felt rather than saw its white wings passing over his head. He knew that there would be a piton already in place at the top of the crack. If he failed to climb the roof, it would have to hold him. He found the peg, clipped on one end of a long runner and then called down, 'Tight rope', and felt it tighten. Looking down and using the tension on the rope for balance, he reached round the roof with his right hand and felt for a hold on the wall above. After thirty seconds of anxious scrabbling he found it, and then one for his left hand. Swinging into the air, he pulled up on his hands, found holds for his feet and got back into balance. He put another runner over a flake of rock and clipped on. He was secure.

And now there was no more anxiety, only a remembered joy. The rest of the climb was steep but the rock was clean with good holds all the way to the top. He hauled himself over the edge of the cliff and lay for a moment, exhausted, with the smell of earth and grass like a benison and the sand gritty against his mouth. He got to his feet and saw Kate coming towards him. Looking into her face, radiant with relief, he had to resist a ridiculous impulse to rush into her arms.

She said, 'Congratulations Benton', then turned away as if afraid to let him see what the strain of the last half-hour had done to her.

He found the nearest large boulder, made a belay, clipped in, took hold of the rope and called down to Jago. 'Climb when you're ready.'

Kate, he knew, would have dealt with the evidence while Jago was at the bottom of the cliff. The stone and the remnant of torn latex would already have been sealed in an exhibit bag. And now Jago's life was in his hands. He felt an old exhilaration like a surge of the blood. This was what it was about: the shared danger, the mutual dependence, the fellowship of the climb.

With astonishing speed, Jago was with them, hauling up and re-coiling the ropes, carrying the gear. He said, 'You did all right, Sergeant.'

He strode off with his gear towards the buggy, then

hesitated and turned back. Walking up to Benton he held out his hand. Benton grasped it. Neither spoke. They threw the climbing gear into the back of the buggy and climbed in. Kate took the wheel, turned the key in the ignition and made a wide sweep to trundle back towards the house. Looking at her face, Benton realised, in a moment of surprised revelation, that Kate could be called beautiful.

7

All through the rest of Tuesday part of Kate's mind was in that unseen sickroom high up in the tower and she had to restrain herself from phoning Guy or Jo Staveley to enquire what was happening. But she knew that if there were anything to tell her they would find time to telephone. In the meantime they had their job to do and she had hers.

Mrs Burbridge, finding what relief she could in domestic routine from the double peril of a murderer at large and a potentially fatal disease, asked what they would like for supper and whether it should be delivered to Seal Cottage. The thought was intolerable to Kate. To sit at the table where Dalgliesh had sat, seeing his raincoat hanging in the porch, to feel his absence more strongly than his presence, would be like entering the house of the dead. Her apartment in the stable block was small but it would do. She was anxious, too, to stay close to the house and to have Benton next door. It wasn't only a matter of convenience; she admitted to herself that she would feel reassured by having him near. With that realisation came another: he had become her colleague and partner. She told him what she had decided.

Benton said, 'If it's all right by you, ma'am, why don't I move my easy chair and anything else we need into your sitting room. Then we can use your apartment as the incident room and mine for meals. I'm quite good at cooking breakfast. And we've both got small fridges – large enough for milk anyway – which could be helpful if we're working late and need coffee. The rest of the rooms in the stable block haven't. Staff have to take what they need from the large fridge in the staff dining room. I've spoken to Mrs Plunkett and she can send over some salad and cold meats, or we can collect them. Would one o'clock be all right?'

Kate wasn't hungry but she could see that Benton had his mind on food. And the lunch, when he fetched it, was excellent. The salad and cold lamb came with baked potatoes, followed by fruit salad. To her surprise she ate it avidly. Afterwards they sat down to discuss the future programme.

Kate said, 'We have to set priorities. We can begin by cutting down the number of suspects, at least for the present. Jo Staveley wouldn't have killed Boyde and nor, I think, would her husband or Jago. We've always assumed that Mrs Burbridge, Mrs Plunkett and Millie are in the clear. That leaves us with Dennis Tremlett, Miranda Oliver, Emily Holcombe, Roughtwood, Dan Padgett and Mark Yelland. Logically, I suppose, we should include Rupert Maycroft, but we'll discount him for the present. We're assuming of course that there's only one murderer at Combe, but perhaps we should keep an open mind.'

Benton said, 'We've tended to discount Yelland, ma'am, or at least not to concentrate on him, but he hasn't an alibi and he had as much reason to hate Oliver as anyone on the island. And I don't think we ought to eliminate Jago, at least not yet. And, of course, there's still Dr Speidel. We've only his word for the time of the assignation.'

Kate said, 'Let's begin by concentrating on Tremlett, Roughtwood, Padgett and Yelland. All four disliked Oliver but we're up against the old problem as far as the first three are concerned: why wait until this weekend to kill him? And you're right about Dr Speidel. We need to question him again if and when he recovers, but God knows how long that will be.'

They then went through the written statements. As they had expected no one admitted that they had been on the headland after nine o'clock except for the Staveleys, who had had dinner at the house with Rupert Maycroft and Adrian Boyde. Boyde had joined them in the library for his usual pre-dinner tomato juice. He had seemed subdued and preoccupied but that didn't surprise them. He had been more upset than anyone over Oliver's death. Afterwards he had only stayed for the main course and had left, they thought, just before half-past eight. The Staveleys and Maycroft had coffee together in the library, then the Staveleys had left together by the front door for their cottage. They were a little vague about the time but thought it was about half-past nine.

Kate said, 'We'll see all of them individually tomorrow and see if there's anything else to be got out of them. We need to check the times.'

But there were other decisions that were more difficult. Ought they to ask all the suspects to hand over the clothing they had worn last night, and send it to the lab when Boyde's body and the other exhibits were removed?

As if sensing her dilemma, Benton said, 'It seems pointless, ma'am, to start collecting clothes before we have a prime suspect. After all, unless we take the whole wardrobe there's no guarantee they'll hand over what they were wearing. And Calcraft could have stripped to the waist. There was no hurry. He had the whole night to clean up after the job.'

Kate said, 'There could be prints on the taps and the shower in Chapel Cottage, but all we can do there is to keep the place secure and preserve the evidence until the technical back-up arrives, if ever. It almost makes me wish we were back in the old days before our time when the investigating officer would have an insufflator and equipment for fingerprinting in his murder kit and could get on with the job. But we'll bag up the bathroom towels in the hope of DNA and we need to send the cardboard box with the body. I don't think we've got an exhibit bag big enough. We'll have to get a plastic bag from the house. We'll ask Mr Maycroft, not Mrs Burbridge.'

It was three-thirty before the helicopter arrived and, as soon as it landed, they unlocked Benton's apartment and wheeled out the stretcher. They had covered Boyde's body with a sheet, obscuring the cope although they knew it was unlikely that Mrs Burbridge would have kept silent. Kate wished that she had bound her to secrecy. That was a mistake but one which it was probably too late to rectify. Millie would ask about the cope the next time she was in the sewing room and it was hopeless to expect discretion from Millie. They had mittened Boyde's hands to preserve any possible evidence under the nails but had done nothing else to the body. Distanced they watched, standing side by side, as the masked figures zipped it into a body bag and lifted it and the exhibit bags aboard.

Behind them the house was absolutely silent and they had no sense even of eyes watching from the windows. It was in curious contrast to the morning when there had been constant activity as people moved into the house and the stable block. The buggy had lumbered to and fro, laden with the bags and books which Emily Holcombe considered necessary for her stay and the luggage from Peregrine Cottage, with Tremlett driving and Miranda Oliver sitting bolt upright in the buggy, every inch of her rigid body expressing disapproval. Yelland carried his bags, striding in through the back door of the house and speaking to no one. Kate thought it was as if the island were expecting an invasion, the barbarians already sighted, and everyone was seeking sanctuary in Combe House, preparing to make a last stand.

But then both the Staveleys came out of the house and Jago appeared driving the buggy. Kate saw with a lurch of the heart that oxygen cylinders and two large boxes, obviously of medical equipment, were being carefully unloaded and that Jago and Dr Staveley were receiving them and placing them in the buggy. A table had been placed at some twenty yards from the helicopter on which the formalities could be concluded without risk. With everyone masked and keeping their distance as far as possible, the business, including the handing over of the exhibit bags, took some time. Ten minutes later the helicopter took off. Kate and Benton stood gazing up at it until it was out of sight, then turned silently away.

The day wore on. There was little they could do now as Kate had decided to leave the interviews until Wednesday. The day had been shocking for everyone. They had the written statements and it would probably be unproductive to begin further questioning now.

As daylight faded, she said, 'I'm going up to the sickroom. It's time we learnt what's happening to Mr Dalgliesh and we need to know where the surgical gloves are kept and who had access to them.'

She showered and changed before setting out, then went first to look at the sea, feeling the need for a few minutes of solitude. She both needed and feared an encounter with the truth. Dusk was falling fast, obliterating the familiar objects. Behind her the lights came on one by one in Combe House but the cottages and all the stable block, except her and Benton's rooms, were in darkness. The lighthouse was the last to disappear but even when its shaft had blurred into a pale spectre, the waves were still a white curdle against the blackening cliffs.

She unlocked the side door and passed through the hall to the lift. Moving upwards, she stared at her image. Her face seemed years older, the eyes tired. With her fair hair tightly brushed back, her face looked vulnerable, stripped for action.

Jo Staveley was in the surgery. It was the first time Kate had seen it, but she had no eyes for the details except for the steel cabinets with their meticulously printed labels.

She said, 'How is Mr Dalgliesh?'

Jo Staveley, white-coated, was standing at a desk studying a file. She turned to Kate a face from which all vitality had drained. Closing the file, she said, 'I suppose the orthodox reply is that he's as well as can be expected, or I could say comfortable. Only he isn't comfortable, and his temperature is higher than we would like. It's early days. An erratic temperature may not be atypical. I've no experience in nursing patients with SARS.'

'May I see him? It's important.'

'I don't think so. Guy is with him now. He'll be here in a minute. Why don't you sit down and wait until he comes.'

'And Dr Speidel?'

'He'll live. Decent of you to ask. Most people seem to have forgotten him.'

Kate said, without preliminaries, 'What happens if visitors need something from the surgery – pills, a bandage, something like that?'

The abrupt change of subject, the almost peremptory question, obviously surprised Jo. She said, 'They'd ask me for it. There wouldn't be any problem.'

'But is the surgery open? I mean, could they come and help themselves?'

'Not to the drugs. All the prescription drugs are locked up.'

'But the surgery door isn't locked?'

'Even so, I can't see people wandering in and out. If they did, they couldn't do any harm to themselves or others. I keep some of the over-the-counter drugs like aspirin locked up too.' She was looking at Kate now with frank curiosity.

Kate persevered. 'And things like bandages or surgical gloves?'

'I can't think why visitors should want them, but

they're not locked up. If they did want them, I imagine they'd ask me or Guy. That would be courteous as well as sensible. They'd hardly help themselves.'

'But you would know if any were missing?'

'Not necessarily. There were things we needed when we were nursing Martha Padgett. Mrs Burbridge helped occasionally. She'd take what she needed. Why all this curiosity? You haven't found drugs, have you? If so, they didn't come from this surgery.'

'No, I haven't found drugs.'

The door opened and Guy Staveley came in. Jo said, 'Inspector Miskin wants to see Mr Dalgliesh. I've told her I think it's unlikely to be possible tonight.'

'I'm afraid not. He's resting quietly at the moment and it's important he's not disturbed. Perhaps sometime tomorrow if his temperature falls and if he's still here. I'm thinking of transferring him to the mainland tomorrow morning.'

Kate said, 'Didn't he tell you that he wanted to remain on the island?'

'He was pretty insistent about it, which is why I asked for the oxygen and other equipment I might need. Jo and I can cope at present, but if his temperature is still high in the morning I'm afraid he'll have to be transferred. We haven't the facilities here for a dangerously ill man.'

Kate was sick at heart. She thought, *And you'd rather he died in hospital than here.* She said, 'If he's adamant he wants to stay, can you really transfer him against his will? Isn't he much more likely to die if you do that?'

There was a trace of irritability in Staveley's reply. 'I'm sorry but I can't take the responsibility.'

'But you're a doctor. Isn't it your job to take responsibility?'

There was a silence then Staveley turned away. Kate saw that Jo was looking intently at her husband, but neither of them spoke. Something to which she, Kate, could never be privy, was being communicated. Then she heard him say, 'All right, he can stay. And now I have to get back to him. Good night, Miss Miskin, and good luck with the investigation.'

Kate turned to Jo. 'Could you give him a message when he's well enough?'

'I can do that.'

'Tell him that I have found what he thought we might find and that it's been sent to the lab.'

Jo said, without apparent curiosity, 'Yes, I'll tell him that.'

There was nothing else Kate could do and she found nothing else to say. Now she was faced with a second call to Emma. She could tell her that AD was resting quietly. That had to be good, that would surely give her some comfort. But for Kate, walking out into the darkness, there was none.

8

At five o'clock on Thursday morning Kate was awake after a restless night. She lay looking out at the darkness trying to decide whether to turn over and attempt another few hours' sleep, or to accept defeat, get up and make tea. It promised to be a frustrating and disappointing day. Her exhilaration at the discovery of the stone was waning. The forensic biologist might be able to identify the blood as Boyde's, but where did that get them if the fingerprint expert couldn't raise prints from the stone or the remnant of glove? The lab was giving the case top priority but Kate had no hope that any bloodstains would be discovered on the cope other than Boyde's. This murderer had known his business.

It was all conjecture. Of the four suspects she and Benton were concentrating on, Roughtwood and Padgett were the ones who could get most easily to the lighthouse unseen, using the under-cliff. Tremlett in Peregrine Cottage north of the harbour wouldn't have had that advantage, but he was the suspect most likely to have read Speidel's note. He could have seen Oliver leaving the cottage early and followed him, knowing that, once in the lighthouse, he would have to act quickly but that there was little chance of immediate discovery. He would have had the security of that bolted door and would probably have depended on what in fact had happened: Speidel, finding he couldn't get in, had given up and gone away.

Turning restlessly, she tried to plan the priorities for the next day, weighed with an almost overwhelming conviction of failure. She was in charge. She would be letting down AD and Benton as well as herself. And in London Harkness would already have been discussing with the Devon and Cornwall Constabulary what back-up could be provided on Combe without risk of infection, might even have discussed with the Home Office the advisability of the local force taking over the whole investigation. He had talked about giving her until Friday night. That was only two days away.

Getting out of bed, she reached for her dressing-gown. It was then that the telephone rang.

She was downstairs in the sitting room in a matter of seconds, and heard Jo Staveley's voice. 'Sorry to wake you so early, Inspector, but your boss wants to see you. You'd better come quickly. He says it's urgent.'

9

Dalgliesh's last disjointed memories of Tuesday morning were of disembodied hands supporting him into the buggy, of being jolted over the scrubland under a sky which had suddenly become scorching hot, of a white-coated figure in a mask helping him into bed and the comforting coolness of the sheets being drawn over him. He could recall reassuring voices but not their words, and his own insistent voice telling them that they had to keep him on the island. It had been important to get that message across to these mysterious white-clad strangers who seemed to be in control of his life. They had to realise that he couldn't leave Combe. How would Emma find him if he disappeared into this threatening nothingness? But there was another reason why he couldn't leave, something to do with a lighthouse and a job that was unfinished.

By Wednesday evening his mind was clear but he was weaker in body. He had difficulty in shifting his head on the high pillows and throughout the day he had been racked with a cough which wrenched the muscles in his chest, making it difficult to breathe. The intervals between the paroxysms became shorter, the episodes harsher until, on Wednesday afternoon, Guy Staveley and Jo were busy around his bed, tubes were inserted in his nostrils and he was breathing a stream of oxygen. And now he was lying peacefully, aware of the ache in his limbs, the heat of his fever, but blessedly free from the worst of the coughing. He had no idea of the day or the time. He tried to twist his head to glance at the bedside clock, but even this small effort exhausted him. It must, he thought, be night-time, or perhaps early morning.

The bed was at right angles to the high windows. So, he remembered, it was in the room next door where he had stood looking down at Oliver's body. And now he could recall every detail of that scene, recall too what had come after. He lay trapped in the darkness, his eyes on the two pale panels imprinted on the wall which, as he gazed, were transformed into high windows patterned with stars. Below the windows he could see an easy chair and a woman in a white coat, her mask about her neck, leaning back as if dozing. He remembered that she, or someone like her, had been there every time he had woken. And now he knew that it was Jo Staveley. He lay quietly, freeing his mind from conscious thought, relishing the brief respite from the racking pain in his chest.

And suddenly, with no sense of revelation and no exultation but with absolute certainty, he saw the answer to the puzzle. It was as if the wooden pieces of a spherical puzzle were whirling wildly about his head and then, piece by piece, clicking together into a perfect globe. The truth came to him in snatches of conversation, the voices as clear as if they were being spoken into his ear. Mrs Plunkett in her kitchen: *More likely he'd be sitting in the cabin. Proper scared he was.* Dr Speidel's voice in his carefully precise English: *I knew that Nathan Oliver visited quarterly. He revealed that in a newspaper article in*

April 2003. Millie's high young voice describing her meeting with Oliver as if she had learnt it by rote, his own voice speaking: *But that was in another country: and besides, the wench is dead.* Padgett seeing the smoke from the chimney of Peregrine Cottage. Nathan Oliver's one paperback among the popular romantic fiction in Puffin Cottage.

They had all been looking at the case the wrong way round. It wasn't a question of who had arrived on Combe since Oliver's last visit and by their arrival had been the catalyst for murder, it was a question of who had left. None of them had remembered that helpless dying woman who had been carried away from Combe in her coffin. And the blood sample dropped overboard by Dan Padgett, was that an accident or deliberate? The truth was that the sample hadn't been lost – it had never been in the bag. What Dan Padgett had let slip into the sea had been nothing more than old shoes and handbags and library books. Those two events, Martha Padgett's death and the incident of the blood, both seemingly irrelevant, had been at the heart of the case. Padgett, too, had been telling the truth, or at least part of it, when he said that he saw the smoking chimney just before eight o'clock. He had seen the rising smoke, but from the platform of the lighthouse not from his window. In the half light of the sickroom, Boyde's pain-filled eyes looked again into his, willing him to believe that on his walk over the headland on Saturday morning he had seen no one. But there was someone he should have seen. He had called at Puffin Cottage to talk to Padgett and Padgett had not been there.

Their thinking had been accurate in one premise: the

motive for the murder must have been recent. Before she died, Martha Padgett had confided her secret to the one person she could uniquely trust: Dan was Nathan Oliver's son. She had told Adrian Boyde, who had helped minister to her and whom only she and Mrs Burbridge had viewed as a priest, a man she could confide in under the seal of the confessional. And what then? Had Boyde persuaded her that Dan had a right to know the truth? But Boyde was bound by the secrecy of the confessional. He must have persuaded Martha that she had to be the one to tell her son that the man he hated was his father.

And that, of course, was why Martha Padgett had been so anxious in her last months to come to Combe. She and Dan had arrived in June 2003. It had been in April of that year that Oliver had said in a press interview, widely disseminated, that he made regular visits to Combe, breaking an agreement with the Trust that information about the island should remain confidential. Did Martha hope that somehow her son and his father would meet and that some relationship would develop, that even at the end she might persuade Oliver to acknowledge his son? It was in giving that ill-advised press interview that Oliver had set in motion the almost inevitable concatenation of events which had led to two violent deaths. Why hadn't she taken action earlier, why remain silent through the years? Oliver was a famous man; his whereabouts couldn't be concealed. At the time of Dan's birth, DNA testing hadn't been discovered. If Oliver had told his lover that he wouldn't acknowledge the child and that she couldn't prove it was his, she might have continued to believe that all her life and only in the last years been faced with two new facts: the public knowledge of DNA testing and, much later, the realisation that she was dying. It was significant that she had kept, and obviously re-read, only one of Oliver's books. Was that the one in which he described a seduction, perhaps even a rape? Her seduction, her rape?

After the murder Boyde must have suspected Padgett. He couldn't reveal what he had heard as a confessor, but finding that cottage empty on Saturday morning, that damning fact could have been told to the police. So why hadn't he spoken? Did he see it as his priestly duty to persuade Padgett to confess and heal his soul? Was that the confidence, perhaps the arrogance, of a man who had been used to exercising what for him was a unique spiritual power? Had he called at Puffin Cottage on Monday night to make a last attempt and in doing so had ensured that he would be silenced for ever? Had he suspected that? Had he perhaps even known it? Had he returned at last to the chapel instead of to his cottage because he was aware in the darkness of those following feet?

Fact after fact clicked into place. Mrs Plunkett's words, *He fairly tugged it out and I could see the look on his face, which wasn't really what you'd call loving.* Of course he didn't cut the hair. He must have been told that you needed the roots for DNA. And there could have been resentment, even hatred, for the mother who by her silence had condemned him to a childhood of misery and humiliation. The team had accepted that the death of Oliver could have been impulsive not premeditated. If Speidel's note had been altered, the appointment would have been changed to a time more convenient than a mere thirty minutes earlier. Padgett, perhaps from his top window, perhaps because he was outside his cottage, had seen Oliver walking purposefully towards the lighthouse. Had he seen this as an opportunity to confront him at last with the truth of his parentage, to tell him that he had proof, to demand that Oliver acknowledge him and make financial provision? Was that at the root of his confidence about a different future for himself? With what jumble of hope, anger and determination he must have set out impulsively on that short secluded walk along the lower cliff. And then the confrontation, the quarrel, the fatal lunge at Oliver's neck, the hapless attempt to make homicide look like suicide.

Dalgliesh had lain there so still, but now Jo moved quickly to his side. She laid a hand on his forehead. He had thought that nurses only did that in books and films but the touch of Jo's cool hands was a comfort. Now she said, 'You're an atypical case, aren't you, Commander? Can't you do anything by the book? Your temperature soars up and down like a yo-yo.'

He looked at her and found his voice. 'I need to speak to Kate Miskin. It's very important. I have to see her.'

Somehow, despite his weakness, he must have conveyed the urgency. She said, 'If you must, you must. But it's five o'clock in the morning. Can't it wait at least until it's light? Let the girl have her rest.'

But it couldn't wait. He was tormented by fears that he realised were not entirely rational but that he couldn't banish – the cough might come back, he might get suddenly worse so that they wouldn't let Kate see him, he might lose the power of speech, he might even forget what was now so abundantly clear. And one fact was clear above all others. Kate and Benton had to find that phial of blood and the lock of Martha Padgett's hair. The case hung together but it was still conjecture, a precarious edifice of circumstantial evidence. Motive and means were not enough. Padgett had cause to hate Oliver, but so had others on the island. Padgett could get to the lighthouse unseen, but so could they. Without the blood and hair the case might never come to court.

Then there was Mrs Burbridge's belief that Oliver had died by accident during an experiment. There was enough evidence to suggest that this was the kind of thing he might well have done. Dr Glenister would testify that the bruises on Oliver's throat couldn't have been self-inflicted and, given her reputation, her opinion would carry weight. But the post-mortem examination of bruises, particularly some time after death, could be controversial. There would be forensic pathologists for the defence with very different views.

He said, 'Please. I want her now.'

10

To begin the search of Puffin Cottage before daylight would be to invite speculation and possible interruption. With all the cottages dark, one light would shine out like a warning beacon. It was vital that Padgett didn't know that the search was under way. If the evidence wasn't in the cottage that betraying light would give him a chance to remove the blood and hair or even to destroy it. But never had the early hours passed so slowly for Kate and Benton.

When the time was right, they passed quietly and speedily out of Kate's apartment and sped across the headland like a couple of conspirators. The door of Puffin Cottage was locked but the keys were clearly labelled on the bunch Maycroft had given them. As Kate quietly closed and relocked the door behind them, she felt a familiar qualm of unease. This was a part of her job that from the first she had found disagreeable. There had been so many searches over the years, from stinking hovels to expensive immaculate apartments, and she had always felt a twinge of irrational guilt, as if she were the one under suspicion. Strongest of all was the distaste at violating the privacy of the victims, rummaging like a salacious predator among the often pathetic leavings of the dead. But this morning the unease was momentary, subsumed in the euphoria of anger and hope. Recalling

Boyde's mutilated face, she would have happily torn the place apart with her hands.

The cottage still held its atmosphere of dispiriting conformity, and with the curtains drawn the sitting room was as gloomy as if still in mourning. But something had changed. In the strengthening light Kate could see that all the ornaments on the mantelpiece had been cleared away and the bookcase was empty with two cardboard boxes beside it.

Benton said, 'I thought it might be useful if I read that novel, so I borrowed it from the library. They've got hardbacks of all Oliver's books. I finished it at about two o'clock this morning. One of the incidents is the rape of Donna, a sixteen-year-old girl, on a school trip. The writing is extraordinary. He manages to give the two viewpoints, the man's and the girl's, simultaneously in a fusion of emotions which I have never known in a novel before. Technically, it's brilliant.'

Kate said, 'Spare me the literary technique. Let's get moving. We'll start with the bread oven inside the fireplace. He could have removed one or more of the bricks.'

The iron door of the bread oven was closed, the interior dark. Benton fetched a torch from Kate's murder case and the strong beam illumined the empty interior.

Kate said, 'See if any of the bricks are loose.'

Benton began working at the grouting between the bricks with his penknife while Kate waited in silence. About a minute later he said, 'I think I've found something. This one comes away and there's a cavity behind.'

Putting in his hand, he drew out an envelope. It contained two sheets of paper: the birth certificates of Bella

Martha Padgett, born 6th June 1962, and of Wayne Daniel Padgett, born 9th March 1978. On Dan Padgett's certificate the space for the father's name had been left blank.

Benton said, 'I wonder why he bothered to hide these.'

'He saw them as damning evidence. Once he had killed Oliver his relationship was a danger, not a meal ticket. It's ironic, though, isn't it? If his aunt hadn't insisted on Padgett and his mother not using their first names, she would have been called Bella. I wonder if that would have struck a chord in Oliver's mind. Is there anything else there?'

'Nothing, ma'am. I'll just check the rest of the bricks.'

The search revealed nothing more. They placed the certificates in an exhibit bag and moved into the kitchen. Kate placed her murder case on the work surface next to the sink and Benton put his camera beside it.

Kate's voice was as low as if she feared to be over-heard. 'We'll try the fridge. If Padgett's got the blood he probably thinks it has to be kept cold.'

Benton's voice was more natural, confident and strong. 'But is it necessary for it to be fresh to get DNA, ma'am?'

'I should know but I can't remember. Probably not, but that's what he'd think.'

They stretched on their search gloves. The kitchen was small and simply furnished with a wooden table and two chairs. The work surfaces, the floor and the stove were clean. Beside the door was a foot-operated rubbish bin. Benton opened it and they gazed down on the smashed remains of the china figurines. The woman with the hoe had been decapitated, her head incongruously simpering on a heap of torn pages.

Benton stirred them with his finger. 'So he destroyed his mother's last possessions and Oliver's paperback. The leavings of the two people he blamed for spoiling his life – his mother and Nathan Oliver.'

They moved to the fridge which was the same type and make as in Kate's kitchen. Opening it, they saw that it contained a tub of easy-to-spread butter, a pint of semi-skimmed milk and half a loaf of wholemeal bread. But there was discordance between the contents of the fridge and the kitchen, which looked as if it had been unused for weeks. Perhaps Padgett had given up cooking for himself since his mother's death and was relying on the staff dining room for his main meals. They opened the small freezer compartment at the top. It was empty. Kate took out the wrapped loaf. The eight remaining slices were still fresh and, separating them, she checked that nothing was pressed between them.

Replacing the bread, she carried the tub of butter over to the table. Neither spoke as she prised open the plastic lid. Underneath was a sheet of greaseproof paper with the name of the brand. It looked untouched. Kate folded it back to reveal the smooth spread of the butter. She said, 'See if there's a thin knife or a skewer in one of the drawers, will you Benton.'

Gazing at the tub, she heard drawers being quickly opened and shut, then Benton was at her side holding out a meat skewer. He watched as she gently pierced the butter. The skewer went in for less than half an inch.

She said, unable to keep the excitement from her

voice, 'There's something in here. We need photographs from now on – the fridge, the tub.'

Kate waited while Benton began to photograph, then gently scraped away the top layer of butter on to the lid of the tub. She dug a little deeper to reveal a sheet of foil and beneath it two small packages neatly wrapped also in foil. Benton took another photograph as Kate carefully peeled off the foil. In one was a phial of blood with the label giving Oliver's name and the date still attached. In the other was a sample of hair wrapped in tissue paper.

Benton said, 'There would have been a paper detailing the tests Dr Staveley wanted done, but Padgett wouldn't have bothered to keep that. The label will be enough. The name and date are handwritten so we'll get clear identification.'

They looked at each other. Kate could see on his face the smile of triumph which she knew matched her own. But this was a moment for controlled activity, not for rejoicing. Benton took the final photographs, including the contents of the bin, and Kate placed the phial, the hair and the butter tub inside an exhibit bag and sealed it. They both signed the label.

Neither could say afterwards what it was that alerted them to the fleeting face at the kitchen window. There had been no sound but it could have been an almost imperceptible dimming of the light. He was gone before they could be sure of anything except two terrified eyes and a shorn head.

Benton swore and together they rushed to the door. Kate had the bunch of keys but it took three seconds to identify the right one. She cursed herself for not having left it in the keyhole. Now trying to thrust it in, she found she couldn't. She said, 'He's blocked it with his own key.'

Benton tore back the curtains across the right-hand window, pulled up the latch and thumped the wooden frame. The window was stuck fast. He tried twice more, then ran with Kate to the second window. This too had stuck. Pulling out one of the chairs he battered its back against the frame. The window burst open with a tinkle of glass.

Kate said, 'You get him. You're faster. I'll see to the exhibits and the camera.'

Benton hadn't waited to hear. He had immediately pulled himself up and was gone. Snatching up the camera and murder case, Kate ran to the window and swung herself through.

Padgett was sprinting towards the sea with Benton gaining on him, but those thirty or forty seconds' delay had been enough. Padgett would have been out of sight if Jago hadn't suddenly appeared round the corner of the house. The two collided and both fell sprawling. But before the dazed Jago could get up Padgett was on his feet again. They were racing towards the lighthouse with Benton now only about thirty yards behind. Breasting the mound, Kate saw with horror that they were too late. And there was something worse. Walking round the edge of the lighthouse came Millie. There was a second in which time seemed to be suspended. Kate was aware of the two flying figures, of Millie standing stock still, eyes wide with amazement, before Padgett scooped her up and flung her through the lighthouse door. Seconds later they reached the door in time to hear Millie's scream and the scrape of the bolt as it shot home.

They stood panting. When she could speak, Kate said, 'Take the exhibits to the safe, then get Jago here. He'll need help. I want the tallest ladder he's got and another shorter one to reach these lower windows.'

Benton said, 'If he takes her up to the gallery, no ladder will reach him.'

'I know, but if he does take her up to the top, and I think he will, he'll know they can't reach him. But he'll enjoy watching us make fools of ourselves. We've got to keep him occupied.'

Benton sped off at once, and now there was the sound of voices. The chase must have been seen from the house. Roughtwood and Emily Holcombe appeared with Mrs Burbridge and Mrs Plunkett behind them.

Emily Holcombe said, 'What's happened? Where's Padgett?'

'In the lighthouse and he's got Millie.'

Mrs Burbridge said, 'Are you saying he murdered Adrian?'

Kate didn't reply. She said, 'I want you all please to keep very calm and do what I say.'

Suddenly there was a high scream like the shriek of a gull, but heard so briefly that at first only Kate looked up. Then the others raised their eyes and Mrs Burbridge let out a moan and sank down, her face in her hands.

Roughtwood gasped, 'Oh my God!'

Padgett had lifted Millie over the gallery rail so that she was standing on the outside ledge no more than six inches wide, clutching at the rail and shrieking while Padgett held her by the arm. He was shouting something but the words were lost in the breeze. Slowly he began edging Millie along the ledge towards the seaward curve of the lighthouse. The little group below followed, hardly daring to look up.

And now Benton was with them. Panting he said, 'The evidence is in the safe. Jago's coming with the ladders. He'll need some help with the longer one. It needs two to handle it.'

Already they could see Jago running across the forecourt of the house. Kate said, 'Go and help him.'

Her eyes were fixed on the two figures. Millie's frail body seemed to be drooping in Padgett's grasp. Kate prayed, *Oh God, don't let her faint.*

And now she heard feet, a scrape of wood and, moving round the lighthouse, saw that Jago, Benton and Roughtwood had arrived with the taller ladder. Tremlett had also arrived and was behind them with a smaller one, no more than twelve feet long.

Kate spoke to Benton. 'We've got to keep him calm if we can. I don't think he'll throw her off without an audience. I want Roughtwood and Jago to put the taller ladder against the wall. If he moves round, follow him with the ladder. Everyone else out of the way, please.'

She turned to Jago. 'I've got to get in. We can't use the buggy to batter down the door, it's too wide. Is there anything we can use as a battering ram?'

'No miss, that's the difficulty. I've been trying to think of something we could use. There's nothing.'

She turned to Benton, 'Then I've got to get in through one of the lower windows. I think it'll be possible.'

Roughtwood and Jago were moving the larger ladder round the lighthouse and she followed them while they were trying, with difficulty, to set it up. At one time it slipped against the lighthouse wall and crashed to the ground. She thought she could hear Padgett's jeering laugh and hoped she was right. She needed the diversion.

She ran back to Benton. 'You're the quickest. Go to the sickroom and find Jo Staveley. I want the biggest tin of Vaseline they've got. Any grease will do, but Vaseline's the most likely. I need plenty. And bring a hammer.'

He was gone without replying. She moved quickly to the little group now waiting in silence by the lighthouse door.

Maycroft said, 'Shall I call a rescue helicopter?'

This was the decision Kate had been dreading. It would be the safe choice. No one would blame her if, unable to get into the lighthouse, she called in a rescue helicopter and the experts. But wasn't that just the kind of audience Padgett would welcome as he flung Millie and himself into the void? She wished she knew what AD would have done. She was aware of the little group standing helplessly, their eyes on her face.

She said, 'Not yet. I think it might panic him into taking the final step. If he does decide to throw her off he'll do it either when he has an audience or when he's frightened.' She raised her voice. 'Will the women please go back to the house. I don't want Padgett to have too big an audience. And tell Dr Staveley we may need him if he can leave Mr Dalgliesh.'

The little group dispersed. Mrs Plunkett with her arm round Mrs Burbridge, Emily Holcombe walking very upright, a little alone.

And now Benton breasted the hillock carrying a hammer and a large tin of Vaseline. Kate inspected the windows. Those at the top of the lighthouse looked little more than slits and those nearest the ground were the largest. Benton placed the ladder against the one nearest the door and some twelve feet from the ground, and climbed up. Gazing up, Kate estimated that the window was some three feet high and about eighteen inches wide with an iron bar down the middle and two horizontal parallel bars at the base.

Benton broke the glass and began hammering on the bars. He slid down the ladder and said, 'They're deeply embedded in the stone, ma'am. No chance there. It's going to be a tough squeeze getting through one of the segments.'

Kate was already taking off her clothes, leaving only her pants and bra, socks and shoes. She prised open the lid of the tin of Vaseline and began scooping up the shining mess, smearing it thickly over her body. Benton came to help. She wasn't aware of his moving hands, only of the cold slabs of grease spread thickly on her shoulders, back and hips. And now she became aware that Guy Staveley was there. He didn't speak but stood silently watching.

Ignoring him, Benton said to Kate, 'Pity he didn't grab you, ma'am, instead of Millie. We could have had that kid through the gap in no time.'

Kate said, 'If I need shoving, for God's sake shove. I've got to get through.'

It would have to be feet first, she couldn't risk dropping on her head. She had no idea how far down the chamber floor would be but the lower bars would give her a hold. It was more difficult edging her body in sideways than she had thought. Benton was behind her on the ladder, holding her with strong arms at the waist, but her body was so slippery that it was difficult to get a purchase. She grabbed his shoulders and edged herself through. There was no problem with hips or the soft tissue of her breasts, but at the shoulders she became stuck. She knew the weight of her dangling body wouldn't force them through.

She said to Benton, 'For God's sake push,' and felt his hands first on her head and then on her shoulders. The pain was appalling and she felt the dislocation of her shoulder, a precise and excruciating moment which made her yelp in agony. But she managed to gasp, 'Keep pushing, that's an order. Harder. Harder.'

And then suddenly she was through. Instinctively she grasped the lower bar with her one good arm and let herself slide to the floor. There was the need, almost overwhelming, to lie there collapsed, her left arm useless, the pain from torn muscles and the scraped raw flesh almost intolerable. But she scrambled to her feet and half fell down the single flight of steps to the bottom chamber and the barred door. As soon as, with difficulty, she'd shot back the heavy bolt, Benton came in, Staveley behind him.

Staveley said, 'Can I help?'

It was Benton who replied. 'Not yet, Doctor. Stand by if you will.'

Staveley turned to Kate, 'Are you all right, can you get up the stairs?'

'I've got to. No, don't come. Leave this to us.'

Benton was carrying her trousers and jacket,

impatient to get moving. She tried to get her arms into the jacket but couldn't without Benton's help. She said, 'Come on, leave the trousers. I'm decent,' then heard his quiet voice. 'Better put them on, ma'am. You may need to make an arrest.'

He helped her on with these too, and half-carried her after the first flight of stairs. The climb to the top storey seemed endless, the half-familiar rooms unnoticed. And always stairs, more stairs. At last they were in the final chamber.

Benton said, 'Thank God the door's on the island side. If he's still where he was he may not have heard us.'

They were on the gallery at last. The daylight almost blinded her and she rested for a moment against the glass of the lantern, dazzled by light and colour, the blue of the sea, the paler sky with its high trailing clouds like wisps of white smoke, the multicoloured island. It all seemed too much for her eyes. She steadied her breath. There was absolutely no sound. They had only a few feet to go before they would know whether Millie was still alive. But surely, had he thrown her down, they would have heard even at this height a cry of horror from the men with the tall ladder watching from below.

She said to Benton, 'I'll go first', and they moved quietly round the gallery. By now Padgett had heard them. He was holding Millie by one arm and with the other was grasping the top rail as if he too were in danger. He turned on Kate a blazing look in which she detected fear and hatred, but also a terrible resolution. All pain was forgotten now in the extremity of the moment. What she did, what she said, would mean life or death for Millie. Even deciding what to call him could be the wrong choice. It was important to speak quietly, but at this height the breeze was erratic. She had to be heard.

She moved a foot towards him and said, 'Mr Padgett, we have to talk. You don't want to kill Millie, and you don't have to. It won't help you. And you'll be sorry for the rest of your life. Please listen.'

Millie was moaning, a low tremulous sound broken by sharp little cries like a kitten in pain. And then a torrent of words came at Kate, a spitting stream of obscenities, violent, filthily sexual, full of hate.

Benton's quiet voice was in her ear. 'Better let me try, ma'am.'

She nodded and he moved past her and edged round the rail more confidently and purposefully than she had dared. Seconds passed. And now he was close enough to shoot out a hand and grab Millie's arm. He held it and began speaking, his dark face close to Padgett's. Kate couldn't hear what he said, but there was no interruption from Padgett and she had a ridiculous vision that she was watching two acquaintances speaking together with the ease of mutual understanding. Time stretched, and then the talking stopped and Benton moved a little back and, with both arms, lifted Millie over the rail. Kate ran forward and, bending down, held the girl in her one good arm. Looking up over Millie's sobbing head, she saw Padgett's face. The hatred was still there, but there was something more complicated – resignation perhaps, but also a look of triumph. She turned to Benton, who took Millie from her, then made herself stand upright and, gazing into Padgett's eyes, spoke the words of the arrest.

II

They put him in Benton's apartment with Benton guarding him. He sat on an upright chair, his manacled hands between his knees, staring into space. Only when Kate was in the room did he show any emotion, directing on her a look of mingled contempt and disgust. She went into her own sitting room and rang London and then the Devon and Cornwall Constabulary to arrange for his transfer. SARS or no SARS, he couldn't be kept on the island. Waiting for a return call she could imagine the consultations that were taking place, risks that were being weighed, the legal procedures that would have to be followed. She was grateful that the decision was out of her hands. But the risk of removing Padgett was surely small. He hadn't been interviewed by Dalgliesh and neither she nor Benton was showing symptoms of the disease. The call came in a comparatively short time. It was agreed that Padgett had to be moved. A helicopter would arrive in about forty-five minutes.

And now she made her way up to the sickroom where Dr Staveley and Jo were waiting. With Jo supporting her, Staveley pulled on her arm and the joint clicked back into the socket. They had warned her that it would hurt and she resolved to endure it without crying out. The pain was agonising but momentary. Almost as painful and more prolonged was the dressing of the raw patches on both arms and on her thighs. It was hurting her to breathe and Dr Staveley diagnosed a broken rib. That, apparently, had to be left to heal itself. She was grateful for their skill but the treatment would have been easier to bear had it not been for their kindness and gentleness. She was trying hard not to weep.

The removal of Boyde's body had been done almost in silence with only herself and Benton present and no watching faces at the windows. Today, when Padgett was lifted off, was different. Staveley and Maycroft stood at the door and, behind them, Kate was aware of watching eyes. She and Benton had already received congratulations. Residents and visitors were flushed with the euphoria of relief. The weight of suspicion had been lifted, their peace restored. Only Dr Yelland seemed comparatively unaffected. But their congratulations, although heartfelt, had been muted. Everyone, even Millie, seemed to realise that they were celebrating a success but not a triumph. Kate half-heard the murmured voices, briefly pressed the eager hands, braced herself to keep going, not to collapse into tears of pain and exhaustion. She had accepted Jo's painkillers but hadn't swallowed them, fearing they might befuddle her thinking. She had to report to AD. Until that happened she couldn't relax.

Walking back to the incident room with Benton after the helicopter had lifted, she asked, 'While you were guarding him, what was he like?'

'Perfectly quiet. Rather pleased with himself. Relieved, of course, as people usually are when they don't have to fear the worst any more because it's happened. I think he's looking forward to his moment of fame, but

443

half-dreading it. He can't quite take in the enormity of what he's done. Prison probably seems a small price to pay for his triumph. After all, that's where he's been for most of his life. An open prison anyway. He was resented and humiliated from the day he was born. That awful aunt, her impotent husband – they even made him change his name. His mother too. Bella, of course, would never have done for Auntie.'

Kate said, 'She probably thought she was doing her best for them. The usual excuse. People mean well when they're doing their worst. Did Padgett tell you what happened when he confronted Oliver?'

'Oliver went up to the lantern and Padgett followed. He poured out his story and all he got was contempt. Oliver said, "If you'd been a child I would have assumed some responsibility for your support. There was nothing else I would have given you. But you're a man. I owe you nothing and you'll get nothing. If you think a moment of stupidity with a randy schoolgirl is going to saddle me with you for life, then think again. After all, you're hardly the son a man would be proud to own. I don't deal with contemptible blackmailers." It was then that Padgett flew at him and fastened his hand round Oliver's throat.'

There was a silence. Kate said, 'What did you say to him?'

For a moment she was back on that high gallery, forcing her torn body to stand upright, her eyes dazzled by the shining colours of earth and sea and sky. She added, 'Up on the gallery.'

'I appealed to the strongest emotion he felt – hatred for his father. And to something else that mattered to him, the need to be someone, to be important. I said, "If you kill Millie you'll get no sympathy from anyone. She's done nothing to you. She's innocent. You killed your father and you had to kill Adrian Boyde, that's understandable. But not Millie. If you want to get your own back, now's your chance. He ignored and despised you and your mother all your life and you couldn't touch him. But you can now. You can show the world what he was like, what he did. You'll be as famous as he was and as long remembered. When they mention his name, they'll think of you. Are you going to throw it all away, a real chance of revenge, just for the satisfaction of pushing a kid to her death?"'

Kate said, 'Clever. And cynical.'

'Yes, ma'am, but it worked.'

How little she knew him in his mixture of ruthlessness and sensitivity. She recalled that scene outside the lighthouse, his hands smearing her half-naked body with grease. That had been intimate enough. But his mind was closed to her. And not only his mind. Did he live alone? What was his relationship with his parents? Did he have siblings? What was his motive in joining the police? She supposed he must have a girlfriend but he seemed detached from all relationships. Even now, when they had become colleagues, he was an enigma to her.

She said, 'And what about Boyde? How, if at all, did he try to justify that killing?'

'He claims it was impulsive, that he took off his jacket and picked up the stone before he followed Boyde into the chapel. That isn't going to wash. He came prepared with the gloves. They were among the nursing impedimenta left in his cottage. He says that Boyde was on his knees but got up and confronted him. He didn't try to escape or to protect himself. Padgett thinks he wanted to die.'

There was silence. Then Kate asked, 'What's on your mind?'

It was a common enough question but one Kate rarely asked, seeing it as an invasion of privacy.

'A verse by Auden. *Those to whom evil is done do evil in return.*'

'That's a cop-out. Millions of children are illegitimate, ill-treated, resented, unwanted. They don't all grow up to be killers.'

She tried to feel pity, but all her imagination could stretch to was a modicum of understanding tinged with contempt. She tried to picture his life: the ineffectual mother fantasising about a love which had never been more than a joyless seduction, or at worst a rape; a single act of violation, planned or impulsive, which had delivered her, pregnant, penniless and homeless, into the power of a petty sadist. She found she could picture that bleak suburban house, the dark hall, the front parlour smelling of furniture polish, kept immaculate for the visitors who never came, the family life lived in the small back room with its smell of cooking and failure. And the school, a burden of gratitude because some philanthropist got his kicks from exercising power and had paid an annual pittance to make him a charity child. He would have done better at the local comprehensive, but that, of course, would never have done. And then a succession of failed jobs. Unwanted from birth, he had been unwanted all his life – except on this island. But here too he had felt the grievance of the under-regarded and unqualified. But how could he have done better? Unhappiness, she thought, is a contagion. You carry the smell of it as you carry the detected stink of a dreaded illness.

And yet he had been a child of the 1970s, a decade after the liberating '60s. His life sounded now more like a nightmare from a distant past. It was difficult to believe that people like his unloving aunt could still exist, could wield such power. But, of course, they could and did. And it needn't have been like that. A different mother, one with intelligence, confidence, physical and mental strength, could surely have made a life for herself and her child. Thousands did. Would her own mother have done as much for her, had she lived? She remembered with dreadful clarity the words of her grandmother, overheard as she pushed open the door of that high inner-city council flat. She had been talking to a neighbour. 'It's bad enough having her bastard foisted on me, but at least she could've stayed alive and looked after the kid herself.'

Her grandmother wouldn't have said the words to her directly. She had known from childhood that she was seen as a burden and only at the very end did she realise that there had been love of a kind. And she had escaped from Ellison Fairweather Buildings, from the smell and the hopelessness, and the fear, when the lifts were again vandalised, of that long upward climb with violence lurking on every floor. She had made a life for herself. She had escaped by hard work, ambition – and, of course, by some ruthlessness – from poverty and failure. But she hadn't escaped from her past. Her grandmother must surely at least once have mentioned her mother's name, but she couldn't recall it. No one knew who her father was, and no one ever would. It was like being born without an umbilical cord, floating free in the world, weightless, a nothingness. But even the upward climb, the promotion, was tainted by guilt. By choosing this particular job, hadn't she broken faith with – even betrayed – the people to whom she had been irrevocably bound by the fellowship of the poor and the dispossessed?

Benton said, so quietly that she had to strain to hear him, 'I wonder if childhood is ever really happy. Just as well, perhaps. To be blissfully happy so young would leave one always seeking to recapture the unobtainable. Like those people who were happiest at school or university. Always going back. No reunion ever missed. It always seemed to me rather pathetic.' He paused, then said, 'Most of us get more love than we deserve.'

Again there was a silence. Kate said, 'What was that quotation, all of it? You know it. After all, you got a degree in English, didn't you?'

Again that small prick of resentment from which she was never entirely free.

He said calmly, 'It's from Auden's poem, "September 1, 1939". *I and the public know/ What all schoolchildren learn,/ Those to whom evil is done/ Do evil in return.'*

She said, 'Not all of them. Not all the time. But they don't forget and they do pay.'

12

Jo Staveley was adamant. After enquiring about Kate's injuries, she said, 'He's not coughing at the moment but, if he begins, put on this mask. I suppose you have to see him, but not both together. The Sergeant can wait. He's insisted on getting out of bed, so try to make it brief.'

Kate said, 'He's well enough for that?'

'Of course he's not. If you have any influence with him you might point out to that blasted man that I'm in charge in the sickroom.' But her voice was warm with affection.

Kate went into the room alone. Dalgliesh in his dressing-gown was sitting beside the bed. The oxygen supply tubes were no longer in his nostrils but he was masked and as she entered he rose painfully to his feet. The courtesy brought the hot tears stinging to Kate's eyes but she blinked them away and took her time walking to the other chair which Jo had placed carefully distanced, trying not to move stiffly in case he realised how much her injuries were hurting.

He said, his voice muffled by the mask, 'We're a couple of crocks, aren't we? How are you feeling, Kate? I've been told about the broken rib. I expect that hurts like hell.'

'Not all the time, sir.'

'And Padgett, I take it, is off the island. I heard the helicopter. How was he?'

'He gave no trouble. I think he's enjoying the prospect of the notoriety. Shall I make my report, sir? I mean, are you feeling all right?'

He said gently, 'Yes, Kate. I'm all right. Take your time.'

Kate had no need to consult her notebook. She was careful to make her report factual from the discovery of the blood and hair in the refrigerator, Padgett's capture of Millie and what had happened almost minute by minute at the lighthouse. She made as little as possible of her own part. And now it was time to say something about Benton. But how? Sergeant Benton-Smith's conduct has been exemplary? Hardly. Too like an end of term report commending the goody-goody of the fourth form.

She paused, then said simply, 'I couldn't have done it without Benton.'

'He did what was expected of him, Kate.'

'I think he did more, sir. It took courage to go on shoving me through that window.'

'And courage to endure it.'

It wasn't enough. She had undervalued Benton and now was the time to put things right. She said, 'And he's good with people. Mrs Burbridge was deeply distressed after Boyde died. I didn't think we'd get anything out of her. He knew what to say to her, I didn't. He showed humanity.'

Dalgliesh smiled at her and it seemed to Kate that the smile went beyond approbation, the fellowship of the job completed, even friendship. Instinctively he held out his hand and she moved to clasp it. It was the first time they had touched since, years earlier, torn with remorse and grief, she had run into his arms after her grandmother had died.

He said, 'If our future senior officers can't show humanity there'll be no hope for any of us. Benton's part won't go unnoticed. Send him in now, Kate. I'll let him know.'

He got up with painful slowness and, still distanced, walked to the door with her as if he were showing out an honoured guest. Halfway there he paused and swayed. She walked back with him to his chair, no longer apart, watchful but careful not to support his arm.

Seating himself, he said, 'It hasn't been one of our successes, Kate. Adrian Boyde shouldn't have died.'

She was tempted to point out that they couldn't have prevented his murder. They had no evidence to arrest Padgett or anyone else, no power to prevent people's movements and not enough man-power to keep a surreptitious twenty-four-hour watch on all the suspects. But he knew all that.

At the door she turned and said, 'Padgett thinks Boyde knew what was coming to him and could have prevented it. He thinks Boyde wanted to die.'

Dalgliesh said, 'I'm tempted to say that if Padgett was capable of understanding even one part of Boyde's mind he wouldn't have murdered him. But what makes me think I know more? If failure teaches us anything, it's humility. Give me five minutes, Kate, and then tell Benton I'm ready.'

Epilogue

I

Even while she lived through them, Kate knew that she would look back on the days between the arrest and the expiration of the quarantine period as the most surprising and some of the happiest of her life. Sometimes, remembering what had brought her to the island, she felt spasms of guilt that grief and horror could be so quickly subsumed in the physical exhilaration of youth and life and an unexpected joy. As some of the company would be witnesses in any trial, it was agreed that there would be no discussion about the murders, nor were they spoken of except between individuals and in private. And the team, without it seemed any policy decision, were treated as VIP guests who were on Combe for peace and solitude, the only relationship to visitors which the island was apparently capable of recognising.

Gently and quietly Combe exerted its mysterious power. Benton continued to cook breakfast and he and Kate collected what they needed for lunch from the kitchen, then spent their time alone or not, as the fancy took them. Millie had transferred her affections from Jago to Benton and followed him about like a puppy. Benton took to rock-climbing with Jago. On her solitary walks along the cliff, Kate would occasionally look down to see one or other of them precariously stretched against the granite crags.

When he was able to walk, Dalgliesh removed himself to Seal Cottage. Kate and Benton left him in peace, but she would occasionally hear music as she passed and he was obviously busy – boxes of files from New Scotland Yard were delivered regularly by helicopter and taken by Jago to the cottage. Kate suspected that Dalgliesh's phone was seldom silent. She disconnected her own and let the peace of Combe do its healing work on mind and body. Frustrated at not getting through, Piers Tarrant wrote one congratulatory letter, light-hearted, affectionate and slightly ironic, and she sent a card in reply. She wasn't ready yet to confront the problems of her life in London.

Although most of the daylight hours were spent apart, in the evenings people would congregate in the library for drinks before moving into the dining room to enjoy Mrs Plunkett's excellent dinners, good wine and each other's company. Kate's eyes would rest on the lively candlelit faces, surprised that she could be so at ease, so ready herself to talk. All her working hours and most of her social life had been spent with police officers. The police, like rat-catchers, were accepted as necessary adjuncts to society, required to be immediately available when needed, occasionally praised but seldom consorting with those not privy to their dangerous expertise, surrounded always by a faint penumbra of wariness and suspicion. During the days on Combe, Kate breathed a freer air and adjusted to a wider horizon. For the first time she knew that she was accepted as herself, a woman, not a detective inspector. The transformation was liberating; it was also subtly gratifying.

One afternoon, wearing her one silk blouse in Mrs

Burbridge's sewing room, she had said that she would have liked a change for the evening. She had just enough clothes with her; it would be unreasonable to expect a helicopter to bring in anything more. Mrs Burbridge had said, 'I have a length of silk in a subtle sea green which would suit your hair and colouring, Kate. I could make another shirt for you in two days, if you'd like it.'

The shirt was made and on the first evening she wore it Kate saw the appreciative glances from the men and Mrs Burbridge's satisfied smile. Amused, she realised that Mrs Burbridge had detected or imagined some romantic interest in Rupert Maycroft and was indulging in a little innocent matchmaking.

But it was the more voluble Mrs Plunkett who confided to her the discussions about the future of Combe. 'Some of the Trustees thought it should be a holiday home for deprived children but Miss Holcombe won't have it. She says enough is done for children in this country already and we could hardly bring them in from Africa. Then Mrs Burbridge suggested we should take in overworked city clergymen as a kind of memorial to Adrian, but Miss Holcombe won't have that either. She thinks overworked city clergymen would probably be young and keen on modern forms of worship – you know, banjos and ukuleles. Miss Holcombe doesn't go to church but she's very keen on the Book of Common Prayer.'

Was there, Kate wondered, a hint of irony in the words? Glancing at Mrs Plunkett's innocent face, Kate thought it unlikely.

Mrs Plunkett went on, 'And now previous visitors

are writing to enquire when we'll re-open, so I expect that will happen. After all, it wouldn't be easy to vary the Trust. Jo Staveley says that politicians are so used to sending hundreds of soldiers off to be killed in wars that a couple of dead bodies won't worry them, and I daresay she's right. There was talk that we were to prepare for some very important visitors and they'd be on their own, but seemingly that won't happen now. A relief all round if you ask me. I expect you've heard that the Staveleys are going back to the London practice. Well, I'm not surprised. He's quite a hero now with the papers all saying how clever he was to make that SARS diagnosis so quickly. Thanks to him the whole outbreak was contained. He shouldn't go on wasting himself here.'

'And Millie?'

'Oh we'll still have Millie. Just as well with Dan Padgett gone. Mrs Burbridge and Jago's friend are trying to find her somewhere to live on the mainland, but it'll take time.'

The only visitors who kept themselves apart were Miranda Oliver and Dennis Tremlett. Miranda had announced that she was too busy to join the party for dinner; there were affairs to discuss by telephone with her father's lawyers and with his publisher, arrangements to be put in hand for the memorial service, her wedding to be arranged. Kate suspected she wasn't the only one to be glad of Miranda's absence.

It was only in bed at night before sleep that this strange, almost unnatural peace was broken by thoughts of Dan Padgett lying in his cell and indulging his dangerous fantasies. She would see him again at the committal proceedings and at the Crown Court, but for now she resolutely pushed the murders to the back of her mind. On one of her solitary walks, on impulse she had gone into the chapel and found Dalgliesh there staring down at the stains of blood.

He had said, 'Mrs Burbridge wonders whether she should ask someone to scrub the floor. In the end she decided to keep the door open and leave it to time and the elements. I wonder if it will ever completely fade.'

2

Three days before he was due to leave Combe, Dr Mark Yelland at last replied to his wife's letter. He had earlier acknowledged it, saying that he would give it thought, but after that had been silent. He took out his pen and wrote with care.

These weeks on Combe have shown me that I have to take responsibility for the distress I cause, to the animals as well as to you. I can justify my work, at least to myself, and I shall continue at whatever cost. But you married me, not my job, and your decision has as much validity as has mine. I hope our parting can be a separation not a divorce, but the choice is yours. We'll talk when I come home, and this time I mean that. We will talk. Whatever you decide, I hope that the children will still feel that they have a father, and you a friend.

The letter had been sent, the decision made. Now he looked for the last time round the sitting room which, in its emptiness, had become suddenly unfamiliar. He would face what he had to face but he would be back. Shouldering his bags he set off vigorously for the harbour.

3

In Peregrine Cottage Dennis Tremlett had taken no more than ten minutes to take from their hangers the few clothes he had brought with him and meticulously fold them into his canvas holdall. He left it, zipped, in his room ready to be taken down to the harbour with the other luggage. Miranda, after a calculation of the relevant cost of train fares and taxis, had ordered a car and driver to meet them at Pentworthy.

In the sitting room Miranda was still fitting Oliver's books into the small cardboard boxes in which they had come. Silently he began removing the last of them from the shelf and bringing them over. She said, 'We won't be coming back.'

'No. You wouldn't want to. It would be too painful. Too many memories.' He added, 'But darling, they weren't all bad.'

'They were for me. We'll holiday in hotels that I went to with Father. Five stars. I'd like to see San Francisco again. It'll be different in future. Next time they'll know who's paying the bill.'

He doubted whether they would care provided it were paid, but he knew what was in her mind. Now she would be the rich bereaved daughter of a famous man, not the resented hanger-on. Kneeling beside her, he said on impulse, 'I wish we hadn't lied to the police.'

She swayed back on her heels and stared at him. 'We

didn't lie. Not really. I told them what Father would have wanted me to say. He'd have come round in the end. He was upset when he first knew, but it was just the shock. He'd have wanted me to be happy.'

And shall you be? Shall I? The questions were unasked, the response not given. But there was something else he needed to know, whatever the risk of asking. He said, 'When we got the news, when you realised that he was actually dead, was there a moment, no more than a second or two, when you were glad?'

She turned on him a look in which he could identify each fleeting emotion with a horrible clarity: surprise, outrage, incomprehension, obstinacy. 'What a terrible thing to say! Of course there wasn't. He was my father. He loved me; I loved him. I devoted my life to him. What made you say something so hurtful, so awful?'

'It was the kind of thing that interested your father, the difference between what we feel and what we think we ought to feel.'

She slapped the lid of the box down and got to her feet. 'I don't know what you mean. Get the sellotape and scissors, will you. I put them in the top of that small grip. I suppose we ought to seal these down.'

He said, 'I shall miss him.'

'Well, we both will. After all, you were just his employee; I'm his daughter. But it's not as if he was young. He was sixty-eight. He'd made his reputation. And there's no point in your getting another job. There'll be plenty for you to do with the house to arrange, the wedding, and all the mail we'll have to reply to. You'd better ring the office and tell them the cases are almost ready. We'll need the buggy, of course. I was going to say that Padgett could bring it. Funny to think that he's gone. I'll never forgive him. Never.'

There was one last question which he dared not ask and didn't need to; he already knew the answer. He thought of the galleys, the margins crowded with Oliver's precise almost illegible handwriting, the careful revisions which could have made his final work a great novel, and wondered if he would ever be able to forgive her.

He stared at the denuded shelves, their emptiness reinforcing his own sense of loss. He wondered how Oliver had seen him. As the son he never had? That was an arrogant presumption which only now, with Oliver dead, had he allowed to lodge in his mind. Oliver had never treated him as a son. He had never been more than a servant. But did it matter? Together they had engaged in the profound and mysterious adventure of language. In Oliver's company he had come alive.

Following Miranda to the door he stood in silence, taking a last long look at the room, and knew that here he had been happy.

4

The day came when they were at last able to leave Combe Island. Dalgliesh was ready early, but waited in Seal Cottage until the helicopter was in sight. Then he placed the key on the table where it lay like a talisman promising that he would return. But he knew he would never see Combe again. Closing the door, he made his way across the scrubland to the house. He walked in a confusion of emotions – longing, hope and dread. Emma and he had spoken only rarely during the last two weeks. He who loved language had lost confidence in all words, particularly those spoken by telephone. Truth between lovers should be written, to be weighed at leisure and in solitude or – better – spoken face to face. He had written once proposing marriage, not a protracted affair, and thought he'd had his answer. To write again now with the same request would be to badger her like a petulant child, while to have done so while he was still sick would have been too like inviting pity. And then there was her friend Clara who didn't like him and who would have spoken against him. Emma was her own woman, but what if Clara was only echoing her own half-acknowledged misgivings? He knew that when they met Emma would say that she loved him. That at least he could be sure of. But what then? Phrases from the past spoken by other women, heard without pain and sometimes with relief, came into his mind like a litany of failure.

Darling, it's been the best ever, but we always knew it wasn't meant to last. We don't even live in the same city. And with this new job I can't keep mucking up my free evenings.

What we've had has been marvellous, but your job always comes first, doesn't it? Either that or the poetry. Why don't we face the truth and make an end before one of us gets hurt? And if there is hurt you can always write a poem about it.

I'll always love you, Adam, but you're not capable of commitment, are you? You're always holding something back and it's probably the best of you. So this has to be goodbye.

Emma would find her own words and he braced himself to hear the destruction of hope with dignity and without whining.

The helicopter seemed to hover interminably before finally setting down precisely in the middle of the marked cross. There was another wait until the blades finally stopped spinning. Then the door opened and Emma appeared and, after a few tentative steps, ran into his arms. He could feel the beating of her heart, could hear her whispered 'I love you, I love you, I love you', and when he bent his head the tears were warm against his cheek. But when she looked up into his eyes her voice was firm.

'Darling, if we want Father Martin to marry us – and if you're happy, I'd rather like that – we'd better set a date quickly or he may say he's too old to travel. Will you write to him or shall I?'

He held her close and bent his dark head to hers. 'Neither. We'll go to see him together. Tomorrow.'

Waiting at the rear entrance to the house, bag at her feet, Kate heard his exultant laugh ring out over the headland.

And now she and Benton were ready to leave. Benton lugged his bag on to his shoulder and said, 'Back to real life.'

Miranda and Tremlett had left by boat with Yelland the previous day but Dalgliesh had had final arrangements to discuss with Maycroft and the team had been glad of these few hours to themselves. Suddenly the rest of the little group was with them. Everyone had come to see them off. Their private goodbyes had been said earlier and Rupert Maycroft's to Kate had been surprising.

He had been alone in his office and, holding out his hand, had said, 'I wish I could invite you to come back and visit us, but that isn't allowed. I have to abide by the rules if I expect the staff to. But it would be good to see you here again.'

Kate had laughed. 'I'm not a VIP. But I shan't forget Combe. The memories won't all be bad. I've been happy here.'

There was a pause, then he had said, 'Not so much two ships passing in the night as two ships sailing together for a time but always bound for different ports.'

Dalgliesh and Emma were waiting for them, standing side by side. Kate knew that, for her, something had finally ended, the vestige of a hope which, even as she indulged it, she had known was almost as unrealistic as her childhood imaginings that her parents were not dead, that any day they would arrive, her handsome father driving the shining car which would take her away from Ellison Fairweather Buildings for ever. That illusion, cherished in childhood for her comfort, had faded with the years, with her job, her flat, the satisfaction of achievement, and had been replaced by a more rational but still fragile hope. Now she let that go, with regret but without pain.

There was a low cloud base; the brief St Martin's summer had long since passed. The helicopter lifted as if reluctantly and made a final circuit of the island. The waving figures became manikins and one by one turned away. Kate gazed down at the familiar buildings which looked as compact as models or children's toys: the great curved windows of Combe House, the stable block where she had lodged, Seal Cottage with its memories of their late-night conferences, the square chapel, still with that stain of blood, and the brightly coloured lighthouse with its red cupola, the most charming toy of all. Combe Island had changed her in ways which she couldn't yet understand, but she knew she would never see it again.

For Dalgliesh and Emma, sitting behind her, this day was a new beginning. Perhaps for her, too, the future could be rich with infinite possibilities. Resolutely she turned her face to the east, to her job, to London, as the helicopter soared above a white tumble of clouds into the shining air.